THE Suicide Motor Club

Titles by Christopher Buehlman

THOSE ACROSS THE RIVER

BETWEEN TWO FIRES

THE NECROMANCER'S HOUSE

THE LESSER DEAD

THE SUICIDE MOTOR CLUB

THE Suicide Motor Club

CHRISTOPHER BUEHLMAN

BERKLEY BOOKS, NEW YORK

BERKLEY
An imprint of Penguin Random House LLC
375 Hudson Street, New York, New York 10014

This book is an original publication of Penguin Random House LLC.

Library of Congress Cataloging-in-Publication Data

Names: Buehlman, Christopher, author.
Title: The suicide motor club / Christopher Buehlman.
Description: First Edition. | New York, NY : Berkley Books, 2016.
Identifiers: LCCN 2015050513 | ISBN 9781101988732 (hardback)
Subjects: | BISAC: FICTION / Horror. | FICTION / Fantasy / General. | GSAFD: Horror fiction. | Fantasy fiction.
Classification: LCC PS3602.U3395 S85 2016 | DDC 813/.6—dc23
LC record available at http://lccn.loc.gov/2015050513

FIRST EDITION: June 2016

PRINTED IN THE UNITED STATES OF AMERICA

10 9 8 7 6 5 4 3 2 1

Cover photographs: car © Michael Krinke / iStockphoto; sunset © Clint Spencer / iStockphoto; tree © hutchinsonphotos/Shutterstock.
Cover design by Judith Lagerman.
Interior text design by Kristin del Rosario.
Interior art: Road © Maciej Bledowski / Shutterstock; Vertical tire track © Denys Tokar / Shutterstock; Horizontal tire track © LongQuattro/Shutterstock.

Penguin
Random
House

For Jade

PART ONE

Judith

May—September 1967

1

"DID YOU SEE THE MOON?" JUDITH LAMB SAID, HALF TURNING HER FACE TO LOOK at her boy in the backseat. Glendon continued coloring, not out of rascality, she knew, but because he would want to finish whatever task he had set himself. His aunt Patsy, an expert colorist, had lately taught him how to outline, and he was probably laying down some border or other with the stubby blue crayon he bore down on. Outlining was what kept the colors apart, made the picture look grown-up. Scribbling was for small children, not five-year-olds like him. *Five and a half* he would say; he was still at an age where half years mattered, and his birthday in December seemed impossibly far away.

"Glendon, I'm talking to you," she said, affection sweetening her voice even in rebuke. That she would spoil him seemed a foregone conclusion. He furrowed his brow and kept on; this was not a boy who suffered interruption gladly. It was easy to mistake Glendon Lamb for an entirely serious child, his father's child, watching him like this, but Judith knew better.

"Major Nelson, this is mission control. Do you see the moon? Over."

"I'm coloring, Mom. Over," he said, but he smiled. She had him. He loved *I Dream of Jeannie* so much that she could get him to do almost anything if she crossed her arms and nodded decisively like Barbara Eden issuing a spell.

"It's okay," she said. "You look at your book. It's just that the moon's a color like the milk in Apple Jacks, and it won't be for much longer. In fact, it never will be exactly that color again."

"Won't it never?"

"Won't it *ever.*"

"Won't it ever?"

"Never, Master!" she said.

He laughed and looked up. If he had his father's worry lines, the boy had her eyes, cornflower blue and tilted handsomely down at the corners. His eyes resembled hers so closely, in fact, that finding them handsome struck her as a species of vanity.

She put her arm out the window, into the warm dusk air blowing hard against it, and aimed her finger at the just-past-full moon where it shone faintly against a lavender sky rapidly filling with dark. The moon itself glowed just a bit less pink, just a bit more yellow than it had when she first called the boy to look at it, but it still held magic. Glendon Lamb put his arm out the window like a smaller shadow of his mother's, pointing his finger where hers pointed.

The sun had been down perhaps fifteen minutes.

Judith glanced at her husband.

If Robert Lamb noticed the operations of the dusk sky, he gave no sign beyond pulling out the headlamp switch, frowning at the road before him like a man working at some equation. The '65 Falcon he washed and waxed every Sunday purred east on I-40, gobbling up New Mexico on its way to the Amarillo motel he'd called ahead for.

"Wow," Glendon said. "Wowee!"

Judith withdrew her arm, fished a cigarette from her purse, and lit it. Rob looked now, saw the moon, and lit his own cigarette, a Lucky Strike. Judith smiled at him. She was no fool. She knew something ominous moved in the waters past the shallows of his eyes, but she preferred to let him tell her in his own time. If she was lucky, it would have to do with his bid to become junior partner at his firm. If not? That was too dark to think about. Perhaps it would go away on its own. Perhaps she would be lucky enough for him never to tell her. At least he had made an effort to be present on their vacation: at the Alamo on their way west, but especially at Dodge City, where he had faked death so extravagantly at a freckly boy's "Ka-pow!" and finger-shot that Glendon had giggled for a full minute after. If Robert submerged within himself on the return trip, at least his son had a bag of little plastic cowboys to play with now.

They passed a hitchhiker, a young Negro wearing a dirty white T-shirt, greasy jeans stuffed down into combat boots that he might or might not have marched in recently. It was getting harder to tell the counterculture folks from the ex-soldiers, the ones who wore fatigues ironically from those who owned little more than their government-issued clothes. Robert thought about stopping, his father's knee-jerk bigotry skirmishing with his desire never to be his father. He might have stopped if he hadn't had his family with him; he had done some hitchhiking on summer trips while he was in college and knew what it was to rely on kindness. Judith loved it that she knew those stories, loved it that she knew he was tempted to stop for the man as well as why he didn't. She put her hand on his knee, turned her wild blue eyes to search for his, caught them, got a smile from him. Was every marriage a seesaw of joy and disappointment? She thought so.

If marriages didn't need divine assistance to survive, weddings wouldn't be held in churches.

We'll be okay, she thought.

I'm imagining things.

The little boy was alone with the moon, his hand now planing the air up and down, a dolphin riding waves of wind.

THE BLACK CAMARO CAME FROM THE CLINES CORNERS EXIT WHERE ROUTE 285 intercepted Interstate 40. Santa Fe lay to the north on 285, but this car nosed its way onto the ramp that came from the south, from the scrublands leading up from Encino. Just half an hour earlier, its driver and two passengers had been sleeping in an abandoned gas station off 285, wild with weeds and painted with rust, as had the occupants of the red GTO racing to catch up with it. Well, one of those two had slept in the gas station. The driver had been sleeping in the trunk.

The first car opened up when it hit the highway, its 350 V-8 growling high and pushing it toward the rising moon. The second car followed after.

The Camaro's taillights flashed when the driver saw the hitchhiker, but the driver said "Dirty" and kept on. The Pontiac slowed too but didn't stop, its driver too proud to take the first car's leavings.

The highway, relatively new, yawned east with little traffic on it, and the two muscle cars plowed on at better than ninety, unafraid of patrolmen, unconcerned that a javelina or armadillo might wander out laterally from the scrub. They passed a pickup truck full of sad-eyed Mexicans, this going so slowly it seemed to be standing still when the twin comets streaked by it, the driver of the red car flicking his glowing cigarette behind him as he passed, the butt erupting in a shower of sparks against the pickup's windshield, earning a bird finger from the driver, a fellow with a nearly formless cowboy hat and a road map of wrinkles. The gesture seemed so funny coming from such a wizened figure that the GTO's driver laughed, as did the man riding shotgun, a very large, very pale individual with a filthy neck brace.

The next car they crept up on was doing a fair clip itself, perched in the fast lane like nobody would ever want to pass. A newish Ford Falcon, bone white, its perfectly round taillights looking to the driver of the Camaro less like a raptor and more like the wide-set eyes of a disinterested fish. He was fairly sure the Falcon's driver wasn't even aware of them yet.

The Camaro's headlights were still off, sleeping behind the hideaway doors in the grille; the tiniest bit of light remained in the sky to the west, though the sun was twenty minutes down.

A young boy's arm jutted out from the Falcon's rear passenger-side window.

"Lookee-lookee," said the Camaro's driver, a small, boyish man with a blond James Dean cut, licking his lips. He slid into the right lane without signaling, backed off his speed, eased up into the Falcon's blind spot. He said "Feel like fishin'?"

"Yeah," the tall man in the back said.

The driver pulled his seat all the way forward, hugging the wheel almost against his chest under his chin. The tall man in the back crouched, ready. The prettyish young woman in the passenger seat drooled all over her shirt.

JUDITH HAD ONLY BEEN PERIPHERALLY AWARE OF THE CAR SNOUTING UP BESIDE them on their right. Now she looked over, caught a gasp in her throat. Her first feeling was concern—the other driver, a smallish figure crowded up against the steering wheel, looked too pale to be well. He offered her a cordial "Evenin', miss."

At that instant, Glendon yelled.

A man had him by the arm.

A long, lean man hunching forward from the backseat of the other vehicle.

The man was *pulling him out of the car.*

"NO! NO!" Judith screamed, grabbing his left leg before the boy disappeared entirely, though he was mostly in the other car now. She had her hips against the door, yanking so hard on the boy's leg that her nails dug tracks in it, the nail of her little finger tearing half off.

"ROB!" she screamed.

Her husband stared, uncomprehending at first, shouting, "What the FUCK! HEY!"

Judith pulled with all she had, recognizing the danger Glen would be in even if she did wrench him from the white hands that gripped him, realizing with the animal genius that wordlessly grasps physics how fast and strong she'd have to be to keep the boy from tumbling into the road or the back wheel.

Anything would be better than letting him go into that car. That car was death, driven by the dead. She saw with true eyes, saw what they were. Saw the catlike reflection in their eyes, saw the driver's smile, his foxlike canines, the wolfish teeth on the one wrestling with her. Saw the sharp red hole that was the woman's mouth, the teeth in it the teeth of a biting gar. All in a flash.

"STOP!" she wailed. "LET HIM GO!"

The ones in the car laughed.

"ROB, DO SOMETHING!"

"How'd you know my name? That his name, too?" the one pulling her son said, massively entertained by the coincidence. Now a red car loomed up, very close to the tail of the Camaro. The Camaro accelerated, jerked forward.

"NOOOO! NOOOO! NOOOO!" she wailed as her son was wrenched from her grip, her hand clawed around his little blue Keds shoe. She shrieked, clutched the shoe to her chest. Her Rob shouted, punched the gas, gave chase.

The Camaro pulled away.

The Falcon's needle topped one hundred, one hundred ten, and still the other car receded. Now Judith spared a glance at the other car, the red one, hoping to find an ally or a witness. Its driver, a balding, pale scoundrel of a man, offered no such comfort. He grinned at her, showed her his teeth. The same killing teeth the others had. He knew she wouldn't be able to see them because almost none of the living saw them with true sight; even if she could see, he didn't mind showing her what he was because she would die soon.

Even if she didn't, nobody really believed in vampires.

The GTO now nosed up almost to the rear wheel of the Falcon, then changed lanes, pushing sideways into it, sending it into a spin that soon turned into a violent roll. The GTO moved smoothly the whole time, as if immune to the harsh kinetic laws to which it had exposed the other car. Its driver slowed, meaning to pull over and see to the occupants of the Ford, which had only just come to a rest on its roof, junked beyond recognition, dust caped behind it, but his very sharp eyes detected the twinkle of headlights coming. More than one car, more than a mile off, but he knew he had better "git." Especially if he wanted a taste of that plump little kid.

He glanced once more at the wrecked Ford.

The one in the neck brace looked questioningly at the bald one.

"Deader'n hell," he said.

The GTO accelerated and sped off in the direction of the moon.

The driver turned the radio on.

THE FIRST CAR ON THE ACCIDENT SCENE ARRIVED NINETY SECONDS AFTER THE Falcon came to rest on its crumpled roof. The driver had just picked up a hitchhiker. The former man, a loquacious undergraduate who was likely to declare a major in anthropology, had been talking his passenger's ear off since the young colored had climbed in. The latter man had done a tour as a combat medic with the second infantry in Vietnam, distinguishing himself in a firefight near the Michelin rubber plantation half a year before, half a world away. August Lively had only been stateside for three months, tuning out for a while, traveling light, trying to smoke and fuck some of what he had seen out of his brain before going back to school on Uncle Sam's dime.

"Holy shit," the driver said, holding the corner of his horn-rimmed glasses as though this might help him peer through the gloaming and understand the column of dust rising in the scrubland to his right, the saffron moon echoed below by a single, occluded headlight.

"Shit, man," Lively said, "better pull over. Yeah, pull over now, NOW."

For the second time in five minutes, the driver found himself ambling his beat-up '59 Galaxie to the shoulder of the interstate, the first time to pick up the slightly built black man in the jungle boots, now to eject him. Lively had the door open and had started running before the Galaxie stopped moving.

"Flag somebody down, man!" he shouted behind him, sprinting the sixty yards to the hulk of the Falcon, saying *dinky dau dinky dau dinky dau* under his breath because he thought it made him run faster.

Had it been ten minutes later, the darkness might have obscured the wreck, the Galaxie might have kept on toward Amarillo, where the driver knew a girl with an ever-simmering crock of mushroom tea and a bundle of hashish in a Monopoly box. In that version of events, the Falcon's driver, whose spine had been crushed and whose left arm had been all but severed, would have almost certainly died on the spot. As it was, the hitcher managed to tourniquet his arm with strips from his own T-shirt and a loose drumstick; he then soothed the man until first the New Mexico State Police and then an ambulance arrived.

"My wife, she's dead, right?"

"No, sir, she's hurt, but I think she'll be okay. You'll be okay, too."

"Did you see it?"

"No, sir."

"Not the wreck. I know there was a wreck, right?"

"Yes."

"But did you see it?"

"See what, sir?"

"I forget. I can't feel my legs."

"You're just rattled, you'll be okay. Help is coming. Be strong for me."

"I know what it means when you can't feel your legs."

"Sometimes, yeah, but not always."

"Can you get me out of here?"

"I don't think so."

"My head hurts."

"They're going to need to cut you out," Lively said. "They're coming."

"I fucked up, you know?"

"Be strong."

"I can't."

"Be strong for her. She needs you."

"No. She doesn't."

The hitcher stroked the man's sweaty hair, even kissing his hairline, anything to comfort him, keep him present.

"She does, man. Believe me. You hold on."

Robert looked at the moon, thinking he was in a dream where a malevolent quarter hung over the desert like a badge of judgment, thinking he was the serpent and that God had taken the use of his legs. Thinking God had also sped up the script and slain Abel.

Not Abel.

Glendon.

Something about Glen going out the window stirred in his memory, made him start to hitch and sob.

"Where's Glen?"

Silence.

"I need to see my son."

Lively saw a torn coloring book, saw blood on it, probably the mother's.

But maybe not.

Oh shit a kid, a kid got thrown. Or is he in that mess somewhere? I can't leave this guy but where the fuck is the kid?

"He's fine."

Feeling his own panic rising up in him, August Lively turned on his internal loop, saw a Vietnamese boy in tap shoes and a top hat singing *this is dinky dau, dinky dinky dinky dau, this is dinky dau, dinky dinky dau*. The kid in his head was like a little god of madness; his holy message conveyed in idiot song was that everything was fucked up and ridiculous and that all you could do was your best. That your best was never going to be enough, that was okay, that was number one, panic was number ten.

If only somebody could radio in a chopper—an ambulance was going to take a month of Sundays, and if neither of these folks had internal injuries, he'd eat his own shorts.

Where the fuck is the kid? Probably dead. Don't let this guy die, too.

"Where are you from?" he asked the stricken man, stroking his head, gritting his teeth, scanning the very dark land for the little boy he knew he wouldn't find. Blood bubbled from the inverted man's nose, a drop running along the side of his nose toward his eye. The hitcher intercepted it with a thumb.

Finally, flashing red lights coming, a siren. Probably the state police. Thank Christ. Thank Buddha. Thank Bugs Bunny. The college guy had done okay.

If cops came, he'd stay with the man and make them look for the kid. If paramedics came, he'd look for the kid. *Dinky fucking dau.*

Would he be a suspect? Shirtless, bloody, scruffy, six dollars and a roach in his pocket? Nobody but two semiconscious accident victims and a mildly stoned UNM sophomore to vouch for him?

Stranger things had happened.

The semiconscious woman sobbed.

Then she laughed.

IT SEEMED TO JUDITH THAT THE MOON HAD SHONE IN THE WINDOW AS THE CAR rolled, that she saw it exactly twice as it revolved wildly around the crumpling axis of the Falcon, whose interior was mad with the scrambled gravity of purse and coins and sand and crayons. She would never forget the noise of it, the earsplitting sound of everything breaking, her husband's shout stomped flat by the composite heel of dashboard, roof, windshield. When everything settled, she had something like an out-of-body experience, only she wasn't a disembodied spirit—she experienced the scene through the eyes of another person. She saw herself from above and feared she was dead, with her shirt wrenched halfway around and blood in her eye, her black hair matted and plastered to her cheek. She was upside-down, resting on her neck. She knew then that she wasn't herself but a man; she used hands the color of cocoa to grab her own white limbs, pulling herself free from the impossibly flat, impossibly twisted Falcon. Her new hand cradled the small head that once belonged to her, supporting it in case the neck was broken. A small boulder that should have dashed the brains from her had instead sheared off the door and propped the chassis up to give her the space she needed to live, and the man she was now stooped and shouldered her body past this. You shouldn't move accident victims, this man she was knew better than most, but the angle at which she had come to rest seemed to put weight on her neck, and he wanted to see the rest of her body, see where all the blood might be coming from. That she saw herself from another human being's eyes didn't surprise her so much—she had dreams that came true sometimes, and this experience, while different, seemed cut somehow from the same cloth of unreality.

When she came back into her own body, she knew it was for a period of trial and great tragedy. She had the idea that her son was dead, and this seemed cruel to her, or random, and neither cruelty nor happenstance seemed compatible with the idea of a benign and responsible God. She believed in God, she *needed* him. Now was no time to doubt his motives, wrecked in the desert at night. She sobbed. Then she realized how foolish she was being, taking a dream so seriously. It had to be a dream, because she thought monsters with shining eyes had taken Glendon. Monsters! It was ridiculous. A black man's broad face loomed down at her, kind and wise. She thought she smelled pot. She laughed.

Then everything went away.

2

SHE WOKE UP AFTER A LONG DITCH OF NOTHING.

Her eyes wouldn't open all the way.

The lights, the tray with a water pitcher, the curtain, all suggested hospital. The next face she saw staring down at her belonged to her little sister, Patricia. She wore a shirt Judith didn't recognize, a pretty coral-colored shirt with a frilly collar. It took Jude a moment to remember that she didn't live at home anymore, that she wouldn't know when Mom got Patsy a new shirt. Nobody in the Eberhart family had wanted to call her Patsy; it was the kind of name to invite teasing, with its connotations of gullibility, especially for a girl like her, but she had preferred that to Patty or Pat, introducing herself as Patsy from the age of five. She wasn't a little girl anymore, but she lived at home. She would always live at home. How old was she? Twenty? Older? Judith was starting to remember something else, something troubling.

"Um," the young woman said, looking agitated.

Judith tried to say her name, but it came out *Passy*.

"Um. Jude. Mom's not here."

Judith just watched her. Something horrible was trying to assert itself in Jude's memory, but she fixed on the bright coral fabric of her sister's shirt.

"Mom's in the bathroom. She'll be right back."

Patsy looked to the hallway, looking for their mother. There was something Judith needed to know, something Patsy didn't want to tell her. Her mother would say the words. Or the man. What was the man's name? Robert. There was a word for what Robert was to her, a word like *lover* or *buzzer* or *hug*.

It would come to her later.

Patsy looked at her now, then looked down, shifting from side to side. She liked Patsy's face. A little like hers, framed in shoulder-length black hair, but thicker in the jaw, her nose turned up. It was a plain, trusting face, the face of a girl who would never stop liking milk-shakes. The eyes heavy-lidded and brown, not blue like hers. Like the boy's.

What boy?

"Um. Mom's coming right back, okay? Okay, Jude?"

"Okay," she managed.

"Your face is bruised a lot."

"I'm sorry."

"I don't like how much your face is bruised. It's green. Except your eyes are black like you been in a fight."

"I guess it's good I can't see my face."

"It's bruised bad. And it's cut."

"It'll get better."

"I know. Mom said."

Patsy rested her head on Jude's shoulder, touched her cheek with her fingers. Lightly, so lightly. Was anyone as loving as Patsy? She'd never deserved the ugly words other kids had used about her. Jude had never tolerated those words. Billy Verne had shouted *mongoloid* from his bike just across the street from the Sacred Heart Academy and sat there looking tough with a cigarette, but Jude had pushed him off that bike and kicked him with the hard toes of her polished Mary

Janes. Kicked his shins so hard they bled through his khakis. She got suspended for that, but Billy Verne never shouted anything at Patsy again, not from his bike, not from a school bus, not from a second-story window. When Mother asked Father Grogan to talk to her about what she did to Billy, he said, "I'm sure you know our Lord Jesus, who told us to turn the other cheek in the face of violence and ignorance, never would have done such a thing." Then added, "But, if I'm honest, I doubt he would have stopped you."

People who knew Patsy loved her.

Especially the boy.

The boy with the coloring book.

"Oh God," she said, her eyes welling up. "Oh God."

Patsy patted her cheek.

That was how their mother found them.

JUDITH KNEW HER MOTHER HAD NO GIFT FOR DELIVERING BAD NEWS.

When Judith had been fifteen and Patsy ten, the family dog, an affable little mutt named Chester, was buried in the backyard with great pomp after being "struck by a car." Actually, Chester had been killed by a neighbor's Bedlington terrier. The truth emerged (for her, not Patsy) when her mother got tipsy one night not long before Jude's wedding. On that September day, the kids were at Sacred Heart, their father working at the watch factory. Janet Eberhart had seen the other dog coming. It had finally worried a second plank out of its fence two doors down and wriggled free, and this escape coincided with one of Chester's smiley, ambling tours around the yard to water the heaps of raked leaves. When Janet saw the Bedlington streaking across the next-door neighbor's lawn, her first thought had been *My, that sheep runs fast*, but then the wretched, curly thing had grabbed poor, screaming Chester by the neck and started shaking him like one of the knotted socks her dog so enjoyed tugging tugs-of-war with. Janet had fetched a rake from the porch and tried to swat the other dog off Chester, but she hit the victim as often as the aggressor. The Bedlington's owner, a neurotic drama teacher whose wife took long trips away, came bounding across the yard separating their properties and, to Janet's astonishment, ducked under her rake to shield his dog, tugging impotently at the thing's collar. The murderer's name was Brando, and she would dream that name for years. "Brando," the little man said again and again, "Brando, Brando, please!" as if admonishing a good but stubborn child. When Brando finally let drop his prey and suffered himself to be led home, his owner, receding across the lawn with his captive, babbled a barely punctuated apology at Janet without meeting her eyes, "I really don't know what got into him I'm so, *we're* so sorry, of course I'll compensate you it's just awful I've been meaning to fix that fence but I'm not handy like your husband I should have just paid somebody to do it I guess oh what will the girls think I'm beside myself I'm sorry I'm sorry I'm sorry you bad bad dog I'll never forgive you." Janet had just held her rake and watched them go, the terrier proud of itself, the man ridiculous with his cheeks, his lime-green shirt, his European scarf all speckled with blood, his own hand bleeding from a bite. And Chester just limp and finished near a pile of poplar leaves.

She took the dog to the vet and left him there. When the girls got home at three, she told them Chester had run off, but not to worry. Their father would take care of things. Patsy believed her, of course, but Judith had been old enough to sort out that Chester wasn't coming home alive. If the dog had run off, Mom would have set the girls making signs to nail up on light poles while she called every shelter in Fresno. Judith knew "Dad's taking care of things" would mean coming up with a story and presenting a body. She had excused herself to cry in her room so Patsy wouldn't know.

WHEN HER MOTHER TOLD HER, "GLEN'S NOT DEAD, HONEY, HE CAN'T BE," AND "Robert's banged up but the doctors are hopeful," and "Nobody can believe how lucky you were; aside from the concussion and the cut on your face, you were barely injured," Judith knew she'd have to wait for a doctor to tell her something like the truth. Her father would talk straight to her, but her father was still in California.

It turned out the last thing her mother said was correct; she really was lightly injured for the violence of that wreck. The worst pain she had came not from her lacerations or bruises, but from a twisted ankle that was expected to heal without future impediment. The paramedic who loaded her onto the ambulance came to see her in the hospital, told her, "There just wasn't room enough for a person to live in that car, but you did. There was only one place on the ground your head could have gone without busting on a rock and you found it. I keep trying to tell myself it's just luck but I can't. I hadn't been to church in ten years but I went after I saw you. You weren't just lucky. You were *spared.*"

He left a pamphlet next to her water pitcher.

She started to read it but then put it in her drawer, next to another religious pamphlet a visiting nun had left her. She liked the nun's pretty Catholic pamphlet better with its illuminated manuscript pictures—the paramedic's was a Protestant cartoon about heaven and hell, and in very poor taste, but she thought she should give it a chance, too.

I'll read them both when I get my son back. That's the deal.

But there was no deal.

Glendon Lamb was declared missing. The Torrance County Sheriff's Department and almost a hundred volunteers, mostly church folks from Albuquerque and Pueblo Indians from Isleta, combed the scrubland near Clines Corners. Paint scrapings confirmed the involvement of a red car, but Judith's testimony about the people with the shining eyes made the officer who took her statement stop writing. State troopers in New Mexico and their counterparts in west Texas set up roadblocks looking for Glendon, as well as for a black Camaro and a red sports car, possibly traveling together, the latter possibly driven by a bald Caucasian suspect.

Judith had been out for three days.

Her account of the abduction made no sense.

"Their eyes were *shining*. Shining how, Mrs. Lamb?"

"Like a cat. Like cat's eyes in the grass by the side of the road."

"Shining."

"Yes."

The first man on the scene never saw the assailants with the shining cat's eyes.

The trail went hopelessly cold.

MEANWHILE, ROBERT LAMB LAY DYING.

His fragile body would never be able to handle the trauma of surgery, nor his split liver the burden of a general anesthetic; even surgery might not stop his brain from swelling. He lingered in a dimly lit room for nine days. Judith came to see him on day five. He had been waking up intermittently, sometimes to cry, sometimes to roll his eye around. When Judith limped into the room and sat down by the bed, she took his remaining hand in hers and he opened his eye. His yellow eye sat mounted in a sunken triangle of yellow flesh where the bandages had been cut to let him see. He fixed that eye on her and she grew cold knowing he was going to say something she didn't want to hear. It is possible to think that she needed to hear the words he slurred around his tube over the next hour, that his brief lucidity was in itself a sort of rough providence. Without the toxic words he poured into her ears, her hopelessness might not have been complete, and she might not have taken steps to become what she became.

The man with the yellow eye told the bruised woman a story.

3

CARLA HARRIS WALKED INTO THE HOSPITAL HOLDING HERSELF LIKE A WOMAN who had done a great good deed. She had driven nearly twenty-four hours, not counting half a night of barely strung-together naps in the parking lot of a truck stop diner, her car close enough to the building to be visible under the lights, but not so close that thick-faced men in work shirts would leer at her on their way to eat chili dogs. Her hands still smelled ferrous from clutching the tire iron.

"Mr. Lamb is in very grave condition," the woman with the thick horn-rimmed glasses and cheap lipstick said from behind her desk. "Are you family?"

Carla had been prepared for this.

"Yes."

"What is your relationship to the patient?"

"Sister."

"Name?"

"Emma Lamb."

Robert had mentioned a spinster sister in Philly or Pittsburgh, Carla wasn't sure if it was Emma or Ellie, but this bookworm girl with the big forehead wouldn't challenge her unless the actual sister was here, and the odds weren't good on that. Robert said they weren't close. Robert wasn't close with a lot of his kin, but she understood that because it was the same for her. Not that she had much against her own relations except that they were people, and she never could stand people for too long. That was the problem with family—they just kept being family.

Carla stared at the egghead receptionist, half hoping she'd try to give her guff, but she passed Carla a clipboard and asked her to sign in. The pen didn't write well.

Carla was glad she was going to get a chance to say good-bye to Robert; she didn't feel good about the way they'd left things.

"YOU'RE GOING TO HELL," SHE HAD SAID, AND SHE MEANT IT, EVEN THOUGH SHE wasn't sure she believed in hell.

He was calling her from some phone booth in Covington, where he always called her from. It had occurred to her that a phone booth would be a good instrument in which to cook a man, and there simply had to be cannibals in hell. She imagined them lined up like Zulus in that British movie, an army of them stamping out a cannibal dance in the fire, waiting for Robert Lamb to plump up in his glass-walled rectangular pot, waiting for the windows to crack from the heat and for his juice to run clear like a roast chicken's juice so they would know he was done and come for him. She thought all of these things in the silence after she spoke.

"Are you still there? Did you check out on me? That's your favorite move, isn't it? Checking out?"

She had caught her own reflection in the living room mirror, standing the way she always stood when she spoke on the phone, one foot crossed over the other, her free hand fingering the coils of the phone cord the way she might have fingered a rosary if she were Catholic like Robert's prize hen. She knew she was thinking mean thoughts, but she didn't care. She had a *right*. And meanness was her thing. It turned on a certain kind of man. She knew very well what she was to Robert—the sharp-tongued bartender at the watering hole across from his law office; the cute blonde with a vocabulary just big enough to hide her ignorance. She felt bad for the people who loved her no matter what she said to them; some people are just so pretty you pretend until you can't anymore, and she was one of those people. She would learn to be nicer when she got ugly. But she would probably die before she did that.

No matter what inchworm did to her figure.

"I . . . Yes. Yes, I checked out on you. I'm sorry."

"Sorry," she had said, spitting the word back at him so he could hear how dead it was.

"I am sorry, Carla. More than I can tell you."

"Maybe you are."

She had paused, savoring the words she was about to use.

"Or maybe you'll just say anything now to protect *her*. The fucking . . . *wife*."

"Yes," he said. But the truth was worse than that. He wanted to shield Judith from this; of course, he *did* love her. Carla could detect love the way the deaf can feel music. But the truth was that the thing he dreaded most about Judith finding out wasn't her pain. It was his inconvenience. What a sunless, lightless fucking drag the whole weeping world would become when it got out that golden boy had put his horse in the wrong stable. A few wrong stables, if the truth were told, but this one had caught fire.

At the time she made the phone call, it had pleased her to think that if she couldn't be a wife to Robert, at least she could drive one away.

Robert had asked for this. It had been *his* drunken intimations that he might not be married for much longer that had gotten Carla to invite him up for "an after-drink drink." *His* suggestions that his wife was unfaithful had coaxed her panties off. At least, that was the way she let it seem to him. Truthfully, once she set her eye on something she had to have it—she would have screwed the handsome, serious-looking lawyer if he'd been married to a saint.

What finally ended the affair was Robert's refusal, even drunk, to come inside her. She had already admitted to not being on the pill, that she wanted a baby, even out of wedlock. When that seemed to scare him, she had changed her story. She told him she *was* on the pill, a new kind that you didn't have to wait to kick in. To his credit, he had been too smart to buy that one. She was trying to trap him, so he *checked out.*

She accepted this at first, she really did.

If she followed him in her car once or twice, it was his own fault. He had gotten her good and hooked, he knew exactly what he did to women. If it took her a few weeks to let go, that was to be expected.

Then it happened.

She saw him pick up the boy at kindergarten.

His boy, a wild-haired little thing with the most piercing eyes she had ever seen. She had screamed in her car, pounding the steering wheel while the oblivious philanderer drove his son home.

He had never once mentioned having a son.

She thought about telling her other regular lover, a bookie with a red devil tattoo on his ass, about her affair with Robert, knowing the hothead would beat the hell out of him. Just drive to the law firm and beat the ever-loving shit out of him in his own office, his tie flying up, his coworkers running and leaving him to gasp like a fish in his own blood. But then Rob would *really* never see her again, the bookie would go to jail, and she'd have to patch things up with the fry cook.

Instead, she put a note under Robert's windshield.

CALL ME TOMORROW AT THREE.
IF YOU KNOW WHAT'S GOOD FOR YOU.

The clock in her kitchen read ten after three when she said, "I'm going to flip a coin, Bob."

"A coin."

"That's right. A quarter. Your marriage rests on a quarter, how do you like that, you cheap bastard? If it comes up heads, it means I tell her. But when, right? So I flip it again. Heads, I tell her now. Tails, I tell her later. Maybe much later, you won't know."

"And if the first one's tails?"

"Let's just say you won't have anything to worry about. Not in this world, anyway."

"Don't say something like that. You're not going to do anything of the kind."

She had let him stew in that for a moment, and it was a good moment.

"What if I was? Would you want that?"

She had softened her voice a note.

She would no more shoot herself than the man in the moon, but she would make him say she mattered to him. By God, she would.

"Carla . . ."

"Yes, *Bob*. I know my name, *Bob*. You're just spinning your wheels because you haven't got the sack to tell me you wish I'd dry up and blow away."

"No, I . . . don't want that."

"Okay, so you'd rather I told her."

She remembered that she had heard a truck go by just then, in Covington or wherever he was, and she had the idea it was a garbage truck. People were full of garbage, and telephones were just another way for them to dump it on each other.

"Yes," he said at last, forcing the syllable out. "If the alternative is you hurting yourself, yes."

She didn't respond for a moment.

She let him hear ice in her glass; women who drink in the afternoon are wild horses, they could trample you.

"Well," she said. "That's something. The thing is, Bob, I don't believe you."

She twirled the cord, thrilling to the power it held, what she could do through it.

"Carla, listen," he said.

"No, Bob, you listen."

That was when she flipped a coin on the table so he could hear its potent *chink* and wobble. She had looked at herself in the mirror as she did it. She looked good holding a phone, threatening a man. She could have been on *All My Children*.

"Well, that's interesting," she had said.

"What? What was it?"

"Heads or tails, you mean?"

"Yeah."

Silence.

"That's for you to find out."

She had hung up.

That had been a month ago.

Now her lover was all banged to hell and the car he loved so much was junk. The wife was in a coma or something, the paper had said so. Now Carla was here, ready to stand tall and healthy over Robert's bed and let him see what he missed. Ready, if he was going to die, and it sounded like he might, to send him out of the world thinking about her.

She walked into his room.

God, he looked worse than she had imagined.

His *arm* was gone; the paper didn't say that.

"Oh, Robert," she said.

So many bandages, like a mummy.

It was almost funny.

His eye was a closed slit in a patch of yellow skin.

He was out.

"Robert," she said, moving toward his bed.

God, the tubes, the IV bag, this was like a movie.

She made her face look sympathetic and concerned. This was where he would open his eye and see her. She put her hand on her belly, gently, significantly, so he would know about inchworm in a glance, never mind that it was almost certainly not his. Robert always pulled out. She and the bookie had both been too drunk to know if he had pulled out, which meant he probably hadn't.

"Robert, look at you," she said a little louder, letting her voice hitch.

This was his cue to look at her.

Robert wasn't opening his eye.

He didn't move at all.

But something moved to her right.

A woman had been sitting in the chair, blocked from her view by the open door. Could it be the wife? She had imagined her prettier, though, to be fair, she might look okay if not for the swelling and the wicked paint job the bruises had done on her.

The woman stood.

Was she trembling?

Carla felt her eyebrow rise, the way it always rose in confrontations. She didn't like the eyebrow. It made her look smug and, even if she felt that way, smug wasn't a good way to look. She tried to put it down, but it wouldn't go.

The woman's eyes were blue like the sky in a fairy tale.

The whites white as summer clouds.

Eyes like that boy's.

"You must be Judith," she said, brightening her voice a little too much when she said her rival's name.

The woman looked her in the eye, then dropped her gaze to where Carla's hand lay on her belly. She looked at Carla's eyes again.

Carla got her eyebrow down.

The woman was standing with the help of a cane.

Carla got the idea that the woman wanted to beat her to death with that cane. As if reading her mind, the woman carefully set the cane on the chair.

Carla knew she should talk now.

"I just want you to know that I'm so . . ."

The fist loomed up overhand, fast, so fast.

Carla heard her own nose break.

Sat down hard.

4

"DO YOU HAVE VIOLENT EPISODES OFTEN?"

"I wouldn't say often."

The man wrote on his tablet. His legs were crossed at the knee, the toe of an expensive shoe pointing up. Overhead lights reflected in his eyeglasses.

"And you said she isn't pressing charges."

"Not if I pay for her nose job. And see you once a week."

He smiled a practiced smile.

"Do you think she felt remorse?"

"I think she didn't want to look like a whore at the trial."

"You mentioned she was at the funeral."

"That's right."

"Tell me how you feel about that."

"I don't feel anything."

A silver angelfish with black vertical stripes cruised by in the aquarium to her right. A very bright red hermit crab ducked into the shell it had been carrying when the fish passed.

The doctor watched Judith for a moment, but she didn't elaborate.

"Do you prefer to talk about . . . Glendon?"

He had looked at his papers to check the name.

She watched him do it, then blinked hard and looked at the ceiling.

"No."

"I think it would be good for you. These other things we're talking about are peripheral."

"Yep."

"I'm assuming there haven't been any new developments."

"I said I didn't want to talk about it."

"That's right, you did."

"But no. No developments."

The fish cruised by again, rolling its big eye around. Its eye was orange like a tiny full moon rising just past sunset. She remembered Robert's eye swiveling in the triangle cut in the bandages.

She didn't speak.

"Okay. We don't have to discuss Glendon if you're not ready. What do you want to talk about?" the doctor said.

"Honestly, nothing."

The toe of the expensive shoe bobbed up and down.

"I heard that was quite a right hook you gave her."

"Right cross."

"Are you a boxing enthusiast?"

"My father was a middleweight."

"Professional?"

"Briefly."

"What happened?"

"He figured out he wasn't ever going to get a title shot. At his best, he was the guy people beat up to get a shot at a title shot."

"That must have been disappointing."

"Do you think so?"

The doctor wrote in his notepad.

"Good. I like your sarcasm. I like it when you show a little life."

"You don't sound like you like it."

"You mustn't read too much into tone. You were talking about your father's frustrations with his boxing career."

"Yeah. Anyway, there was steady money at the factory."

"But he taught you. To box."

"He wanted a boy. First he got me. Then he got Patsy. Patsy seemed like time to quit, I guess. He stuffed an army duffel full of old shirts and sawdust and hung it from a tree in the yard. He used to pay me a quarter for every half an hour I'd hit it, but only a dime if he caught me punching sloppy. He said girls not knowing how to fight was why they got taken advantage of so much. Mom hated it, said he was giving me boy's hands. I already had boy's hands. He was looking forward to . . . yeah."

She stopped herself.

The doctor got up and poured her a glass of water from a pitcher on a small table. She looked at him while she drank the whole thing, and he had the impression that she was reassessing him, though whether for better or worse seemed unclear.

"We've got two more months of this," she said.

"That's right."

"I don't think I'm going to make it."

"Make it, how?"

"Hold together."

"Do you have to hold together?"

"Do you only ask questions?"

"Mostly."

"Do you like it? Your job asking questions?"

"Most days."

"But not today?"

"Today's not so bad."

"Would you tell me if it was?"

"Not in so many words."

"Why not?"

"If you think you're getting my paycheck by asking the questions, you're mistaken."

He was smiling again. She tried to smile back but she didn't think the expression her face made was exactly a smile.

"Why do you think you have to hold together?"

"I just do."

"That's interesting."

She heard the sound of his pen scratching at his notepad. It seemed to go on for a long time.

The hermit crab was walking around again. She watched it, waited for the angelfish to circle around and swivel its eye at her. How many loops had that goddamned fish made while she was sitting here? How many would it make in the months or years before the good doctor found it floating at the top of the tank? Was there an angel in charge of angelfish who knew that number? Would there be two numbers, one for clockwise, one for counterclockwise?

The doctor was working his lips because they were about to dilate and birth another question disguised as an imperative. He was going to say, *Tell me again about the people with the shining eyes and the sharp teeth.* They were forty minutes into their hour and that was when he usually tried to get her to talk about her car monsters. She had begun to say that she wasn't sure she saw them, that the trauma of the accident and Glen's disappearance must have made her remember things that weren't there. This was the answer he wanted to hear, but he wanted to believe her and he didn't yet.

She would scream if he made her lie again. She would scream if he asked her another question of any kind right now. She needed at least one more fish-lap before she got another arbitrary, time-wasting prompt from this overeducated, overpaid, deeply sad man.

His lips parted. The tip of his tongue mashed up against his palate, he was about to manufacture the *tuh* in *tell*, and if he did, she would shriek so loud the angelfish's brain would swell, it would leak blood from its head and circle the tank leaving a murky wake, a depth-charged sub, a shot-up fighter plane, a car rolling on the desert floor throwing coins and potato chips.

She had to intercept that *tuh*.

They spoke simultaneously.

"Tell . . ."

"I want to be quiet now. I just want to sit here and be quiet."

5

THE DREAM WOKE HER. SHE GASPED. SHE LIFTED HER HEAD FROM THE PILLOW she had wet with drool and looked around her room. Morning's first light bled in through the curtains, just too bright for her to blame the streetlamps. She found herself bunched up to one side of the bed as though she still had to share it with her husband, but he was three weeks in a box. Her T-shirt clung to her here and there where she had broken out in a night sweat, but she heard the fan on the dresser and felt it cooling her. The dream had made her sweat.

A man had been in her bed, but it wasn't Robert. Then the same man had been hitchhiking, but it wasn't the black man who pulled her out of the car. It was a dead man, long dead, his skin fish-belly pale and an almost pleasant stink on him like faraway skunk. But when he opened his mouth, fireflies came out. What was he doing in her bed? Was that why she had pushed herself over to one side, to give this corpse room to lie with her? Perhaps they had been speaking. It didn't seem to have been a sexual dream, but she couldn't reason out what had made her sweat. It had all the ingredients of a nightmare, but something about it made her feel . . . what? Alive, perhaps. Whatever had passed between them, he had gone out the window and started walking away from her toward the highway with his thumb out. His fireflies went with him and left her in darkness so profound and hopeless that she gasped.

Judith went to the bathroom and looked at herself in the mirror. The face that stared back at her struck her as some relative's face, an older cousin's face. The stitches were out, but the scar traversing her nose and cheek still looked pink and raw, like a slash of war paint in a bad western. She wouldn't be doing any face cream commercials soon. Or ever. But she wasn't hideous. Her mother would be glad of that, at least. Her mother worshipped at the church of grandchildren and even now, even with Glendon barely cold, if cold he was,

I'm in the trunk, Mom! I'm in the trunk but there's no rush.

the old woman would already be sizing up Judith like a brood mare. It made her want to march down to the hospital and demand a hysterectomy. She missed Glen too much for another infant, even a hypothetical baby ten years out, to seem like anything but a reptile posing as a child. She had been grateful when he stopped screaming so much and learned to sleep the night through, but now she would do anything to hear that high, rattling scream, so particular to him. So different from any other infant's.

"Stop it," she told herself, and squinted away the tears that wanted to come.

She thought about going back to sleep to finish that odd dream, but she didn't think it would return. She feared sleep would bring another crash nightmare, the variations of which were like various tentacles of the same malign octopus: Sometimes she rode in the backseat of a driverless car just beginning to careen out of control, unable to get to the steering wheel before it gained speed and smashed a guardrail, or wandered across the line into the grilles and headlights of oncoming traffic, and she woke shouting. Sometimes she cradled

Glendon in her lap while the Falcon teetered on the edge of a mountain pass or a bridge, and the boy crawled away from her and out the window; when she went after him, her shifting weight made the car fall, and it rolled while it fell, and she woke shouting. Sometimes Robert drove them slowly through a crowd of people with shining eyes like cat's eyes staring in at her because they knew her husband was a liar, and when she asked him what he was lying about, he floored the pedal and smashed the car into the crowd and arms came off and heads knocked the windshield and she knew the brains inside those heads would swell and she woke shouting.

These were ordinary nightmares, she knew, common to victims of trauma. Nothing to fear, just some nocturnal yelling. Now that she was alone in the big empty Craftsman on Coventry Street, she could shout to her heart's content. She considered shouting now, at her own scarred face in the mirror, just to prove she could. She even took a sharp breath in.

She let the breath out.

"You're going off your rocker," she told her face, and the face didn't disagree.

She wanted to go back to bed and dream of the dead man with a mouth full of fireflies, but she knew she would dream of crashing.

She knew she would dream of shining eyes.

Too dark in here, even with the sun inching closer.

She didn't like the dark anymore.

im in the dark now mom but i dont mind the dark or the cold because nothing can hurt me in the trunk lets both get in the trunk and not be hurt

"Stop it!" she told the voice, not really Glendon's voice, she knew, but some part of her own brain that wanted to torment her. Or maybe it was something worse—maybe her mother was right. Janet Eberhart really believed in the devil, devils in plural, and angels, and she hadn't been sure she believed in devils, but now.

Oh, but now.

Judith turned all the lights on in the house.

She put coffee on and sat at the dining room table, glad for the sound of its percolation. She knew she shouldn't look at the kitchen clock because she wasn't going to like what it said, but of course she looked almost immediately.

Five forty.

Even when she had a husband and child, the house would have been still now. She used to cherish the mornings she woke up first, how precious that hour or half hour of silence had been. At six thirty Robert's alarm would have gone off and he would have started the gruff industry of morning. Glen would have woken up when he heard the bell on Dad's Westclox, and even though he liked to wallow in bed and play with this or that toy under the sheets as if in a tent, he would have tromped downstairs by seven in his footie PJs, mad for cereal. Maybe if she listened hard enough she would hear his feet, just the sound of them, not a ghost precisely but a crack in this false, still new world the accident had made. If she heard that sound and believed hard enough, maybe the actual boy would knit himself up from the ankles, hop into the kitchen like a bunny, and drag a chair across the linoleum so he could reach the cupboard and, on the bottom shelf, his bowl with cowboys on it.

She folded her hands under her nose and talked into them, saying, "Just take it back, I won't tell anybody you changed your mind so they'll expect it too. Just take it back and it'll be our secret and I'll do anything you want. I can find that paramedic's church and turn Protestant, I can even forgive Robert if you just do this for me please please please."

She turned off the coffee urn so she could hear better and she bent her head and listened for Glendon but all she heard was birds, and after half an hour she was starting to hate the birds, so she turned the coffee back on.

"I HAD A WEIRD DREAM THIS MORNING, MOM, LIKE A FEVER DREAM," JUDITH SAID.

"Did you sweat?"

"Yes."

"It wasn't about lemons, I hope."

"Not lemons."

The two women were boxing the last of Robert's clothes for the church thrift store. His side of the closet was empty now, and the same was true of the medicine cabinet and the pantry and the refrigerator. Neither Jude's father nor mother dared suggest she should start paring down Glen's things; it had only been a month. Nobody in authority held out any hope the boy might be recovered, but Judith kept staring at children on the street who resembled her son in any way. Once she had seen a boy with little red pants just like Glendon's and she followed that boy into the library, so full of mad hope she made a soft squeal in the back of her throat. She knew good and well those pants were in Glen's drawer because she had washed and folded them for the third time that morning, but when the library boy turned around with the wrong face, the strength of her anger and betrayal astonished her. She turned on her heel and marched herself out the front door before she could slap the strange boy—she wouldn't have stopped slapping him until somebody pulled her off, or until he did what she wanted and turned into Glendon.

box my clothes up too mom im a big boy like daddy i wanted to be just like him and now i am

STOP IT!

"Do you have a fever?"

"I don't think so."

"Let me feel your forehead."

Judith obliged her.

"No, you're not warm."

Judith's mom looked at her with wary eyes; she remembered the night sweats that came on when Jude turned thirteen and started her monthlies, and she remembered the dreams that came with them.

In June of her fourteenth year, she had awakened her parents sleepwalking. Her top had been soaked. When her father asked her what she was doing, she had said she didn't want to go to "Lemons" because "Lemons" wasn't safe. They burned cars and threw them at people and they died. Although she didn't remember the conversation, parts of the dream had stuck with her. Her dad had asked her who told her Lemons wasn't safe, but nobody told her—she had seen a lettered sign, and a flying car, and fire. Days later, the worst auto racing accident in history took place at Le Mans when a hurtling car struck the barrier separating the crowd from the track and somersaulted over, burning and beheading scores of spectators.

Mom's face sagged as she thought about the echo here, how another layer of coincidence had been piled on to that distant event by circumstance. Judith the girl had dreamed not only about an event taking place later that week, but also about the way Judith the woman was destined to lose her family. Had God really shown a child a glimpse of the awful turn her life was going to take and given her no chance to escape it? It was all too much. She folded a shirt.

"I have to get out of here, Mom."

"I think that's probably a good idea. You should come back to California."

"I don't know what I'd do there."

"You could still test for the post office. In Fresno. Weren't you going to do that anyway now that . . ."

She swallowed the words *Glen's in school* but Jude heard them anyway.

"They're giving all those jobs to vets."

"Not all of them. And you'll test really high, I know you will. They pay."

"I don't think I can just go to California like nothing ever happened."

"What will you do here? There's nothing holding you to Ohio now. Just his people, and his people are . . ."

Judith wasn't sure if the next word was going to be *untrustworthy* or *cold*, but she couldn't have argued with either one.

"There's something I'm thinking of."

"Surely you see that coming home is natural. In these circumstances."

"No, Mom, listen to me. I just have to get out of here, and Fresno's not going to help. At least I don't think so. I need . . . I just have a big hole where my heart was. Everything's falling into it."

Mom taped the box shut, but her hands were shaking and she stuck the tape to itself. "Oh shucks," she said. "Now I've done it."

Judith helped her separate the tape.

"Where will you go?"

"Someplace I guess I never thought about. But I just want to see."

"Can you tell me?"

"You'll laugh."

"I think my laugher's busted for a good while."

"Anyway, I just want to see."

"Where, Jude?"

"Here," she said, getting to her feet in a fluid way the older woman simultaneously envied and felt guilty for envying. She came back with a paper triptych showing a medieval-looking woman holding a flower.

"It's just for a weekend. Just to see what it's all about."

Her mother unfolded the brochure, looked at it, then folded it back. She gave Judith a dubious look.

She only said one word.

"You?"

6

"A LOT OF YOUNG WOMEN SIT IN THAT CHAIR ONCE. ABOUT HALF OF THEM SIT IN IT twice. Very few come back for a third interview."

"I understand."

"Do you?"

Judith had to struggle to look at the older woman's eyes. However kind they were, they were also hard. They were the eyes of a woman who had been disappointed innumerable times, and knew you were likely to do it to her, too. They were eyes that withheld their true sparkle for those who surprised her.

"I hope I do, Mother Superior."

The older woman nodded. Judith had the impression she was pleased to hear a measured answer. She noticed for the first time that she sat higher than the nun with whom she spoke. The older woman had intentionally chosen a lower chair for herself than that her guests sat upon.

"You don't owe us anything, you know."

"I feel I do."

"Nonsense. Helping others is our chief calling, and there is no question in my mind that you needed help. Help we were uniquely qualified to give you. It was our duty to shelter you from the world that has been so very . . . brisk with you. It is why we have a guest house in the first place."

"I was able to sleep here. You quieted my mind."

"It was not us who gave you rest, but him we serve."

"Then I thank you for being . . . his instrument."

"The pause is telling."

"I'm sorry."

"The pause is not significant because you doubt. Everyone doubts, even our Lord at Gethsemane. Rather, it tells me you are honest. You pause because you want to make sure you mean what you say. That is a virtue."

Judith looked again at a large charcoal sketch of St. Peter's Basilica that hung in a simple frame on the wall opposite the window. It was a good sketch, earnest if not sophisticated. Something seemed important to her about that drawing, and she couldn't say why. Her mind went to a drawing Glen had made of their church; in it, the cross on top had migrated to the side, stuck jauntily out. He had made marks that looked like chicken feet to represent the roof tiles, and that struck her as rather advanced. Had her pride caused them all to be punished? Were her pride and Robert's transgression enough to cause God to withdraw the gift he had given them?

You're being ridiculous

She realized then that she had been spoken to and was expected to respond.

"Pardon me, Mother Superior?"

"Are you quite well?"

"Yes, I'm fine."

She blinked, looked deliberately away from the drawing.

"Vatican Two. I was fortunate enough to be sent with a group representing the American Order of Cistercians of the Common Observance. I saw His Holiness in person and even got to practice my Italian on an archbishop. Over cappuccino. I know that smacks of pride, but it was a very pleasant interlude. I think God gives us foretastes of the pleasures awaiting the faithful, and that we honor him by recognizing them as such and then going back to hard work and poverty. It's the going back that trips up so many of us."

"Yes, Mother Superior."

All this Mother Superior business, as if the younger woman were already a postulant.

"Judith."

"Yes?"

The woman leaned closer, spearing Jude with those eyes that missed so little.

"I meant what I said about you not owing us. I understand that you feel gratitude toward us, but make no mistake; the course you are proposing is nothing short of marriage. To Christ. And gratitude is a poor reason to marry anyone."

"It's more than that."

"You're quite sure, are you?"

Judith pinched her left finger, felt where her wedding ring used to sit.

"Yes."

"There it is. That refreshingly honest pause again."

"I'm sure."

"I think you very much want to be sure. But I'm not convinced you are, and I must be before I go further with your application."

Judith looked down.

The Mother Superior gently raised Judith's chin so their eyes met again, then sat back.

"I think you mistake affection for vocation. Our order is in some peril. Our numbers are flagging, hence the brochures. The retreats. The average age here is 58.4, I worked it out on my calculator. Oh, we get applicants, not in droves, but we get them. Modern life makes so many of us strangely empty. Yet, of the several girls who have presented themselves to us this year, you are one of only two I would seriously consider. There are other sisters in positions of authority who want me to accept anyone who isn't promiscuous or violent. But I would rather see us close our doors than harm young women by setting them up for failure."

"I won't fail, Mother Superior."

The woman seemed to chew the inside of her cheek.

"You could simply be our friend, you know. Buy our candles. Come to stay for a weekend once a year. Write us letters or send us Christmas cards, we very much like Christmas cards, especially Sister Agatha, who just had her cataracts removed in Dayton. My point is that you are a woman of the world. You have had the blessings of family, which is, despite what some of the sisters tell themselves, just as pleasing to the Lord as a life of contemplation and prayer. Yes, those blessings were taken from you, quite savagely, but, once you do the hard work of grieving, you will still be young enough to . . ."

Judith took a shallow in-breath and held it.

"There."

The Mother Superior pointed at her.

"You wanted to interrupt me because I was about to say something ignorant and presumptuous, something it wasn't my place to say. You would have been within your rights to interrupt, but you checked yourself. Your natural honesty is tempered with the good manners so often missing in girls your age. I like you, Judith. I don't think you're right for us, not yet, or rather I don't think we're right for *you*, however much moments like that make me doubt myself. We'll talk about your application, and pray on it. But I tell you candidly that I think joining our order now will do you great injury."

7

BIRDS SANG IN THE DOUGLAS FIR AND LODGEPOLE PINES A FEW MILES OUTSIDE Fresno, California, as Judith walked behind her father on a path they both knew well. Riley Eberhart carried an olive-drab duffel slung over one shoulder. Despite his nearly sixty years, he walked with the amiable slouch of a rancher's boy skipping church. Judith carried a shopping sack and the .22 rifle she'd been plinking cans with since she retired her pellet gun at ten.

He turned his head to flick an ice-blue eye at her, the hollow where the cancer bit his jaw making him look older but tough, like a bone the dogs had a gnaw at but couldn't splinter.

A robin hopped near the path, beaking now and again after some morsel wriggling in the brush. Dad spied the bird, too, and each knew what the other was thinking about. When Jude was nine, she had shot a robin with a pellet gun and stood transfixed while it thrashed, flying up and falling, flying up and falling.

What'd you do that for? You meanin' to eat that bird?

No.

Shoot him again.

I don't want to.

Have to.

Please, Daddy.

Ain't no please about it.

She tried to look away but he turned her head around.

Do it.

I can't!

She started crying then and put her gun down. Riley picked it up and put it back in her hand.

You gonna leave him like that?

Maybe he'll get better.

He won't.

You do it, Daddy.

No, ma'am. I'm not the one shot him for fun.

So she pumped the lever of the air gun until it was hard to pump, crying all the while. The bird had mostly stopped thrashing, and when she shot it again, it shivered hard once and stretched out its wing and lay still.

Can't unshoot a gun, Jude.

She had cried harder and he held her.

You won't never do that again, will you?

No, Daddy.

Then be sad for this one. But you be happy the next time you see a robin, because a robin taught you something you needed to know.

JUDITH'S DAD UNPACKED HIS DUFFEL, SETTING FOUR SODA CANS AND TWO WHITE jugs up on the hacked-flat top of a fallen log they had laid against a primeval mound of dirt and brambles they called Boot Hill.

"Your mom switched us off'n the glass to these new plastic milk jugs. 'Jug-a-Moo,' ain't that a peach? Some feller probably got him a corner office and a shiny new tiepin for comin' up with that one. What's the milkman s'pose to do now? They're always dreamin' up new ways to fire people."

"Least nobody's fired you."

"No, ma'am. Work too hard. Lot harder'n them lazy-ass milkmen anyway. Ten yards to start?"

"Sure."

"Pace 'em off," he said in his best John Wayne.

"Your feet are closer to a foot," she drawled in response. They had been doing that routine so long she couldn't remember if it was from a movie or not.

He handed her a .38 revolver from his duffel and fished out a box of shells. They stuffed cotton in their ears. Judith aimed and popped holes in the cans, dumped the shells, loaded the gun for her dad.

"What's wrong with the jugs, you scared of 'em?" he asked her as she set the cans back up.

"Nah. You hate 'em so much I thought I'd let you do the honors."

Riley made the Jug-a-Moos hop and wobble. Once they had warmed up, they took turns throwing cans for one another and shooting them just before they hit the ground. Riley was better at this, but not much; Jude hit about every other one at ten yards. After they finished the .38 rounds, then backed up and burned a box of .22 long rifles with her Winchester, they meandered over to a sunny break in the trees where a creek could be heard. Riley sat down next to his daughter on a massive oak stump gray with age and weather. "We've been polishing this old man with our butts since Ike was in office, haven't we?"

"Yep."

They shared warm beer and the deviled ham sandwiches Patsy had made for them, cutting off the crusts with great care and pride. Patsy never came to Boot Hill; she hated loud noises.

Riley rolled a cigarette from a pouch on his belt and fixed Judith with a long look.

"I just don't see it, you a nun. I know you're hurtin' and you've got hurtin' still to do, but it just seems like runnin' to me. What about Patsy?"

"What about her?"

"She'd be in seventh heaven if you moved back. Your old room needs a paint job, but I'm sure we could tackle that together. You could just get off the plane in Cincinnati Tuesday, pack up what you need, and drive on back. We could be right here plinkin' next week."

"I've got my own life to live, Dad."

"Reckon we all do."

"Anyway, are we talking about Patsy or you?"

She took a long swig of her Pabst and watched him sort out what he wanted to say next.

"They said no, right?"

"They haven't answered. But I think they might say no."

"They say no, you gonna find another one?"

She looked down. She didn't tell him about the other cloistered order in Detroit she had written to.

"I don't know. I'm still hoping about this one. I mean, I *felt* it and it felt right."

"Guess the Lord speaks to some. Me he ain't never had a conversation with, least not in clear words. Maybe holdin' you the first time he was tellin' me somethin'. Maybe seein' your mom and her friend at that park, he was sayin', *You pick careful now which one of them pretty gals you tip your hat to,* and I guess I did. Maybe I heard him growlin' when the *Missouri* opened up her big guns, man I never got used to that. But nothin' like a, what's the word, *calling*."

Judith looked at her dad's forearms, the fuzzy blue-green anchor tattooed on one, the cross and swallows on the other.

"You believe in evil, Dad?"

"I've seen evil deeds done. That what you mean?"

"I mean like the devil."

"That's a tricky one."

"Mom believes in the devil."

"Oh, sure she does, I know it."

"So if there's evil, there's got to be good, right?"

"I saw some things on the islands. I just don't know if there's enough good to balance them things, least not on earth. But I never saw nobody with horns and a tail. Just big white men and little yellow men doin' the worst things they could think of to each other. Then the lucky ones goin' home to their wives and tryin' to teach their kids not to kill birds just because."

He mussed her hair when he said that.

She looked out at nothing for a long moment.

Then she said, "No."

"No what?"

"I guess I just won't be a nun."

8

Dear Mrs. Lamb,

Upon review of your application and after careful discussion of your situation, I am happy to tell you that you have been accepted as a postulant at the Our Lady of the Gleaning monastery.

Orientation will be Friday, September 8 at nine A.M. Please bring no more than you will absolutely need, as living space is shared and clutter is not permitted. Dungarees or other work clothes and one set of ordinary clothes are recommended, and sufficient underthings to last one week between launderings. Your habit will be provided, as will all kitchen goods, linens, towels, et cetera. Up to five books are permitted, provided they will serve you in your journey at a cloistered order and will fit neatly onto a three-foot shelf.

Family visits will be permissible once per month, though we remind you that you will not be permitted to leave the grounds.

In hopes that your journey toward the bridegroom will be as rewarding as it is challenging,

Yours in peace,
Reverend Mother Mary Catherine

P.S.: Perhaps I ought not share this with you, but last night, after much prayer and contemplation, I had written you an altogether different letter, one reluctantly declining your request to join our house. I folded my glasses on my night table and tried to sleep, but sleep would not come for many hours. When at last it did, I dreamed of Our Savior, and when I have had such dreams in the past, they have usually been a comfort. Last night, however, he had his blessed back to me and would not turn to face me no matter how I pleaded my love for him. No, he would not look at me. I became aware of a field of corn wherein, at such a great distance I could scarcely recognize her, I saw a young girl I had refused entry to the order some years ago, a girl of tragic circumstances similar to your own only in their severity. I learned, some years later, that this girl had married badly and subsequently taken her own life. At the time, in my pride, I thought I had been correct to refuse her because she had shown such weak character, and I put thoughts of her away. I know how harsh that sounds, but it will perhaps not surprise you to learn that nuns are just as prey to sin as others, even if their temptations come in different forms. Now, seeing her in this dream, I understood that I had done her, and perhaps the order, a great disservice in turning her away at her time of need; I had let her need make me see her as a beggar rather than one with great gifts to offer. I feel now that I am compelled to welcome you. I accept the task gladly, confident that you will give to the order more than you will take, and hopeful that we will give you more than we demand.

PART TWO

The Killers

1969

9
Ohio

"THE PRESIDENT DOESN'T CARE ABOUT GOD, MAN. THAT'S WHAT THEY ALL TALK about to get the Bible-thumpers on board, but Nixon, Kissinger, McNamara, they only go to the church of the military industrial complex."

George sat in the corn with Mandy and their new friends as if they were kids about to play duck-duck-goose. The protest at the university had ended at sunset with the quiet reading of the names of war dead. It had been well attended and peaceful. Too peaceful, to George's mind. So he had painted *HONK TO IMPEACH NIXON* on his rear windshield in white shoe polish, leaving the relative urbanity of Wright State to cruise the farmland around Xenia, honking at other motorists and flashing the peace sign. He had gotten more insults and bird fingers than honks, and one flung bottle of Labatt's that had chipped his windshield, but he considered this a success. People needed to be woken up, and hanging around with like-minded folks wasn't going to do any good. He had to take it to God's country. When the sun went down, he had pulled into Pap's bar off 68 to wet his whistle. Mandy sat near him, hugging his arm with both of hers, while he ordered himself a beer and her a Coke with a cherry in it. She didn't like beer, though she had tried to like it for George. She felt the same way about pot.

And politics, but she had determined not to give up on that yet. Expressing anything but disapproval for the fascist regime in Washington would cause him to point his big vocabulary at her and fire it again and again till her head blew off and all she could do was nod and say, "I guess I hadn't thought of it that way" or "I'm sorry, I just don't read enough." Then he would talk sweetly to her like a teacher or, when he was drinking, some kind of prophet, but both of those things were better than being shot at with words. What she really cared about was horses. She had worked all last summer at a riding camp before shipping off for her freshman year at Wright State, teaching wealthier girls how to ride and then brushing down the beautiful quarter horses and Appaloosas and that sweet-eyed bay named Percival. She had tried to get George to meet Percival, and he promised to, but somehow they never found time.

"Johnson wasn't much better. Just kept lying, acting like he had it under control. Acting like he was just a good guy doing his duty when he took the oath of office. How else do you shoot a president in broad daylight and nobody's got a good answer how, unless it's an inside job? Oh, he didn't give the order, maybe, but whoever did had Johnson in his pocket. And Nixon's their golden boy, war, war, war, bombs, bombs, bombs. Carpet bombing, how's that for a nice term? Like, we're just laying down some carpet, never mind that all these simple people who just want to get by are in the way of that carpet. Coca-Cola has to be sold. Hanoi needs to drive Fords and smoke Camels, right?"

His new friends just smiled and looked at him, dark under the night full of stars, and the stalks of the corn were dark. No wind blew at all and crickets sang hard.

The three strangers, a pretty woman, a bald man, and a big man with a neck brace, had walked into the bar not long after George and Mandy. They had taken the three stools on the left of the couple, the bald man closest. He asked were they the ones who wanted Nixon impeached, and George had thrust his chin out and said yes. The bald man slapped him on the back and smiled, bought him a shot of whiskey.

"Aren't you having one?" George said. The man wished he could but he had an ulcer. Southern accent. George didn't usually like southerners, but this one had seemed friendly and open-minded, even if he did fish his hand around in the bowl of peanuts, put peanuts in his mouth and after a minute spit them on the floor wet like he just wanted the salt. George wouldn't have been able to say why he thought the man was open-minded, they hadn't talked about anything, but that was the impression he got the moment they shared a glance. When they traded names, George said, "Hope you didn't take my windshield personally." The man found the situation funny, admired George's spunk, asked if he liked to get high. George allowed that he did.

That was how the five of them left the bar together, though not before the bald man said something to the barkeep that made his mouth hang open, made him stand there looking confused. Then the man whisked them all out the door. George saw a souped-up red car parked in the far corner of the dirt lot, but before he could ask about it, the stranger woman suggested George drive because they had a lot of junk in the backseat. George drove them to a stretch of 68 near a tumbledown barn, its weedy land separated from the high cornstalks by barbed wire. Mandy hadn't wanted to get into the car with these folks, and she definitely didn't want to sneak under fences into strange cornfields with them. When she whispered as much in his ear, he whispered back, "How are we going to influence people if we don't trust them? This man is open-minded. He's ready for revolution."

"How do you know that?"

"He told me with his eyes."

NOW THEY SAT IN THE STILL, HEAVY AIR, GEORGE SMOKING AND OFFERING TOKES the others took, but not deeply, blowing out fast. George didn't form an opinion about this but just kept talking as the others listened and approved. The approval of others was a drug George coveted even more than grass or righteous indignation.

"Right on," the woman said after each of George's declarations, smiling at him with bright, gleeful eyes.

When he said he thought Humphrey wasn't a great man, but that he'd take anybody over Richard Nixon—he was careful now to say "Richard Nixon" or "the president," not just "Nixon"—Mandy yawned a theatric yawn, hoping George would notice and take her back to her dorm. Instead he ignored her and asked the bald southern man whom he'd voted for. He confessed that he hadn't voted in a long time. George asked the big man with the neck brace, who hadn't spoken once, what he thought of last fall's election, and the man shrugged. The bald one said his friend was not political.

That was when the bald one pulled out a small revolver and shot George in the temple at an upward angle.

Mandy made a guttural sound like a bark and stood up, but the woman grabbed her hand harder than anyone had ever grabbed it and yanked her down. Now Neck Brace held her head against his chest from behind, almost gently, his big, cold hand over her mouth, while the woman took out a knife and started poking deep holes in Mandy's chest and stomach. She thrashed and kicked, kicked so hard one shoe flew off and into the corn, but then shuddered and lay still. Neck Brace peeked over the high corn to see if anybody had heard the small gun's pop while the other two put their mouths to the damp holes in Mandy's sweater and drank. Then it was Neck Brace's turn. Two others appeared from the corn shadows and they also drank from the dying girl. The bald man remembered seeing George drink beer with his right hand, so that was the one he grabbed. He wrapped George's fingers around the knife, unwrapped them, put the gun in George's hand, threading his finger through the trigger guard and pressing while he held the hammer in place. The five of them slunk through the corn to where their two cars waited and drove north on 68 toward Springfield.

Back at the bar, the bald man had looked Pap in the eye and said, "These two here came in alone and left alone. They was fightin' bad. Hissin' at each other. She was getting friendly with some jock, there's always some jock around, ain't there? He said he was the only man she was ever gonna have. You hear?"

Pap heard.

That was how Pap told it.

10
Indiana

BUDDY'S LIQUOR LOUNGE PACKED IN A BIG CROWD ON A FRIDAY NIGHT. A MOSTLY black clientele dominated Buddy's, but white guys from the hospital or from the university would come in twos or threes when a good band played and things mostly stayed peaceful. This particular evening, a scuffle broke out when a burly fellow named Jack claimed a skinny blond boy with long hair had pinched his ass. Actually, the boy *had* pinched him, rather hard, on the instructions of a tall, pale man in a ball cap who had promised him five dollars if he did it. Jack pushed the blond kid out into the parking lot, then pushed him down, kneeling over him with a fist cocked.

"You want to play sissy games? Huh? I'll play. How 'bout I whup your ass and call that playin'?"

Jack had worked all day on his hands and knees laying carpet for the remodel of the Indianapolis Power and Light building, getting told what to do by younger white guys who didn't have half his experience; getting fucked with by this scrawny kid with hair like a Meridian Hills cheerleader at *his* bar right at the start of *his* weekend was *not* on the menu. Buddy came out and pulled Jack Smalls up, asked the younger man what he did; he knew Jack and had never seen him steamed without a good reason. The kid went to explain about the guy with the cap, but nobody else had seen such a man and this fresh nonsense provoked Jack a second time.

"Just once, Buddy. Just let me tap him once. I'll barely lean into it."

"Don't waste knuckle skin on this fool," Buddy said, helping the kid up, then giving him a less-than-friendly shove toward the street. "Go home, fool." It all seemed funny to the ass-pincher, who was on his second mushroom cap and waiting for the main attraction to start in his head, but he made himself not laugh and so avoided his date with the head nurse in charge of stitches at IU Health Methodist.

Jack seethed. He neither heard the band (a cover band with a fat, coal-black front man who should not have sounded like Smokey Robinson but did) nor tasted his next four Buds. When midnight came around, he drove his cherry-red Nash Rambler home, trimming a few leaves off the hedge near the driveway as he parked. He went to the skillet and pried a disc of sausage from its bed of whitish grease. He turned on the TV and sat down, watching Johnny Carson telling fortunes with a huge turban on his head. Johnny Carson made him chuckle for the first time that night. He lit a cigarette and fell asleep, his cigarette burning a hole in the arm of the sofa but then burning itself out in a curl of smoke. He was dreaming about a girl he'd kissed in eighth grade and how she had strawberries on her dress. He never saw the shadows move into his driveway and up the sidewalk.

The knock woke him up at 1:15 A.M.

The television hissed with snow.

BETSY TRAUTMANN KEPT LOOKING AT HER FRONT DOOR. IT WAS AN UNREMARK-able front door, pine painted white with three little windows you could peep through to see who was knocking. On the outside a plastic wreath hung, bright with plastic flowers. That one would stay up through summer, replaced by plastic autumn leaves in the fall and plastic holly in December. She knew the right wreath was on the door, but she had the impression she had forgotten something.

She cleared her plate from the table, scraped the fish bones and two shriveled green beans into the wastebasket, and put on her dish gloves. The water heater was set at 130 degrees, as it had been since the kids had grown up, so she scalded the hollandaise sauce off her plate, soaped it, washed it, rinsed it, and set it in the drainer. Outside, the shadow of the poplar tree that stretched long and longer while she cooked had now dissolved into general shadow. The sun had been down perhaps fifteen minutes. The streetlights ticked on. Somewhere a mother called for a boy named Tommy.

Saturday nights were hard for Betsy since she lost her husband. She taught typing and German at the high school. She liked teaching German even though she knew it was temporary; as soon as Herr Mueller's hip was healed, she would be back to typing, spending her two free periods smoking and reading in the teachers' lounge. Herr Mueller had grown up in Germany (although one didn't talk about what he had done there), so his German was better than hers, of course. Yet the children liked her more, she knew it. Mueller was a harsh, secretive man, and not one person on the faculty approved of his thick, walrussy mustache. Still, no girl from the prairie was going to out-German a native of Düsseldorf, so she tried to enjoy every minute of her time drilling the kids on verbs, helping them pair articles with nouns, sprinkling her lessons with anecdotes about her trips to Switzerland and Austria before the war. Not that children loved the anecdotes of their elders, but they certainly preferred them to drilling. Herr Mueller drilled them like SS soldiers, and, from what she'd heard, he just might know a little something about that. It was wrong to hope his hip healed slowly, but she did. It was so nice to have a break from the clacking of the typewriters, so pleasant to interact with the kids without some fussy old machine between them. *Schreib-*

maschine. That was German for "typewriter." And it was *die*, not *das* or *der*. It was always best to learn the sex of the article the instant you learned the word.

Tür was the word for "door."

She looked at the door again, but it just stood there, still and serene, as white as cake frosting. What did she expect? She went over to the door, *die Tür*, and peeked out the windows. Nothing out there, of course. Just a boy on roller skates, cruising by with a bright orange hula hoop around his waist. Probably Tommy.

Was she expecting somebody? She wasn't even sixty yet, too young to be getting senile. She turned the porch light on, slotted the door chain in. That relaxed her a little.

She opened the freezer and cracked grape juice ice cubes from the tray, plonked these into a glass. Poured grape juice a little too fast; a drop splashed up and dotted her white, flowered blouse.

She wondered what was on the television, but a noise stopped her hand before she reached for the *TV Guide*. Had something shifted in the attic? It was such a faint sound she was tempted to disregard it. And yet it had not been a creak or a groan or any of the normal sounds an old house makes. Something had shifted. A box? She stood still with her ear cocked up toward the ceiling for a moment, then reached for the *TV Guide*, shaking her head at her skittishness.

A creak now, coming from the second floor.

She moved to where she could see the door to the attic in the hallway above the landing. As she watched, a black, rectangular mouth opened in the ceiling and the ladder came down. Her heart beat fast. A pair of white feet came down the rungs. What to do? Dirty toenails on those feet. Call the police? Get a knife from the kitchen? That was ridiculous, she could never stab a person. Not even the woman with the mousy hair who was now walking down the staircase as a pair of dirty work boots started down the attic rungs. So *that* was where the dirt on her rug had come from, she thought, realizing that her mind was fixing on anything it could to avoid the subject of the strangers in her house.

The girl went around now, weasel-quick, and pulled all the curtains. Something bad was about to happen. She was in a crime, a real crime. She should yell for help but couldn't. All she could make herself say was "What . . . ?" Her heart banged so hard in her chest she thought she might faint.

That was when she got a good look at the owner of the work boots.

She relaxed when she saw him, realized she recognized him, although it was hard to say from where.

"Hello?" she said.

The man answered. Was it that man? The man who didn't want breakfast? Her legs shook and she wondered again if she should go to the telephone, though now the woman had placed herself between Betsy and the kitchen.

She didn't look at the eyes of the woman, a skinny creature who smelled bad and looked like she'd have relations with anyone at all, but she did look at the man's eyes.

"Are you the man who didn't want breakfast?" she said.

He'd said he never ate breakfast, but it had been kind of her to ask.

"You were here this morning," she said. "I let you in."

He thanked her for doing that. Told her it was nice to meet somebody unburdened by suspicion. Asked her to sit down. She did.

She didn't know why her chin was wet, but it was. Now she saw a tall man in a ball cap helping a confused-looking colored down the attic ladder. The colored had something in his hand. The bald man with the work boots told him to walk over to Betsy, saying he wanted to make introductions. The colored took the steps slowly, his minder behind him, holding his shoulders steady. Now he stood over her, swaying, empty-eyed, spit running out of his mouth. Should she get up and run? She wasn't a very good runner.

She remembered a little bit about these people. Someone had rung her doorbell at five in the morning; she remembered looking out the window to see who was there and then everything went hazy.

She had forgotten them, just as they asked her to, but seeing them again jarred them back into memory.

What had she done all day? Had she even left the house?

Now she saw the dirty girl rooting under her sink, saw her stand up with Betsy's biggest pot, the wide one she made pot roast in, saw her start walking toward the couch. A dark suspicion tried to form in her mind but she pushed it down. It came up again anyway, attached to a memory from the farm in Kansas. A huge, mottled pig hanging upside-down over a bucket, flies in the air.

She opened her mouth now, meaning to scream, but the bald man took the *TV Guide* from her hand, rolled it into a tube, stuck it in her mouth. He said she should hold it and bite down so she did, her saliva soaking the newsprint.

Now a big man with a neck brace had her ankles and she went upside-down, awkwardly bumping her head on the cushions. She nodded because she had been right about the pig, making the magazine go up and down. She saw carpet, shoes, the girl's bare feet, plumbed with eely veins. She saw the black man's faraway eyes, his shiny chin, then looked along his powerful forearm. His wrists were raw, like he'd been tied.

The bald man whispered in his ear, smiling.

The bald man had sharp teeth, like a dog's.

She saw what the black man was holding.

A carpet knife.

"Sorry," he said, bending to her but not really looking at her. "I'm sorry."

He said it the whole time.

THE RAMBLER WAS FOUND PARKED ONE BLOCK AWAY.

Jack Smalls remembered nothing that happened in the Trautmann house, not even how he got there, why he stayed in the house. He had been found at the kitchen counter eating bacon he had fried up himself; a neighbor had seen his dark face through a gap in the curtain. His public defender swung between hopelessness and exasperation. Bail was set so high even Buddy's Liquor Lounge wouldn't serve as collateral on the bond. Buddy told everyone who'd listen how Jack had been framed, that he was a good man, that something real fishy had happened, though his theories on what changed from week to week.

Betsy Trautmann was laid to rest that Thursday in a white casket, next to her husband. Six of her typing students got permission to come, though only two of them did. Erich Mueller attended in a wheelchair pushed by his teenaged son, the German instructor's mustache oiled for the occasion.

As dictated in her will, Betsy's headstone read

DEVOTED WIFE

GELIEBTE LEHRERIN

11
Missouri

"MY NAME'S NIXON, JUST LIKE THE PRESIDENT, BUT I'M NO TRICKY DICK. MINE only knows one trick. Okay, two. My name's Luther, and that rhymes with . . . well, just Luther. If I were older than you, I could be long-in-the-toother. Huh? If your mom watched a play I might John-Wilkes-Booth-her. Huh? Right?"

Did this jerk really just talk about his dick to me?

Barb blinked once, slowly, letting her eyelids rest shut for a half second as if praying for the angel of removing nuisances to whisk this tiresome, pale man away from the sidewalk table she and her cousin had unwisely chosen. She pushed her fingers through the table's wrought-iron curlicues. She didn't know she was doing it. To Barb's horror, her cousin, Peggy, actually seemed pleased that someone was paying attention to her.

"Right," Peg said to their guest. Now she nodded at the long red muscle car he had pulled up in not three minutes ago. "Nice ride. That yours?"

Peggy was actually *encouraging* the jerk. It wasn't as if she were desperate. Sure, Peggy was a little wide in the hips and tried too hard to look like the teenagers, wearing her pink lipstick and headbands, but she had a pretty face. Not like the man who had set his glass of boozy ice on their table, as if by accident, responding to Barb's flinty gaze by saying, "Sorry, I thought you were my friends." There was nothing pretty about Luther Nixon.

"Maybe we are your friends," Peg had said, "only you just haven't met us yet." It had been all Barb could do not to roll her eyes. Luther had wasted no time pulling up a heavy iron chair, dragging it on the bricks as if to make sparks.

Peggy was a lightbulb to the mothlike Luther Nixons of the world, and it was working Barb's nerves. She loved her cousin but didn't love these beery postdivorce forays into downtown St. Louis. Not that men bothered Barb that often—despite her svelte stewardess's build and high cheekbones, there was something hawkish and unattainable about her that steered men of small character away. Straight into Peggy.

"It *is* my car," Luther Nixon said, nodding proudly at the machine whose tires kissed the curb near their sidewalk table. "Wanna ride?"

"No, thank you," said Barb, even though the question was clearly not directed at her. She did not care for this man. She did not care for the one-size-too-small shirt he had stuffed his almost-muscular shoulders and chest into, nor for the weak, thin lips that jerked around the botched fence of his teeth. Nor for his baldness. Her pity for balding men extended to those who parked toupees upon their bare crowns and also to those who did not. Of the latter sort, the overcombers were most pathetic, followed by the au naturel types who allowed their remaining hair to congregate on the back and sides in a sort of fat horseshoe. Somewhat better, though too often criminals or sex fiends, were the glossy-domed full-baldies who razored it off in the shower. Better still, most noble of a sad lot, were the military types and realists who buzzed it close, as this man had done, reducing all of it to varying densities of stubble. Luther Nixon's stubble silvered at the temples, and silver shone in the odd little rogue hairs on his neck that caught the streetlight unflatteringly. She didn't like it that he was close enough for her to note those fine hairs.

She let her eyes fall contemptuously on his bald pate, let a sneer seep onto her face, and he noted this. Damned if he didn't, but who cared? Perhaps he would be offended enough to leave. It was really all Barb wanted.

"What kind of car is it?" Peggy asked.

"It's big. And red," Luther said, suggestively enough that it was clear he meant something else, but not so suggestively that Barb could call him out for it. Peggy laughed. "Besides being big and red, *that* is a super-cherry '67 Pontiac GTO with a cordova top. GTO stands for *Gran Turismo Oh-lookit-her-go*, but I just call her a goat. Four-hundred-cubic-inch V-8, but I done some things to it. It ain't what you'd call slow. Hood tachometer, Hurst shifter, but I don't want to bore you ladies with boy talk. Let's just say it's the meanest, sweetest piece of metal since the *Enola Gay*." Barb fished in her purse for her Virginia Slims, turned her face deliberately away when Luther produced a lighter, lit it herself.

"Whoa, horsy!" Luther said. "That's a hot, sassy horse, there! Look over here, horsy."

Luther grinned at her then, and, aside from the off-center gap or notch in his teeth, Barb remarked something odd about his smile. It blurred like a bad photograph. She had been about to say something sharp to Mr. Nixon, but the hazy quality of his smile stopped her short, made her forget the words. How could the teeth of a real, live man blur like teeth in a picture? She looked up into his eyes. She hadn't noticed how warm they were, how his fine crow's feet hinted at an inner kindness he covered with crude jokes and poor manners. *Don't believe him it's a trick he's like a devil look away look away he's gonna kill if you don't it's a trick trick trick trick.*

"Would you like to see a trick?" he said, drilling harder into her eyes with his own.

"Sure," Barb answered, confused about the word *trick*, but then remembering how kind this man's eyes were, this man whose dick knew two tricks. She tried to take a drag of her cigarette but noticed it was too wet. Her brother would have said she had *nigger-lipped* it, and, as much as she disliked that term, and her brother, she couldn't help thinking that every time it happened. Did that make her a racist? She hoped not, she didn't care for racists. Her mouth was really full of spit tonight; she tried catching the excess with the back of her hand, but it didn't work, and a strand blobbed out onto the table, pooling near the crumbs from the fried chicken she had eaten earlier. Luther handed her a napkin. Thought about it. Handed her a second.

"Thank you," she managed. She glanced at Peggy to see if she had noticed her predicament, but her cousin was drooling, too. Drooling and smiling at Luther. She felt like smiling, too, so she did. "Sorry," she said.

"Nothing to be sorry about. Everybody niggie-lips a ciggy from time to time."

He plucked her drenched cigarette away, tossed it into the street, smiled again with his blurry teeth. He was drooling a little, too. How strange! Three droolers drooling away at a sidewalk table outside Honey's Bar and Grill. She laughed a little despite herself. She had been too hard on Luther Nixon. He offered her a Marlboro. She took it, suffered him to light it.

"The way you're feelin', that's called bein' *charmed*. Least that's what I heard someone else call it and it stuck. You didn't charm so easy 'cause you're kind of a cunt. This other'n fell off like a fat man off a pony. Know who doesn't charm worth a good goddamn? Injuns. I once rolled up on some wigwam gas station and country store, this was out in the desert some'ers, an' this buck said, 'Nothin's on the house 'cept for family and you don't look Comanche to me—you gonna pay for that gas or what?' This's after I looked him in the eye and told him it was on the house—I ain't paid for gas since I was takin warm shits. So I beat the fuck out of him with a can a' tomaters or something, just beat him till one of his eyes bugged. Don't think I kilt him, but if he wins a spellin' bee that'll be a neat trick."

"Were you going to show me a trick?" she said. She felt like a four-year-old at a party, a very lucky four-year-old at whose table the clown had chosen to sit. She became aware of pressure in her bladder, wondered how much trouble she would get in if she wet herself, decided not to.

Barely.

"Right!" Luther said. He lit a cigarette for himself, then plucked a toothpick from the porcelain bee holder that smilingly offered a belly basket of toothpicks from its post between the salt and pepper shakers. "Watch! It's magic."

He checked to left and right to make sure nobody else was watching, then took a deep drag from the cigarette and held it. He displayed the toothpick as if inviting inspection, then, smiling all the while, poked it into the tough meat of his trachea.

The women gasped, delighted. Luther removed the toothpick, discreetly sheathed the bloodied end in a napkin. A drop of blood started rolling down his neck, making for the collar of his too-tight shirt. Now he strained, blowing first a fine, grapelike cluster of bubbles and then a plume of smoke from the prick in his windpipe. It sputtered and stopped as the hole closed and went away entirely. He caught the runner of blood with a napkin and wiped his throat clean as though nothing had happened.

"That's terrific," Barb allowed, crying a little at just how rare and terrific it was.

"Yeah," Peg echoed. "Really groovy."

"Groovy," he said. "Fuck, how I hate that word. I never want you to say it again."

"Okay," Peg said, smiling and starting to drool again. Luther wiped her chin, then licked his hand, staring straight at a waitress who saw the whole thing. She wrinkled her mouth in distaste and hurried a teetering plate of rib bones inside, dropping a fork with a *ting-tank*. The waitress thought she saw sharp teeth on him but wasn't sure, never told anyone, not even when she saw the papers in the morning. The police would ask her what she remembered about the man, but the truth was she remembered nothing about him. Several people who dined at Honey's that night offered careful descriptions of the women, right down to their pumps and the white piping on Barb's mod but tasteful crimson dress, but nobody could say who the man was or what he looked like. Only one remembered the car, though any who heard him start it might have said it grumbled like storms coming, like the beginning of a biblical plague, that it was a noise Pharaoh would have noted and hardened his heart anyway.

Luther Nixon stood up.

Barbara Atwater and Peggy McMullen stood up, too, watching him.

"You girls pay already?"

They nodded.

"You park close to here?"

They nodded again.

"Where?"

Barb pointed at a bottle-green two-door across the street and one block down.

"Chevy Nova. Small-block V-8. Sixty-three?"

Barb nodded.

Luther Nixon pointed at it and a large, hairy-looking fellow in a neck brace and sunglasses appeared from an alley and walked over to it, leaning against the trunk like it was his.

"Not too shabby. What's your name, sassy horsy?"

"Barbara."

"Barb," he said, leaning close so only she heard, "you nickel-plated bitch, I'm going to watch you shave all that pretty blond hair off your head tonight and then you're going to die, and die bloody. That cool with you?"

"Sure."

"Groovy," he said, flicking his cigarette at a passing car. "Let's go for a ride."

12

THE SLIGHT, YOUNG-LOOKING WOMAN MADE HER WAY THROUGH THE TALL GRASS close to the shoulder of Route 66, carrying her messenger bag, her Indian-print dress wet with night dew. Her face shone white beneath a chip of moon floating over fast-moving clouds. The wind made the trees hiss. She waited until she saw headlights, only one set, then mounted the shoulder so her pale skin would blaze in the headlamps and the driver could not help but see her.

The car that pulled over was a Chrysler Windsor; she knew it by the big grille like the fat half of an upside-down triangle. The driver was fat, too, and when she leaned down to the window she smelled his stink of sadness and loneliness even under his excess of after-shave. He was an ordinary man well into homely middle age, with his friar's crown of salt-and-pepper hair, a second chin starting under the first, a belly blooming out over the belt that seemed to bisect him. A sticky-looking coffee mug lay on its side on the passenger seat next to a tie like a dead snake. A worn briefcase slouched on the floor as though it had been kicked there.

"I don't normally do this," he said, "but you look like you might be in trouble."

"I am," she said, smiling like she and trouble were friends.

"Where ya headed?"

"Depends. Where are *you* headed?"

He stiffened. She had played the wrong card. She saw the wedding ring now. She had to catch his eyes before he drove off.

"I don't mean any offense by this, but you aren't a—"

"No," she interrupted. "I just meant that I have to get away from here. They hit me."

"Who?"

"They," she said, "here." She pointed just above her left eye and, while she knew there was no mark on her, she hooked his gaze with hers. She pulled him with her thin-ice eyes, so gray they were almost clear, and he fell through them and into her. It was almost as though he knew she was going to say, "Open the door," almost as though he were saying it with her.

She looked at his gas gauge, then tossed the coffee cup into the grass she had emerged from and sat down, shutting the door. She dug for the safety belt and cinched it tight around her tiny waist, buckled it.

"Drive," she said, and he did.

A preacher station babbled on the radio, almost out of signal range.

"Ruth was a beautiful woman. But it was not just for her beauty that Ruth was allowed to glean from the corn, and in these days (pfffft) less fortunate could take some part of the corn that fell, so that they should not starve. The greater part of (pffffft) was given this privilege, her beauty notwithstanding (pfffft) shown kindness unto her mother-in-law. For the lord Jesus knows, doesn't he, that this is not always easy."

The radio preacher laughed at his own joke.

The woman turned the volume knob so hard she nearly broke it, and the radio fell silent.

"Jesus, Jesus!" she said. "You like Jesus?"

"I love him," the big man slurred.

"You love him like you wanna give him big wet sloppy kisses?"

"No," he said, "I just lub him."

"You *lub* him, huh? You sure? What's your name?"

"Edgar."

"Edgar, mash that gas harder."

"Where are we going?"

"Straight on. You just keep going straight on, and I'll tell you when to turn."

She watched the needle float a hair nearer to the *E*.

"Talk to me, Edgar, and tell me everything you're thinking."

"Why?"

"Did you grow up on a farm, Edgar?"

"No."

"So you never killed a chicken?

"No."

"Never cut its head off?"

"Uh-uh."

"Poke a nail in its eye and fish around to see what its brain looked like?"

"Uh-uh."

"Me neither. Not a chicken, anyway. I grew up in Amish country, they had all the chickens. Start talking."

"What about."

"I dunno, how about me."

"What's your name?" he said, drooling a wet one on his collar. She used his tie to wipe his chin.

"What's your mother's name?"

"Janice."

"Then my name is Janice. What did you think when you saw me? Just talk and don't leave anything out."

"I thought, what's a hippie girl doing out by herself at night so far from town, the Munger Moss Hotel is a bit back in Lebanon and I almost stopped there for the night but then decided I'd try to get home to Shirley it'd make her happy . . ."

"Hell with that cow. Talk about me, I said."

"Sorry. Thought hippie girl kinda like Cleopatra with all that makeup on your eyes and them beads sewn in your hair, thought maybe you was a whore then maybe you had a gun but that didn't seem likely and I wouldn't feel good about myself I left a skinny girl alone in the night when she was askin' for help so I pulled over thinking maybe you were sick maybe a junkie that skin on you too white and I couldn't see your mouth right, like your teeth were blurry and when you leaned in close I smelled them hippie oils on you but under that something like a dead thing or dirt in a basement and I knew you'd smell worse if you were hot but you aren't, you aren't no warmer than the night air outside . . ."

"Yeah, but am I pretty? Did you think I was pretty?"

"At first I guess but I don't like skinny girls too much that way, but yeah you got a pretty face I thought until I smelled that smell and I knew it was a trick you're a trick like a new paint job on a car that's been wrecked but it was too late because I looked at you in the eyes and stuck like on flypaper and my mind ain't right now and I wish you'd let me go from whatever you're doing to me and why are you laughing, what's funny Janice, what's funny, can I stop talking now 'cause I can't keep spit in my mouth it keeps falling out."

The woman had been laughing, laughed even harder when he called her Janice.

"Jesus, Jesus!" she said. "Okay. Now shut up and keep driving. I want to go fast."

He pressed the pedal.

The needle floated up from forty-five to fifty-five, reached the zenith of the arc-shaped speedometer at sixty.

"Faster."

The needle struggled to sixty-five.

"That's good," she said, watching the fuel gauge.

A hill bled some of the speed from Edgar's car, and at the top of the hill they passed a billboard showing a tangly-headed youth, the legend to his right reading

BEAUTIFY AMERICA—GET A HAIRCUT

Edgar was so focused on the road and the speedometer that he didn't really see that. Nor did he see the car behind the billboard, sitting still with no lights, a shark in the murk, a shadow on the lung. She saw it, though. Her eyes saw lots of things his missed. They rolled on into the night for another ten minutes, taking Interstate 44, then diverting onto Route 66 again near Waynesville.

The fuel needle had reclined left, kissing the *E*.

"They're after us, Edgar. The people who did this to me. Get me away from them. FAST!"

He looked at the rearview mirror, and, though he saw no headlights in the distance, he mashed the gas all the way down to climb a steep hill.

Now the road descended and the needle arced down the right side of the speedometer to seventy-five.

Eighty.

The man knew this was wrong, even deeply in thrall, and he let a small, fearful noise escape his throat.

"Shhh," she said into his ear, turning up the Patsy Cline song starting on the radio, then resting her hand on his where it white-knuckled the steering wheel.

"Flash your lights, Edgar."

He did as instructed. She looked at the rearview mirror, waited for the car running dark behind them to flash its lights in answer. It did.

Nobody else on the road.

At the bottom of the long downward grade, a telephone pole loomed, solid and real, black with creosote at its base. A copse of young trees stood behind it. It was far enough off the road that the headlights never swept it, but she saw it anyway.

"My name's actually Calcutta," she said. "It's a pleasure to meet you."

She moved the wheel to the right, the Chrysler bucking violently on the grass and gravel.

"Please," Edgar said, his charm wearing off at the last second, too late to fight her for the wheel, too late for anything.

Calcutta, if that was her name, steered the careening vehicle expertly, jerking the wheel fractionally right at the last instant so the car would slam into the pole at something like a forty-degree angle. The pole would catch the Windsor just behind the engine well, just in front of the rearview mirror, all of its brutal counterforce bull's-eyed into the driver's section.

At the last possible instant, the woman ducked her head between her knees, cupping her hands over her eyes.

Edgar had pressed his lips together again to form the *puh* in *please*, but that wasn't the awful, wrenching sound that exploded into the world.

CALCUTTA ENTERED A BLACK PLACE AND THEN CAME TO A PLACE OF SHOCKING pain. She might have screamed if she had any air in her lungs, but she did not; they had been speared flat by her broken ribs. Now that she was still, the damage done, things began to shift back. The lungs pushed the ribs out and those ribs found their bone-stems and became whole, this in the darkness of her body, which lay in the darkness of the mangled car. Something hot spritzed her face, though whether it was blood or radiator fluid she hadn't the apparatus to determine with her jammed-shut eyes and her flattened nose. Her right ear picked up the hiss of steam, the spinning of a wheel, a harsh rasp she could not identify. With her mostly whole right arm she felt where the roof had peeled back like the tongue of a shoe, felt night air on her skin. That was when she heard the doors of the Camaro chunk shut.

They were coming.

"Beautiful," Rob's voice said, meaning the spectacular wreck she had created.

"You don't mind if we start?" Cole said to her. "Though that's kind of a rhetorical question, seeing as what kinda shape your mouth's in."

Calcutta's less-damaged right eye came in enough for her to see something moving against the stars, a blurry image that soon clarified into the compact form of Cole, his boyish face pale, his slender body moving through the goldenrod with foxlike grace. He ran his fingers through his wavy central mass of hair and stepped out of Calcutta's limited field of vision. Rob followed behind, taller, less forceful, his hangdog slouch a counterpoint to Cole's vulpine slink.

"Oh, he's not quite there, is he?" Cole said. "Good, good."

Calcutta now realized that the rasping sound to her left that she had taken for some dying part of the car actually belonged to what remained of its driver.

"Hey, mister. How're they hangin'?"

The rasp again, louder.

"Naw, I ain't gonna kill you just yet. Better that heart of yours keeps the tap runnin' a minute or two."

Calcutta's insulted legs unfolded themselves from beneath her, and she found she was able to draw them forward. Her left eye tuned in just in time for her to see Rob remove the one intact windshield wiper blade, hand it to Cole. She heard him squeegee it across the hood, heard him slurp what he had squeegeed. Rob did the same. Her pain diminished, started giving way to hunger. Now Rob loomed into view, squinting at her forehead, his chin bibbed in blood. He laughed.

"No shit," he said. "You don't see that every day."

So saying, he pulled something from her head, something that ground on the way out, held it before her eyes like a magician showing a card. A tire pressure gauge, her blood and hair on it. Even as she watched, the hair disappeared. She felt her skull weave itself whole. She had to flatten out one of her hip bones to wriggle out of the busted architecture that enclosed her, retearing the skin on her thigh and calf, shedding her ruined dress like a husk as she wriggled nude through folds of crumpled steel. Once free, and once she had removed every shred of her bloodied dress from the wreck, she joined the other two and fed on the driver. They did not bite him—there was no need. They licked, they sucked, they took up pieces of torn metal or broken glass and cut, then squeezed to milk the cut. They undressed, rearranged, yanked free, got at all parts of the wheezing, rasping man where blood yet moved. His wide eye watched them until his heart at last gave out and the eye froze and dimmed, and still they fed, Cole sated enough to slow his ministrations and say "Good" or "Damn good" in between.

When she had taken her fill, Calcutta wrestled her messenger bag out of the wreck and removed the brick-red dress and denim jacket she had rolled inside, climbing into these. Her belly pooched out from the blood she had taken in, made her look four months gravid. Her hair shone and her eyes sparkled and she knew she looked alive, healthy, womanly. She opened her mouth, showed her teeth to the stars, felt the night breeze in the wet hole of her mouth, held her arms up. Somewhere in the sparse woods to the north, a coyote yipped.

She drew in the first lungful of air since the wreck and answered it in a high, yipping voice of her own.

"Jesus! Jesus!"

13

WOODS HAD BEEN IN THE MIDDLE OF A DREAM ABOUT TORNADOES WHEN HE FELT the slap on his face. Little wonder that tornadoes figured in so many of his dreams since his hometown of Beasley, Michigan, had lost its general store to one in April 1956, during a freak outbreak in the upper Midwest. When he remembered the tornado in waking hours, he saw a still image of it, the one in black and white that made the paper, but in his mind's eye the iron-black funnel lay silhouetted on a sky the dirty green of creek water. He remembered wind and yelling. He remembered how angry his little brother was that his father wouldn't look for Flash, their dog, before shutting them all in the basement. He especially recalled the sound of his mother singing "Jesus, be good to us," over and over again as if it were the chorus of a song, though he was pretty sure she made it up. She had keened it like a spell, as though the storm would spare them if she could keep singing that refrain loud enough to be heard over the wicked engine of the wind. Aside from turning Manny's General Store into a pile of kindling, the thing had flipped a police cruiser, dropped a tree through the barn roof at Becker's Dairy, and snatched the slide in the park clean away. Becker's Dairy was visible from the road, and Woods remembered marveling at the spectacle of that upside-down tree, its roots pointed straight at the sky, exactly in the middle of the barn, as though an engineer had measured everything beforehand. Nobody died, not even cows. Flash had come back when everything was over, tail between his legs, head low, blinking like he expected to be swatted on the ass for whatever it was he had done wrong to make such a noise and mess. Maybe his mother's spell had worked. Maybe she was a sort of witch. Woodrow Fulk certainly didn't think the chaos of April 3, 1956, had much to do with Jesus.

The truth was, Woods liked tornadoes, and his dreams about them were less like nightmares and more like eerie adventures. He knew that he was in mortal danger when he saw them, six or eight at a time, at all compass points, kicking up giddy flights of debris; yet he always felt that they would pass him by. Diving into a basement was out of the question—they would hold his fear in contempt and destroy him if he tried. No, the only way for him to negotiate these malign, black stovepipes was to stand amid them and trust them to harm only others. Not only would they harm others, they would let Woods watch.

It didn't take a genius to figure out what these tornadoes meant—they represented his new friends. The fact that he'd been having these dreams ever since the clouds bent and roughly kissed Beasley, Michigan, only pointed to a sort of intelligent symmetry. All things were measured out in advance. All the gears were set. No fault could be found in his actions, thoughts, or deeds, since the same engineer who plunged a tree through the Beckers' barn roof had set him on this path. If he caused harm, he was the tip of a spear thrown by another hand.

The hand that slapped his chin was cold.

He had been standing on top of a playground slide, laughing and watching a quintet of soot-black funnel clouds kick the shit out of Beasley, Michigan, and now he was lying . . . where?

Oh, yes. The abandoned house. He had scouted out a house in the middle of a young wood, overgrown with bushes, birds nesting in the attic, but the roof sound enough to keep out sun, if not rain. The house lay about a mile and a half down a dirt road off Route 66. He had taken the two stakes and the banner out of the truck, posted it facing the dirt road, not so as to call attention should the rightful owner drive by, but so only those who pulled over might see its legend:

No Trespassing
Explosives in use
Risk of death!

The hand squeezed his chin harder.

"Wake up, daybitch."

"I'm up," Woods said, lighting the stub of candle near the blanket he slept on.

"So?" Cole said.

"I set you up in the bathtub," Woods said, getting to his feet and using the candle to help him pick his way around the broken chairs and over the dirty snow of couch stuffing, the couch itself capsized near a vine-cauled window. Cole followed him, grunted with mild satisfaction when he saw the sleeping bag and towels he would be cocooning into while June's fat sun baked the green hill country all around them.

Woods liked Cole least. His Yankee ears weren't keen to the variations between Cole's slower Georgia drawl and Luther's hard-plucked Carolina twang, so Cole struck him as derivative of the older creature, something that had been caught in Luther's tailwind and now tried to fly like Luther.

Outside, Woods heard the sound of a bristle brush on leather, knew Rob would be cleaning his bomber jacket with water from the jerry can they kept in the trunk. Calcutta emerged from the shadows near the door, stepped over a dust-colored dollhouse, clipping its roof with a bare foot and scattering a fire drill of spiders.

"Calcutta, I got you in that bedroom, Rob in the kitchen, Neck Brace and Luther in the basement."

"Why not all of us in the basement?"

"No room. 'S full of junk."

"Fuller than this?"

"See for yourself."

She shook her head and smiled. She looked east, saw the beginnings of first light, pulled Woods by a hand to the filthy stairs, brushed splinters and broken glass off these, set Woods down. Took the candle from him and set it down as it started to flicker. Birds sang in the trees now. He liked the way she was looking at him. He liked her shadow dancing to the candle's strobe.

"We have time?" he said.

She didn't say anything, just unbuckled his pants, flipped him half erect out of his shorts. Traced a fang on his tenderest skin, put the tip of it in the hole.

"Ah," he said. "Careful."

She smiled around him, then sucked him.

She took the candle stub he had set on the stairs, belled her mouth over it like a fire eater to heat the air therein, but he stopped her.

"Right," she said. "I forgot you *like* it cold. Old habits."

Sucked him again.

"My flower," he said, quietly enough so the others wouldn't hear and mock him. "My night flower."

DAWN PUSHED UP TOWARD THE HORIZON, PAINTING THE SKY LAVENDER WHERE IT showed between knots of wormy trees. A retaining wall of cloud would delay the sun's crowning by a handful of minutes, and Woods knew Luther Nixon would wait until the last possible moment before retreating into the bolthole the young man had made for him down the dry-rotted stairs and among the boxes of broken plates, unrecognizable tools, and corrupt toys that cluttered the basement. Whether Luther and Woods were alone on the porch was a matter for philosophers; the other vampires had already wound themselves in blankets and tucked into the darkest joints of the house, but a woman slumped in the porch swing next to Woods, still wearing the stiff clothes she died in. Her scalp shone pale and razor-burned where she had been shorn, paler even than her bloodless flesh. No effort had been made to disguise the punctures on her neck and arms; she would not be found until the beetles had done their work.

"You remind me of somebody," Luther said, leaning back in the chair, a peeling chair that had once been blue, then red, now mottled and dry and ready to break. The way he leaned you had to watch him, because you were sure he was going to fall, though he didn't. Woods waited to find out who Luther was talking to; it might just as easily have been the cadaver.

"The way you are with the ladies, I mean," Luther said.

Woods laughed uneasily.

"Quite the stud, aren't you?"

"I don't know about that."

"No, I watch the chickens look at you, and I don't mean Kamikaze Jane in there. I mean the live ones. They like you."

"I guess."

"I see 'em at the bar leanin' heads together hopin' you'll ask 'em to dance, hopin' you'll buy 'em a drink or somethin'."

"I guess."

Luther looked at the dead woman, then at Woods.

"I guess you are kinda a handsome couple."

"I don't want to talk about it."

"Barb."

"What?"

"Her name's Barb in case she's shy about tellin' you. She kinda reminds me a' somebody, too, if the truth be told. I ever tell you about Dolores? Nah, you don't want to hear about Dolores."

Woods just looked up at the sky, saw a planet there, night's last holdout.

"You think that's Mars or Jupiter or what?" Woods said.

Luther didn't look.

"Fuck if I know. How old are you, what, twenty-two?"

"Twenty-three."

Luther smiled and nodded hard.

"Yeah. Yep. I remember what that's like."

Luther talked then.

Luther liked to talk.

14

I USED TO THINK I'D DO ANYTHING TO GO BACK TO THOSE DAYS, BACK TO BEING *twenty, twenty-three years old, running shine into Asheville and Spartanburg. You know, I was handsome then. You won't believe it, but I had just hanks of hair, honey-colored hair the gals'd say. There was always girls then, all proper on Sundays in a clean yellow dress, or robin's-egg blue, in church with Mammy and Pappy, but they was only thinking about one thing just like the boys was, couldn't wait to get you back behind the garage and go hoistin' up that Sunday dress, push your head down there, lookin' over their shoulder for a place to lay flat and fuck you. They'd come by thick as flies when I was bootlegging, one'd be walkin' up to the gas station to meet me, watchin' another one leavin' thinkin' huh, that little gal's got a look on her face like maybe she just fucked but no, even Luther wouldn't be bare-assed bastard enough to stand on that porch and wait for one when he just diddled another, but she was right the first time. Yep. She was. Part of it's havin' a big cock-a-doodle-doo, they talk you know, them little church hens, they can't help it. They get with a fella packin' a hogleg and they can't wait to tell the other girls, all coverin' their mouth and lookin' around like they hope the wrong person don't hear, but they're sittin' there tellin' the wrong person 'cause every one of them little Baptist gals is now thinkin' she's gonna get her legs around that Luther Nixon if she has to die to do it.*

And that's the friends she's got. Born down in the holler with a broke-ass daddy drinkin' shine outta soup cans, only book in the house is a Bible full a' finger smudges and pressed weeds, gonna have to ship off to Charlotte and work in a munitions factory when we go to war with Tojo, but that's later. Now she's just tryin' not to get lice and chicken pox off her nine little brothers and here come Sally and Jane to fuck her man out from under her. Life's a whore, huh? Only I wasn't never her man to start with, any more than the spittoon owns the fella spittin' in it. Luther Nixon didn't belong to nobody except maybe the devil, and did he ever come to claim me, but not in them days. Them shine days. I was goddamn good at it, too. Sheriffs'd lay for you, revenuers too, tryin' to bust you on not payin' tax, but they couldn't afford to mail in parts from California to soup up their cars, no sir. And didn't none of them want to die just to take you in. That's the difference. You go shavin' the curves on a twisty-ass country road, and those roads weren't nothing but packed mud, you gotta know what you're doin' and you gotta be ready to die. The shine'd throw you, too, like a lard-ass square dancin', you had to know how much weight you was carryin', put special springs on your back wheels to help the shock, but an assload of eighteen, twenty cans of hoss eyes'd roll you right over if you fucked up. Burn you, too. Fella named Clem Welsh went and cracked up near Pigeon Lane, and he packed his load right, big drums of it, none of this mason jar shit—that's how you tell an operator from a shit-nose, but you had to put it in the big cans, right? Yeah, Clem had him a bunch of blankets all between them cans to cushion 'em and he'd soaked them blankets in horse piss to mask the corn smell in case the revenuers come makin' him pop his trunk, figurin' nobody'd want to go putting their hands in horse piss. But I don't guess the devil minded too much, because he got him a load of shine and a skinny white boy on Pigeon Lane that night. Wasn't nobody even chasin' Clem, he was just showin' off for his brother, rumbling down the road bigger than hell, clippin' them curves, but his wheel hooked and wouldn't come back and he rolled, cracked them cans. That was good shine, too, not boss eyes, but damn near, hunnert and twenty proof or more, but something sparked and he went up like the Fourth of July, blowed all the leaves off them trees, made a black char mark they say won't never grow back. I didn't see it. I was in the jailhouse that night, first time I went. Mitch Lily came and got me out, did it because I was makin' him too much money, and the sheriff was scared of Mitch. Hell, everyone was. Mitch said, "Hey, kid, did you hear about Clem?" "No," I said, "is he dead?" and he said, "Yeah, how'd you know?" "Just the way you said it," I said, "ain't nobody alive when somebody says 'did you hear about so-and-so,'" and he said, "Yeah, well he might have been in jail or beat up, or maybe he got the syph, and I'd'a said the same thing," and I said, "Yeah, but it's the way you said it. I just knew." And he punched me in the nose real hard for bein' smart, and that was a good lesson. You can be smart all you want, until you go makin' somebody else feel dumb. Especially somebody stronger than you. And Mitch was stronger than everybody. Except Hitler. Hitler shot his ass out of the sky over Romania somewhere, Ploesti, that was the name of the place, bunch of oil fields, and here I still am, though Hitler fucked me up pretty good there too for a while. I loved Mitch. But I fucked his woman. And she didn't tell him 'cause he'd'a killed us both. Women today, they'll cheat on a fella and then tell him about it to show him she's stronger, but it wasn't like that in those days, not in the mountains. You cheat on a hard-ass operator like Mitch Lily, and you'd better sew that mouth up with iron wire or you'd get found ass-up in a well and everyone'd know why and nobody'd say boo. She was fine, too, freckles on her like cinnamon dust, red hair curly and thick and it smelled like clean laundry on the line and pine sap and river gravel all at once. Yeah, I miss those days some. But all I gotta do is get a whiff of blood, anybody's blood, and all those days of sunlight on girls' hair and sunlight on chicory flowers and the hot wind blowin' in your face and shine money and sheriffs swearing a blue streak 'cause I cut their tires, all of it just blows away. If Mitch Lily was still alive and walked in some bar, I'd drink with him and talk about old times for as long as I could stand it, and then, when that hot brick of hunger started cookin' my guts, I'd ask him what he's drivin' now, and he'd say, "Aw, nothing like in them days," and I'd say, "Show me anyway, Mitch Lily," and out we'd go to the parking lot and I'd bend him down between two cars and first he'd think I was playin' a joke and I'd laugh, too, and then he'd try to stand up and say, "Quit horsin'," and say, "I ain't," real cold and he'd smell death in my mouth under the whiskey and he'd get a little scared and start tryin' hard to stand up and push me off and he'd be surprised that he couldn't stop me and I'd open up his throat and drink. Because as strong as he was, I'm stronger now. And as good as those days were, these nights are better, and the reason is blood and blood and blood. No shine, no pussy, and no love of Jesus ever tasted as good as the dirtiest nigger junkie's blood, and that's how it is. And that's all right. Life, or whatever this is, is all right.

"BUT I KNOW IN MY BRAIN THAT IT AIN'T THE SAME AS BEIN' HOT MEAT AND twenty-three. I know you want you a . . . *promotion*, and that might could happen, but you should enjoy the ride where you are now. There's time for the other, and there ain't no takin' that back."

"Yeah," Woods said, but he thought,

And as soon as you turn me you don't have a daybitch, and who's gonna find your knocked-down barns and rusty old junkyards? Who's gonna ditch your skins and carry your shitty bags of clothes? Who's gonna pitch a pup tent in the field across the way and watch your asses through the scope of his Garand? I'm stuck here till one a' you eats sunshine or you find another sucker to drive that truck.

"That's right, old hoss," Luther said, and, as was often the case between them, Woods wasn't sure if Luther had read his mind or if he was just talking. He knew they could put thoughts in your head, but could they reach in and fish them out?

You know what I'm thinking, you dirty old redneck? You dead old possum-fucker?

Luther looked at him.

There's worse things than fuckin' possum popped into Woods's head, but he wasn't sure if Luther put that there or if he thought it himself. Either way, it was true.

Woods looked at the woman on the porch swing next to him. He was tempted to pick up her wrist and see if she was getting stiff already, but he didn't want to let Luther know any more than he already might. He knew Woods disposed of their leavings; he might ask where and how, but he never asked what happened to them before. Woods liked the look of this woman, with her hawkish face freckled with dried blood, her half-lidded eyes that seemed to be watching something in the middle distance, something he couldn't see yet. Her eyelashes looked like bits of plastic or rubber, like the nibs on new bike tires. He might pull those off first.

He began to feel a pleasant pressure under his fly.

This was not like after prom, when the girl with the green sequined dress had worked and worked with hand and mouth in the backseat of his borrowed car until her lipstick was wrecked and his thighs were covered in cool spit and she cried and pleaded to know what was wrong with her. This was not like it was with Donna, who would come home to their shared studio apartment behind the garage after her shift at the diner and swear at him as a limp-dick and a queer and make him lick her until she held her breath and turned purple and came. The turning purple was the only part that turned him on, made him twitch just a little, but by then it was too late and Donna had gotten up to stand in front of the icebox and eat from the bag of vinylly french fries she had brought home from work, lit up by the fridge light, her ludicrous false eyelashes blinking with every third chew. He had been able to get off while she was gone, imagining her shot in the head and thrilling to the desecration of putting it in the hole. Then he had met Calcutta, pretty as a living girl, cool as a dead one, her whole body a wound. Calcutta was a walking desecration. She shouldn't be moving, but she was. He could take her with her head in a bathtub the whole time, her smile beaming under the water like a mermaid's smile, like a drowned nymph. He could strangle her as tight as he liked with an electric cord and she would noiselessly throw those bony hips. Cuts in her flesh would close up around whatever was put in them, and that felt like nothing else in the world; she didn't permit this often, but when she did, it only took him seconds. Best of all, she didn't mind if he had other girlfriends. She never said a thing about it. And neither did they.

15

THE FIRST THING WOODS SAW WAS THE VERY THING LUTHER TOLD HIM TO LOOK for. Tilted, rusted, not a big Ferris wheel to begin with, it slouched above the foothills wearing a shawl of vines, several of its once-white cars missing like baby teeth. Next he saw the jet fighter, a Korea-era Sabre jet with its wings swept back and its intake gaping in an idiot O. The jet, once the terror of MiG Alley, now listed to its right as if lame; it now wept rust from the cracked, verdant bubble of its cockpit, its skin pocked with absent panels. A statue of Jesus Christ stood nearby. He was twice as tall as a man, his hands resting on a sword that he seemed intent on pulling from the ground, more resembling King Arthur than a prophet, except for the halo and the incongruously beatific expression on his linebacker's face. Old paint flaked on his mighty chest and biceps, as it flaked on the sign beside him.

The Avalon Garden of Wonders and Motor Lodge stood on the Missouri side of the Oklahoma border, just a bit east of Hornet, Missouri, not far from the Devil's Promenade. Built in 1948 by Arthur Britton, who called himself "King of the Brittons," it enjoyed a brief spasm of popularity in the early fifties but found itself closed when the interstate opened and starved Route 66 of cars. Like many roadside attractions, it suffered from a lack of identity—not that it would have necessarily survived had it declared itself a military museum, or an amusement park, or a botanical garden, but the grafting together of all three provoked a sense of unease in even the youngest visitors. The greenhouse seemed, even when it had all its panes, too fragile to exist near the gaping mouth of the Sabre jet parked outside, as if the engine might roar to life, breaking the glass of the greenhouse and inhaling the stargazer lilies, birds of paradise, and other rare biota. The Christ, even when his white paint gleamed, had seemed embarrassed to stand before the cluster of motel rooms, as though he knew what sort of things went on behind their blue doors even as freckled boys shouted *Marco!* and *Polo!* at one another in between splashing and peals of laughter.

As Woods idled the F100 truck through the rubble that had once been a driveway, he considered the pool with its cracked and grassy lip, the trumpet-mouths of three stray tiger lilies blaring at him in the golden light of early evening. The motel rooms sagged, mired in their thickets of chicory, Queen Anne's lace, and other less photogenic weeds. Some of the doors stood open, inviting him in. 9. 12. 17. The chipped and water-stained door to 9 seemed to open just a little farther, the darkness beyond revealing no hint as to what had moved it. He looped the pickup around the pool, starting as a great black shape flew up from it. He jogged the steering wheel in surprise and nearly drove into a mossy stone bench.

"HUH!" he cried. The winged thing flew up past the lip and then back down again. A vulture. Overcome by curiosity, Woods veered closer to the pool to see what else was in there. Three black-cowled carrion birds hunched and shouldered each other out of the way to get at the pink-gray, stringy guts of a doe. The carcass was flat, dried up, the fur of the neck dyed crimson. Luther had told him deer blood was second best after man's.

Could there be another one of *them* here? Luther always told him to watch out when scouting ruins, that they weren't the only creepy-crawlers hiding from daylight in shamble-down buildings.

Number 9 opened a little farther.

He accelerated then, his tires spraying gravel till they caught. He lumbered blindly from behind the hedge of brush that hid the motel from the highway so that he nearly drove beneath the wheels of a semi bound for Tulsa. It blared its horn at him in a long, flat blatt that rang Woods's ears; he fishtailed but stayed straight, gunned the engine, veered past the truck in the left lane, and went on toward the Stuckey's gift shop west of Joplin. He would meet them at the Stuckey's. Luther, Neck Brace, Rob, and Calcutta. Even Cole. His monsters. And they would protect him.

16
Missouri

CLAYTON BIRCH LIKED HITCHHIKING AFTER DARK. HE WAS A GREGARIOUS CREA-ture, and, of all human society, he most enjoyed the company of the brave and the mad. Who else would stop for a short, ill-shaven young man standing by the side of the road with an antique leather pack at ten P.M., eleven, midnight? It was imprudent; he looked like trouble, and he was. He wore his chestnut hair longish, after the fashion of the generation he appeared to belong to. His dress suggested a thrift shop habit, but he in truth he had purchased some of his dated clothes new. He had hitched from Florida in a series of short jaunts that introduced him to a recently paroled safecracker, a Black Panther with a trunk full of tear gas grenades stolen from the Georgia National Guard, a divorcée on her way back from a séance, a homosexual with a lazy eye and six cats, and, most recently, three flower children in a repurposed and wildly painted milk truck. Of these, he had bitten all but the flower children, whose blood-stew of LSD, cannabis, and Beefeater gin promised a rarefied headache and a hard morning piss, besides making the driver, an unfortunately featured young woman who looked like nothing so much as Ringo Starr's fraternal twin, too enthusiastic to charm. He had given them five dollars for gas, accepting and pocketing the fat joint they offered him in parting; it would make excellent currency with a certain sort of motorist, and he hoped to be in California by midmonth, if nothing more interesting presented itself in the meantime. He had not seen San Francisco since shortly before the quake, news of which had depressed him so that he could not bear to see its ruin, recoiled from pictures of it filling up with boxy, soulless buildings. Only now that the nation's youth had been pouring in and filling it with music and art did he think he could accustom himself to its new face.

Clayton liked people and did not enjoy killing them. Killing, Clayton felt, was often foolish, usually unnecessary, and always inconvenient. Sometimes, however, it was unavoidable. The divorcée had died as he fed, and he wasn't sure why. Shock? The unhappy coincidence of an aneurysm? The postséance wrath of some importuned spirit? He hadn't taken more than a mugful of the woman's lonely, floury blood, he was certain of it, but still she had started to shake and, in the end, vomited all over her own lap and expired in a great, wet wheeze that sounded uncannily like disappointment. He was disappointed, too. He had been forced to dispose of her by driving her car into a nearby lake, which he had spent the remainder of the night in finding. Standing on the sandy shore, Clayton had been so aware of his silence as the car frothed and bubbled and filled that he had shamed himself into saying a few ceremonial words:

"God or gods, such as you are, I did not know this woman. I did not mean to kill her. I blame you completely and utterly for her untimely passing, which, as I am powerless to punish you, is certain to occasion a belly laugh on Olympus, in heaven, or hell, or wheresoever you currently abide. You are a bastard or a pack of bastards, if you exist. If you do not, then I am a fool for speaking to you. Take . . . damnation, what was it, anyway?" He had rummaged in his pocket here, fishing out the Florida driver's license bearing her wan smile. ". . . Cheryl into your care, or do not, but do not let it be said that her sad death went unremarked upon, for I remark upon it here. Amen and yours sincerely, C. Birch, of the Boston Birches, upon whom you have liberally shat. Also, please let there be no alligators in these waters, for I am in no mood to witness carnage."

So saying, he undressed as a wary great blue heron looked on, hiding clothes, hat, and pack under a mess of brush. At first light, he knifed into the piss-warm, murky water, swimming into the flooded backseat of the car, curling into a fetal ball behind the lap-belted, still-bleeding body of Cheryl Heffner, dental hygienist, owner of three Ouija boards, and, until very recently, the youngest resident of her Clearwater, Florida, apartment complex. Suppressing a vampire's intense dislike of water had been one of the most useful disciplines Clayton Birch had mastered, but it was not the only one.

That had been weeks ago.

Now, just past sunset, Clayton walked backward down Route 66, just southwest of Lebanon, Missouri, smiling his biggest smile, gouging the warm summer breeze with his thumb.

When not one but two cars, both loud and grumbly, pulled over, that surprised him. The driver of the first car, a cagey, bald fellow of coarse manners and poor breeding, eyed him from shoes to hat. The passenger, a large, hairy man in a neck brace, did the same, but it was the bald fellow who spoke. He raised his voice to be heard over the engine.

"You need a ride, mister?"

"Maybe."

Clayton walked to the driver's side, his intuition telling him this man fought the impulse to step on the gas when he passed in front of the bumper. This was a car with blood in its very seams.

As he got closer, the bald man squinted his eyes at him.

"You what I think you are?"

"A Seventh-Day Adventist?"

"Jocular fellow. I like that."

His eyes didn't say he liked it.

"What precisely is it that you think I am?"

"A sumbitch," Luther said, dropping the charm that hid his fangs.

"You, sir, are correct," Clayton said, not returning the courtesy of showing his fangs.

The two dead men eyed each other. Clayton, despite his almost scientific curiosity about other *nocturnals*, as he called them, had just been about to walk into the field and away from this vulgar specimen. Luther, not impressed with this northern smartass, was on the fence about whether to invite him along or to grab his head and drive.

Calcutta craned from the passenger seat of the black car, appraising the newcomer.

"He can ride with us," she said.

17

"SO WHAT DO YOU HAVE IN YOUR BAG?" CALCUTTA ASKED. "YOU CAN TELL A LOT about somebody by what they carry with 'em, especially when they travel light."

"Shrunken heads from the island of Borneo."

"Tell me really."

"The lost diary of William Shakespeare."

Behind them, something banged in the trunk.

Thump

"No, tell me."

"Watercolor paints and brushes."

"Are you gonna tell me for real or are you gonna make me open up that sack and see for myself?"

"I prefer not to."

"You know, I thought you were gonna be fun when I said come along. Being secret's just not neighborly, not with family anyway."

Thump

Cole flicked an eye into the rearview mirror, said, "Man don't want to tell you what's in his pack, he don't have to. But I do believe he is a painter. Painter's fingers on him."

"Well, that's boring," Calcutta said. "How long till we gas up? I gotta call my momma before she goes to bed."

"What, being a painter's boring but you calling your dried-up old momma's a party? We'll stop before long," Cole said. "I got a quarter tank left, but I'll bet Luther's eatin' fumes."

"Your mother is still alive?" Clayton asked.

"Yep."

"You must be young."

"Luther stopped my clock seven, eight years ago. Luther made us all, all but Neck Brace. Why, how old are you?"

"I'd rather not say."

"What, like fifty?"

Calcutta turned around in the front seat to look at him.

"Not like fifty," he said.

"I oughta be thirty-three, I think, but I lose track."

"That's normal. I lose track, too."

"Liar," she said. "You don't seem like the track-losing type. So tell me something."

"Like what?"

"Like what's the first thing you remember."

"My mother holding my hand out the window to feel the rain."

"That's sweet. But something that tells me what year it was. Like what kind of car you rode in."

"John Quincy Adams's cologne smelled of ambergris and leather. I sat on his lap."

"Huh," she said, her eyes betraying her brief but unsuccessful attempt to place John Quincy Adams. "Who made you?"

"She never gifted me her name."

Thump Thump

Cole said, "I'm about sick of that shit."

"Stop and charm it."

"I ain't stopping."

Cole jerked the steering wheel back and forth, causing the weight in the trunk to shift side to side. Something squealed and kicked hard.

THUMP

"It don't learn."

Cole jammed down on the brake then let up, jammed down and let up, bucking the car, rolling the contents of the trunk forward and backward. Then he fishtailed side to side again. After a moment of this, he slid into neutral, his sharp ears listening past the engine's throaty idle to pick up muffled crying.

"That's right," Cole said. "Less bangin' and more boo-hoo."

Clayton suppressed a wince.

He knew it was their intention to keep the one in the trunk alive until the following night. He also knew they were an undisciplined gang of thugs and that if they did chance to murder their guest, they would simply invite another one. Shortly after they had taken him on board, they had gone hunting in the suburbs of Springfield, Missouri. He had watched with mixed shock and admiration as Calcutta, attracted by the turquoise glow of a pool light, had bellied up to the fence of a suburban house and peeped over. The pops and shrieks of amateur fireworks could still be heard from all compass points, along with beery guffaws and the fuzzy jangle of electric guitar on someone's backyard radio.

"Want to go to a party?"

"I . . . I've got friends coming over. Who are you?"

"Your new friend," Calcutta had said, the charm finally taking. "Your best friend. No, you don't need your shirt. Let's go!"

The attractive blond woman, wearing only a red polka-dot bikini, had stumbled dripping from a side door in the fence, her eyes bloodshot and her skin reeking of chlorine, and climbed into the open trunk as if settling in for a pleasant nap. A man from the house called the woman's name, but he wasn't concerned yet. He never looked over the fence.

It happened just that fast.

"I'M GONNA LIGHT IT."

"Wait till midnight," Cole said.

"It is midnight, slow horsy."

"It's almost midnight. We said *midnight.*"

"Well, midnight ain't the Fourth of July no more and I want some Fourth of July in this sumbitch. Lady Liberty should be holdin' her torch high and proud tonight, yessir."

Luther lit the sparklers, their reflected image twinned in the mirrored aviator's glasses he wore to protect his eyes from sparks. Luther in his overalls and lace-up leather work boots, some dead soda jerk's soda shop shirt on, the collar off-white from blood and bleachings. He liked that it said *Mike* on the shirt and he wasn't Mike. Mike was in a patch of woods near Erie, Pennsylvania, all tied up with bicycle chains and rolled in office carpet. Just to be funny, Luther had written *NOT MIKE* on Mike's chest with Calcutta's eyeliner. That woman had no shortage of eyeliner.

That had been last year.

Now the two monsters and the dying woman sat in a wobbly car just at the top of the Ferris wheel. Luther wished there were a bleeder in every car, all moaning as their lives pulsed out into vampires' mouths, and this made him think of dates at a drive-in, everybody doing the same thing, private but not private. He had another thought that made him angry, a thought about a drive-in, but he shook this away.

"I'm a golla," Lady Liberty mumbled, drowsy with blood loss.

"You are a golla!" Luther agreed, securing the hissing torch of sparklers in the beer can taped to the woman's palm, just above where the wrist was taped to the broomstick holding her arm aloft. Her plastic Lady Liberty crown, purchased at the Stuckey's where they met up with Woods, sat crooked on her head. Her head drooped.

"Hold that crown up now, you luscious golla you."

She tried but couldn't.

"I think she said *goner*," Cole said.

"I know it. But I like *golla* better."

Luther held her head up for her, hearing Calcutta and Rob's cheers coming from below them. Woods watched in awe and glee, looking very like he did the first time he ever saw fireworks. Neck Brace stared with all the animation of an Easter Island moai.

The sparks made Lady Liberty wince; she turned her face away from the crackling light in her hand, her brutalized throat now illuminated, along with its runners of drying blood.

She turned her groggy head back to face Luther.

"Tay mee um," she slurred, her head lolling, but her open eyes fixed on the reflective plates of Luther's sunglasses, where doubled eruptions of sparklers blazed.

"You are home," he said with something in his voice that might have been regret.

"Tay mee um," she said again. "UM!"

Luther's voice hardened again.

"Give me your poor, your sick, your huddled masses."

"I wa go um."

"And I'll light sparklers in AAALLLL their asses!"

"Um. Mleeze."

"*Mleeze*, huh? I was never one to resist a lady with good manners. Home you go," he said, sucking hard from her gouged neck, so hard he arched his back, until her legs shook and the only part of her that did not wilt was the arm taped to the broomstick. Cole pulled her leg wide and attached himself at the femoral artery. Her heart stopped shortly before the sparklers died, and Luther did not light more.

"IF Y'ALL WANT ANY, YOU'D BETTER GET IT WHILE IT'S WARM," THE BALD ONE WITH the mirrored shades said from the top car of the Ferris wheel where the smaller, well-dressed one silently fed. The tall one called Rob skittered up the rusted wheel's frame, making Clayton think of a roach running up a drain pipe. The biggest one just watched, standing near the oddly martial statue of Christ, fingering under his dirty neck brace as if he had an itch. This one, despite his size, tended to eat last and least, which probably made him the youngest. Clayton had yet to hear him speak. Of the victim, Clayton only saw a limp spill of blond hair; Liberty's crown, now askew; and a dead arm taped aloft to a broomstick. These killers favored macabre spectacle, and this would be their undoing. None of them had been nocturnal more than two decades. They would not see three. Clayton determined to part company with them the next night, or perhaps one night later. He would make them talk to him, if he could, and he would write down what he learned for posterity's sake. He might well paint the girl on the Ferris wheel once he was clear of them and had a place to work unmolested.

Hypocrite, he thought, *at least these are honest ghouls.*

He caught the diurnal they called Woods looking sideways at him from beneath the cheap Indian bonnet he had shoplifted from the Stuckey's where they met and fueled up.

"I really do like your headdress," Clayton said. He felt jealousy pouring off the disturbed young man-child in waves, and he understood that this came from some attachment to the female who had invited Clayton to ride along. He also understood that this creature was serving to watch the dead by day, and that alienating him would be unwise. He stepped away from Calcutta and put his arm around Woods. "The actual headdresses of the Plains States war chiefs were impressive things, or so I've seen in photographs. They had to earn each feather through an act of hardship or loyalty, so a man whose headdress reached the ground was a man to be reckoned with. Of course, I know yours is just a bit of panache, but there's little enough of that in the world anymore."

The hostility Woods had felt a moment before dampened considerably now that the boy felt himself acknowledged and respected. Calcutta sensed the tension ease as well and gave in to the hunger that propelled her toward the Ferris wheel and the exsanguinating young woman in the crown and swimsuit.

"You're not talking about photographs at all, are you? You're talking about things you've seen."

"Maybe so, maybe not."

"Tell me."

Clayton allowed a gleam to visit his eye as he said, "There was a minor chief named Smiles at Horses who wore a bonnet that stood straight up, all in a circle around his head. Not so many feathers as other chiefs had. It was said he kept the others under a bear skin in his teepee, that he would not wear them all, for he wanted men to judge him by what he did now, not what he had done before."

"Did you see the buffalo?"

"Which buffalo?"

"The great herds."

"I saw a buffalo."

"You didn't see the herds?"

"Alas, no. I also once saw Buffalo, in New York. Does that impress you?"

Woods smiled a crooked smile. Clayton clapped his arm in fraternity, then wandered off. He would find some house and charm the occupants therein, take his necessary tribute and leave unremembered, sheltering with this pack through one more day, two at most. Why did these insist on killing? He had been tempted to scale the carnival ride and take his share, perhaps more tempted than any of them—older stomachs rumbled louder, and he did not gorge himself lionlike as these did, which might see him through two or three nights of fast—but he felt no kinship with them and would not break bread with them unless expediency demanded it.

"Hey," Luther said from his perch as Clayton wandered off down Route 66. "Where the hell're you goin?"

"Nowhere I shall not soon return from, sir."

"Just see that you come back alone."

"I shall deserve your every confidence."

"What?"

"I will come back alone."

"Yeah. Or not at all would suit me, too."

Cole said, more quietly, "Shut up, asshole, I kinda like him."

Clayton heard them tussle now, but good-naturedly, and not so hard that either would be pitched from the squeaking car lest Cole should tear his shirt.

There's something more to these two than friendship, Clayton thought. *Or there was.*

TWO HOURS LATER.

Luther and Clayton sat on the floor of the mold-furred room Luther claimed as his own. He had brought Luther half an RC Cola bottle full of blood as a peace offering.

"Who'd you take this off of?"

"The daughter of a squash farmer two miles off."

"It's good. She's as pure as North Carolina rain."

"Her father was no less tainted than she. Baptists of the rare variety, and by that I mean observant."

"You're a funny bird, you know that?"

"How so?"

"Way you talk."

"I can't seem to help it. In my household we were punished for lazy speech and rewarded for sounding like gentlemen. They were trying to make senators and rail barons of us, and our sisters the wives of such."

"What happened?"

"Smallpox. Scandal. Vampirism. We were already undone before I was whisked off into the night. My last remaining brother succumbed to fever at Andersonville while enjoying southern hospitality."

"I ain't from Georgia, Cole is. Anyway, that's before my time."

"And after mine."

Luther raised his RC bottle in salute, swirled it to discourage coagulation, then throated it back. He picked up a bottle of Old Crow bourbon and rinsed it around in his mouth, seemed to think about it, then swallowed. Clayton looked at him with some surprise.

"I love the shit outta whiskey. I still swallow it sometimes. Mostly spit it out but sometimes it's worth a headache and pissin' fire."

"There we disagree."

"Not just about that, I reckon."

Luther swigged bourbon again, but this time spat it out on the floor.

"I reckon the same."

An awkward moment passed between them. Luther broke it.

"Had a little fun while you was gone."

"Did you?"

"Sheriff rolled up askin' about fireworks and was we squattin'. Course I charmed him into getting on the radio sayin' he'd checked the place and there weren't nothing to see. Then just for fun I said, 'But how's that little itchy spot doin' on your face?' and he said, 'What spot?' with spit runnin' down his chin, and I said, 'That'un there,' and touched his cheek. 'Got a tick in it or something, but the tricky kind you can't hardly see. I'll bet it itches a little now, but by morning you'll be ready to scratch your face plum off from it.'"

Clayton considered Luther, wondered how much of his sadism came from his condition and how much had been natural to him. It had been Clayton's observation that vampirism amplified certain traits, chief among these narcissism and psychopathy. This specimen seemed to be wealthy in both.

"Tell me something, Mr. Nixon."

"Yeah?"

"How did this come upon you? The curse, I mean."

"You really want to hear all that?"

"I do."

Luther spoke.

Luther liked to speak.

18

YOU BEIN' A YANKEE AND ALL, YOU PROLLY DON'T KNOW NOTHING ABOUT DIRT *track racin', old NASCAR shit. Lot of us moonshiners fell in love with Mr. Henry Ford and his big, growly V-8s before the war and, well, after we came back we needed someplace else to drive fast for money. I got knocked around a bit in Italy, okay, more than a bit. Pile a' busted-up bricks called Cisterna di Latina. That was in '44. That day in Cisterna, me and three guys on patrol went into this busted-up church, you know, daylight coming through the roof and pigeon shit everywhere. There was an angel holding a pretty wood cross that looked loose in its hand. Had gold on it. I wondered why had nobody taken it, so I jiggled it, but the sergeant called me a Philistine, how'd'ya like that word? An' he said don't go givin' us bad luck. But we had just been through hell tradin' that town back an' forth, and we was pissed off generally because of all them rangers gettin' kilt, and I guess I felt like I had something good comin' to me. I wanted that thing, figured I could sell it, send it to my momma, give it to a whore, somethin', so I gave it a good tug. Now the major had already told us how Fritz had rigged up every little thing in Naples with explosives and not to touch nothin', but that was different. That had been the year before, and way down south. They had lots a' time there, they knew we was comin'. Here, the fightin' had been real fresh and they only just turned tail, and us all over 'em. So I wasn't thinkin' that* *way. Guess I wasn't thinkin' at all. "Private Nixon, I gave you a order," he said. It hadn't sounded like no order, it sounded like advice, but I guessed now it was a order, so I left that cross be. But whenever I settled it back in the hand, that's when the fuse finally caught. Boom. And not no little boom, neither. I got knocked back in the pews, both my legs broke, blinded too. But that didn't last. Anyway, I shoulda been dead. The other guys were. All of 'em. Sarge, Jumper, the new kid that smoked a pipe like a old man, I forget his name. So back home I went on a hospital ship. Hadn't even been in Italy but a month. Never shot nobody, well, mighta coulda 'cause I shot at 'em, but I didn't never see it. I think that was the biggest thing seemed wasted to me. All that trainin' and yes sir no sir and I end up getting sent home lookin' like roast beef off a booby trap and never once got to plug me a kraut. I guess you can see why I was okay with kickin' a little ass on the stock car circuit. Guess you could say I maybe had a little chip on my shoulder. That was in '44. By the time I could get around okay again, it was '46 and I was thirty years old and meaner'n a badger with a bad haircut. I got picked to drive a car in Daytona, they had a course there on the beach wasn't just an oval, right turns too is what I'm sayin', an' I had just won a race up in Georgia on a track like that. So I was thinkin' I had a chance even though Roy Hall was in the game, and that was a crazy, rare fucker. I loved that ole boy, handsome like Clark Gable and he'd whoop you at racin' or shining or shoot ya if you made him. But this city fella comes up to me the night before and says, "I got some people bettin' on somebody," and I says, "If these is smart people, I hope you mean me," and he says, "Nossir, but this bag a' dollars says you'll help the one they's bettin' on," and it was a pretty bag a' dollars. I was hurtin' for a new place to live, on account of a lady friend kicked me to the curb. Besides which, I had a little morphine monkey on my back, too, and I know you know what I mean, you look like you mighta had a suck on a opium pipe once or twice. Anyway I took that man's money and found myself not racin' to win but playin' wingman to a gimp flyboy named Red, gimped up even worse than me, had to nail his fucked-up leg to the clutch, but the boy could definitely drive. Just not as good as Roy Hall. An' as much esteem as I had for Roy, it was him I had to do wrong to. After he sprayed some wet sand back at Red—and I mean this track was right on the water—I came up on his left and nudged him off'n the other side of the track so his wheel sheared off and he almost went plowin' into bystanders—they didn't have no raised bleachers—but instead he took a jump and tumble into a bunch a' scrub palms. Me, I kept my wheels on the track, but I fell good'n behind. Red Byron won the purse that day, but I made more money'n him, and it makes me wonder just how much the fellows that paid me bet on the thing if they was cutting me that much. I'm pretty sure I'd'a ended up in the Atlantic if I'd fucked up. Roy swore he'd kill me but he never did. Fellow killed me did it in Atlanta. Turns out I had a talent for wreckin' other people. Truth was I liked it. The papers started callin' me "Blitz," like "Blitz Nixon sent Barney Childress into a spin on the second-to-last lap." Oh, I won a few smaller purses down the way, I had a talent for third place, but I made my big takes when some fella'd come outta the shadows with a paper sack. I killed a fellow once, I ain't proud of it, and a spectator or two, but I never got disbarred because by then I was good at makin' it look like a accident. Or enough like one. And I think them fellows with the paper sacks had a talk with some of them NASCAR and AAA boys. But there it was 1955 and all these rules comin' in and I was pushin' forty, never goin' to be nothing but a dirt track racer. I was lookin' for one more big score. Well, I was runnin' this race in Pennsylvania, got told to take out a fellow named Penry Carlisle, ain't that a hell of a name? Ole Penry had a future. Prettier'n Roy Hall had been, Roy was in the pokey now, though Penry was not near as hard as Roy. Penry wouldn't a' hurt a fly. But Lordy could he thread the needle in a stock car. He was getting ready to make the switch and try to qualify for Indy, and here he was out on a clay track in Amish country, the stands all full a' pretty girls. He was like Elvis, makin' 'em scream when he waved at 'em, and that didn't make me love him no more. Old dogs don't like young pups takin' all the soup bones.*

So I did it. Near on the thirtieth lap I hooked his bumper and flipped him pretty, spun him into another car and caused a big ol' pileup. Fellow was supposed to won won, so I guess the paper-sack boys was happy. But I messed up that Carlisle kid. Burnt him. He didn't die, but the only woman was gonna wave back at him now was his momma. NASCAR banned me. I got a death threat or two—ever notice that most death threateners ain't good spellers?—and I decided maybe I should make myself scarce, like Mexico scarce, but didn't do it quick enough. One night I was drinkin' at the Black Mill, that was the bar down from Little Five Points where I was livin' in Atlanta, and the bartender gives me this extra shot of Jack Daniel's. I said, "What's that for?" He said, "Fella bought it for you." "What fella?" I said. "Penry Carlisle," he said, but with no sass on it, like he was just deliverin' a message. I looked around and didn't see no burnt-up pile a' goo, so I said, "Well, where'd he go?" and he wiped his chin and said "Who?" so I said, "Penry Carlisle, man, who do you think?" and he said, "Mister, I don't know what you're talkin' about." So I knew somebody was messin' with me. I asked him for a cherry in my glass and he gave me one, and I lifted up that shot of Jack Daniel's to the crowd, lookin' right at everyone who looked at me, and I drank it down, and I ate that cherry, too, with big chews. I put the stem in the glass like putting a bow on a package and I walked out with my chin up and a smile on like Fuck you, coward, if you can't call me out to my face. *I walked home watchin' over my shoulder a little but I never saw nothing. Not that I was likely to, knowin' what I know now. When I got home, where I was livin' by myself because ol' Dolores give me the boot, I turned on the radio and started listenin' to a ball game and lit myself a cigarette. I about shit myself when I saw him. He'd been there all along, just watchin' me, kind of a older man in a hat and coat, standin' in the corner. I said, "How'd you get here," and he said, "I spoke to your landlord," and I ain't entirely slow, so I said, "Thanks for the drink," and I'm thinkin' how can I get to the .38 I got in a shoebox under my bed but now he comes walkin' over and I stand up thinkin' he's going to shoot me but I can see both of his hands. So I rush at him and then he's just not there and I bang my head into m'own closet door. Where the fuck did he go, right? So I go divin' in my room under the bed to grab the shoebox but he was already under the bed waitin' for me. I yelled and I could smell his breath like onions and ants, you know how ants get that formaldehyde smell? That was what it smelled like. And he grabs my face with a hand like a wooden Indian's hand and it's dark and I can't hardly see but his eyes are bright and he says, "Penry Carlisle was important to me," and I says, "Was? Ain't he alive?" and he said, "I fed him a pillow last night. Some kinds of living aren't living. You'll learn all about that," and that's when he did it. You know what he did. There under the bed, he did it. And took me away and left me alone under a bridge to figure out what I was now. Course, once I did, first one I went back for was that paper-cut lesbian bitch Dolores. Anyway, "Blitz" Nixon disappeared. You mighta seen it in the papers if you follow racin'. But I don't guess you do.*

19

"NO," CLAYTON SAID. HE THOUGHT FOR A MOMENT BEFORE HE SPOKE AGAIN.

"It seems to me that you might have had a promising career had you not preyed on other sportsmen. And now you jeopardize your peace by killing those you might simply steal from. Why?"

Luther tilted up the bottle and tongued out the very last drop before he spoke.

"I'd rather show you than tell you."

Clayton knew what Luther would do at the very instant Luther did. Luther whipped the bottle at him. Clayton ducked, but the bottle broke against the wall, a piece of it nicking his cheek. Now Luther was on top of him, licking blood from his face, laughing. Clayton threw him off with great force, smashing a discolored chair neither of them had thought fit to sit on. Luther laughed even harder, then spat blood and a front tooth. He sprang again, but this time Clayton rolled away and took up a leg of the chair, rising to his knees. Luther, up already, kicked him in the head, driving Clayton's face against the wall and breaking his nose. He pushed away from the wall and turned, whipping the chair leg down so it broke the arm Luther blocked it with, then ducked and whipped it even harder, splintering it against Luther's leg, which broke as well with a sick, wet crack, tumbling Luther to the ground. Clayton grabbed the Old Crow bottle and nearly brought it down on Luther's head but then, as an olive branch, set it carefully down on the floor. Now Cole came in with a camper's hand ax and Neck Brace loomed outside the window like he was about to jump through it. Luther stopped them both by raising his good hand. He looked at Clayton, his hurt arm thrice-jointed, his mouth smeared, smiling as though he'd been caught stealing cherry pie.

The arm made a gristly noise as it reset itself. He slithered forward and took the bourbon bottle, swigged from it and made himself swallow. Sat up again. Winked at Clayton.

"There, now. Wasn't that more fun than just sittin' talkin'?"

CLAYTON WAS HAVING HIS FIRST GOOD DREAM IN MONTHS, MAYBE YEARS. HE LAY in the lap of a beautiful woman who was sitting in a cool, clear stream, such that only his face remained above water. This was important because in this dream, he was alive and breathing. He knew the woman was beautiful even though he could not see her face because of a bright light behind it. The sun. She bent over him, backlit by bright sun, and he did not burn. He saw his own white limbs in the running water, little fish or maybe tadpoles moving in the current, and he lay still. He had no thought of leaving this place, which might have been Eden, and no care to ask the woman's name or intentions toward him. He breathed in and out without thinking about it. He blinked automatically, not by act of will to mimic the living. He smelled plants and sap and heard the muffled sound of the water. Nothing had ever been so sweet as this, just breathing in, breathing out. Just feeling cool water on his limbs and sun on his nose and cheeks.

He wanted a good look at her face; perhaps it was his mother as a young woman, perhaps it was Anna, his wife. He knew the woman was nude, but hers was the nakedness of the meadow, not the boudoir. The fringe of bright sun about her lit her hair so it might have been brown, black, or blond, he could not tell. It did not matter. He breathed in, breathed out, and it seemed from the rise and fall of her belly that her breathing matched his. She opened her mouth and he thought she was going to ask him a question, or say his name—he had no doubt that she knew it—but she did not speak. Instead, a curious noise came out of her mouth, a noise like a dry croaking or ticking, an electric noise. He understood then that the waking world was intruding on his dream, and he fought against it. Since the real world had found him here, he thought he might flee with her to some other place.

"Let us go to Jamaica," he wanted to say. "Let us break sugarcane and chew its stalks and walk in the sea together." But the ticking or static grew louder, then faded away. He became aware of a rotten hotel room mixing with his stream and his platonic ideal of woman, making a rude palimpsest.

"No," he said. "I am not ready."

But now Eden or Elysium was gone, and the woman with it, and even though he knew that someone was moving outside his room he ignored this fact lest it grow too solid and scatter the memory of the dream.

"Go away," he whispered into the shawl he had wrapped his head in, but now it seemed urgent that he should investigate. He wasn't lounging in some subterranean parlor where he was known and protected; he was sheltered above ground among strangers, and not altogether friendly strangers, at that.

I am in Missouri!

He did not know the exact hour of the day, but his sick feeling and the weakness in his limbs told him it was bright afternoon outside, the killing sun at its lordliest post.

Someone is outside this room!

He tore off the cloth and reached for his backpack, fetching out his sunglasses, putting these on. He approached the warm rectangle of the window, where old and stinking towels had been nailed in place. His window faced north, as all the rooms the vampires had settled in did, so the sun's rays did not beam directly on the cracked pane, nearly black with dust.

He peeled back the edge of a towel, opening a long diamond of indirect light that sickened him but did not burn, and he leaned as far back in the shadows as he could to observe the intruder.

A slight man with a blond mustache stooped at Luther's door now, having passed by his, listening to the ticks produced by some machine he held, these ticks growing louder as he wanded it close. He nodded at some compatriot behind him and stepped back.

They were hunted, which suggested they were known.

This was bad.

Clayton was aware of his head hurting, this caused by his squinting into the furnace of sunlight even through shaded spectacles and a dirty window.

A second window he remembered in the rear bathroom might allow egress, but, again, into sunshine, and it was so small he would lose half his clothes pouring through it. Might he towel up and try to kill the intruders, then run for the pine woods? Might he charm them and then run? That seemed the best of bad options; with luck, he could make it without direct burns, but what then? The woods were not so deep as to be fully proof against the sun, though a cave or abandoned structure might offer itself. Plausible if he were not hunted, but he was, and even if he charmed or killed the first one, he could not know how many more remained. Where was the watching-lad who thought himself an Indian? What had gone wrong?

He had trusted in fools, that was what.

Now another fellow stepped up where the ticking-machine man had been, a middle-aged man with the body of a former athlete or laborer gone soft about the waist. He held in his small hand a nozzled can Clayton only too quickly recognized.

Gasoline!

"So this is it," he said quietly, stepping back from the window.

"You were my own death," he said to the woman from his vanished dream. The soft sound of splashing came from two doors down—Luther's door. Clayton lay down on the dead hotel's floor among the dry husks of insects and cigarette butts left by vagrants; substituting his backpack for the absent death-mother's lap, he tried to assume the posture he remembered from the stream in Eden. He was not surprised to find that it was vaguely cruciform. He smiled.

He heard Calcutta saying, *"Luther! Luther!"*

"That one, too," someone stage-whispered outside.

Now his door was splashed.

He closed his eyes.

An image came to him of his father's horse groom smoking out a hornets' nest in the stable.

"All right, then," he said. "Let it be so."

"Hurry," the outside voice hissed.

Then everything changed.

The man by his door let out a yelp of pain and surprise at exactly the moment another sound rang out, rolling after as if from some distance.

A gunshot.

Clayton opened his eyes.

PART THREE

The Bereaved

20

"SISTER CLARE, YOU HAVE A VISITOR," NATHALIE SAID. HER VOICE SOUNDED strange in Jude's ear even though she was technically Jude's best friend.

"A visitor?"

"Yes."

"Who is it?"

"A man."

"Is it my father?"

"He didn't say he was your father. He told me a name and it's gone right out of my head. And I even had a trick to remember it." Her voice seemed to be swallowed by the oaken joints of the hallway outside the chandlery.

"Thank you, Sister Anne," Jude said. The two young women addressed each other by their new names as often as possible to help one another remember. Jude still thought of herself as Jude, and she was sure the same was true for the girl who used to be Nathalie. It would take getting used to. As would the silence. Sister Clare had not heard Sister Anne speak, prayers and singing aside, for two days now.

The other novice turned to go, but then she turned back and faced her friend. She dropped her voice to a whisper. "It was something to do with a candle, I should certainly be able to remember that, as many as we make. Chandler? No. Wicklow. That's it. His name is Mr. Wicklow."

"I don't know a Mr. Wicklow," Judith whispered back.

"Well," Sister Anne said, "he seems to know you."

"Did he say what it was about?"

"Not a hint. Except that it was urgent."

"What about Mother Superior? Will I be allowed to see him?"

"You weren't supposed to be. He spoke first to me, and I did my best to shoo him off, but he wasn't having any. I heard Mother Superior speak to him although I didn't hear the words. Whoever he is, he's very persuasive."

"Am I to miss Sext?"

"No, of course not. You'll see him just after. You'll have to miss lunch, but I'll save you some. I hear it's beets."

"We had beets yesterday."

"Apparently we didn't eat enough of them. The Lord has made us rich with beets."

"Well, yes, please save me what you can. Where did you put him?"

"On the bench in the visitation room. I told him it would be better if he came before Vespers, and he said a very odd thing."

"Which was?"

"He said Sext was better, he knew what Sext was. He seemed like a priest."

"Maybe he is. That's not so odd," Judith said.

"That's not the odd part."

"Tell me already."

"Patience is a virtue."

"So is silence," Judith said, "and we're not doing so well with that."

Nathalie smiled. Judith liked her smile. The women stood so close their heads nearly touched.

"He said he wouldn't come at Vespers because he'd come from far away."

"So?"

"He said he wouldn't drive at night."

"Is he old?"

"No. He has glasses, but not like Mr. Magoo."

"I still don't see what's so odd."

"He said he wouldn't drive at night because it wasn't safe for him."

Judith held her breath.

She saw that her friend was going to speak again.

"Sisters," Mother Superior called from down the hall as she passed on her way to the office. Brightly but with a note of rebuke.

Judith's eyes begged Nathalie to tell her more.

When she saw that the young novices had not separated, Mother Mary Catherine stopped her busy walk and faced them. "Our Lord keeps no company with whisperers," she said.

"Sister Anne," Judith said.

Nathalie bowed and turned her feet as if to move away.

"Nathalie," Judith hissed, imploring.

Mother Superior started walking toward them.

Nathalie spoke.

"He said *you* would know why it's not safe to drive at night."

Judith ran toward the visitation room.

THE MAN SAT ON THE BENCH LOOKING PHYSICALLY SMALL BUT SOMEHOW LARGE, as though he exceeded the boundaries of his skin. His small, wire-frame glasses intensified rather than diluted his gaze, which settled on Judith and made her flush with warmth. He closed his eyes in an over-long blink, less from fatigue or shyness than from courtesy; his was a gaze that might stir dust devils from a heap of ash. She walked to him in fast, long strides and he stood, taking his hat in his hands, then setting it on the bench, meeting her eyes again. He had the dark hair and good posture of a man of thirty-five, but he had seen too much of something and he carried it. He smiled, and the smile was brightened by the darkness he carried behind it. He offered his hand through the iron grate that separated them—how like a cage it looked—and, even though she knew it was against the order's rules, she took its cool, uncallused strength in hers. She opened her mouth to speak but didn't know what to say, so he spoke.

"Judith Anabelle Lamb?"

She nodded.

"My name is Phillip Wicklow. I am one of a group who call ourselves the Bereaved, and with good reason. I have come to tell you that the statements you made to the Arizona State Police concerning what you saw on the night of May 13, 1967, are accurate. Your husband was murdered by people who died some time ago but who persist because they prey on the living. Your abducted son, Glendon, is almost certainly dead, but we intend to find and destroy the beings responsible for your tragedy, and we believe you can help us do that. We have evidence that your status as a nun, even a novice, will grant you some power to harm them. Are you interested in that? Harming those who took your family from you? Stopping them from harming others?"

She mouthed a word but gave it no voice.

Yes.

"Excellent. Then I'll need you to pack your things, if you have any things, and come with me. Try to appease the good woman I see politely monitoring us through the window and get her to grant you a leave of absence from the abbey. If you can't, we hope to strike before you are formally expelled for abandoning your post, which could take a month or more. Even if you are expelled, your faith and your familiarity with sacred paraphernalia still make you dangerous to them. Mrs. Lamb, are you in or out?"

"How long do I have to decide?"

"Do you see the car just across the street from the property?"

She looked. A nondescript yellow car sat hunched against the new, green corn.

"I'll need you in that car within the hour. If you come with me, you will have difficult and dangerous work to do, and you will find out things about the true nature of creation that you cannot unlearn. If not, the world needs candles, too. But I will not be back, and you will never find me."

She felt a breeze on her face, warm and faintly sweet with rot; a trio of crows hopped and gathered near a grayish smear on the pavement.

"May I ask you a question?" she said.

"Whatever you like."

"Are you a priest?"

He looked down and away, aiming his gaze at the crows and their banquet.

"I was."

"MY FIRST THOUGHT IS THAT I DON'T KNOW WHAT I'LL DO WITHOUT YOU."

Nathalie said it as Jude made her bed again, yanking the corners crisp and tight. The room seemed very small, what with the whole world outside breathing on the window glass.

"Aside from a mountain of penance for missing Sext and maybe lunch while I say good-bye. Now you say, 'Who's saving beets for *you*, Sister Anne.' Except you're too upset to joke. That man upset you, of course he did. It's why your hands are shaking. It's why you're leaving. It has to do with your tragedy, doesn't it? Of course it does. He brought bad news that sounds like good news, brought it like a bee bringing pollen in its baskets. I would ask you to stay and think about it, at least until I could sit and listen in the chicory and Queen Anne's lace. Maybe I would hear God's little voice telling me if you are really supposed to go or not. To whatever place you're going, someplace that scares you, that much is clear. Don't forget to be safe. Don't forget to write me, please. We're like sisters, blood sisters, I mean. We started together. I guess I thought we might always be here, gardening, singing. That we would always know each other. Maybe Sister Mary Monica would say this was right, you leaving, I mean; that being close to you distracts me from prayer and contemplation. That it delays the trial of solitude that makes the silence from which we hear God's bigger voice. But that's all right for her, she has Sister Columbine, and those close friendships are permitted for the older sisters. I guess they're afraid, well, you know what they're afraid of. Oh, it hurts me to see your hands shake like that. Are you still Sister Clare? Or are you Jude again? I suppose you're always going to be Jude for me, which is a sin of some kind, I'm sure of it, but I'll sit with that until you're Sister Clare and I'm Sister Anne and even the Reverend Mother can find no fault in us. If you'll stay. Will you stay? No, of course you won't. Is it your son?"

Jude nodded. Sat on the bed. Looked at Nathalie.

"Maybe we're neither one of us meant for this. Maybe Sister Mary Catherine was right the first time. She nearly refused me, too, you know. Said I reminded her more of a wild hermit mystic than a Cistercian, but that there was nothing wrong with that. Maybe my mind's too busy to quiet down and make candles only and only pray. To be around people and not talk, it's so hard. We sign to each other around the other sisters, just like they do, that's permitted, and everything I have to say to them I can say with my hands. But there are no hand signs for how much you mean to me. This didn't turn out at all like I thought it would. I thought a contemplative order would let me hear God better, it was all I wanted. I felt so sure once. Did you feel sure, or were you just hiding here?"

Jude looked at her, the tremors going through her getting smaller.

"You don't know, do you?"

Nathalie sat next to Jude. A bell sounded.

"There's the end of Sext. An hour, you said. An hour isn't enough. I promise I don't talk like this to anyone else, the words just pour out of me when I'm with you. It's your eyes, your sky-colored eyes, I fall into them. I suppose I also fall into the hole that's in your heart, there's such a vacuum there, maybe now you'll find whatever you need to make you heal. Maybe you'll find that it's here after all and come back. Will you at least think about that? Coming back? You wouldn't be the first to leave and then return, though so few leave. It's nice here, after all, away from traffic and wars and the radio, so much noise on the radio. Will you take your sandals? Of course you will, you can't walk out of here barefoot. And your socks, though it's not cold now, only a little at night. Oh, Jude. May I hold you?"

Jude nodded. Nathalie put her thin arms around her friend, rested her head on her shoulder. Sister Columbine walked by, holding a rosary and whispering, glancing once into the door Jude had left blamelessly open. She walked on, still whispering, her face innocent of approval or disapproval. It was Sister Mary Monica and the Reverend Mother who thought these birds nested too closely, but they, too, passed by without comment.

Jude gripped the smaller girl hard now, her boyish hands all but hurting Nathalie's shoulders. Jude kissed her temple once, long, her nose filling with Nathalie's faint scent of garden sweat and black tea. Jude rose from the bed in her work clothes, put on her socks and sandals. She took her habit and rosary in a small handbag. Just before she moved out the door for the last time, she kissed her fingers, then turned her palm to Nathalie, something between a blown kiss and a kiss of peace. Nathalie sensed that her friend was heading into a profound darkness full of biting and broken bones; that she was going there to stand in the stead of innocents; that she was the closest thing to a saint Nathalie would ever meet; that they would never meet again in person, or, if they did, they would not recognize each other.

The young woman stared at the emptiness where Jude had been. The tears were not long behind, and when they came she would savor them, she would kiss them from her own fingertips. She had no stomach for lunch, not for beets, not for honey, not even for Sister Columbine's cheese and potato casserole.

The hanger that once held Jude's habit still swung gently.

When it was still, Nathalie would let herself cry, but she would shut the door. Her grief was between her and Jude. Or, now that Jude was gone, between her and God. This was what it was to be a cloistered contemplative; to lose everything but God, and to do nothing about it. To be passive as a lamb.

"You're not a lamb at all," she told the hanger. "You're a wild boar. And someone's going to get the tusk."

21

"IT'S BRAVE OF YOU TO TAKE THIS STEP," THE MAN WHO CALLED HIMSELF WICKLOW said. Farms drifted by outside the car windows, their soil fertile and sweet on the air that buffeted her through the quartered window. Classical music played over static, Judith wasn't sure what song or composer it was, she didn't know classical music. She had been meaning to correct this since she wept at Beethoven's Moonlight Sonata when her tenth-grade English teacher, Sister Henriette, played it for a roomful of acneous sophomores on a cheap picnic record player. What Beethoven, who was German, or Henriette, a mousy French-Canadian who sounded like a duck, had to do with English class Jude never knew, but she wept at the relentless fall of the piano keys, each note driving at something mute and powerful and sad that grew in the center of her and was perhaps only now flowering. Cows lined up at a sagging wire fence, probing the air with their gentle tongues, calves shouldering into mothers' legs, tails swishing in light that had just matured into something like gold. Now the sun, well behind the speeding car, ducked behind a raft of clouds.

"Are we in Pennsylvania?"

"It's better if you don't ask questions about geography. Try not to look at town names."

She nodded. He smiled at the road, and she guessed that he was proud of her silence, that he saw strength in it. She wanted to ask why but decided to practice patience. God had taken the reins now. That God existed she had no doubt; her only questions were questions of character.

"They can make you do things. Did you know that?"

"No."

"They can also make you say things. That's why no one of us should know more than necessary."

She nodded again.

Her eyes asked a question.

"You know what they are."

"I do?"

"You just don't want to say the word because it sounds ridiculous."

The thin one in the Camaro the tall one in the backseat the woman like the whore on the beast's back the teeth on them the eyes that held light like coins on dead eyes quarters quarters quarters the teeth on them could bite holes in cans.

"Evenin', miss."

They came out after dark like dark brought them like junebugs stupid butting into lights could they help themselves it didn't matter they bit hard they were for smashing she would smash them if she could oh please let this man be real oh please don't fool me anymore like when you said I should be a wife like when you put that baby in my arms when his gums hurt my breast and my nipples turned tough and brown for nothing oh please arm me sanctify me I'll believe what you tell me I'll say that movie-monster word and if you fool me again then stop telling people about Jesus stop the book at Malachi because all you have in your pockets is Passover and the baby on the rock and the knife in Daddy's hand.

She said the word.

He said it too.

She turned the corners of her mouth down and laughed, but she was also crying. He laughed, too. He put his hand on her shoulder and drove like that until he had to shift gears.

BY DAY, THE BARN RESEMBLED ANY NUMBER OF BEAT-UP OLD BARNS ONE PASSES on rural roads without sparing a second glance. A stone foundation and waist-high stone wall gave way to weather-grayed planks that brightened to faint red in a foot-wide band beneath the roof. The trees that once separated the property from a neighboring cabbage farm had been cut, leaving sight lines open for hundreds of yards in each direction. Unremarkable terrain stretched out for miles around the barn, punctuated by a lonely gas station here, a general store there. A fertilizer plant hulked just past the one-stoplight town, making a once-pristine little jewel of a river undrinkable, this despite the prayers of the Amish in the next county. Judith had been nearly asleep when the car approached the barn's gate, the wood of which looked much older than the cross that sat atop it.

A small white house with black trim sat just north of the barn, a cross over each window.

"Welcome to All Souls Ranch," Wicklow said.

At that, three border collies sprang barking from the shadow of the barn and ran to the gate, followed by one amiable-looking stout man with a silver cross around his neck and a holstered pistol. He walked from the darkness of the barn in no particular hurry, at last squinting into the window of the car. He smiled, betraying missing teeth near the back, and opened the gate. As they drove in, Judith had time to notice that the single strand of rusted barbed wire atop the fence had been hung with tiny bells, all of them painted black.

"You're just in time," the man shouted after them. "Supper's at seven."

"WE ARE THE BEREAVED," THE MEN SAID, STANDING AROUND THE RAW PINE TABLE with their heads bowed, their hands clasped. "We unite in hidden knowledge to act for the good of others. Our works will go unseen. We shall not love our own lives, but shall lay them down in the name of good works."

"Have you witnessed proof of evil on the earth?" Wicklow said.

"I have," the stout man said.

"I have," each man in turn said, four besides Wicklow, starting at his left and going around the circle until they got to Judith, who sat next to him. They looked at her.

"I have," she said.

Light from the failing sun leaked in between the planks at the barn's west side, throwing stripes of golden sunlight across the floor.

"Have you lost beloved flesh through the machinations of evil?"

"I have," each man said.

Judith said, "I have."

"Will you use any means at your disposal to destroy unnatural agents who work evil in the world, and also those who knowingly serve them?"

"I will," each man said.

and also those who knowingly serve them

Judith paused at the thought of destroying anything other than one of these monsters, meaning *a person,* even if that person served them. This was her first time speaking the creed. Nobody rushed her. She examined the word *knowingly,* found it just reassuring enough. At length, she met Wicklow's gaze and spoke.

"I will."

She heard her own voice as if from afar.

Did I just promise to kill somebody? Am I really here? Did I die in that wreck and pass into purgatory? Is anyone praying for me to get me out of here? I cannot believe the course I'm on. I can't turn from it, either.

"Then let us sit thankfully and break bread, as our enemy cannot," Wicklow said.

Judith remained standing.

I'm in the trunk, Mom.

I'm ready to come out of the trunk.

YOU'RE NOT GLENDON

no

GLENDON'S DEAD

Yes

IT'S JUST ME IN HERE ITS ONLY ME MAKING YOU TALK IN MY HEAD

Yes, Mommy.

"Judith?"

Wicklow's voice.

She opened her eyes.

She smelled vegetables and garlic. An older woman with pillowy bosoms ladled soup from a steaming pot into the mismatched earthenware bowls that sat before everyone's place. The others looked up at her where she stood sweating.

"Judith, do you require assistance?"

"No," she said, and sat at her place.

This isn't purgatory. I'm nuts. I'm finally losing my mind. Maybe I lost it before and Robert and Glen are living at the house without me because I'm in the nuthouse and none of this happened.

Except that it did.

She took a spoonful of soup and held it, inventoried it. Tomato and chicken broth with carrots and potatoes and onion. Threads of meat; the soup was thick with threads of canned corned beef. She looked again at the faces as six mouths opened around spoons or chewed or got wiped by napkins. Wicklow, intense and certain, like some killing clergyman, some armed prophet doing God's dirty work. She looked at the eyes of these men.

If I am nuts, I'm at the right table.

She took the spoonful of food and ate.

"We await one more," Wicklow said. "Upon his arrival, tomorrow, we begin preparing, and we must prepare in earnest. Bram Stoker, quoting the poem 'Lenore,' said, 'The dead ride quickly.' That has never been more true than now. When that phone rings," he said, pointing at a wall-mounted telephone that looked quite out of place in the barn, "in whatever state of readiness we find ourselves, we act."

"Who's on the other end of that phone?" Jude said before she could stop herself.

Wicklow smiled pleasantly at her, and, in a disarmingly mild tone, said, "You will never ask me that question again."

NIGHT.

My name is not Wicklow, but it is the only name I have now. When you speak to the others, do not ask them their last names, do not tell them yours. I would not want members of your family to come to harm because another is taken. This is not a request.

That was one of the first rules Wicklow had taught her while they drove.

Breaking that rule was also one of the first things the stout man from the gate did when they sat down to talk on the back step. He and Judith were the last two who had not retired to the house.

"My name's Pete, but everyone calls me 'Lettuce.' I picked that up in the air force. Airman 'Lettuce' Pettis. Don't tell me your last name, I don't want to know. I only told you mine because my family's gone, so they can't go looking for anybody if they get you. Not that they'll get you."

"I would have been okay with Pete."

"Yeah, but I answer better to Lettuce. Or Pettis. But I didn't want you to think I was named for actual lettuce. Nothing exciting about lettuce. Not that I'm trying to excite you, it's not like that. Sorry, I always talk too much around pretty girls. You make me nervous. Pretty girls, I mean. You really a nun?"

"A novice, yes."

"Is that a special kind of nun?"

"It's a new nun. A temporary nun."

"Like on probation?"

"No, that's a postulant. Being a novice is more like leasing before you buy."

"Gotcha."

Lettuce took a drink from a small flask, and the smell of whiskey rose in the air.

"You don't seem like the type, or I'd offer," he said. "But you just sing out if you do want a nip."

"I thought we weren't supposed to do that."

"I can't sleep without a little. I don't need much, just a bit to take the edge off. He knows. It's really more of a suggestion than a rule. Least for me. I been with him the second longest. After Hank."

"How long's that?"

"Two years. When I say with him, I don't mean physically with him. You go home. He calls. It's like that. I've probably only spent thirty or forty days with him altogether, and not all at once."

She processed that for a moment. Pinched her hand like a claw to ask for the whiskey flask, took just a capful of its bright warmth into her mouth and swallowed.

"So, none of you are very experienced at this?"

"I guess you could say we're all *novices*."

She smiled. A question wormed its way into her mouth.

"Have you ever . . ."

He watched her, pretty sure what she was asking but waiting anyway.

"Destroyed one?" she said at last.

"No."

"Oh," she said.

"He has, though."

"I certainly hope he has."

"He has," Lettuce said. "Not here."

"Where?"

"Cuba."

22

MORNING.

Judith had lain awake half the night with the silence of the house heavy on her, looking at the red line of light beneath her door. An infrared bulb burned in the hallway and remained on even when sunlight leaked into the frosted panes of window glass; the panes in all the bedrooms but Wicklow's would allow one to discern shapes and shadows but were not sufficiently opaque for a hypnotic gaze to lock a wakened sleeper's eyes and render him vulnerable to command. One they called Somchai walked the house for the last watch; a Buddhist monk before Wicklow found him, half Thai and half British, Somchai was hoped to be proof against mind control because of his meditative discipline. Judith got the idea that this, too, was theory.

During the night, she once again thought she heard music coming from somewhere below, so faint she couldn't place it except that it sounded weirdly familiar, weirdly like a pop song. Wicklow's was the only downstairs room, but she couldn't picture the deadly serious man listening to anything so frivolous.

The knock came shortly before sunrise, stirring her from dreams of taking cake from the oven with no mitt, the pan burning her hand.

"Rise and shine," Somchai said to Judith and the others he had roused. "The last man is here."

Jude was the first down the creaking stairs to the kitchen, where coffee hissed and bubbled in a percolator and fresh sunlight streamed through the drapes. A heavily tattooed man sat at the cramped table, a steaming cup before him.

"You must be the nun," he said when he saw her.

"I'm Judith," she said.

He nodded and went back to his coffee. She now saw that his tattoos were all of crosses, or of Christ, or of the Chi-Rho. His neck was all crosses, big, black ones over the carotid arteries.

"I'm Hank," he said, after Judith thought they were done talking.

Lettuce said, "He's the driver."

IN THE BARN, WICKLOW HAD COVERED THE LARGE PINE TABLE WITH NEWS CLIP-pings and photographs, all arranged in overlapping stacks that made sense only to him. The six men and one woman gathered close, took seats.

Wicklow remained standing.

He spoke.

"While you should know as little as possible about one another, I will share with you most of the relevant information we have about our quarry so that the knowledge might survive. We believe we have the names and living identities of three of those traveling in what we'll refer to as the Suicide Motor Club, a group of murderers who roam the country abducting women and children, provoking lethal automobile accidents and literally feeding on the blood of their victims. These killers have themselves already died a bodily death and risen from this death to live again unnaturally. Have you witnessed proof of evil on the earth?"

"We have," the others said together.

"We have," said Judith.

"We have," said Hank.

"And so have I. The group of news clippings I'm about to show you features a man named Luther Nixon, a North Carolina bootlegger turned auto racer. Look well at his photographs, particularly this last one."

Here he held up a black-and-white image of a balding man with a closely shaven head smiling broadly and holding up his hand in a victorious wave. A red number 10 had been written in the top corner of the picture. Judith clutched her stomach.

"You might think the man in this picture had just won his race, but he didn't. Nixon intentionally collided with the lead vehicle and ran it into oncoming cars. The ensuing fire burned a promising young racer over seventy percent of his body. Luther Nixon was unhurt, as he was in six of the seven other crashes he caused over his bewildering career. I would go so far as to say there was probably no one in the country more practiced at causing and surviving high-speed wrecks. Now, of course, he doesn't have to survive them. Judith?"

"Yes," she said. Her face had gone completely white.

"Do you recognize this man?"

"Yes," she said. Then she walked to the barrel they used for trash and vomited up her coffee and oatmeal.

"I SHALL NOT TELL YOU HOW WE TRACK OUR QUARRY. IF ANY OF YOU WERE TAKEN, your . . . inevitable . . . confessions would alert our nocturnal friends to our methods, and they would disappear, perhaps for good, before or after turning on their pursuers. What I can tell you is how we come to identify them. The methods are exhaustive but crudely effective. We look for newspaper stories and police reports involving missing persons and stolen bodies. When we find such a story, we rank the likelihood that the individual has joined the ranks of the undead on a scale of one to ten. One through fives are simply filed; daylight abductions, for example. People who went missing in the wilderness, or while swimming or boating. That leaves us with nighttime disappearances in reasonably populated areas, still a very large body of data. Most missing children are rated as fours or fives. Unfortunately, vampires are not the only servants of evil, and children are routinely preyed upon by the malign or unwell. Children come to grief while exploring. Parents kidnap children from spouses and flee the country, or go to ground. Older children run away. Those few who are taken by the undead, we believe, are not normally turned, but simply . . ." Here Wicklow searched for a word that might be less painful for Judith but found none. "Consumed. If strange phenomena accompanied the disappearance, they become at least a six. If reliable witnesses claim to have seen them at night after a living disappearance, they become a seven. If a missing body is later seen alive, or if the victim can be associated socially or geographically with another vanished party rating six or higher, that victim is promoted to an eight. Where possible, and prudent, we attempt to speak to any surviving friends or family members about those rated eight or higher. There are less than a dozen nines in all of our files, two of them in the group we're chasing. Nines are strongly believed to be vampires. Take this young man."

Here he held up a yellowed, careworn newspaper clipping preserved in plastic. "He died of blood loss at Beth Israel Hospital in Manhattan in 1933. His body went missing that night, and a nurse was murdered, along with a teenaged boy. Nobody was able to say what happened, not even people who were in the same room. His mother says a cousin of the boy's contacted her years later and swore to have spotted the young man in the subway unchanged after thirty years. Even taking into account the mother's several stays in Bellevue following nervous breakdowns, we can be reasonably certain this boy is or was undead. Now we come back to our ten. A known vampire. Luther Nixon, the Alpha driver. We don't know the identity of the Beta driver."

Here he produced a newspaper clipping.

"The *Asheville Times*. September 13, 1955. 'Blitz Nixon Vanishes,' it says. In Atlanta. Now let's look at this one. From the *Savannah Morning News*. January 4, 1926. 'Crime Figure Missing. Harris Carlisle, fifty-eight years old.' I'll just skim this . . . Racketeering, petty theft, murder, nice fellow. Vanished into thin air, his car still running. So what, a petty southern crime boss gets bumped off, right? Except that his grandson is Penry Carlisle, the promising race car driver Luther Nixon disfigured. And Penry died of suffocation around the time Luther was last seen. It's possible some relative of the boy euthanized him, then shot Nixon and dumped his body into a ditch—Mr. Nixon had something like that coming for a very long time. Except that we have fourteen different car accidents from 1958 through 1968 resulting in exsanguination or abduction wherein the victim's vehicle was flipped or steered off the road and a witness identified a bald man as the driver. In seven of those cases a second car was reported to be involved. In three of those cases, a witness reported seeing shining eyes. And now," he said, nodding at Jude, "one with true sight has seen their teeth. Also, there's this."

He passed around a series of pictures of a man at a bar.

"This was found on a roll of film developed from a Vitrona camera, a very fancy electronic flash camera, found near the wrecked car of a Danish tourist in New York State, just south of Niagara Falls. The camera bag had been thrown clear, the camera itself ruined. Much like its owner."

The man in the photos was clearly bald, but his face was badly blurred. From his body language, he appeared to be telling a joke, mugging to the camera. Hands up like a monkey. Fists to his head as if pulling hair he didn't have. Leaning toward the camera as if telling some vulgar secret. Turning away as if laughing.

"Now look at this."

So saying, he passed around a fifth photograph from the Vitrona series. In it, the same blurred bald figure stood with its arm around a jovial, ruddy-looking blond man with pale blue eyes. The blond man's image was so clear you could count his laugh lines. The bald man appeared to have been caught moving fast, even those parts of him that had clearly been still. The images did not seem to be part of the same picture, but they undeniably were.

"The dead, it seems, do not photograph well."

GUNSHOTS RANG OUT ON JUDITH'S THIRD DAY WITH THE BEREAVED. SOMCHAI HAD taken the van, a newish Chevy in need of its first brake job, to buy all the honeydew melons and cantaloupes from an Amish couple who ran a roadside fruit stand just on the other side of the county line. Lettuce had gone to town to make other purchases. Now the men were shooting the Amish melons in the field bordering the woods. A portable basketball hoop with a rotten net stood nearby, as did a trio of scarecrows set up like tackle dummies.

First the shooters shot honeydews on the ground. Then they fired as the cantaloupes swung back and forth from a length of rope dangling below the basketball hoop. Not many of the men could hit the melons while they were in motion; just Lettuce with his short, double-barreled shotgun and Hank with his .45 revolver.

Judith watched with her arms crossed.

She had not been given a gun nor invited to borrow anyone else's.

I shoot better than most of these guys.

Lettuce had assumed command of the firing exercise. After he shot, he stood near a large canvas tool bag and smoked.

"I'd like to shoot, too," Jude said. "Have you got an extra gun?"

"You won't be a shooter. You have another job."

"You might want me to have something, just in case. I'm really not bad. I could show you."

"We can't waste ammo," Lettuce said, seemingly disinterested, stubbing his cigarette out on the bottom of his shoe. Judith felt at least half of their whiskey-sharing camaraderie burn away at that. The last man emptied his gun and said, "Clear." Lettuce walked away from Judith and spoke to the group.

"Now, the reason I got you shooting melons is because Mr. Wicklow tells me a head shot will stun an undead. Not for long. But long enough to do this."

So saying, he reached into the tool bag and took out a long, very sharp wooden stake that looked to have been made from a baseball bat. He charged one of the scarecrows and rammed this into its chest while Hank grabbed a mallet from the bag. Lettuce ducked, still bracing the stake, while Hank swung, driving the wickedly pointed, fire-hardened wood deep into whatever comprised the scarecrow's chest. Putting the mallet down, Hank ripped the shirt free to reveal a large half-frozen ham lashed to the frame.

"What are the others doing?" Judith asked.

Lettuce said, "Covering us, I hope."

"No," Judith said. "I meant the other vampires."

23

DAY FOUR.

Judith rubbed her eyes, trying to stay awake in the hot barn where Wicklow had left her to read files. He had gone to town to pick up a registered package from overseas, something important. Something for her. Flies, their numbers seemingly undiminished by the coils of fly tape hanging near the walls, lit on her or buzzed near her with impunity.

She read from a typed piece of paper, its back still lumpy from keystrokes.

> Katherine Louise Cutter, b. 1936. Arrested for shoplifting, assault with a deadly weapon, and resisting arrest, Lititz, PA. 4/30/1962. Bradley's Gas Stop and Market, Kenneth Roy Bradley, prop. At approx. 9:30 pm Miss Cutter was observed sneaking liquor (type not specified) into her purse. When Mr. Bradley confronted her, she claimed the bottle was hers. He took it from her and shoved her toward the door. She went behind the counter, presumably looking for money or a firearm, but only found a pair of scissors, with which she stabbed Mr. Bradley

about the face and head. His son, Kenneth Bradley Jr., hearing the commotion, came from the trailer behind the store and helped Bradley subdue her. Officer J. M. Landrey of Lititz Borough PD made the arrest, and was en route to jail with Miss Cutter when he was summoned to pursuit of a red Thunderbird suspected of fleeing a fatal crash. Landrey made contact with the vehicle, reported that it looked scraped up and had a wobbling tire. He could not read the plate, which had been intentionally obscured with mud. The station lost radio contact with Officer Landrey at this point and had no further news of the Ford or its driver, a white male wearing a hat. Approximately an hour later, Officer Landrey was found parked on train tracks seated in the backseat of his duty vehicle in only his boxer shorts. The officer was reading *Field & Stream* magazine. He had no memory of the chase, nor of arresting Miss Cutter, nor was he unduly concerned about the possibility of being struck by a train. Miss Cutter was not seen again, though her mother claims she is not deceased. After a medical exam ruled out trauma or illness, Officer Landrey was fired.

Judith rubbed her eyes. Someone had written in red pen above the words *fatal crash*:

Flip & bleed

The red penman—was it Wicklow, or the one on the other end of the phone?—also wrote on the bottom of the page:

PFC John Morris Landrey US army 4th Inf.
KIA Dak To 6/22/67

Requiescat in pacem †

Everyone suffers who meets them

In the same manila folder, Judith found a yearbook picture of a chestnut-haired or dark-blond girl who was pretty in a sneaky, cute way, like a sexy squirrel. Bangs framed a tan face captured in a three-quarter turn, smiling hard at the photographer's command. This was a boyfriend-stealer and shoplifter, perhaps, but girls who stab clerks don't wear lace collars, do they? Of course, she was only a senior in high school, eighteen years old. A lot could change in, what, five years? Was this healthy but sly Pennsylvania teen the pale, gaunt, wild-haired thing with the red hole for a mouth she had seen riding shotgun in New Mexico? She could be sure about Nixon, and maybe the Camaro driver if they got a picture of that fine-boned, young-looking monster.

And of course she would never forget the long, horsy, dead face on the thing that took Glendon. The tall one that poured his arms out of the car. The one that won at tug-of-war.

She looked one last time at Katherine. The number 8 in red had been scratched through and replaced with a larger 9 on the top corner.

Almost certainly a vampire.

She yawned with the early summer heat.

Dreams had batted sleep away at least four times the previous night, and her damp pillow suggested one of those dreams might have been significant. Was it the car crash, in which she rammed headfirst into a train that had been heading for hell but now derailed? Could it have been the saloon dream that found her winning a poker game with four skeletons? She strongly suspected the moon mission dream, but everyone knew a real moon mission was coming up. She had been atop the parapet of a white sand castle, its walls notched like a castle she and Rob had helped Patsy build on a summer trip to Myrtle Beach.

Glen stood with her on the moon-castle, getting on tiptoes to peer over the wall at tiny astronauts climbing out of their rocket. Stars shone icy and cold above them. It dawned on her that she was not supposed to be on the moon, that there was no oxygen here, that she and Glen would suffocate and it would be her fault, but it was too late. She yelled at the astronauts, who could not hear her, and then found that Glen was gone. She had still felt his tiny hand in hers.

When she had gone downstairs at dawn (following Somchai's second knock), she drank three cups of black coffee in a row, cooling them with water from the tap to get them down faster.

Now she put down Katherine's file and picked up one labeled *Robert Odom.* She held it in her hand for a moment, a tremor of hate and fear going through her: not fear of him or it exactly, but fear of what seeing its human face would do to her. She didn't know if her frame was sound enough to contain the scream Robert Odom's face might draw from her,

How'd you know my name? That his name, too?

and she was done reacting like a woman. No screaming, no crying, no vomiting at the sight of those she must destroy.

I will be strong, she thought. *I will fortify myself with psalms and wafers, wafers and psalms. He leadeth me in the paths of fast cars. He maketh me to lie down on white gurneys.*

STOP IT.

My blood runneth over.

ENOUGH

I never blasphemed even in my mind at the convent.

Or did I?

Have I been misled in coming here?

Nothing seems real or matters.

I've lost it.

I've lost it.

I've lost it.

JUDITH SMELLED SMOKE, THE HIGH, CHEMICAL SMOKE OF SUMMER BARBECUE grills before the meat goes on. She walked to the door and saw a burning figure sagging on the grass past the men. A young man named Shane now squirted liquid from a square can all over a second scarecrow and ducked aside while Somchai, coming from behind him, struck a stove match and tossed it at the dummy. The speed of their movements suggested they had been drilling at this for some time before they were given lighter fluid. The dummy erupted in flames nearly invisible in the noon sun, but a whitish cape of smoke drifted up, casting a hazy shadow on the grass. A third scarecrow patiently awaited its immolation while Lettuce soaked the first with a garden hose.

Shane drenched the last dummy with fuel.

Shane, she knew, believed he had lost a son to one of them as well. His little blond moustache and carefully parted hair suggested a bank manager, but he moved with purpose and she could picture him burning one. Holding the point of a stake to one while a bigger man slammed it home. Maybe shooting one, though he was a pathetic shot even with stationary targets.

Now Hank ripped a match from the box and tossed it on the false man. Lettuce spoke while he doused the flames.

"Good! You know how to shoot, you know how to stake, you know how to burn. We'll work in twos to make our movements harder to predict. We'll drill to get it in our muscles so when the fear and adrenaline hit, we just do it and don't think. That's the key to staying alive. Don't stop to think. Tomorrow we'll work on beheading. Not the most pleasant thing to do, but we're gonna get real good at it. Wicklow says it works."

How does he know?

What did he do in Cuba?

"Of course, this is all backup. We're gonna try to hit them during the day. Even under cover, they're supposed to be weaker while the sun's up. And if we can get sunshine actually on 'em, that'll do our work for us sure as hell. That's the plan."

Maybe they would be able to destroy their enemies.

But what was her role in this? Was she to pray? Sing psalms?

Hopefully she could keep her mind better focused than she had today.

She just needed sleep.

And faith.

God give me faith. I was hoping to pray my way to you in the cloister, but now I need you to find me. Help me. I don't know how deeply I believe you care about us; you know my heart, you know I want nothing more than to be sure. Do you hear me? Please show me that you hear me.

The dogs barked and she knew Wicklow was back.

DAY FIVE.

The elderly priest made his way toward the altar with a pained gait; he had to be at least seventy years old, probably closer to eighty. Wicklow sat to Judith's right. He had told her about Father Klaskow, how he was forgetting himself these days.

"He'll make the sign of the cross at the absolution during the penitential Mass," Wicklow had said as they walked in. "The missal was changed in April this year, but nobody has the heart to correct him."

Now she was watching for it.

"May Almighty God have mercy upon you, forgive you your sins, and bring you to life everlasting. May the almighty and merciful God grant us pardon, absolution, and remission of our sins," the old priest said. Here he crossed himself and most of the congregation did the same, though a few did not. One young woman checked her missal.

Wicklow winked at Judith and smiled.

She smiled uneasily back at him, then felt ashamed for it.

As the choir started to sing the Kyrie and the congregation joined in, Judith's mind wandered.

Is this man devout? What would make him wink like that if he's serious about this? Am I still serious? I pray to be, I pray to be in a state of grace.

Even as her mouth moved around the words of the Kyrie and the Gloria, words she had been saying since she was old enough to walk, she thought about what Wicklow had unpacked in the barn.

This is holy water. The bottles are antique, you'll see the image of Our Lady of Guadalupe engraved on the silver part of these six, which are full of blessed water from the River Jordan. These six with the crown contain blessed water from Lourdes. You will use the empty one to practice with.

What does it do to them? Burn them?

Yes. It may also blind them if it gets in their eyes.

Do you know this for fact?

I do.

How?

I can't tell you. But I know. If the one who casts the water is devout, it will do great harm to the unholy living dead.

And if she's not?

We believe the water itself has enough power to do some harm, but that this will be greatly amplified in a believer's hands.

She did a decent job keeping her mind on the service during the liturgy of the Eucharist, right until the moment she began to sweat.

No, she thought as they knelt for the *Sanctus.*

Not here just let me be one with you here at least please give me peace.

She saw a church deserted, wind blowing through its broken windows, its candles strewn about the aisles, Wicklow in priest's robes crucified upside down like St. Peter.

She shook her head. The image dissolved. She wiped her brow with her sleeve.

Wicklow took her elbow, escorted her to the altar and knelt beside her. It was nearly impossible for her to take communion without remembering an irreverent non-Catholic boy she had dated briefly during her senior year of high school. Her mother hadn't been pleased to meet the young man, Jimmy Dell, but couldn't forbid it outright since she herself had dated Riley Eberhart. Riley had been an indifferent Baptist, before, as Janet saw it, her careful rationing of premarital intimacies had turned him into an indifferent Catholic and conjured an engagement ring. Jimmy Dell had accompanied the family to Mass one Sunday, which scored a point or two with Mom, but then blew the whole thing spectacularly when he had to stay in the pews while the Eberharts filed toward the altar to receive the body of Christ.

"Bring me back a wing," he said, just above a whisper.

Mother had heard. Riley heard, too, and covered his mouth with his hand; it might have been a cough but Jude suspected it was a laugh. It had been all she could do to keep from laughing, too, but she was a teenaged girl then.

She wasn't anymore.

The old priest stood before her and she looked into his big, watery eyes before she closed her own. She felt the wafer on her tongue and Father Klaskow said, in his hoarse, sterile voice, "The body of Christ." She believed as hard as she could that it was literally true and said, "Amen."

When she opened her eyes, they went immediately to the tenth station of the cross. *Jesus falls a third time.* She thought again about the barn, and the imported cross she was to use as a weapon.

This cross is from an Italian church destroyed by German artillery during the war, just south of Rome. The image of Christ is bronze, the wood is cedar. You'll see the gold leaf vine pattern, and here, where nicks in it actually caused by shrapnel have been filled in and covered with gold leaf. It is significant that this cross stood against evil and was not itself destroyed.

The cross had felt awkward in her hand, just a little too wide for her grip. It was not meant to be held by a hand her size.

After Mass, and after they had both gone to confess, Wicklow drove her back. She closed her eyes as requested so she would not see the town's name but felt the car stop sooner than she expected; he had pulled over.

"Open your eyes," he said.

When she did, his image had barely come into focus before he slapped her face. Hard. His eyes remained impassive.

She suppressed the urge to strike him in return, grabbed the fabric of her dress. A tear of pain wormed its way out of her left eye, the one above her stung cheek, and she felt ashamed of the tear. She did not want him to see that he had hurt her.

"Why did you do that?" she said, the corners of her mouth turned down, her hands still grabbing the dress so they would not form fists.

"Because you smiled when I mocked a priest."

"What?"

"You heard me," he said. He winked at her.

"You had no . . ." she said, choking on the next word.

"I had every right. I am forging you into a weapon. Your desire to please another even at the expense of your devotion is a flaw in that weapon's temper. I strike you as a blacksmith strikes a sword, not in anger, but in defiance of those you are consecrated to destroy."

She swallowed hard. She hated that what he said made sense to her. She hated that she felt guilty for hating it. She wiped her cheek with the back of her hand.

NIGHT 5.

Jude woke.

She had the impression someone had softly closed her door.

The crack beneath the door was black.

The bulb's off. Is someone out there?

She reached for the vial of holy water she kept by her bed, prepared to break its seal and throw water in a cross pattern, prepared to say certain Latin words she had memorized.

She also took up the Italian cross, clutched it to her.

Nothing moved in the hallway, at least not so far as she heard.

But why is it black out there?

Did I lock the door? Of course I did, I must have.

She glanced at the heavy old iron door key on her nightstand.

The crickets outside stopped their chirring.

What time was it? Her stomach still felt full from the rich dinner of venison stew the Bereaved had eaten together.

"It isn't deer season," Jude had said when Maryanne served them.

"It's frozen," Lettuce had said. "We've got a meat freezer."

From the profound silence of the house, up from the basement perhaps, she heard the music. That pop song, tinny and just too far away to identify.

Now the crickets sang again and obscured the music.

She set the cross on her dresser and took up the room key, padding across the old wood floors in her bare feet. She thought she heard the boards in the hallway creak, but it might just as well have been her. She held the vial of holy water one-handed, its cap in her teeth, ready to twist it open and throw.

What would she do if one really came through the door right now, white and lamp-eyed and wicked, showing its obscene teeth? It seemed like a fairy tale that they should be out there, hunting in the night unrecognized by men, even though she knew they were.

Have you witnessed proof of evil on the earth?

I have.

Evenin', miss.

She tried to remember a psalm but only got the chorus.

Thou art with me for thou art with me for thou art with me.

She fitted the key into the hole, tensing as metal slid barely audibly on metal. She turned it.

It was already locked, just as she knew it would be.

The keyhole looked black.

She thought she heard a hushed voice but couldn't be sure. Was she missing Nathalie and their late-night conferences, their "diet of whispers," as Nathalie called it?

Nathalie with her wild mane of hair and her wholly innocent eyes.

Even her overbite was oddly charming, the way her upper lip had to curve down and back when she said a *p* or a *b*. Gentle, half-mad Nathalie. Judith felt the absence of a friend now more than ever. How much she would give for someone's hand to hold, someone to compare notes with.

Did you hear it? Did you hear it, too?

She withdrew the key.

She bent to the keyhole and peered out.

Black.

Her nose filled with a pleasant, musky scent.

Aftershave? Too nice for aftershave. More like incense.

She stayed where she was, squatted down on her heels, listened to her heart hammering in her chest.

I'm jumping at shadows.

Now the keyhole went red. She saw the far door, Shane's door bathed in eerie infrared.

Someone must have changed the bulb, that's all.

But the bulb hung in the center of the hall, just near her door. Whoever changed it would have to stand in her line of sight, turn another light on to see.

Somebody just switched it on, then.

The switch was nearer to Hank's room.

Why was it off?

Just as she was about to stand up, a shadow crossed her eye's path.

She couldn't be sure, but the impression she had was of a priest's black vestments.

Wicklow.

Did he lie?

Is he still a priest?

She went to sleep only after a long vigil troubling herself with how little she knew about those to whom she had entrusted her life.

And perhaps her soul.

24
St. Petersburg, Florida

THE OLD MAN STOOD IN THE MAP ROOM, SWEATING THROUGH HIS CLOTHES. HE could have afforded an air conditioner, but it killed him to spend real money he could save simply by being uncomfortable. Life was uncomfortable, and the harder you worked to keep discomfort at bay, the more you suffered when your efforts failed. And they always failed.

The old man pushed the button that started the tape again. There was a good deal of static on the line. The private dick he used in Pennsylvania didn't have high-grade equipment—he was mostly just an adultery-and-minor-lawsuits guy, but the old man could make everything out. This was his second time listening, so this time he took notes. The private detective spoke first.

> "Milner, James. Milner Information Services, Pittsburgh, Pennsylvania. Client, T. Calvert. Conversation between Katherine L. Cutter, whereabouts unknown, and Anne Cutter, Lititz, Pennsylvania. 9:21 pm, July 4, 1969. Begin tape."
>
> *(static)*
>
> "Hello?"
>
> "Happy Fourth a' July, Momma."

"Katherine?"

"It's Calcutta, Momma, I told you."

"I can only call you Katherine."

"Call me what you want, Momma, but it's Calcutta."

"Where are you, baby?"

(static)

"On the road."

"Like always. But where?"

"Missouri, Momma."

The old man stopped the player and picked up his yellow legal pad, scribbled on it, pressing *play* when he was done.

Missouri

"Someplace safe?"

"Nice hotel with Jesus out front. I been there before."

AVALON GARDEN!

"When you comin' home?"

"Soon, Momma."

"How long's it been since I seen you?"

(static)

"A year."

Says one yr since seen mother—bullshit

"It's been more than a year. It's been . . ."

"It's just been a year, Momma, you get confused."

"Oh. How old are you now, baby?"

"Never mind that, Momma, I just called to see if Ray's been coming over like he said he would."

"You sound like you always did. In your voice."

"Ray, Momma, did my brother come over with your medicine?"

"And I know you shouldn't sound like that no more 'cause it's been so long, but I just love you so much and I love your voice."

"I love yours, too."

"Have you met a boy? Is that why you're callin'? Oh, I hope it is."

"I met a boy, yeah."

"Is he nice?"

"I wouldn't date a boy wasn't nice."

"Good girl. He isn't stayin' with you in that hotel?"

"Different room, Momma. I'm not like that."

"Hotel's okay when you're married. Everything's okay when you're married, everything that makes babies, anyway."

"I need to know about Ray."

"You would have such pretty babies."

"No babies, Momma, I hate 'em."

"Hush now, you don't."

"I do."

"Ray's boy's drivin' now."

"Eddie."

Eddie/Edward Cutter (nephew) 17 y/o, dope user

"Eddie's drivin' his daddy's car, yes he is. Drove over to see his grandma all by himself."

"Did he bring the medicine?"

"I have all my medicine."

"'Cause Ray's not always good at doing what he says."

"I know it."

"And you need somebody now."

"I need you, baby. Baby Katherine, I need you. When you comin' home?"

"Soon, Momma."

"Why do you call me and don't come home?"

"I would come if I could, Momma."

"Tell me what's happening, Katherine. Please."

"Don't get upset, Momma."

"But why?"

"Don't cry. You cry, I'm hangin' up."

"No."

"I will."

(static)

"No."

"Should I not call anymore?"

"I couldn't stand it if you didn't call."

"I should throw this number away."

Bullying/control w/emotional threat.
This girl probably a jerk before.

"No. I need my baby girl."

"I know it. That's why I call."

"Please don't not call."

"Please don't ask me when I'm comin' home."

"Why, baby?"

"Just don't. You don't ask and I'll keep callin'. That's our deal."

"I can't help it."

"I know. But try."

"I'll do better. Are you seein' anyone? Romantically, I mean?"

"A nice boy."

"That's good. You eatin' good?"

"Getting all I need."

"You was always skinny."

"I am still."

"It's getting hard to remember what you look like. It's been so long."

"It's been a year, Momma."

"No . . . It's been . . . '63? '64? I was still in the blue house."

Blue house Magnolia Street, Mannheim PA
1947–67

"A year, you hear me?"

(static)

"You there, Momma?"

"I'm here. I just drooled on myself. Like a baby. Like my mouth don't work no more."

Aural Mesmerism—dangerous—ask W can they all do that?

"You just drool sometimes, Momma."

"I know it."

"It ain't nothing."

"Don't get old, Katherine, it's rotten getting old."

"I won't."

"You sound good."

"You takin' your medicine? How many kinds a' pills now?"

"Five. I think five. Ray makes sure."

"Liver pills, heart pills, blood pressure pills, right?"

"Two kinds a' blood pressure pills. I was a hunnert eighty over a hunnert."

"Is that real bad?"

"Pretty bad. But not no more. Ray makes sure."

> Health poor, 5 meds, stroke risk? Time limited (mine too—ha ha)

"He still at the plant?"

"Yeah. You should call him."

"I don't call Ray."

"You should call him, because he confuses me about you."

"Tell me again what I looked like when I was a little girl."

"You looked like you had cinnamon in your hair, and cream for skin, and your feet were so tiny you coulda worn bottle caps for your shoes."

"I like that, Momma. You always say pretty things."

"Baby, why does Ray say you're dead?"

"Ray's ignorant."

> Ray knows

"Why would he say that? I'm talkin' to you right now."

"You are. It's better you don't talk about me to Ray. Or nobody else."

"Katherine, baby . . ."

"I gotta go, Momma."

"He nice to you, that boy?"

"He likes the same kinda things I do, 'cept we keep different hours . . ."

The old man raised a white eyebrow, reached for the button to stop the tape.

". . . but he ain't really anybody. You hear? He ain't anybody."

He hesitated, then forgot what he was going to write down.

"What?"

"Nothin, Momma, I didn't call."

(static)

"I didn't call."

(static)

"Hello . . . Is someone there? Who is this?"

(click)

25
All Souls Ranch

DAY SIX.

Judith stood behind Shane as he aimed.

"Put pressure on it from both directions. Push a little with your back hand, pull a little with your front. That'll keep you steady."

Shane jerked a bang out of the gun, sending up a panache of dirt six inches behind and to the right of the pale green honeydew.

"Relax," she said, "You can't jerk it. Just breathe and squeeze."

Bang!

Better, but still a miss.

Lettuce called from where he cleaned his shotgun and smoked.

"I already told him. Just let me handle this."

"Wait," she told Shane. "Don't shoot just yet but keep it aimed."

She put her hand on his right forearm and it felt more like hard, humming wood than flesh.

"There's your problem right there," she said. "Give me the gun."

He handed it to her dutifully.

"Hey," Lettuce said.

"Now shake your arms out, Shane. Like a dog after a bath."

He grinned a little at that.

"There you go, smiling's good. All that hate's got a purpose, I know it, but you can't let it get in your muscles when you shoot. This is easy, right?"

Shane shook his arms out good.

"Hey, really," Lettuce said, standing up. "I mean it. You're not supposed to touch a gun."

"I'm not."

Judith handed the gun to Shane.

"Now aim again but this time your arms are wet spaghetti. You don't use any more strength than you have to, and you breathe. Don't shoot till I tell you."

Judith cut an eye to where Lettuce started his approach, looking very much like a bull trotting up to see who was putting a leg over his fence.

She focused on Shane.

"Now line it up. Can you see just a sliver of daylight on either side of the notch?"

"Yeah," he said.

"Good. Hold it. At the end of your next out-breath, before you breathe in again, you just squeeze that trigger easy like you got all day to do it."

Lettuce stood a few feet off, ready to physically pull the insubordinate girl away if he had to, but not until the man shot. Safety was safety.

Bang!

The honeydew rocked, a neat hole appearing not in the center, but at about two o'clock on the dial. Had the melon been a head, the bullet would have thumped solidly over the left eyebrow.

Lettuce breathed out through his nostrils.

He locked eyes with Judith.

Judith stared back.

"Your student," she said, walking away.

She saw Somchai coming out of the barn with heavy garbage bags.

The dogs jumped and wagged around him, so he showed them something and then threw it hard and far. They chased it and he loaded the van and drove off. As the border collies ran, play-fought over it, and ran again, their contest took them just in front of her and she saw what Somchai threw.

A deer hoof.

"Nobody freezes a whole deer," she said to nobody.

Nobody agreed.

LETTUCE SPOKE TO WICKLOW NEAR NIGHTFALL ON THE SIXTH DAY. JUDITH STOOD near them in the barn, her arms crossed. When Lettuce finished, Wicklow spoke, seeming to stand over the larger man.

"Did she shoot the gun?"

"Well, no. But she handled it. You said she wasn't to handle it."

"She wasn't."

"And I told her not to."

"Why not?" Judith said.

"Because firearms aren't the most effective tool against them," Wicklow said. "I don't want your power as a holy vessel compromised by touching an instrument for killing."

I don't feel holy

"Is that what we do to them?" she said. "Is it killing?"

"That's a thorny question. We destroy them."

"And how many have you destroyed?"

"You're changing the subject."

"I need to know."

"Do you see what I mean?" Lettuce said. "Insubordination."

"She's not the only insubordinate. I like her zeal for action more than yours for the flask."

Stung, Lettuce flushed a deep red from his collar to his scalp.

Judith pressed.

"How many? One?"

"No."

"More than one or not even one? Because if it's not even one . . ."

"More," he said, as close to shouting as he ever got, "and that's the end of your interrogation. You trust me or you don't. We go after them together under my command or you go back to your grate and your prayers and your chandlery. If they'll have you."

She fumed but said nothing.

"Courtesy is a good start," he said. "But I require obedience. You swore it once, to your order."

"And broke that oath."

"That's right. Because your purpose is here, and God knows that."

"Do you speak for him now?"

"In matters touching the malevolent dead, I do."

Lettuce said, "Not following orders gets people killed."

"I agree with that," Wicklow said, then looked at Judith. "Do you?"

She furrowed her brow.

"I do," she said. "Is this man my superior?"

Wicklow said, "Yes."

Judith looked at both of them.

"In or out, Sister Clare."

Judith pressed her lips together at that.

Both men stood completely still, waiting for her to speak.

She opened her mouth.

The telephone rang.

26

SITTING ON THE FLOOR OF THE VAN WAS NOT EASY FOR JUDE. SHE HAD LITTLE TO hold on to in the Chevy's spartan interior save the wheel well she rested her tailbone against, hunching forward to hold her knees. The absence of windows had left her mildly carsick. She wore her habit, as instructed, but it was hot and constricting. Worse, she felt like an impostor. It might as well have been a Halloween costume for as much as she felt like a "holy vessel."

I'm lost I can't do this I'm on a fool's errand.

The motion of the van and the hum of the motor lulled her nearly to sleep, but every time she got close she started awake as she feared the van was rolling, in the desert, under the moon. "Huh!" she would say, and lurch this way or that, but still the van hummed on under the stars, through and past the intermittent glow of oncoming headlights, the floor ever harder under her ass. Lettuce was having no difficulties, snoring in that distressing, hitching way particular to the stout and middle-aged. His leg touched hers, but it was not awkward. After the call had come in, something had changed in him. Something had opened. He was no longer a gruff, prickly bear defending abstract lines of authority; now he was a soldier and she, irrespective of her sex, rode with him into the valley of death. The very little bit of talking done in the closeness of the van had been between the two of them.

"Know how I lost my back choppers?" he had said.

"Tell me."

"Bit down hard and cracked them on a bad landing, same one that gave me the limp. Korea, '52. I had been flying a C-47 transport ship. I really wanted to do fighters, everybody did, but that wasn't what I pulled. So I flew me a gooney bird and dumped flares for night bombing or hauled supplies, mostly hauled supplies. One night an engine flamed out, no reason, just old. But it was raining. That, plus her pulling with the dead engine gave me a bad pitch coming in—I put down on the strip and wham-bang, hit and bounced, skidded, ended up off the runway half in the mud. Broke five teeth, three leg bones, a foot, plus had to get two vertebrae fused. I'd'a got dentures, but I still had enough teeth to chew, and they were in the back anyway. VA takes care of me all right, though. Honestly, I was glad to get home. I didn't feel much one way or the other about the Koreans. Or the Chinese. I liked flying, but I haven't done it since. I guess they had me pegged. Never took fire. Couldn't even land an old prop-job gooney bird in a thunderstorm. I wouldn't have made a great jet pilot. Jet pilot would have got back in the cockpit. Me, I was done. I never wanted to see that ground coming up at me wrong again."

"I can't imagine being a pilot. I don't think I could even drive a car," Judith said. "After my wreck, I didn't want to. Nobody made me."

Now Lettuce was sleeping and Shane was awake, stealing glances at her when he thought her eyes were closed. She knew she had some physical beauty, but for most of her life it had seemed a burden. Now she envied older women their invisibility to men.

I'm not for that anymore Shane don't think about me keep focused what we're doing is dangerous so very dangerous.

Even Wicklow had gone white when the phone rang. He had picked up the receiver, stuck it between shoulder and ear, scribbled notes on a steno pad hanging from a nail nearby.

"It's Missouri," he had said. "You drive in one hour."

And so they had.

Near dawn, she finally slept, though not for long. She woke up just past the Missouri border, soaked in sweat, making guttural noises that were building up to a scream. Lettuce grasped her shoulder.

Before she knew what she was saying, she looked up at him with mad, wide eyes.

"Don't touch me!" she said. "You're dead! You're dead! You're dead!"

THE CHEVY VAN DROVE WEST ON ROUTE 66, SLOWING JUST A LITTLE AS IT PASSED the Avalon Garden motel. The time was shortly after two P.M. Lettuce, who had moved up to the passenger seat, scanned the brush not far from the building, though his eyes were drawn back to the Sabre jet decaying near the ruin of the greenhouse. He snapped his eyes back to the brush, said, "I see the Alpha car." Hank nodded. The Pontiac GTO had been poorly hidden, its solar-red paint showing through gaps in the young trees it sat behind. "Holy shit, that's really it," Lettuce said, his hands starting to shake.

"Keep it together," Hank said. "We can't have two people freaking out."

"It's together."

Hank eyed Lettuce for a moment longer, then wheeled the van around to make a U-turn.

Judith sat in the back, her arms folded, trying to look strong.

"I'll go," she said.

"No," Hank said, "You won't. You'll watch the van and *I'll* go."

She didn't say anything.

LETTUCE MIGHT HAVE BEEN IN CHARGE, BUT HANK WAS THE STRONG ONE. WICK-low had recruited Hank through his uncle Tracy, a former FBI man, even though Hank had grown up on the other side of the badge.

He had been convicted of robbing a movie theater, a vacuum cleaner repair shop, two banks, and a used-car lot before he was twenty. His lawyer hadn't been able to make the insanity plea stick, but the jury clearly had doubts about the faculties of a boy who claimed the devil used to visit his momma in her bed and finally took her out the window with him. That his accomplice, a hardened criminal, had been able to manipulate such a weak-minded boy was no surprise. He was out in six years, even though it might have been his bullet that paralyzed the car salesman who tried to defend his cash box with a hammer. Hank was a good getaway driver, but an even better shot. In prison, a Mexican tattoo artist of some talent had covered him in religious tattoos, the most striking of which portrayed a somewhat Mexican-looking Jesus praying at Gethsemane, a circle of crosses around him. This was on his angular, rather bony chest. Wicklow had come to him the day before his release.

After Judith woke from her dream, she had tearfully done everything in her power to explain to Hank and Lettuce that the mission was doomed, that some if not all of them would die. Shane listened in silence.

"I know how I sound, but you have to believe me. Look at the sweat on me; when I sweat like this the dreams I have come true. How can you believe in *them* and not believe in other things that shouldn't be?"

"Bad dreams aren't enough to scrub the whole mission," Lettuce had said. "They give me bad dreams too, every night, but I still say we go after them."

"Call it off, please," she had said, hating how weak and tremulous her voice sounded, hating that she couldn't cut the dream from her own mind and graft it into theirs. Nothing short of that would turn them, but it was beyond her power.

"Listen," Hank had said. "You know how many times I made this drive, trying to find this group? Three. You know how many times we actually found them sitting? One. *This* one. You saw the files. *That's Luther Nixon's fucking car.* You don't want to go, that's fine. I don't want you to. I had my doubts about bringing a woman along anyway. Especially you. What with your kid . . ."

Lettuce shot him a warning glance.

"Yeah. Oops. But if you think I'm turning my happy ass around and letting them get away because *you* remembered you had a pussy, you're wrong. You stay in the van. Just give me the fucking holy water."

27

THEY EASED THE VAN OFF THE ROAD AND INTO A COPSE OF TREES A HUNDRED yards west of the motel. They sat now, the engine ticking, watching the building for movement. They took in the scene.

"Cloudy," Shane said.

Lettuce nodded.

"Can't be helped. This is our shot."

Hank said "Look over there. Patch a' sunshine coming."

"More clouds behind it," Lettuce said.

"Yeah, and more sunshine behind that. Probably be like this all day. What do you say? Go now and try to torch it before the sun hits? Or wait and see if we get a bigger break?"

"I don't feel good sitting here. They could see us."

"They sleep."

"Maybe they get restless. Do you sleep the whole night?"

"Actually, I do."

"They could look out the window."

"The big windows are in the front; all they got on this side are the little bathroom windows."

"They could look out those windows."

"What are they doing in the bathroom?"

"I don't know. Do they use the bathroom?"

"How the fuck should I know?"

They sat and watched the motel. A little breeze blew up, rustling the leaves in the poplar and juvenile maple trees. One car on the Ferris wheel rocked.

Shane, trembling a little, tied a sheaf of stakes to his belt. Hank checked the load in his revolver.

"Can they come outside when it's cloudy?"

"Yes," Jude said.

"No," Lettuce said, louder. "It makes them sick, even when there's clouds."

"I say we go when the sun hits."

"That's soon."

"Yeah."

"All right, gear up. We go in two minutes."

Hank went into the back of the van, moving around Judith like she wasn't even there. He slipped the handle of a mallet through the back of his belt, just next to the wickedly sharp Ka-Bar knife and the little pouch of tools that never left his belt. He tucked a box of stove matches into one pocket, and into his other pocket he slipped a vial of the Guadalupe holy water. He held his .45 in his hand. Lettuce wore his shotgun on a strap, carried a jug of gasoline. Shane took kerosene, matches, and stakes, holstered a pistol. Then he picked up the Geiger counter.

Judith watched him do it, remembering perhaps the most surprising thing Wicklow had said during his several lectures in the barn.

It is believed that some of their favorite lairs are in abandoned underground uranium mines and near uranium tailing ponds, where people will be unlikely to bother them. There is no reason to believe radiation harms them. Fences are no obstacle. Any personnel onsite may be mesmerized into forgetting them, even helping them. We believe the undead, like many predators, have cycles of feeding and rest; that they gorge themselves more some months and less other months. We believe one of their favorite lairs is a very dangerous abandoned site near Albuquerque containing both tunnels and radioactive sludge pools. They spent daylight hours there, sheltering in the mines themselves or in shelters near the tailings, just this last March. It is also probable they were on their way to or from this site when they happened upon Judith's family farther east, near Moriarty. Some of these sites are radioactive enough that anything they brought with them—shoes, personal effects, perhaps even their physical matter—will have absorbed enough for a Geiger counter to pick up. Not enough to harm anyone, at least not in the short term, but enough to make our little friend tick and crackle. Should you find a lair with many possible hiding places, you may locate them in this way. It's the stuff of drive-in movies, don't you think? "Radioactive Vampires from Planet X." But this movie has been playing for a very long time, and will continue to play until brave men and women end it.

28

ONCE THE MEN IN THE VAN HAD ARMED THEMSELVES, THEY WAITED IN THE REAR for Hank, who had climbed back in the driver's seat, to signal them. He watched the bright patch of sunlight make its way toward them, a lake of gold flooding the brambly woods and foothills. He raised his hand, had almost flicked a pistol finger at the squat form of the motel when he hissed, "Wait!"

The sun hit the road just as the cruiser drifted east, light winking on the chrome and glancing off the windshield. The Jasper County sheriff turned his head to look at Hank, his mirrored shades revealing nothing of what he made of the parked van, the tattooed man behind the wheel. Hank felt the weight of the pistol on his lap like the devil's hoof, ready to press him and his prior convictions right through the van seat and asphalt straight into twenty years of hell. He didn't tell the others why they were waiting any more than he told them that if the cop had stopped, he would have shot him in the face. The cruiser rolled east, around the curve in the road but still visible, small, smaller, gone.

"Now," he said, pointing. He slid out the driver's door while the others chunked open the rear doors, making Judith blink as light flooded the cargo area. Shane was the last one out, and he hesitated before he shut the doors.

"Come on! Now!" Lettuce said from outside. Shane slid his .38 revolver along the van's floor to Judith, who dropped the cross she had absently held and took up the gun. The doors shut, obliterating Shane's silhouette and throwing her back into darkness. She crawled into the driver's seat to watch Shane and the other men file across the road, crouch down in the brush opposite while a station wagon rolled by, its driver oblivious, a child in the backseat turning his head toward the van, or slightly behind it. Judith's left hand crossed over her body; the fingers drifted down to make sure the keys were in the ignition. Her right hand, out of sight, clutched Shane's gun. Her eyes stayed fixed on the Avalon Garden motel.

She nearly jumped out of her seat when the strange man stepped up to the window.

A young man, baby-faced even,

Shoot him

wearing an ersatz Indian bonnet, sunlight blazing on the white feathers,

Shoot him!

holding something in his hands.

She thought she should raise her right hand, point it at the man, but couldn't.

He's not one of them

"Are you really a nun?" he said, squinting in the strong July sunlight.

He's a human being

NO shoot him now now NOW!

She started raising her right hand

Too slow

but he was already moving, his question just a distraction

this is going to hurt

and he jabbed the stock of his rifle up at her with the speed and violence of one new to manhood. It caught her on the right eyebrow, and she thought she smelled rubber, but maybe she was mixing that up with the time an older boy threw a basketball into her head and knocked her down, and then she saw the floor of the van, fuzzy, out of focus, and then she saw nothing.

WOODROW FULK HAD BEEN JERKING OFF IN HIS TENT, LESS BECAUSE HE WAS horny than because he needed to sleep. It was a hot day, at least when the sun was out, but he had stayed up too late with his friends. Staying up with them always meant losing half the next day, but it would still give him time to scout ahead and find them a safe roost, provided he could catch some sleep now. He was too tired to drive and scan the fields for overgrown buildings. He was too tired to do anything but fish around in his boxers and fondle it, thinking about women who didn't blink and seawater gushing out of drowned wombs and other things that would turn most men's stomachs. He thought about the one he had enjoyed just last night, how her butt and the bottoms of her limbs had darkened where the blood pooled, how the little muscles of her hands and feet had locked but her legs had still opened. Then of course he got fully charged and the play turned earnest. There was nothing like a sweaty, hot nap after sexual release, and this was the only kind of release he was going to get during daylight hours. That was when he heard the gentle squeal of brakes on his side of the road. Woods had always had keen hearing.

"Oh shit," he said, tucking himself back into his shorts and writhing into his jeans. He left the shirt but donned the Indian headdress, this to bewilder his enemies and give him power. He took up the Garand and slinked off from his tent's position behind a small rise and through a stand of young maples, wishing he had put his boots on, as a thorn or maybe broken glass found the tender sole of his foot. He heard doors shut and hurried his pace.

A van!

Shit, shit, shit!

He saw nobody in the driver's seat when he came up on the van's passenger side, but someone was moving in there, and by the time he limped around its rear to the left window, a woman had taken position behind the steering wheel. Sort of a pretty, beat-up-looking woman with a scar across her nose and cheek. Funny that he noticed her looks before he noticed she was a nun, if she was a nun. What was a nun doing in a van out in the middle of nowhere? Fuck him if this was a nun, he wanted to shoot her in the chest (not the face, her face was nice to look at and Luther might let him keep her), but it wouldn't be smart to fire off a gun until he found her friends.

Coldcock her, that's the ticket.

She blinked at him.

Shoot her and come in her chest hole later.

The sun, which had just come out, made him squint.

"Are you really a nun?" he said.

She started to raise her far arm

Bitch has a gun!

but he cracked her in the forehead with the Garand's stock real hard—the thing weighed almost ten pounds; she lurched back on her seat and stared at the ceiling before she dove for the floor, it was kind of funny, it reminded him of a dolphin. He peeked in. She shifted once, couldn't seem to get up, then lay still. Blood pooled under her. Good.

Hit her again to make sure? Take too long.

Now he went around the front of the van, looking at the hotel. Three men broke from the brush and trees across the road, making for the motel. He saw that one had a gas can, another had a gun.

Oh God this is it this is it.

His heart hammering, he ran back into the maple trees, his injured foot forgotten. He cut left and ascended the short rise, dropped down on his belly behind the tall grass, exactly the place he had chosen to cover the motel. Now he saw the men crouched near the doors; the big one was splashing gasoline.

He'll burn them up oh no can't have that can't have that

Woods watched him through the scope now,

can't burn my friends fat boy

pressed the safety catch away from the trigger guard

can't burn my cold pretty Calcutta

settled the crosshairs between his target's shoulder blades

fuck your back I'll fuck

started to squeeze the trigger, saw a flash of motion,

cars!

waited while a line of three cars flashed by in the sun, close enough to suggest they were caravanning

picnic lazy fucks off on a picnic

and then they were gone. He looked left and right to make sure nobody else was coming, then peeped through the scope again

fat boy find fat boy

lined up the crosshairs,

you'll die one shot get the tattooed one next

squeezed

BANG

Felt the kick on his shoulder, saw the man jerk backward, drop the gas can, grab his left hip and ass

missed his vitals how'd I miss okay again this shot this shot this

but now the man was moving.

They all were.

29

HANK BREWER KNEW IT WAS A BALLS-UP AS SOON AS THE SHOT RANG OUT. LET-tuce yanked up and almost fell, the gas from his jerry can spilling everywhere. Hank dropped the Geiger counter out of sheer panic. Where'd the shot come from? Had to be the small hill across. Next shot any second, next one would kill if they weren't moving. Needed cover. Behind Jesus, that's rich but that's all there was, that or the pool.

"Run!" he said, hooking Lettuce's right arm around his neck and moving with him toward the big statue just throwing its shadow over the courtyard. Room for two or three behind the wide base, the one his sword sprouted up from into his strong, white hand. Shane beat them there. He saw his and Lettuce's four feet moving under them, his strong, Lettuce stumbling, dropping blood. Something clacked heavily on the cracked asphalt but he kept looking at their feet. Blood on his sneakers from Lettuce, Lettuce was hit deep. That was a big, bad gun out there.

Gotta move gotta move

"Move!" he yelled.

BANG!

The next shot hit Lettuce again, head shot but must have just clipped him. "Aw, aw," the big man moaned. Nobody said anything about guns, it was just supposed to be creepers. Jesus, the top half of Lettuce's ear was hanging. Should they get in the pool? Dead deer down there, probably hit on the highway and stumbled in, no, they'd never climb out with a shooter waiting. Flowers down there too, why flowers?

BANG!

Probably a miss, thank God for small favors.

Jesus let me live let me live

Now they stacked up behind the statue, Shane in front, Hank next, Lettuce leaning on him, heavy on him, bleeding through their shirts, saying, "Aw, aw," but weaker. He would pass out in a minute.

"Shane, you hit?"

"No."

Hank looked around. Motel doors closed, no help. Not sure going in there would be better. To their left, big rotting jet, Ferris wheel farther, one car rocking. Dirty, smashed-up greenhouse between the two. Car behind it, hidden from the road.

Shane peeked up but bobbed right down.

BANG!

"Keep the fuck down, that guy can shoot!"

He thought somebody was holding an ice cube against his left forearm and he looked down, saw blood trickling from a groove of mostly white flesh scored diagonally across black tattoos of crosses and Mother Mary. It looked like Mary's mouth had been shot off.

Guess he didn't miss that other shot after all prick's batting .750.

He remembered the crazy nun yelling, *You're dead, you're dead, you're dead.* Maybe she was right.

They crouched behind the statue, blind and panting. He looked again at the car behind the greenhouse.

Camaro fuck the Beta car this is real they're in there but they can't get us.

Not this second, but maybe soon.

The light seemed weaker than it had. He scanned the sky, saw the next blanket of clouds coming, minutes away.

"Lettuce, I hope to Christ you were right about daytime."

But Lettuce was dead.

Fubar this is fubar

He looked at the motel again.

One door was cracked.

It hadn't been before.

He made a noise like a man who just realized he was on a high ledge and aimed his .45. Nothing moved.

"What's the shooter doing?" Shane said.

"Staying put if he's smart," Hank said. "He's really got our number."

Now Hank crawled to the side of the statue's base, risked a peek and rolled back. Nothing had moved. No shot came. A truck rolled by on Route 66.

The clouds drifted closer.

"Next car rolls by, I make a move," Hank said. "Try to cover me."

"I don't have my gun."

He said it like *Ido'avemygun*, all high and tense and crammed together. He was so jacked up he might have a stroke.

"What? Where is it?"

"Judith."

"What?"

"I left it with her. To watch the van with."

Hank glanced at the van, saw the driver's-side door half open.

The nun's finished shouldn't have yelled at her

Hank thought to look for Lettuce's shotgun, then remembered hearing that heavy *clack* while they ran. The gun lay in the courtyard, twenty yards away. Might as well have been a tennis racquet at this range, against that rifle.

The light dimmed further, the clouds marching on.

He looked at the Camaro again, and, although it was close enough for him to see the SS badge in the center of the grill, it seemed to be a mile away.

"Can you hot-wire a car?" he said.

"No."

"Figures."

Could the keys be in it?

Not likely, and he didn't trust Shane to drive any more than he trusted him to shoot.

"All right, here's the plan. You run for the Camaro. I stay here and cover you. Once you're in it—passenger seat, got me?—I break and come hot-wire it while you cover me."

"Okay."

"Can you do that?"

"Okay."

Hank looked back at the motel. Two doors were cracked now. One shut when he looked.

Oh fuck Oh fuck.

Darkness rolled up the road coming from Oklahoma.

An oil truck came barreling east, riding in shadow but about to break into daylight.

"When I count three, you turn rabbit. You run faster than you ever ran and slide behind that black hot rod like you're stealing home, you got that?"

"Yeah," Shane said.

The truck broke free from the cloud shadow, looming close, light glancing off its mirrors.

"One."

The truck shifted gears, growling as it hit a dip.

"Two."

As the truck mounted the rise, Hank saw the driver had a cowboy hat on.

Yee fucking haw let's do this

He cocked the hammer back, pointed the .45 at the motel doors.

The truck passed the parked van, disappeared from his sight as it roared in front of the statue of Christ.

"Three!"

Shane just crouched there, trembling.

"GO! GO!"

Hank kicked at his hip; Shane staggered almost to his feet but couldn't bring himself to leave shelter and crouched back down, saying, "I'm sorry, I'm sorry."

"Go right now or I leave you here!"

Shane tried, he did. He half stood, shaking.

The frontier of clouds moved over the sun and cast the courtyard into shadow, the golden cape of light seeming to retreat east toward Joplin, toward Carthage.

Shane looked at the motel.

Hank looked at his face, said, "Fucking RUN!" and kicked him again, hard.

His eyes moved down to Shane's crotch, where dark liquid spread as he pissed himself.

Now Hank looked toward the motel.

He almost pissed himself, too.

Instead he ran.

BANG

The shooter's bullet whinnied off concrete and broke a window.

Christ they're so white don't look back but jig, jig

He made himself duck and break slightly left as he ran, something stretching his pants pocket and pressing his thigh

BANG

In my pocket what run faster fast

and Hank ran fast, so fast one sneaker flew off

BANG

Ping!

I know that sound my uncle told me

Shane screamed behind him, from the gunshot or them he wasn't sure and now he was past the Sabre jet, one more gap before the greenhouse and the wicked car behind it.

But the shooter's out that's what that ping was M1 pings when it's dry

Now Hank wheeled and faced *them*, bringing up his gun. He ignored what was happening to Shane—he couldn't process that now—and focused on the closest one. The tall one was almost on him, big ears on him, greasy ball cap, running fast with his long legs. Straight at him. He wouldn't have to move the gun to track the target. Hank aimed just under the brim of the baseball cap and squeezed, the big pistol bucking in his hands. The ball cap flew off, its owner jerking straight and lurching back, putting his hand to his head like he forgot something, matter falling through the greasy hair at the back of his head, and then he sat down hard. The big one with the neck brace was almost on him and he shot that one too. The big one stopped and crossed his arms in front of his face so Hank couldn't tell where the head was and it wasn't coming anymore but now he saw behind the thing.

bald one pulled Shane's jaws apart Oh God save me save me

The female was down on all fours over Lettuce, her face near the shot side of his head, her tongue working like a kid with an ice cream cone. The bald one, holding the lower part of Shane's jaw, kicked her, said, "Later, whore, sun's comin'," and now she ran at Hank. Tears streamed down Hank's face but he shot clean, shot her in the chest and knocked her down with a flat, bloody cough. The tall one had regained his feet but wasn't moving forward yet. The big one was coming, but not fast, the hole in his arm and through his cheek already smaller, but the pain might have made it think twice.

two bullets left

in my pocket something what

He shot the tall one again, he didn't like the tall one, then pulled the round bottle out of his pocket

Holy water!

twisted the cap off with his teeth, splashed it on the big one, who turtled up with his arms crossed over his face again, but this time when the water hit him he made a sound like a deaf man yelling as his arms smoked from many places at once. The others backed up. The bald one, frustrated, threw Shane's jaw at Hank but missed.

A truck's horn blatted from the road but now he could only look at Shane. On his knees, somehow still alive, in shock, his tongue hanging free. Making a sound a man shouldn't have to make.

Christ sorry Shane sorry brother Christ

Hank shot Shane in the chest.

Shane fell back heaving, and then the heaving stopped. Hank ran to the Camaro now, saw the lock tab down, swung with his gun butt meaning to break the window, but only cracked it. He drew back for another swing he never got to take.

Something cold and hard seized him by the other arm, spun him, jerking the holy water loose so the bottle broke on the ground. The fine-boned pale one tried to look into Hank's eyes. Hank knew what that meant, looked away in time, ran months through his head like Somchai had taught him, anything to keep his mind free.

January February March April

He brought the gun around but the vampire slapped it out of his hand, so hard the hand went numb.

May! June! July!

He had one trick left. He tore his shirt open, showing the pale one the tattoo of Christ. One shirt button ticked on the bricks and rolled. The dead one winced at the sight of Hank's chest, then vomited last night's black blood all over the kneeling Christ thereon, obscuring it.

August

Now Hank looked into its eyes.

August august

He couldn't help himself.

"You're okay," it said.

august beautiful so beautiful i'm okay i'm really okay

He went slack and stood helpless before the smaller monster.

The one with the neck brace, his face contorted in pain, stepped up behind Hank, raised a still-smoking forearm and fist. Before it bludgeoned his head into the wrong shape, Luther grabbed that fist and stopped him. The small one put Hank's shirt back on him and popped the collar, covering most of his tattoos, then slipped his arm around Hank's waist and steered him toward the darkness of the motel room. He pushed Hank in by the small of his back, but gently, almost regretfully, as one might usher a naughty toddler into the spanking room.

"You sure fight pretty," Cole said. "But you don't get to touch my car."

The door shut.

30

CLAYTON PEEKED OUT OF THE SLIT IN HIS WINDOW DRAPES NOW, SAW A STRONG, tattooed man helping the stout, injured man away, the latter shot through the hip, a ghastly exit wound under his navel promising death. A smaller man skittered before them to shelter behind the gaudy Christ statue that stood before the pool. The symbolic nature of the event made him smirk just a bit. The stink of gasoline persisted. He felt clouds coming, knew the sun's bright blade would soon be sheathed. A run into the woods out the back window now seemed more plausible, but perhaps unnecessary. The fight had turned. More gunfire, more woe for the breathing. Would the noise bring the constabulary around? Perhaps, but just as likely not. Men shot guns in the country, there was nothing ominous in the sound. Could there be more adversaries in the rear? Unlikely, but smart to check anyway. He crossed the ruined room, peered through the small, filthy bathroom window, squinting against the waning sun, and there, in the middle of the road, he saw an unlikely sight.

A nun in full habit crossed Route 66 in a daze, her head bleeding freely. A van perched behind her, its door hanging open. The clouds came now, robing her in darkness and clearing his vision. He blinked his eyes anyway, unsure if he should believe what he was seeing.

She was beautiful.

Even at a distance of fifty yards or more he could see there was something holy and demanding about her eyes, like God's answer to the fierce interrogation in the eyes of the undead.

He felt as though he were watching a scene from hagiography: St. Mary of the Van, though wounded, crosses the road toward devils; and though he knew he was cast in the role of devil, Clayton could not help but be moved by the tableau. He heard motel doors open, more gunfire banged, closer now; he knew slaughter was descending on the vigilantes.

He went back to the front, let himself out into the sickening but tolerable cloud-light. Now the one they called Cole was descending the Ferris wheel upside-down behind the unsuspecting pistolero defending himself manfully but without real hope against the quartet he was aware of. The other two diurnals had been made ruin of, one tastelessly so. Clayton waded through the overgrown grass and thorny vines encircling the motel, saw a truck heading for the nun. It sounded its great, froggy horn to no purpose, she was half inconscient, but before the horn's echo had faded, Clayton found himself leaping the remaining brambles and sprinting into the road. When the nun saw him, she froze. He grabbed her arm and slung her gracelessly into the brush on the motel side of the road. The truck began to brake now, its great wheels shuddering and smoking, but Clayton jogged alongside until the driver looked at him. He hooked the man with his eyes, said, "Do you like hamburgers?"

"Yes," the man said, licking his pillowy lips.

"Well, good. Drive to Joplin and eat the biggest hamburger you dare. You never stopped here, you will remember nothing of me or the woman."

A man screamed from the motel.

"Or that."

"Okay."

"Can you drive?"

"I think so."

"Then do it, sir! And safe travels."

The truck, which had never fully stopped, now rolled forward faster, woozily crossing the median with its leftmost tires, earning a horn blast from a westbound Chrysler whose driver never saw the man with the Indian bonnet run behind and between the swiftly separating vehicles to start the odious business of cleaning up after the massacre of the Avalon Garden of Wonders and Motor Lodge.

THE WOMAN HAD PASSED OUT. SHE LAY IN THE GRASS CURLED LIKE AN INFANT. Clayton removed her black veil and her white wimple, now sopped bloody down the right side from the vicious cut along her eyebrow. Her eye was already nearly shut.

Head blow, quite a sharp one

Her thick, black hair spilled out and Clayton made a soft noise in his throat. There was something Roman about her, something of the gladiatrix, with her scarred nose and cheek and her well-made limbs. He checked the clouds—sun coming, but spotty; one golden trapezoid moving through the woods across the road looked set to miss the motel. The other monsters were already settling back into their lairs, changing rooms so as not to sleep in the ones that had been splashed with gasoline, dragging the fallen in with them; the false Indian was fetching a shovel from Mr. Nixon's red car, with which he would set to spreading dirt over the blood on the bricks. He would resume his watch when done, and then like as not they would burn this place. And then what?

Clayton was tempted to walk away now, to take his chances in the light woods. But he had not survived so long by giving in to temptation.

Besides, there was the question of the nun. He pulled up her eyelids, the swollen one with difficulty.

Rare color these eyes never seen the like

The left pupil was larger than the right.

"You've got yourself a fine concussion," he told her. "You need a hospital, but not so badly as I need you not to burn us in our stalls."

When he saw that the others had gone in to sleep behind their dry-rotten doors, and that the necrophile with the shovel was occupied in filling up a bucket with dirt, he carried the nun toward his own room.

"Never mind the smell of gasoline—the whole place will burn in minutes if any part catches flame," he told Judith as he carried her through the door. "A wonder lightning hasn't done the deed, or perhaps our savior in the courtyard has warded it."

As he shouldered the door open, looking down into her insensible face, he became aware of how much they might have resembled a macabre bride and groom.

"Your father should demand his money back for that wedding," he told her. He kissed and licked the blood from her face, though it still ran in a stubborn trickle. He knew his spit would stop the blood and help close the wound—this was why bites on living victims closed—but thought it might not be enough for this gash. So he laid her down on his coat and with a sewing needle from his kit held briefly over a match, and with a bit of sage-green thread (to match his vest), he stitched her head while she lay breathing shallow breaths. When his work was done he bit the thread off, then laid her on her side and spooned behind her, one arm binding her, one hand pressed cold against the insulted forehead in lieu of ice. If she woke, he would wake with her and tie her with his belt. If she cried out, he would stop her mouth with his hand. He knew well that she might die of her injury. He yearned to feed from her, but the memory of the Florida woman's death rose up—he did not wish to test the nun's fragile health.

"I promise you nothing, stupid brave thing," he whispered into her ear, "but that I shall try, mind you *try*, to stop them from killing you. And if I can, I shall paint your portrait."

AN HOUR BEFORE SUNSET A KNOCK WOKE CLAYTON. AT FIRST HE WAS BEWILdered to feel his chest and arms so warm, even his chin where it rested on a living head, and then he remembered. The knock came again. He uncurled himself from around the injured nun and took up his sunglasses to peer from the window slit. The queer lad Woods stood there, divested of his Stuckey's feather bonnet, a pile of clouds bulking behind him. The westering sun lit those clouds painfully in Clayton's eyes, even filtered through his shades, so they might have been pillars of molten ore.

"Open up," Woods said. "They want her."

"Whom do they want?" he said.

"The nun."

"Well, they shall have none."

A pause.

"Funny. Open up."

Now Luther's voice came through the wall.

"Do like he says. We need to ask her some things."

"She is not yet conscious."

"Then he'll drag her."

At his peril, he nearly said but choked those words back.

There would be no fighting this bunch. He would be a match for any one of them, perhaps two, but certainly not all of them. What they lacked in age and strength they more than made up for in viciousness. He looked at the woman where she slept, admired the handiwork of his stitches. What would she say if she woke and saw him? He remembered the look of terror in her eyes when she glimpsed him on the road, just before he slung her from the truck's path. He had on several occasions met diurnals who could see through the low-voltage charm all vampires unconsciously ran to hide their killing teeth and present a more pleasant reflection, although that charm wore thin during daylight hours. Would those rare eyes of hers betray him as the corpse he was, even at night?

"No need for that," he told the voice behind the wall. "I shall bring her."

31

JUDITH WOKE TO A ROOM FULL OF THE DEAD. DEAD MONSTERS, ALL LOOKING AT her with eyes that shone faintly in the almost-darkness. Just after sunset. She wanted to scream but bit it back. Where was she? She lay on the raw springs of an old bed so rusty she was nearly falling through. Her arms were bound in front of her. She could barely open her right eye and her head throbbed wickedly. Were her clothes wet?

Monsters.

The last thing she remembered was an Indian standing outside a van's window, but not a real Indian—a white Indian with a weak-chinned face. Her head had exploded then and it still hurt. She blinked, water on her eyelashes. They had thrown water on her to wake her.

The monsters.

She looked at them now.

"Good morning, sunshine," the bald one said.

Oh God help me it's him it's really him they took my boy they took him

He showed her his teeth, the teeth she had seen that night.

God give me strength if you don't what are you for if not now when

"I need to ask you a few questions," he said. He leaned close now, his breath stinking of whiskey and blood, and under that engine oil and rotted meat like in a dog's teeth and the smell of black ants when you crumble them in your fingers. He looked into her eyes. "And you're going to tell me everything you know."

Thou preparest a table for me in the presence of mine enemies

He drooled and it pooled on one of her bare arms, cold and thick.

strengthen me god please youre not doing it youre not im still weak

He showed her the teeth again, and it struck her differently than it did the first time. It was like a bully who kept showing you his fist. A trick. Oh, those teeth had murder in them, she had no doubt about it, but his desire to frighten her had the odd effect of angering her.

They could just kill me but they want to know things

O God Shane and Hank and Lettuce they killed them i know it

Cant think about that yet put it away

"I have a question, too," she said, her voice trembling.

Don't ask them about Glendon don't let them know who you are

The monster raised his eyebrow.

"Really?" he said. "That's interesting. You're an interesting gal."

She kept her eyes locked on the deadlamps in the bald one's face but, peripherally, let her awareness drift to the other monsters now. The tall one who took her boy out of the car, she remembered his cold, long arms, her heels slid up and down a little on the rusty springs with the desire to stomp on his horsy face, to kick those teeth out of his head, to kick his smug, ignorant face until it was nothing.

"Do you like being what you are?"

"Open your legs," he said, staring into her eyes.

In the presence of mine enemies thou preparest thou preparest

"Luther," the smaller blond man with the boyish voice said.

Evenin', miss

Judith stared at the bald one, did not open her legs.

"Huh," he said. It was the sound a man would make if he watched a dog ride a bicycle.

She noticed one among those watching her, more frightful than the rest. The ones from the cars had a dead look about them, with their white skin and pronounced veins, but this one. His skin was darker, deader. His cheeks sank in. His eyes burned brighter than theirs.

I do not remember this one. This one was not there.

"Luther."

"Easy," Luther said. "Just seein'."

He looked Jude in the eye again.

"Now this is only gonna end one of a couple a' ways, and some of them ways is easier than others. Easiest of all is you relax your brain and look at me. Fuckin' look at me. That's right. You tell me who sent you here so we can go pay them a visit. Tattooed fellow already told us some interesting stuff, but I'd like to know more about that farmhouse and barn. Pennsylvania, right? You happen to see a address?"

Judith looked him in the eye and said nothing.

"It's the damnedest thing," Luther said. "This pussycat don't charm."

"Let me try," the Camaro driver said.

"If I can't, what makes you think you can?"

"Let me try."

Luther gestured him forward with an open hand, as if inviting a friend to cut in on a dance.

The smaller blond one sat on the edge of the rusty bed frame, leaned forward, looked into Jude's eyes. Jude looked away. The other grabbed her chin with a cold, hard hand, pulled her gaze back to his. She moved her eyes away, looked at the very dead one.

"Shit, I can't even hook her," he said, standing up in disgust.

Judith noticed the very large one with the neck brace now, saw him holding forearms pocked with angry-looking holes. Like he'd been hailed on.

"We better get on the road," the tall one said, slicking back his greasy, long hair and securing it with a ball cap.

How'd you know my name? That his name, too?

Rob. That one was Rob.

"Yeah," the bald one said. "In a minute."

Luther Nixon. The Alpha driver.

He killed my husband.

The slight one with the James Dean hair was the Beta driver.

Everyone was here but the woman with the red mouth full of teeth.

Luther looked at Jude again. He picked up her hands, sticky with blood that had been lapped off, bound with old, damp rope. He showed them to her. Grinned, showing her his teeth again.

Bully you're just a damn bully

"Big hands on you. You know what that means, right?"

Vulgar damn bully I want to kill you I will

"Look at them big arms on you, too."

You can't beat them with hate be smart

"You a farmer's daughter? Big strong pretty girl, huh? Them arms don't hurt your looks none yet, but if I let you live, you'd be gonna run to fat. I can tell by them arms."

He looked harder into her eyes.

Trying to off balance me make me mad get into my brain

"Bet your momma's got them big ole water wing arms, ain't she? Let me ask you this: When she flops a flapjack, is there a little wobble after?"

Can I get into his brain

"What about *your* mother?"

"Her arms was skinny," Luther said. "Face like a mule, though, and she chawed tobacco. Spat it on me in my crib more than once."

Jude felt sweat start dewing on her temples, her palms.

"No, she didn't."

"How's that?"

Judith looked past Luther, through him. She saw a vision of a woman and knew it was true, though it was long ago. She had never seen the past before.

A slight, pretty woman in a rose print dress

A washtub on a table and the sun just setting

a table for me a table in the presence

"I bet you're lying."

"The fuck do you know about it? Anyway, you ain't got nothing to bet."

Rob laughed.

"Your momma sang to you at night when you had a fever."

"Whores don't sing."

"But your momma did. I'll bet if you think real hard you can remember how soap smelled when she washed you."

Her sincerity goaded Luther.

"She washed me with a rock."

Judith kept looking through him, uncharmable.

Calm.

"I bet she bought the best soap she could afford for you. When you were little."

Luther snorted.

"Before you killed anybody."

"I was born killin'."

"She'd look down at you in the washtub and tell you everything she wanted for you."

He pressed his finger on the gash in her forehead, then removed it. She hissed and breathed in. An involuntary tear rolled down her right cheek, but she wouldn't let herself sob.

"You got this wrong," he said. "I get to talk about your momma. Don't you *dare* talk about my momma."

"She was pretty, wasn't she?"

"Shut up," he said.

"You make jokes about her . . ."

"I'm warnin' you."

". . . because you know it would break her heart . . ."

Luther slapped her laceration like he was killing a roach.

She gritted her teeth but spoke.

". . . to see what you are now. Do you remember her favorite song?"

He put his face very close to hers. He grabbed her nipples with hands like pliers and pinched. The tears came and she started to shudder.

"You can frighten my body," she said, her voice breaking.

"I'll frighten more than your fucking body."

"You can't," she said. "You already took everything."

He's going to tear them off

Please god don't let him it hurts it hurts

She heard the woman in her head sing and she sang after her, looking Luther in the eye.

"Sweet angels beckon me away

Where there's no more stormy clouds arising."

Luther let her breasts go, his mouth hanging open.

"To sing God's praise in endless day

Where there's no more stormy clouds arising."

Luther hit her mouth, hard enough to bloody her lip. The woman in her head went away.

He picked Judith up, put her over his shoulder. When her head went upside-down all the blood rushed there and she almost blacked out from the pain.

"Pop the goddamn trunk," he told the Beta driver, who went before him as he crossed the courtyard with her, past the pool with the dead deer and flowers, past the bloodstained statue of the sword-wielding Christ, past the decaying fighter jet and behind the weedy shell of the greenhouse. The others followed behind. The false Indian and the female came from the greenhouse to see. Jude noticed the van she and the others had ridden in parked near the Camaro, could make no sense of that upside-down van or what it meant for her companions with her screaming head. The Beta driver popped the trunk of his Camaro. Luther threw Judith in and she banged her miserable head again and the floor smelled faintly like chlorine.

"I don't know what you imagine I took from you," he said to her, nodding then at the bag behind her. "But I assure you it was *not* everything."

He slammed the trunk shut, closing her in darkness.

She could still feel his hard, plier hands on her breasts.

They burned like nursing.

"Give me those," she heard, and then she heard a key slot in the trunk's lock and the trunk opened again. Now Luther stood over her, the last light bleeding from the sky above him and a planet over his shoulder.

mars its mars

"No, I don't reckon I'm done with you after all."

He pulled her legs out of the trunk, opened them.

She was shaking too hard to fight.

Her head hurt so bad it took her a moment to realize exactly what he intended.

hey no not this anything but this do you hear me

please god

The false Indian whooped.

The very dead one averted his eyes.

A coldness passed into her, a letting go. Whatever happened next would happen to a doll.

Luther unbuckled his belt.

The Camaro driver walked up behind him.

"Hey," the smaller one said.

"What," Luther said.

"No."

"No *what*?"

"Not *this*," the smaller one drawled calmly, as if reminding Luther of something already agreed between them. "Anything but this."

Luther stared at him, still holding Jude's ankle with one hand. He looked between Jude's legs again.

"Do you hear me?" the smaller one said.

"Yeah," Luther said, fuming. "I hear you. You know what? You can be *real* goddamn boring sometimes."

Luther pulled one of Jude's shoes off, threw it at the Beta driver, then slammed the trunk shut. Judith heard a jingle as Luther dropped the Camaro's keys for the smaller one to pick up.

"Come on, boys," Luther said outside. "We'll drink this bitch in five hunnert miles. We got a nun in the trunk, and we got an old fucker in Florida to kill. Let's motor."

PART FOUR

The Quick

32

DARKNESS. JUDE FELT EVERY BUMP AND SHIFT AS SHE LAY IN THE TRUNK'S CON-fines, unaware that the chlorine she smelled came from pool water shed by the last occupant's skin and hair, unaware of how and how badly the Bereaved had died; that any of them might have escaped seemed unlikely. She had spotted the van parked just past the car they put her in. Where she should feel grief or rage at their passing she now felt nothing. The only feelings she could detect with any clarity were physical: pain, confinement, and thirst. She hated her headache, she hated the sports car's tiny trunk and the spare tire, which crammed alternately into her back or shoulder depending how she turned. Worse, she hadn't had anything to drink since a few mouthfuls of lukewarm water at a truck stop water fountain near St. Louis. Her mouth was so dry she dared not try to swallow. She doubted she could speak, so she tried to pray in her head and found no words that sounded like prayer; only babble and snatches of idiot song. Two verses of a song by a female trio whose name she could never remember kept repeating over and over again. Paisley Bride? Paisley Bird? Some beach-bubble-gum nonsense from the summer of '66 that Glendon just adored, innocent of its clumsy double entendre. That she could only remember two verses was both blessing and curse.

Gimme little lovin'
Got a cake in the oven
And I'm servin' up a piece for you

You can do the icing
If you find a cake enticing
Just as long as you're true and blue

She could still see the sleeve for the 45, in paisley that faded from purple to orange, lying on his dresser. She missed that ridiculous music, missed fitting the 45 adapter onto the spindle to play it, missed his anticipatory smile when he saw her unsleeve the vinyl and set his record on the turntable. When she saw his smile in her mind's eye, it was as often as not red from Kool-Aid or hard candies or a Popsicle, that kid loved anything red. Especially Popsicles. He liked a Jan and Dean song about Popsicles, too, but she couldn't remember how it went through the "Gimme Little Lovin'" concert she was playing for herself. She tried to dismiss the earworm by replacing it with Glendon's voice, but she couldn't even summon his plaintive *I'm in the trunk, Mom* despite the fact that she herself was in a trunk. He had fallen utterly silent. Perhaps he felt no need to speak because she would be seeing him so very soon.

That her captors would kill her seemed a foregone conclusion. It was just a question of when, and how much she would suffer.

The car had stopped shortly into their journey and she had heard doors and voices. Half an hour later they were moving again, and, although she had the impression it might have been in the opposite direction, she couldn't be sure. The Camaro hurtled along at great speed for a while, its motor growling like something that ate human flesh, until at last it stopped quickly, rolling her painfully forward and then slamming her back into the tire again as its driver jammed the pedal down and the car rocketed forward. Somebody above, probably the awful woman, let out a high, yipping war whoop. They were chasing, or being chased. The next minutes were hell—the Camaro swerved and accelerated, collided with something, then stopped, its doors chunking. Then it turned. She heard a confrontation between a man and a woman, a door shutting hard, and then it rolled slowly forward before taking off fast. When it seemed to be at the leash end of its speed, it accelerated again. While her mind told her that dying in a crash would be preferable to whatever fate the dead had planned for her, her heart hammered in her chest all the same, and now the idiot song dissolved and all she could hear was the ear-breaking sound of the Falcon rolling and smashing in the desert.

MINUTES EARLIER.

The red car and the black car had crossed the Kansas border into Galena, where they detoured off the main road and took an old miner's trail Luther knew that led to the remains of unused zinc and lead mines. They had stayed in these mines other times—they were safe, if filthy, with big chat piles to hide the cars behind—but it had been easier to direct Woods to the Avalon Garden motel with its Ferris wheel and ass-kicking Jesus. Tonight they did not stay but they did dump the bodies of the three suckers who attacked them, and Lady Liberty, into a particularly unpleasant mine tailing and shovel chat over them. By the time they were found, man would be colonizing fucking Mars.

Neck Brace and Rob were riding in Luther's car. Calcutta and that piece-of-shit Boston vampire rode with Cole.

The trouble started when they left Galena and doubled back over the Missouri border.

33

JASPER COUNTY DEPUTY STEWART HENSON HELD A LONG-STANDING CONTEMPT for the Avalon Garden of Wonders and Motor Lodge. Even when he was a kid and Arthur Britton himself used to serve hot dogs and hamburgers on Memorial Day, or play Santa Claus when the December sky wasn't spitting sleet or snow, or dress up like a tinpot King Arthur on summer days, the place felt just plain *off.* Stewart had ridden the Ferris wheel at the age of twelve and had observed that even with fresh paint on the outside, the insides of the cars had been rusty and creaky, full of sharp edges that promised lockjaw. Now, fourteen years later, three years into his service with the sheriff's department, he wished somebody would take a bulldozer and knock that damn wheel down, maybe just turn the whole place back into a field while they were at it. It was a magnet for trouble. People were always throwing roadkill into the pool or busting open the motel doors to smoke grass or just plain squat there until fined or, depending on the deputy's mood, jailed. The night before, a known busybody had called in about fireworks there, but the place had been dark and still when his buddy Mike went by, and he said he did a thorough walk-around. Yesterday the same caller had complained of gunshots, but the sheriff had considered the source and ignored the call. Mrs. Jackson would be phoning in again within the week to report motorcycle gangs, or dogs barking, or maybe because the black bear that frightened her in March had come back, once again leaving tracks on neither yard nor porch, nor any mark at all upon the door she claimed he "beat on with his paws."

Now Deputy Henson was stuck working night shift because Mike had had some kind of nervous breakdown. Got the idea he had a tick in his face nobody could see and scratched himself to pieces with his fingernails, then worked himself over with a pocketknife until he needed the ER in Joplin. Had poked himself all the way through the cheek and hurt his gums, they said. This was the kind of thing junkies did, but Mike wasn't like that. His wife had been hysterical from all the blood; she'd never seen anything like that in her life. But then her moving her momma in with them to eat them out of house and home might have had something to do with it; that woman could nag the wet out of water. His own wife knew where he stood on *her* momma, meaning standing on her momma didn't sound like such a bad idea. Maybe with golf shoes. He laughed about that, sitting in his cruiser behind the cottonwood stand two miles east of the Avalon Garden, poking the hard muscles under his shirt, then felt bad about laughing. He wasn't a perfect man, but at least he did sit-ups. Lots of them. That was pride, he knew that, and he felt bad about that, too, but only for a minute. And then he was thinking about the girl he should have married and how big her breasts got after her baby and wondering if maybe her once-pink nipples went brown and how nice it would be if he could see for himself. Before he could feel bad about that, he heard sirens in the distance. The radio crackled.

A red Pontiac possibly associated with a disappearance in St. Louis was heading east on 66 with two officers in pursuit.

Just as he was getting his mind out of Jane Richardson's brassiere, he noticed police lights bathing the fields behind him crimson, saw two sets of headlights coming. First, a dark shape that proved to be the Pontiac in question blew by him at something like ninety-five with his headlights off. How was the driver seeing? Jed Milsap and Otto Van der Meer barreled after him in the other on-duty cruiser, sirens wailing, a Missouri state trooper taking up the rear. Stewart turned his ignition and hit his lights, spraying dirt behind him as he accelerated out of his hidey-hole.

If he'd had his mind on his work, he could have taken that GTO in the side as it went by, but then he didn't know if he really had the stones to ram a car going that fast; a guy doing forty on a country road was one thing, but anything could happen when you started kissing metal on the high end of the speedometer. He didn't much like the idea of getting shot at, either, but he'd take a shoot-out over a high-speed wreck. His right hand absently touched the wooden butt of his service revolver, then went back up to the steering wheel. He fell in behind the speeding cars, pushing his big Dodge 880 as hard as he could, wishing he had Milsap's lighter, newer pursuit-package Fury—that thing screamed.

He rushed by a couple of civilians who'd pulled over to let the chase go by, braking before the sharp curve near Outlook Road, then jamming it down again when 66 leveled out. That GTO was really eating up road. He had nearly caught up with the state boy playing caboose when he saw a dark shape nosing up behind him on his left, using the opposite lane.

A black Camaro SS with its lights off and tucked.

He barely had time to think *Shit they're together!* before the wicked thing had pushed into his rear bumper and spun him into a bewildering kaleidoscope of dust and receding sirens and oncoming headlights. He found himself sitting halfway across the seat with one shoe off, his tie up over his shoulder, and his hat on the passenger-side floor. The Dodge had stalled. Headlights filled his rear window, and soon a middle-aged guy with tortoiseshell glasses was peering at him through the dust, asking him was he okay. He fumbled back into his seat, said, "Yeah, thanks, buddy, just get clear."

The Good Samaritan was backing up when a white shape rushed up and knocked him down. A smallish man. The Camaro driver.

Henson reached for his service revolver but now his door was open and the man sat on his lap, looked him in the eye.

"Wow, big soft brain on you, huh?" he said. The thing's eyes took Deputy Henson in, welcoming and a little sad, eyes like Jesus in that Gethsemane painting but shining a little.

"Yes," Henson said.

Henson felt safe and warm, as though the pale young man on his lap knew all his worst secrets and approved. The creature spoke and the words were alarming but made sense. He got off Henson's lap, spoke some more, and pointed at the road. The deputy stumbled first into the corn, then remembered his new job and waited by the road for headlights. He hoped he would survive. He was grateful for the messenger who was even now driving off in his cruiser, thank God for him. Bad things were afoot in Jasper County. Maybe the worst things ever.

LUTHER NIXON, NECK BRACE, AND ROB PICKED UP THE FIRST TAIL SOON AFTER they crossed into Missouri; the deputy probably just wanted them for speeding—the GTO had been doing about eighty. Luther swore colorfully and started to pull over, putting on his blinker like a good boy, meaning to charm the cop and be on his way. Then he peeked in his rearview mirror and noticed a second cop riding shotgun in the cruiser, a quick-looking little '64 Fury. The charm was maybe still doable if he could get them both to look at him at once. That was when he saw the westbound state trooper put on his lights and make a U-turn. Somebody had been on the radio. Somebody knew his car. That changed the game completely.

"You fellas want to go for a ride?" he said into the rearview mirror, then opened up the four-hundred-cubic-inch V-8 and shot forward. Rob turned around in the backseat and looked at their pursuers, fishing for their eyes—he probably wouldn't be able to get a clean charm at this distance with a distracted subject, but if he did, he might be able to make him pull off or even wreck just by pointing. Neck Brace, sitting up front, grinned a childlike grin, his thick fingers working the pocks in his forearms like rosary beads.

Pretty soon a third cop was on their tail.

"Oh, I don't like this. I don't like three skeeters on my peter. Where th'fuck's Cole?"

They shot around a curve and Luther started to pull away from his pursuers; years on the track and the moonshine trail made him expert at the alchemy of brakes and gas on a tight turn.

"Should I shoot 'em?" Rob half shouted over the bellowing engine.

"Not less you hafta. Wrecks puzzle 'em, bullets stir 'em up."

Luther checked the mirror in time to see the farthest set of headlights wink out.

"There's my beautiful Coley-Cole. That's how it gets done. Two I can get on top of. Whatcha think, big boy? Feel like goin' Geronimo on 'em?"

Luther slowed and downshifted, the big engine moaning, as he let his chasers edge closer. Neck Brace grinned harder, started shifting in his seat. The pursuit Fury, which had been holding a little gas back, now gunned forward and right, partly onto the shoulder, trying to get behind Luther and spin him out.

"Uh-uh," Luther said, "no goddamn way," and he shot into the opposite lane and punched his pedal again, forcing an oncoming car into the far ditch. Now he pulled a car length ahead of the cruiser and eased back right.

Neck Brace flowed out of his seat and grabbed the roof, worked his legs out, all of this much faster than one might have thought possible for a creature of his dimensions. He turned his white moon-mask face back to the cars behind him.

INSIDE THE JASPER COUNTY CRUISER JUST BEHIND THE PONTIAC, DEPUTY MILSAP, the armpits of his uniform sopping wet, said to Deputy Van der Meer, "Oh no. He ain't gonna."

Turned out he was gonna.

The big, pale thing in the neck brace vaulted off the car and spun, awkward in shape but strangely balletic, grabbing his knees in midair, rolling so his back faced the oncoming vehicle. In the split second before impact, Deputy Van der Meer remembered grabbing his own knees just like that as he cannonballed into the pool on Memorial Day to splash his kids. The remembered taste of Budweiser flooded his mouth even as he saw the windshield shoot inward, how like water splashing, and felt his bowels loosen and saw the dirty garment of his long-dead two-hundred-fifty-pound killer so close he could almost count shirt threads.

LUTHER SAW ANOTHER CRUISER PARKED ACROSS BOTH LANES OF ROUTE 66 ahead, so he put the GTO in neutral and mashed the parking brake hard, jamming the steering wheel to the left. Tires screamed and smoked on the asphalt as he spun, whipping his nose around 180 degrees. He put it in gear and drove straight for the oncoming state trooper, who broke and veered right even as Luther went to his own right. The trooper attempted the same bootlegger's turn Luther had just executed but ended up spinning out mostly off the road before he got himself righted and rejoined pursuit of the GTO. The other trooper now joined him. Luther slowed, meaning to try to pick up Neck Brace, who had just pried and unstuck himself from the wreck of the Fury, half naked, covered in the blood of two other men and limping hard, but he waved Luther off and crouched behind the steaming car where it lay on its side near a speed limit sign. Luther drove west, baiting the Missouri troopers rapidly approaching. Just as they passed the dead Fury, the huge, white, bloody thing in the neck brace dove from behind it and folded himself up under the oncoming left wheel of the lead car, which shot up into the air and landed hard on its roof, screaming like a dying thing as it slid, showering the pavement with sparks. The second trooper, skidding away from the big man on the road, who was impossibly reaching a white, hairy hand for his tire as if he meant to pull it off,

why isn't he dead

regained traction and turned his attention forward again just in time to see the oncoming Dodge 880 once driven by Deputy Henson of the Jasper County sheriff's department cross the middle lane. Just before he collided head-on with the other vehicle, the young trooper at the wheel took up the handset of his radio, saw the hawkish white face of the kamikaze barreling at him illuminated by his own headlights, which he had at some point flicked to bright.

He squawked the word "Vampire" into his radio.

And then he died a spectacular death.

THE CREATURE THEY CALLED NECK BRACE HAD A LOT OF WORK TO DO.

When his spine healed enough from the second break (the tire had been much worse than the windshield), he stripped a windshield wiper from the state trooper's vehicle he had flipped and jammed it through the eye of the squirming man still in that car and stirred until he stopped squirming. A farm truck rolled by, slaloming wrecked vehicles, looking for a place to pull over and help, but Neck Brace looked at the driver and waved him on, so he drove on with a spit bubble in his mouth and later couldn't rightly say what he had seen. Neck Brace opened the trunk of the cruiser as much as the angle of the wreck would allow and fished road flares from among the gear that fell out. He lit these and spread them along the road. He gripped the flipped cruiser, gritted his teeth, and heaved, at last and at the outer limit of his strength pulling the car so it blocked both lanes. He walked toward the fire he saw, saw his friend Cole get small, wriggle halfway out of the wreck of two police cars, both of which had started to burn. Neck Brace ran now and pulled Cole the rest of the way out, pulled off Cole's smoldering jacket, pulled him off the road entirely.

"D'ya see that?" Cole slurred, his face half skull, the face of a man killed by road and metal.

Neck Brace nodded even though he hadn't seen.

He held the wet skin of Cole's face back on until it caught and healed. He propped Cole up until he felt Cole's shoulder right itself.

After a moment, Cole stood almost strong, slapped Neck Brace on the back.

"I think I mussed my hair," he said.

He scanned the road for his Camaro SS, which Calcutta should be driving up by now, but all he saw was Luther and Rob in the GTO.

Picking up a very angry-looking Calcutta.

"It better not be," he said. "It just had better not goddamn be."

THE JASPER COUNTY DEPUTY STEPPED OUT OF THE CORN AND FLAGGED DOWN THE young lady in the Volvo. She did not want to stop in such a wilderness, but the uniform reassured her and she complied.

"What is it, Officer?" she said.

"Bad wreck," he said. She didn't care for how wild his eyes were. His name tag said *Henson*. "I need you to pull your car across and block the road."

"Are you quite sure that's necessary, Officer Henson?"

"I need you to pull your car across and block the road."

She got back in her car and angled it as instructed. The officer stood in front of it, clearly waiting to signal other cars. He seemed unaware of her existence.

"Is it very bad? The wreck?"

"It's a bad wreck," he said.

She flinched when she heard a crash and yelling from farther up in the darkness. Emergency lights flashed past a curve in the road.

"Do you know when I might be able to go on my way?"

"No," he said, without looking at her.

Now a serviceman in uniform drove up behind her and then two more cars. A farm truck pulled up coming from the other direction and the officer waved him onto the shoulder and around. The woman looked at his face, saw the same faraway expression she had observed on Officer Henson.

"I hope I don't sound selfish, but I really need to be on my way."

She was roundly ignored.

A fifth car pulled up and, seeing the mess, turned around and went back west toward Kansas and Oklahoma. Now a banged-up black Camaro came from the direction of the accident and skirted over the shoulder just as the farm truck had, a deathly pale young man at its wheel. Once it was past the roadblock, it poured on the gas and roared west.

What have all these people seen? the young woman wondered.

"Officer?"

"The devil's coming," he said, wiping his mouth with his sleeve.

"Excuse me."

"The devil. The real devil."

"I'll just be on my way," she said.

"STAY HERE," he yelled.

Crazy he's crazy

"Hey, buddy, you all right?" the serviceman said.

"Stay in your car, sir."

The serviceman watched him, lit a cigarette.

Now a hellish red car rolled up full of a ghastly crew, the smallest of which, pale and furious, slipped out the window and into an abandoned car that had been sitting by the side of the road. The bald man at the wheel of the red car saw her looking at him, and his hateful return gaze made her look away.

The devil the real devil

Both cars now sped off west, as the Camaro had done two minutes before. From the east, a siren wailed.

A third state trooper, his face ashen, rolled up and, addressing Henson, said, "Deputy."

Thank God, she thought. *Maybe I can get out of this awful place.*

Henson looked at the woman in her car, his eyes even wider. He pointed at the state trooper who had just pulled up, a gaunt fellow clearly stricken by what he had seen up the road.

"See?" Henson said to her, pointing at the trooper. "I told you."

"Deputy," the trooper said again, more urgently. "Did the red car go west? Did you see a red Pontiac sports car?"

Deputy Henson drew his service revolver and shot the state trooper in the cheek.

THE '67 GTO WAS FOUND THE NEXT DAY, ABANDONED IN THE MIDDLE OF A DILAPI-dated stable not far from Hornet, Missouri. Although exhaustive forensic examination of the trunk produced blood and hair matching the women who had gone missing from St. Louis, no body was recovered and the alleged abductors left nothing of themselves. No prints. No hair. Nothing to indicate they existed at all.

It was like the car had driven itself, and had simply decided to stop.

34

HORNIK CHEVROLET SAT ON THE WESTERN SIDE OF DUNN STREET IN MORGAN, Georgia, just between the Daphne Movie Theater, where the legend *The Wild Bunch* stood out in black letters, and Milo's Burger Heaven, whose sexy blond angel and hamburger motif had been hotly preached against by the pastor of the Morgan Baptist Assembly, one block down. This same old reverend, famous for waking the block with shouting night terrors, made it clear that angels, who were our "last and very dear defense against the machinations of the rough beast" ought not be used as "pimps and bawds for the wares of men." The movie theater had received even more liturgical attention than Milo's Burger Heaven, notably during the Sunday sermon following the Friday release of *Barbarella*, "little more than pornography and much less than a godly man demands of his entertainment"; *Rosemary's Baby*, "The devil likes nothing better than to be made familiar to us in film that we may not fear him"; and *The Graduate*, "an adulterer's fantasy made celluloid-real." Not that the reverend scorned all film—he had been observed to leave *A Man for All Seasons* weeping tears of joy, and had declared it "the most moral and intelligent film of our day."

Neither had Hornik Chevrolet escaped the old man's grapeshot.

"Charles Hornik, who goes in the tight pants, turtlenecks, and bobbed haircuts of today's youth, and caters to them with his cars of muscle, and tells them to call him Chuck, shall precede them into hell, and lead them there, too. What young man needs to go at one hundred miles an hour down the road? Where is such a man headed, if not the furnace? A fiery death awaits these hot-rodders, and an even more fiery eternity. If we must drive cars, let us go humbly in cars that do not rumble and growl and screech their tires, that other men might look at us and covet that which we have. Or, better, let us walk. And if we must go to the city, let us ride the bus. Is there any one of us too good to ride the bus? Is there any one of us so important we must race where we go at one hundred miles an hour? If Mr. Hornik thinks I am wrong to warn him, let him come and tell me to my face, but you will not see him here. He stays outside God's house, and, for all his colored pennants, for all his glad back-clapping and handshaking and barbecues for veterans—which I must say is a godly thing, but not enough alone—yea, for all that, when the day of wrath comes, I fear Charles Hornik shall not find his name in the Book of Life, not as Charles, and most certainly, I assure you, not as *Chuck*."

Chuck Hornik's Chevrolet dealership was the jewel in the crown of Morgan, Georgia. Its top salesmen, Hap and Beau, were two of the wealthiest men in town (after Hornik and a retired Coca-Cola executive), and they put keys in the hands of Georgia Bulldog sophomores, Atlanta drag racers, even businessmen from as far away as Miami and Houston. The only dealer in the country that could match Hornik's reputation for putting big engines in light cars was Don Yenko up in Pennsylvania, but anybody south of Virginia who wanted to lay down rubber or roll a real monster into the drive-in came to Hornik. A recent article in *Motor Trend* had bumped sales an additional fifteen percent and inspired Joe Frazier to order a custom 427 Chevelle, which Hornik expected to turn around within the week.

On this particular night, Sunday, July 6, Hornik had long since gone home when the F100 pickup truck and the '65 Impala cruised down Dunn Street, slowed, and kept going. This was near midnight with a quarter moon hiding behind scudding clouds and the crickets just singing hard in the woods and fields nearby. The bank clock's illuminated sign read 90 degrees. The Impala executed a three-point turn in front of the theater and then parked behind the deserted library past Burger Heaven. A smallish figure and a taller one got out and walked to the dealership, looking first at the Z28s and Novas lined up in herringbone ranks up front, finally sidling over to the fence to see what goods might be in the back.

"That's what I was hoping. Yes Lord, I was dearly hoping this."

It sat parked near a lesser Z28.

It was perfect.

Cole wished he had a hat to remove out of respect for whoever had crafted the exquisite vehicle he beheld: night-black, gently curved, resting on fat tires that promised bullfrog-leap acceleration.

"Is that a COPO?" Rob said, holding his own greasy hat in his hands.

"You better believe it. Yeah, damn if it ain't a number 9561. The article said they'd already sold three of 'em this year, two black and a red. Others musta gone. I mean, just *look* at this bitch, and I mean that word in the best possible way."

It didn't take them long to get into the office and find the items they were looking for, keys first of all. Back outside, the stars and Venus peering through the grayish haze of small-town streetlights, they popped the COPO's hood and slavered over what they saw there.

"Iron block 427, that thing'll even burn a Vette. Luther swears himself not a Chevy man, but that's just him being ornery. He's gonna want this one, but he ain't getting it. And they ain't another one all the way to Cocoa Beach, if the magazine's right."

"What're we waitin' for?"

"Nothin. Just getting to know the bride before the weddin's all."

THREE MILES OUT OF TOWN, IN THE NEWEST, WEALTHIEST SUBURB OF MORGAN, Georgia, Chuck Hornik and his wife were up late fighting. She paced in the kitchen of their brand-new house, stopping each time at the place where the linoleum gave way to the den's carpet as if recognizing the perimeters of their respective territories. Chuck sat on the couch he had already resigned himself to sleeping on, staring at the stone fireplace they had never yet lit. Atop the coffee table before him, a marble ashtray held a mass grave of his-and-hers butts, his crumpled and yellow, hers straighter and white but stained with varying intensities of carmine lipstick. A bottle of Squirt soda lay on its side next to this, along with a rocks glass full of watery yellowish liquid that reeked of vodka. Between swigs, Leila held the vodka bottle by the neck as if it were some dead yard bird she had throttled.

"And," she said, "don't think I don't know what it means when Little Miss Something smiles in line at the grocery."

"I'm sorry," he said.

"She knows I'm walking in the door just the same as I know she's standing there."

"I'm sorry, I'm *sorry*," he said, sounding more angry than sorry.

"I don't believe for a minute," she said, seeming to forget what she was talking about, her eyes moving back and forth rapidly, her cigarette going to the vodka bottle hand so she could thumb a small brine of tears and mascara out of the corner of her eye.

"I'm tired of saying it," he said.

She turned her back on him, paced to the oven, turned around.

"I don't believe for *one minute* she just remembered Jesus loved her and smiled that smile. That was for me."

"It's been two years."

"For ME!" she said, jerking the neck of the vodka bottle at herself.

Chuck used the first and second toes of his sock foot to snare the other sock and strip it off, exposing a foot that surprised him with how old and bony it looked. Who put his dad's foot on his ankle? He lit a cigarette and stared at the strange old foot, not sure why his wife had gone quiet but glad for it.

"Course you can come in," she said.

"Come in where?"

He peeked into the kitchen to find that she had zoned out again, just looking out the kitchen window onto the deck. Was she about to get on him about stripping and varnishing the deck? Her piss-off could turn on a dime when she was chicken-necking that bottle. Now she grabbed an oven mitt and blotted her lipstick on it, leaving a huge red smear.

He wanted to refresh his glass but it wasn't worth going in the kitchen to try to unchoke the vodka chicken. He finished the barely cool glass of Squirt, vodka, and melted ice, took off his other sock, and lay back on the couch, covering his eyes with his arm.

"Just go to bed," he said.

"And it isn't like I don't know what it means when you say you're taking a new Chevelle out on Mill Town Road. I know what Mill Town Road means."

She was slurring now, so mad at him in her bleary stupor that her voice took on a strangled quality.

"Man who sells cars has gotta drive 'em," he said, disengaging. The truth was, his drives after work didn't bear close inspection. He waited for her to figure out her next line of attack but instead of words he heard the bottle slosh, heard a gurgle. As much as it grieved him for her to drink like that, it meant her slurs would soon thicken and sleep would follow right behind. She would sleep late the next morning, and that private hour or so before he went into the dealership would be the day's sweetest morsel.

Perhaps she had already slinked off in her bare feet and crawled into bed, settled the sleeping mask over her eyes like a hostage's blindfold.

He nearly fell asleep in the thick quiet of their new house, but then he remembered that he would want to turn the lights off. Leila mocked him for the way he followed her around the house turning out the lights, but she wasn't the one paying the light bill. Not that the utilities were that expensive—all his income decimals had shifted a full numeral right in the last five years—but burning lights in every room when it was just the two of them wouldn't make them any richer.

He sat up and started at what he saw.

His wife stood in the kitchen.

Not alone.

A huge pale man in a neck brace held her wrist to his mouth and sucked it like he was trying to give her a hickey there. A bald man in sunglasses hugged Leila's hips to his, kissing or sucking her neck. Leila was looking right at Chuck, grinning absently and drooling. A woman squatted behind her, holding something sharp and bloody, licking the blood-slick back of her leg just below where her pleated pantsdress ended. A very tall man put Leila's cigarette out in the sink and then leaned against the counter, waiting his turn.

Chuck started to get up, but a cool hand held his forehead and pushed him back down—someone had been standing behind the couch. That someone now moved fast, straddling the prone man's stomach, pushing all the air out of his lungs in a *woof.* The stranger looked into Chuck's eyes. Everything got warm and friendly.

The man spoke.

The man wouldn't stay long.

The man thought his wife would probably be all right.

The man just needed some papers signed.

After Chuck signed the papers the bald man put Leila to bed, saying she was "one hot number" and seeming to find that very funny. The smaller stranger helped the bewildered Chevy dealer back onto the couch and told him to sleep and forget. As the strangers slipped out the kitchen door, then melted into the night between the pine trees, Charles Hornik's eyelids grew heavy. He fixed on a piece of his own letterhead lying on the three-month-old avocado carpet. Beneath his home address, six words stood out in black marker; he drifted off while staring at those words, though their significance eluded him.

TELL US
WE CAN
COME IN

THE F100 HAD ALREADY LEFT, ITS DRIVER RANGING AHEAD TO SCOUT FOR A DAY-time nest, so the brand-new, barely street-legal Camaro rumbled through downtown Morgan followed by the Impala. They rolled down Main Street and took a left on Dunn, heading south toward Interstate 75. When one A.M. fell on Morgan, Georgia, the driver of the Camaro wore a broad, content smile. He punched the accelerator and the car screamed into the night toward Valdosta and Florida, the Impala struggling to keep up. In his lumpy bed at the edge of Morgan's oldest block, the old reverend woke from a nightmare and yelled.

WHEN CHARLES HORNIK SHOWED UP THE NEXT MORNING, HE WOULD FAIL TO notice the shiny finger marks on the dusty grille of the air vent, which was, in any case, too small for a man to crawl through. Hornik's mind would be occupied with the riddle posed by his wife's alcoholism and self-destructive impulses—he had awakened to find his wife smiling serenely in her sleep, the bed sheets spotted with blood. When he pulled these back, he had gasped. A meat thermometer protruded from the back of her thigh.

35

JUDITH FELT THE CAR SLOWING TO A STOP AND READIED HERSELF. SHE COULD taste blood in her mouth; she had bitten her lip during her violent trunk ride. The clanging in her injured head nauseated her, but she would only have one chance and she meant to take it. She lay very still and waited for the sound of the key in the trunk.

CLAYTON PARKED THE BATTERED BLACK CAMARO SS JUST OFF A SWITCHBACK ON the side of a hill. A riot of birdsong heralded dawn's approach, but this part of the Ozark National Forest was so thickly wooded in the summer that Clayton could walk for miles by day if he had to, so long as he picked his way around the occasional searing patch of sun. He didn't really know what to do with the girl in the trunk, if she was still alive. He had been thinking about her all through their drive south, at once puzzled and delighted by the prickling sensation her remembered image caused; it was very like dim memories of infatuation. She *was* beautiful, after a certain Pallas Athena fashion, but not exceptionally so. He had enjoyed the society of opera singers and ballerinas whose looks snared men's hearts as reliably as gas lamps brought moths, and he had always been the charmer, not the charmed. Why was this prettyish, battered thing haunting him? What had she done to him? Was this what they felt, the women he had hooked with his eyes and bound with his voice? It was not entirely unpleasant.

Could he allow her to live?

All of his kind felt a deep directive to keep their existence secret. If a human who had seen them could not be reliably allied with or charmed blank of the memory, then he or she must perforce die. The impulse to kill the injured nun and put her in a hole rose in him again and again, always followed by revulsion at the mechanics of harming her. Her courage in the face of Mr. Nixon's thuggery had moved him; surely bravery of that order deserved more than an unmarked grave in the woods. Could he really shut those eyes of hers and bury them? The pigment of her iris was too rare a food for ants. He had to decide soon.

"Resolved," he said, "that I shall charm this creature into forgetfulness. Failing that, I shall . . . take up the question again."

He had turned off AR 23 just after passing a camping and army surplus store he meant to revisit during business hours, should clouds present themselves. A tent and sleeping bag beneath a rock overhang or in some providential cave would serve to protect him. Unless of course the girl in the trunk harvested a sharp branch and plunged this through the tough meat of his heart. Rope, then. And a canteen—she would need water. And a comfort break.

"Resolved," he said, "that leaving a prisoner in her own filth is a violation of the Geneva Convention and a breach of basic etiquette. I shall let her make water while it is still dark enough for me to chaperone her."

He got out of the car and walked to the trunk, surprising himself with his schoolboyish desire to see her again. He hesitated with the key at the lock, preparing himself for the possibility that the girl might have died without bothering to consult him.

"No, blue eyes," he said quietly, "I should not like to find you dead."

JUDITH HEARD THE KEY CRUNCH INTO THE LOCK, HEARD THE MECHANISM SPRING as the trunk popped. She lay folded around herself, slitting one eye like a child cheating during grace. Weak, tree-filtered predawn light flooded into her steel coffin, blotted in the middle by the figure of a man in silhouette. A dead man with bright eyes. The new one. It frowned down at her.

"Is there a tenant in that body?" it said. "Or have you gone home to your reward?"

She lay still, the spare tire digging into her throbbing back.

"I quite admired your pluck back at that defunct hotel. If you consider yourself my adversary, I may be in trouble."

It reached down now, touched its cold hand to her face. She repressed a shudder. Instead she opened her eyes halfway and reached one hand up to take the dead hand at her cheek. She squeezed it gently, forced a smile. It smiled in return. She rolled over just a little to free what she was lying on. The monster bent slightly, inclining toward her hand, though whether to kiss or bite it she did not know.

A curious thing happened then, and it happened fast. She met the thing's eyes and did not find them hateful. Their unnatural light diminished. The vampire's face seemed to form a double image now, the true image dead and repellent, the false one live and attractive. She did something very like focusing her eyes and chose the true image. The one with the dark, dead skin and the sharp, off-white teeth.

That was the one she swung the crowbar at.

CLAYTON SAW THE NUN'S BODY MOVE AS SHE INITIATED VIOLENCE AGAINST HIM. He saw the hand that had been hidden arc up with the iron bar in it, saw in her face the resolve to do him harm, but he did not move. He realized he was watching the whole thing as a spectator, genuinely interested in the drama of the woman in the trunk lashing out at her supernatural adversary. The impact hurt, of course, rather badly. His vision twinned for an instant; he found himself inadvertently stumbling backward, sitting down hard, aware that his right fang and one other tooth had been knocked half out. His own sluggish, black blood had slimed his cheek; one eye felt wrong in its socket. And here she came again! She had some difficulty freeing herself from the trunk—doubtless her own head injury had left her dizzy—but once she found her feet, she sank into her hips and swung that bar at him again with such force that it occurred to him his head might actually come off. Instinct took over at last. He wrapped his arm around his head and let himself fall with the blow, shunting much of its power. He balled up defensively now, absorbing three more strokes, each weaker than the last. Then she threw the crowbar at him and ran.

ONE SHOE ON AND ONE SHOE OFF WAS NO GOOD WAY TO RUN, BUT ADRENALINE softened the pain. Judith knew she hadn't killed it, knew she didn't have the strength left in her arms to knock its head off. She didn't even know if that would work. She didn't know how fast they could run. She didn't know if sunlight really hurt them. But now she saw weak sunlight painting the east-facing sides of tree trunks near a stream up ahead. She ran for that with all her waning strength, pounding the brambled ground, pistoning her arms for momentum, her gallops seeming to come in threes, keeping time with the shouted locomotive chant in her mind.

please God please

please God please

please God please

The light on the tree trunks ahead grew stronger, took on an orange glow. It looked like heaven to her. God had put it there for her and she would reach it because he was with her and desired her to live.

That was when she felt the hand slip under the back of her belt.

"YOU CERTAINLY RUN FAST FOR A PERSON WITH A CONCUSSION," CLAYTON SAID, sitting in front of Judith under a rock overhang, painting a nasty scratch on the sole of her foot with antiseptic that stained her skin red. Judith winced at the sting, seethed at her helplessness. He looked up as she scanned the trees past him. He noticed this.

"I don't intend to harm you, or anyone else, but I will kill to protect myself. Please keep that in mind before you think to involve any fellow campers you should chance to see."

Her bound hands drifted toward her neck.

"I haven't fed from you."

"Why?"

He furrowed his brow while putting the lid back on the disinfectant. He began bandaging her foot.

"I don't know."

He worked in silence for some time.

She put her hands on her lap, looked at the fresh, new rope there.

She didn't understand why he was ministering to her wounds. Why waste his time if he was going to kill her?

"What now?" she said.

"Now we look each other in the eye and I say things to you."

He put her doctored foot down.

He looked her in the eye.

She met his gaze.

"I don't think I can be hypnotized."

"We call it *charming*."

"I don't think *you're* very charming," she said, almost smiling. If she didn't know better, she would think she actually enjoyed the thing's company.

"I wish that were mutual."

"You're not going to kill me, are you?"

"I don't think so, no."

"I'm sorry I hit you. With the crowbar."

"I know what you hit me with."

"Anyway, I'm sorry."

"And I'm sorry a professional baseball career is not open to you."

She almost laughed.

"You've done nothing but help me. You stitched and bandaged me," she said. "You knocked the woman out of the car and stole it, but you didn't want that car. You did it for me. You're not like them," she said.

"No."

"You're older?"

He nodded.

"You got old because you're not a killer."

"I've killed."

"You've been spared for a reason."

"Let's not start all that."

"All what?"

"All that Calvinist predestination claptrap."

"I'm Catholic."

"I noticed. Anyway, it doesn't matter. Calvinism, Catholicism, they're just two outhouse seats over the same hole."

She opened her mouth in shock, then closed it.

"I suppose blasphemy's the least of your worries."

Her eyes narrowed just a bit as she considered him. That rare shade of blue, with just a hint of lavender to it. Was it possible to become addicted to someone's eyes? He wanted always to see them.

"Do you know why I'm here?" she said. "Why I came after these murderers?"

"I do not."

"I had a son," she said.

She told him about Glendon.

WHEN SHE FINISHED SPEAKING, HER ROPES LAY COILED AT HER FEET. CLAYTON did not remember taking them off her. Afternoon had come, the sun probing odd fingers of light here and there through the forest's murk. Hunger and exhaustion took turns leaning on him.

"I need to sleep," he said.

"What happens if you don't?"

"I get weak."

"We can't have that," she said.

"Why not?"

"You're going to help me kill them."

"Why would I do that?"

She weighed her next words before she said them.

"Because you love me."

He considered this.

"Yes."

They looked at one another.

"Are you toying with me?" he said.

"No."

"Do you share my affection for you?"

"No."

"Could you?"

"I see you as you are."

"Ah," he said. The cosmetic charm a vampire unconsciously ran to mask his true appearance even worked on that vampire—most of the time. Clayton, however, had seen his own true image enough times to know that it would kindle no affection in a living woman's bosom. He had glimpsed himself from time to time in moments of fear or trauma, thinking each time that he looked a little worse, a little more wasted and dark. His shadow had gotten thinner, and it stayed that way. "So we're back to 'Why would I do this for you?'"

She took his cold hand in her warm one and stood.

They were the same height.

"What is your name?" she said.

He told her.

"Clayton Birch," she said, "I cannot love you as a woman loves a man. I cannot allow myself to see you falsely and be deceived into intimacy—I am still a novice sister with vows to uphold. But I can promise not to betray you or hurt you, at least not on purpose. Not until the others are dead."

"And then?"

"I could do something for you."

"Oh, I don't think I like the sound of this."

"Don't you?"

He said nothing.

"How long has it been since you've felt sunlight on your face?"

He watched her. He opened his mouth to voice outrage at her suggestion, but nothing came out.

"If you help me destroy them, if you let yourself be an instrument for good, just maybe you can rest. Don't you want to?"

"No."

"And if there is something up there . . ."

"You have no right."

". . . as I *know* there is with a knowledge that it is beyond my power to communicate, if there *is* a God above us, and you serve him, even now, and I bless you and pray for you . . ."

"Stop it."

". . . and end this false afterlife, this *curse*, maybe then you can go to your maker and be welcomed by him."

"You should sell bridges."

"I am offering you a bridge."

"Well, I won't help you."

"You won't?"

"Have you ever watched anything rot?"

"What do you mean?"

"Have you observed the decomposition of an animal, by the roadside, perhaps?"

"Observed."

"Observed, yes. Noted its decomposition day by day, over time."

"Yes."

"What was it? The particular thing you thought of when I asked."

"It was a raccoon."

"Did anything strike you as especially uplifting about the process?"

"That's an animal."

"Do you think a man looks so different?"

"I suppose not."

"Allow me to assure you that he does not. I killed a man in 1870, with cause, and looked in on him again in 1913. Macabre, I know, but I was born curious. In any event, there he was, just as I left him, only skinnier. So, if a man rots himself flat and gray into the ground and stays there, his meat eaten by beetles, his bones no more than stick piles, how is he different than your raccoon? Why should we think the one has a soul and the other does not?"

"If it were explainable, we wouldn't need faith."

"*Trust me*. That's a liar's evasion."

"Do you forget what you are? I don't—I can see it. You're a *corpse*, and yet here you are talking to me. If there's no mystery in the world and no God running it, how did you manage this?"

"Well, that is a poser, I admit. Are you saying that God claims by default everything that lies beyond the reach of science? Does God then shrink as science grows? We read by lamplight when I was a child. The only men who flew did so in hot air balloons. And now we're going to the moon, where I suspect we'll find more rocks than angels. How long must God retreat with no clear sign of himself before you admit he isn't there at all?"

"So you don't breathe or blink because of what? A germ?"

"Do I not blink?"

"Not always."

"I try to remember to blink."

"Don't bother. What do your cells look like under a microscope?"

"They don't survive to the slide."

"So you mean they're dead."

"I mean they don't make it there at all. They dissolve and rejoin the whole."

"If I cut your arms off you, would they do the same thing?"

"Please don't. But yes."

"How do they do that, Mr. Birch?"

"I don't have a plausible theory."

"But you reject mine."

"Damn it, I don't want to hear this."

She stood up, walked near him.

He saw her bare, bandaged feet, thought it must hurt her to walk on those cut soles he had Mercurochromed. He gestured at a paper sack near the limit of the shadow.

"I got you combat boots. I guessed your size. It's all they had."

"Thank you," she said. She touched his shoulders and looked at his face.

"Help me, Clayton."

He worked his mouth around his fangs, ran his tongue over them as if to assure himself they were still there.

At last he spoke.

"I will. But not because of some fictional old Hebrew whitebeard."

"Then why?"

"I'll do it because they'll kill you otherwise."

"Yes," she said, "I think that's true."

They looked at each other.

"Do you trust me?" she said.

He thought for a long moment before he spoke.

"I do."

"Then sleep the rest of the day. Do you have a dime?"

"Sure," he said, fishing one out of his jeans. "Why?"

She took it out of his hand, then got the combat boots out of the sack and started putting them on.

"I have to find a phone. When I get back I'll watch over you. After sunset, we have to go back to Missouri and find that van."

"Why on earth would we do that?"

"I need the cross that's in it."

36
St. Petersburg, Florida

TRACY CALVERT'S "ACTIVE SENIORS" APARTMENT COMPLEX NEIGHBORED A PUB- lix, separated from the rear of the supermarket by a short cinder-block wall in need of a paint job. From his second-story, screened-in back porch, Tracy could see the loading docks, the Dumpster, the coffee can the employees used as an ashtray. That told him the manager was a hard-ass, that he didn't let people smoke in the break room. He knew the employees, the ones who smoked anyway, so well he could almost set his watch by their movements. At five after three, five after five, and five after seven, the thickset guy from the meat department sat on the stoop and smoked by himself. Too much time in the sun, that guy, but not recently. Probably served in the Pacific theater twenty-some years ago, burned himself the color of roast beef filling sandbags on Tarawa or swabbing down the deck of a destroyer. Definitely a vet, though, the way his back straightened when the fat slob of a manager poked his head out the door to lay down the law on this or that. He used to take his breaks with a gangly kid with a big Adam's apple, a kid who wiped his hands on the front of his apron a lot. The meat guy would sit on the stoop, gesturing with his hands, his Timex glinting in the sun, making the cigarette dance on his lip while he jawed at the kid, who paced around him in a deferential orbit. This was a kid whose dad beat him up—he cut his eyes to the older man to make sure he liked what he was saying the few times he actually spoke. When the kid stopped coming around in April, Tracy guessed his draft number might have come up; that would explain the bonding routine with the older guy, that he was trying to figure out what he was in for. He'd seen the kid bagging in the store—respectful, fast hands, knew when to double-sack, this wasn't a kid you'd fire. And April wasn't a going-off-to-school month. Of course, it could have been anything, a job offer in Peoria for all Tracy knew, but it didn't fit the story the man and the boy told with their bodies, and Tracy had spent his career filling in people's stories.

Now the meat man smoked alone.

This is bullshit you're just occupying your mind 'cause you don't want to think about Hank.

The meat man was just lighting up his five-after-six ciggy when Tracy approached the low wall, scooted his ass up on it, swung his legs over, taking long enough for a drop of sweat to darken the cream-colored polyester pants. The meat guy was watching him, so Tracy issued him a nod, got a wave in return. He wasn't the only old coot who made the pilgrimage from the Bay View Apartments to the Publix. You'd think they would knock down the wall or cut a breach in it just to be sociable; he'd helped Mrs. Clarke, the woman from 318, over that wall more than once before she graduated to a walker. Maybe he would bring it up to the manager, if he could catch him between dressing down his stockboys and stuffing corned beef down his piehole.

You goddamn coward think about Hank the mission went dark they got him the creepy-crawlers ate your sister's kid just like your sister

Shut up wait for the call

Tracy walked around to the front of the store, where two kids on bikes were having a powwow, their Schwinns nose to tail like dogs at the sniff. Probably talking girls or shoplifting, the way they leaned in so nobody else could hear. They both had their shirts off, a sensible uniform given the Christ-awful wallop the July sun was packing. Sweat had dampened the creased legal pad Tracy tucked under his arm while he got over the wall, sweat from his armpit; he wouldn't be writing any love letters on that.

He took the pad in hand now, put it in the top part of a shopping cart he freed from its fellows. He only had one phone call to make today, and it would be a hard one.

In the store proper, he farted near the chickens, saw a woman notice, wrinkle her nose. He picked up a pair of thighs, sniffed them, made the same face she did, put them back. "They used to be fresher here," he said, moving on. He felt more like pork chops anyway. Tracy saw the meat man roll up a piece of ham so it looked like a panting dog's tongue. He came from behind the case, handed it to a little boy who held on to his mother's dress hem while he took it, as if to let go of her dress would invite goblins. "What do you say?" his mother asked him, but he had already stuffed the whole piece in his mouth, made the sounds "mmm-hm," because in kid world thank-yous can be hummed. "That'll have to do, I guess," she said, and wheeled her cart on. The mother and the kid were the youngest non-employees in the store. She was a good-looking head, wore her dress at a decent length, open-toed sandals, nice legs. He saw this gal had cut the back of her calf shaving, a scale of dried blood. Women usually cut their knee, didn't they? His wife had been gone long enough that he looked at other women, but not so long that he didn't feel a twinge of guilt. Tracy himself was turning eighty in August, if he got there.

You won't

He was healthy except for his joints, no funny stools, heart didn't flip-flop around too much, but

The bad guys win sometimes and they're winning now

you never knew when it came to the old ticker. One minute she's humming along, the next minute

You're gonna hear that Pontiac's engine on Bay View Circle

whammo. That's life.

He knew the meat man's name, had seen *KARL* on his name tag, he looked like a Karl, but they weren't on a first-name or any-other-name basis.

"Excuse me," he said, delaying whatever mission Karl was about to launch himself backstage to undertake.

"Yeah, buddy?"

"I used to see a bag boy, tall kid, but I don't see him anymore. He okay?"

Hope he's not dead like my convict nephew

"Army," Karl said, his tone just a little brighter than neutral. Proud the kid went in the service, would have been prouder if he went into the right branch. Definitely a Marine. "Thanks," Tracy said, wheeling his cart around, steering his pork chop toward the registers.

The next thought was selfish.

He felt it coming and couldn't stop it before it formed itself even though he hated it.

Hank knows your address

Shut up

If they took him they know it too

SHUT UP

You haven't got time to cook a goddamn pork chop

Please stop it

Sun's going down in a couple of hours

You have to get in the car and run

Where

Just drive until you see a motel you like

I don't like motels

Go to Naples

"How are you today, Mr. Calvert?" the cashier said.

To hell with Naples

She was maybe twenty-two, a heavyset girl with red hair and a gap between her front teeth. An English teacher had once told the class that girls with a gap like that were "hot to trot," and that stuck with Tracy. From a story about the Wife of Bath. At that age, just the words *wife* and *bath* in the same sentence had been enough to start him on a boner.

"I'm fine, I'm fine, thank you. They treating you all right here?"

"No complaints, Mr. Calvert. I just punch keys and smile."

"Now you're cooking," he said, taking his change, taking the paper sack the bag boy handed him, leaving his cart awkwardly by the register.

Why did I take a cart into the store for a measly pork chop

"Would you like a hand out to your car?" the boy asked.

Distracted I'm just distracted better focus

"I think I can handle this one bag."

"Yes, sir," the boy said, already moving to the next register.

He fished in his pocket for a dime.

I don't want to make this call

Have to just have to

Always knew Hank would end badly but not like this

Forget Hank you're next

Don't think like that Hank was a good kid

No he wasn't

Tough and good aren't the same thing

He set the bag down on the green bench next to the phone.

He picked up the receiver and listened for the tone.

He put the dime in the slot.

He dialed.

37

THE PORK CHOP SIZZLED IN ITS GREASE.

Two more minutes on this side and then he'd flip it and give it four more. Then let it sit for ten.

Tracy looked at the wall clock, a utilitarian thing very like one you'd see in a school or government office. Little wonder, because this very clock had been hanging on the wall at his FBI bureau and, when he retired, the chief had given it to him as a joke—Tracy Calvert had often been the last man to go home.

"Since you never looked at the son of a bitch while you were working, maybe you should get an eyeful of it down in Florida."

His scruffy orange cat, Max, would have normally been watching him from his post under the table, but the cat went shortly after Edna. Edna had named it Marzipan, but that's no name for a cat, so he called it Max. Might as well call them two names, it's not like they listen. Eighteen years under his belt, the fat, two-name scoundrel had been old enough to order a beer. He looked at the clock. Seven thirty. Was this dinner or supper? Both. One of them used to mean lunch, but he forgot which. Didn't matter. It was his last meal in the house for a little while.

Wicklow still couldn't give him specifics, but everything looked bad.

The van had been found and towed to a private lot. Authorities hadn't connected it with the crash and shooting that took the lives of four deputies and one state trooper a few miles down Route 66. Nobody had a good explanation for how the pursuit of a red GTO with an obscured tag had turned into a massive debris field, or why a young deputy had surrendered his vehicle to an unknown party and shot a fellow officer point-blank. According to the tow truck driver Wicklow had spoken to, the radio preacher in Joplin openly blamed the devil, while the one in Hornet blamed the spook light. The spook light theory held a lot of water in Jasper County.

"Tracy, I don't know if we're going to hear anything else. I'm sorry. Hank was a fighter. If anyone could have held out against their mesmerism, it was him, and he knew what to do to keep from being taken alive. But you don't need me to tell you it's best if we assume the worst. We're both compromised, but I'm dug in. Get out of there, and take everything with you. Do it now. If they're coming for you, they could show up tonight. Try to put ninety miles behind you before you stop. Call me again when you're in place."

That had been thirty minutes ago.

Wicklow was right—All Souls Ranch was a hard target, whereas he was a sitting duck. Only Wicklow and Hank had known his location—sending Hank had been a calculated risk. It would have been better not to put him within their reach, but Hank drove well, shot better, and didn't scare easy; it wasn't like the Bereaved were turning people away. Now they were down to, what, eight? Ten? Probably no more than that. Two at the ranch, himself, an unknown number out west. But those were insulated—Wicklow trained them, only Wicklow knew how to reach them, and all *he* had was a phone number. Would Wicklow ask them to come secure the ranch?

Probably not. If one group fell, it was vital that the other group continue—as far as they knew, these dozen or so souls had been the only ones in the country fully aware of the threat.

"This stinks," he told the spot under the table where Max should have been, and then he flipped the pork chop.

The clock's hands pointed at 7:32, the little red second hand doing laps.

It was a bright day; the sun wouldn't set for another hour.

He would be gone by eight o'clock.

He had four minutes before the chop needed to come off the heat, but it would take only three and a half minutes to take another load down to the car.

Why waste time?

He grabbed the suitcase with his winter clothes in it, wrinkling his nose as the mothballs briefly overpowered the more affable smell of cooking meat. He didn't know where he was going to end up, so the sweaters and scarves he had saved from younger days in snowy places might prove useful again. He never wore scarves in St. Pete even on the dozen or so frosty nights each year that passed for winter.

He took the suitcase out the front door and down the steps that led to the parking lot; the elevator would have felt better on his hips and knees, but the steps were faster, even though they would take him past Mrs. Warner, an impossibly wrinkled, gossipy old thing who only left her post on the common balcony to eat, sleep, and produce waste. She had been a pain in the keester before, but it was ten times worse now that her relationship with dementia could no longer be called flirtation. She shouted down to him.

"You going on a trip, Mr. Calvert?"

"Yes, ma'am," he answered without slowing or turning.

"You taking your son with you?" she klaxoned so loudly the landscaper looked up from his ministrations to a *Croton californicus*. The man was new, looked Cuban. A lot of Cubans around since Castro, though more in Tampa. Wherever he was from, he would learn not to look up.

"My son's in Indiana," he said.

"You going back to Indiana?"

"No, ma'am."

He was almost to the car now.

Heat baked up at him from the asphalt, which seemed to want to stick to his sneakers even though the sun was behind the buildings now.

"Now'd sure be a good time to visit Indiana. I was in Terre Haute in February once. No thank you to that."

He popped the trunk of his Caddy, loaded the suitcase, shut it.

"Is it Indianapolis you're going to?" she said.

"Excuse me, but I've got a pork chop," he said, walking back across the blacktop as fast as he could.

"How's that?" she said.

He was almost to the stairs.

"Good evening, Mrs. Warner," he said, giving the gardener a wink as he passed him.

"You drive safely!" she said. "Get some rain tires, it's rainy season up there. And let your son do some of the driving, young eyes are better."

He held the screen door open with his elbow and opened the door, his nostrils widening with the pleasant odor coming from the range. He stepped around the file box and two more suitcases destined for his Cadillac; he was almost to the stove when he stopped and stared. Something was very wrong.

Glass glittered beneath the window.

He walked over to it, checked quickly for a baseball or rock to eliminate benign coincidence, found none.

Turned around to head for the fridge.

His breath caught in his throat.

A young man stood in his kitchen, a black T-shirt wrapped around one fist, blood welling up from a cut on his forearm. He shook the glass off the shirt and put it on, just as casual as you please.

"Who are you?" Calvert said, stalling. Twenty years ago he could have mopped up the floor with this bum. Ten years ago he would have had a fighting chance. But now? He had to get the man away from the refrigerator. Or make a run for his bedroom, but that was a race he wouldn't win without a distraction. The front door was out of the question; there was no balcony out the back window, so the kid must have shimmied up the latticework on the outside of the building—there'd be no outrunning him.

The young man, keeping an eye on Calvert, opened a drawer, peeked in. Shut it.

"I asked you a question," he said, moving closer, angling for the fridge. The meat still sizzled and smoked in the skillet, starting to burn.

"Me no speekee inglee," the man said, peeking in a second drawer. What did he want? Didn't he see the eight-inch kitchen knife sitting on top of the cutting board?

Just let me get near that fridge, kid

Now the intruder's eyes widened like a little boy who'd found his birthday present early. He pulled out an extension cord.

Oh shit this is about to get rough.

MINUTES LATER.

Woods drove the F100 down Fourth Street, heading south to the Banyan Tree Motel, under the canopy of which tree and with the help of a large black umbrella Woods had shuffled his three companions out of the truck and into the suite he'd rented an hour before.

Now he parked behind the hotel as instructed and tried to summon the energy to open the door and stand up. If he could just do that. If he could just get to their room. If Luther would just not be too pissed off about how badly things had gone. His hands were shaking not only from his injury but from fear of what Luther might do to him.

He needed a big favor, and he didn't think Luther was going to be in the favor-giving mood now.

Luther had been *very* clear about what he wanted.

Don't you fuck this up, Woodsy-woods. You don't need to do nothing but keep him there, and I mean don't you dare let him leave. Sun creeps down, we'll be over there and fix his wagon. Now if he starts to load up the Conestoga, you gotta work him yourself. Should be an ole hand at killin' after what you did with that Gee-rand, right? Only you cain't shoot. You beat him, you stab him, whatever, just get a rag in his mouth or something and don't make no noise.

Can I choke him?

Chokin's not as easy as you think.

What is he, eighty?

Somethin' like that.

I just haven't choked somebody before. Not for keeps. I think I'd like to try it.

Try it, huh? You gonna bone him when you're done?

You know I'm not like that.

Right. 'Scuse me. I didn't mean to make you out to be no pervert. Just a clean-cut American injun's what you are. All right, choke the fuck out of him, just remember what I said about it not bein' easy. Man runs outta air he starts getting real enthusiastic. And take the goddamn bonnet off, it's too particular.

People'll remember the bonnet, not my face.

Yeah, but they'll start payin' attention, won't they? "Hey, Mabel, did you see that injun goin' up the stairs? Wonder what he wants!" Damn, you're dumb. You got a handle on this?

I do.

Good. I don't want to be in this dusty old bonestack town no longer than I have to. You see these geezers? I been peekin' out the window since you left and I swear somebody dumped a pile a' mummies up the road. St. Peter's burg is right, half these folks'll be talkin to St. fuckin' Peter by Christmas. Bet the blood around here tastes like wet dust.

Woods didn't have an opinion about the merits of geriatric blood, but it turned out Luther was right about strangulation.

Choking a man, even an old man, wasn't so easy.

Woods started off punching him in the face, knocked his dentures clean across the floor. When the old fellow went to his knees, Woods slipped around behind him and looped the cord around his neck, but his liver-spotty old hand with its big clunky wedding ring got in the way. After he cleared the hand and started choking him for real, the old fellow's adrenaline must have kicked in because he stood up, even with Woods on his back, and leaned forward toward the counter. There was a weird moment when they both looked at an upside-down steel pot, a big bright one, drying on a spread-out dish towel, and Woods saw the guy see himself in the shiny pot all purple with his eyes bugging literally almost out of his head, and Woods saw himself too and hadn't realized he was smiling. That made him embarrassed and mad, so he kicked the geezer's legs till he went back on his knees again, only now he was closer to the stove. Woods knew he was about to get a face full of hot grease and skillet a heartbeat before he did get it, but he pulled tighter on the cord instead of ducking, which turned out to be a poor instinct. The heavy cast-iron thing caught him on the cheek, probably chipped the bone there, and the grease and meat burned the shit out of him. He let go of the cord and it was a good thing he had his Chuck Taylors on because he felt the rubber catch before he actually fell. He stumble-stepped forward for the knife he had seen on the cutting board while the old dude helped himself up, hugging the fridge like a fat dance partner, slipping some himself in all that grease. By the time Woods had the knife and turned, he saw the old guy reaching up high for the wire handle of the fly swatter there, and that actually amused him enough to hesitate and bark out a laugh. But it wasn't a fly swatter he wanted at all. Next thing Woods knew, a snub-nosed gun was coming off that fridge, so he rushed in. The gun went bang loud enough to ring his ears, Woods felt it pinch him in the belly, but then he knocked the old guy against the wall and the gun fell to the floor. He stabbed the old man in the chest until he stopped trying to raise his arms and slunk down, bleeding fast. Woods's biggest thought at the moment was how much trouble he was going to be in for the gunshot and that the police would be coming soon. So he stepped to the bathroom and dropped the knife in the toilet for no reason he could think of, then almost went for the window until he remembered he was supposed to grab evidence. He saw two suitcases and a file box. He grabbed the file box with one hand, grabbed his belly with the other, and out the back window he jumped.

The fall made something move agonizingly in his guts.

He crossed the yard behind the apartment and ducked behind a row of bushes with big round green leaves with bloody veins in them. He was about to splash down into the shallow canal leading to where he parked the truck on First Street when he felt a pain like bad diarrhea he got in Texas once—no, twice—only worse, and his legs got shaky tired. He sat down on a low concrete wall for just a few seconds, hunching over the file box cradled in his lap. Sitting down seemed to help. He noticed a few drops of blood on his white Chucks, but not too much. He might be okay. He didn't want to get up but realized that if he didn't he'd probably sit there until he passed out, so he forced his legs to move. Somebody yelled behind him. He looked and didn't see anybody, but then he was sorry he looked because he saw the huge bloody ass print he left on the wall. There was probably a hole out his back you could put a Ping-Pong ball in. He realized he had registered the wetness there as sweat, but one little corner of his brain had peeped at him that it was weird to sweat hard and fast only down your back and ass-crack.

He felt the seat of his jeans and found they were soaked in the butt like swim trunks.

His hand came up bright red.

He was shot bad.

Real bad.

Dying bad.

Lucky for him, he had friends who could help with that kind of thing.

38

NOW WOODS SQUEAKED THE HINGE OF THE F100'S DOOR AND STAGGERED OUT INTO the twilight, holding his stomach. The sun was nearly down. An ambulance screamed up Fourth Street. Two women with short dresses and sneakers watched it go by, then resumed scanning traffic for lonely male faces. One of them glanced over her shoulder at Woods doing his lame, stomach-clutching two-step, said, "Hey, mister, there went your ride," making the other one laugh. When he approached the room facing the shaded courtyard of the Banyan Tree Motel, he saw the blinds move and the door opened before he could touch the handle.

Cold, hard hands pulled him in.

The door shut behind him, making the curtains jump.

"What in the fast, hard fuck happened to you?" Luther said.

"Sh-shot me."

Calcutta embraced him from behind, helped him sit on the bed, drooling despite herself and licking her wet hand where it touched his back. She scooted Woods so he was lying with his head in her lap; he went *ah ah ah* while she did it.

Rob stood watching, looking impatiently toward the door every few seconds. None of them felt safe in a city—they were better at running than hiding.

"That's disappointing," Luther said. "Well?"

"I got . . . I got a file box."

"What's in it?"

"Don't know. No time. I need help."

"Did you get him?"

"Stabbed him."

"He dead?"

"Stabbed him deep."

"But is he *dead*?"

"Think so. He sh-shot me."

"Yeah, I think we got that part. So that ambulance just went by could be for our boy, huh? Any chance he'll pull through?"

"He shot me."

"He sure did, hoss. That's a bad'n, too."

Woods, as pale as the trio around him, looked up from Calcutta's lap into Luther's reflective sunglasses, where he saw himself tiny and dying.

"I'm ready," he said. "You can do it now."

"Do what, ole hoss?"

"You know what."

"Yeah, I guess I do. I just ain't real decided on that."

"You got to. Please," he said, his voice taking on an unattractive, whining tone.

Calcutta stroked his hair, looked coldly down into his eyes. His eyes stayed on Luther.

"You got to."

"I don't *got* to nothin'," Luther said. "Thing is, they's already five of us dead. Your heartbeat's what makes you special. I drain you dead and then spit some back in, why you ain't special no more, but there your skinny ass is takin' up another seat in the cars, drinkin' part of our share. And I gotta tell you honest, you scout okay and you shoot okay, but you don't drive for shit."

The sun was fully down now.

"P-please. I'm cold. I can hardly see you."

"Well, I can understand a fella wantin' to see me, handsome as I am and all. All right, we gonna put it to a vote. What you think, Rob? Yes or no to old Woodsy-woods?"

Rob looked out the window, watching one of the hookers frown around a cigarette as she lit it. Without looking back he shook his head no.

"Fair enough," Luther said. "Just to make it interestin', I'm gonna vote yes. Mostly based on all your past good deeds." Luther directed his sunglasses at Calcutta. "Sweet cheeks?"

Woods smiled through his pain, relieved.

He closed his eyes.

"Don't put it on me, Luther," Calcutta said.

Woods opened his eyes again.

"Whoa, there's a development!" Luther said. "But it *is* on you. We got us a tie, me and Rob. You are the tie *breaker*."

"I don't want it."

"Well, you got it."

Rob said, "We should get out of here."

"That ain't no lie. Well, Katherine Louise, what do you say? You don't say nothing, I'm gonna assume your tongue's all tied with true love and I'm gonna turn your paramour on your behalf."

He bared his fangs and bent down to Woods, who grimaced with pain as he worked his ruined abdominal muscles to raise his neck toward Luther's mouth.

"No," she said. "I vote no."

Luther stood back up, directed his mirrored glasses at Woods's agonized, betrayed face.

"Well, there you have it, hoss. Tough break. Where're your keys?"

"Why?" he said, starting to cry.

"'Cause I don't feel like hot-wirin' it, dummy. They in your pocket or in the truck?"

"No. Why won't you *turn* me? Calcutta. N-night flower."

"Night flower!" Luther said. "I like that!"

Rob smiled.

"I'll tell you why," she said. "'Cause I don't want a husband, and if I did, I wouldn't want it to be some creepy kid who likes to . . . do all that shit you do. I ain't a night flower, and if I am I ain't yours. Now if you're dying, just hurry up, 'cause we got places to go."

"That was the prettiest grace I ever heard," said Luther.

Calcutta stuffed her fist in Woods's mouth and bit a weakly squirting hole in his neck.

Luther took the wrist.

Rob considered unpantsing him to get at the femoral, then settled for the bullet wound.

After Luther had wet his whistle, he talked.

Luther liked to talk while people were dying.

It was like reading them to sleep.

***FUNNY THING ABOUT DEATH, WATCHING PEOPLE TRY TO GET THEIR MINDS AROUND** it. I mean, you and I both come to this moment in time believing ourselves the star of a movie that won't never end. Problem with that, though, is only one of us can be right. And it ain't you, is it? Nope. I'm watchin' your movie end right now. And the more people I watch get kicked out of what they thought was their own movie, the more I think mine's the real one. Maybe there's other real ones, and maybe I'm just sayin' that so I don't hurt my friends' feelin's while they're havin' their supper. Course I ain't dumb. I know there's a point I can't remember past, and maybe I didn't exist before then, least not in this form. And a thinkin' man might shoot forward from that and see a time when he might not exist once again. I confess I thought* *like that after the war. Peein' through a tube and learnin' to walk all over again, them's what you call humblin' experiences. But gettin' turned, that was something else entirely. A weird zig when I was expectin' a crappy zag. I mean, if this is possible in my little movie house, what else is waitin' around the corner? Every day is any-fuckin'-thing-can-happen day. Martians might come down out of the sky and elect me emperor. The devil might pop up outta the ground and promote me to chief specialist whore-tester in hell, how do I know? I sure didn't see* this *comin'. Can you still hear me? Your eyes is stopped focusin' so maybe no. Maybe you're findin' out for real and true that all them fantasies you had about your own self livin' forever was lies. I don't mind so much they voted you out, I kinda knew they would. See, you're just a creature in my kingdom, created for my entertainment. And you ain't no fun no more.*

WOODROW FULK'S VISION HAD LONG SINCE DARKENED, AND HE HAD PASSED INTO a dream where his truck was picked up by a stovepipe-black tornado that lifted it into the sky; Luther's voice played over the radio as the tornado turned the truck upside-down and shook it. Woods held on to the steering wheel as long as he could, his legs dangling out the door and over the distant patchwork fields below, and at last he fell; not yelling or thrashing, just looking at the farms and woods of Michigan in something like bewilderment on his way down.

39

TRACY CALVERT MANAGED TO CRAWL OUT OF THE KITCHEN, BUT NOT FAR. HE LAY down and bled on the carpet under the table. He was done. Everybody he loved was on the other side anyway, no point in sticking around. His vision went double, and he thought he saw Max, or Marzipan, sitting fat and hungry in front of him; he was lying in the cat's favorite begging spot, after all. Someone banged on the door, but that was annoying. He thought he felt Max's rough tongue on his nose, and he much preferred that to the banging, to the loud voice yelling "Police," but then someone was flipping him over, lifting him up on a gurney. Kids. All young kids. A mask went over his nose and mouth and it got easier to breathe. Next thing he knew he was being wheeled out onto the balcony. A cop with his hand on his holstered gun spoke to him, but whatever he said went away as soon as he said it. It was rough going down the stairs. He closed his eyes and tried to die, but that didn't work. The sun was down now, and he knew that was bad but couldn't remember why. He floated across the asphalt and up into the back of an ambulance where a pretty girl in a uniform sat down next to him, talking to him, he was pretty sure she was saying nice things. The doors chunked shut. He tried to die again and couldn't, but at least the ambulance was speeding away from the apartment, and then he remembered why the sun going down was bad. He got agitated.

"You just relax, we're going to help you."

Where we going, he tried to say, but indistinct mumbles were all he could produce. The pretty girl seemed to understand him, though.

"St. Anthony's."

"Good," he tried to say in response.

It felt like he had burning knives sticking in his chest and a donkey was sitting on it, too.

"You hang on, Mr. Calvert," she said. "You're gonna make it."

She tried not to laugh at his response, a world-weary "Oh shit."

The ambulance sped south on Fourth Street, its sirens blaring, its lights beating red holes into the new night.

And then it slowed.

"Oh damn," he heard the driver say.

The pretty girl looked out the window, where more red lights strobed her face.

She put her hand to her mouth.

"Who is that driving?" she said. "Is that Curtis?"

"I don't know," the driver said, and then spoke into his radio.

Calvert's ambulance sped up again.

THREE MINUTES EARLIER.

Less than fifty yards from the Banyan Tree Motel, Luther walked up to a corner grocery and charmed a woman out of her car. He told her to sit down and forget she saw him, so sit she did, looking the other way, more concerned about keeping her legs together so she didn't flash anybody than about the strange bald man in the sunglasses driving off in her husband's 1962 Chrysler Imperial. Luther took a right, stayed in the slow lane, and crawled toward the Bay View Apartments, listening for sirens. Very soon, an ambulance wailed in the distance, making its way south on Fourth Street.

He made a wide U-turn, earning several horn blasts, and he joined the several cars now pulling over on the far right of southbound Fourth. He waited with them, watched the ambulance approach in his rearview mirror. When it came near him, he pulled out in front of it and gunned the engine. Its trucklike horn blatted in concert with the siren. Luther's door rocketed past the careening nose of the ambulance, though just barely—he had accounted for the driver's likely attempt to pull left—and the big emergency vehicle plowed into the long trunk of the Imperial, spinning Luther into the northbound lanes, where he sideswiped another car and banged his head on the window, starring it.

"You all right, mister?" a man's voice yelled, but he was already out of the car, kicking a rearview mirror out of his way. He moved to the median, where steam was pouring from the ruined front of the ambulance, punched the bewildered ambulance driver in the head, knocking him out, then, simultaneously saying, "Forget me," pushed a concerned citizen down on his ass. Hard. He opened the cracked rear door of the ambulance, ready to pull Tracy Calvert onto the street and kick his old brains out of his ears. Instead, a large, half-naked middle-aged woman with bottle-red hair moaned on the floor, an emergency worker half sitting on her, holding his bleeding head.

"Shit!" Luther said with some venom, seeing that the old man wasn't here. "Sorry, my mistake," he said, shutting the door again. A big construction-worker type grabbed Luther by the collar, but Luther looked him in the eye and said, "Kiss me, sweetheart, then fuck off." The man kissed him chastely on the lips and fucked off. Luther ran south, his back to the headlights of approaching traffic, hearing people shout after him. He approached a little Datsun with its emergency flashers on, opened the door, and pulled a smallish man out by the tie.

"Hi!" he said. "I'm a colored, when they ask." Then he pushed the man down, got in the car, and sped away down a side avenue. Nobody chased him. He heard a siren in the distance, probably back on Fourth Street. He knew in his dead, black heart that Calvert was in that ambulance, but he didn't think he had a chance in hell of catching it in this little rice burner.

He swore a great deal.

He swore even more when he got back on Fourth Street and found himself delayed behind stuck-together slowpoke drivers no amount of honking would dislodge. By the time he found the emergency room of a likely hospital, it was a big Catholic deal with crosses and Jesus everywhere he looked, and he wasn't sure he could make himself go in there if he wanted to.

Old man like that was probably not going to do well with a deep stab wound. Probably dead. Not that that took much sting out of his failure—if he'd only waited another two minutes, he'd have had his man. What the hell were *two* ambulances doing on the street at the same time?

"Goddamn bad luck is all that is," he said to nobody. He ditched the Datsun in the parking lot, then charmed a woman who turned out to be an art teacher into driving him back to the parking lot of some tourist trap called Sunken Gardens, right where he told Calcutta and Rob to meet him with the truck.

"What did you do with the kiddos today?" Luther asked the drooling young redhead.

"Taught them how to make paper," she slurred.

"Huh," he said, not sure if making paper was dumb or brilliant.

After they all had a mouthful or two off the woman, they sent her on her weaving way, saw her get pulled over by a cop no doubt looking for whatever poorly described troublemaker had caused all the ruckus, and even waved at the cop on their way north toward 275. They had a four-and-a-half-hour drive back to Tallahassee, where, presumably, Cole and Neck Brace waited with the other two cars, their trunks and backseats full of all the gear they'd moved out of the truck to give the three vampires sleeping room for the race farther south.

They wouldn't be able to pull double-shift stunts like that without a daybitch. Woods's loss had cut their legs short and left them day-blind and unsafe.

Rob drove the F100 over the bridge and through Tampa.

He was probably going to be driving this pack mule from here out, and he wasn't going to like it.

Where they went after Tallahassee depended on what they could find out about the Bereaved, as Hank Calvert had called them before they drank him dead.

"Bereaved, my ass," Luther said. "I'll give 'em somethin' to be bereaved about."

He started going through the file box almost immediately.

40

JUDITH WALKED BACK THROUGH THE WOODS THAT LED DOWN THE HILL TO THE switchback where Clayton had parked the '67 Camaro. During her long confinement in the blackness of the trunk it had been possible to suppress the knowledge that this was indeed the vehicle that had swallowed her only son; but now, looking at it

Evenin', miss

from the driver's side, just as she had when it nosed up alongside her husband's Falcon

That his name, too?

it looked like some evil black fish that might yet have one more bite in its jaws.

Evenin' evenin' evenin' missss

She touched its cool, steel hide as if in absolution, thinking it was just a tool now, thinking she would use it against them, thinking she would make them as sorry to have seen it as she was, but it was hard not to hate it. How it looked. What it could do. It had been welded and screwed together in Michigan with a big motor that sped easily away from cars with mommies and daddies in them to take children off to witches' pots.

She knew she might have to drive it, and she dreaded that like poison. Jude had only driven a handful of times since the accident, and each time she had felt her heart racing and her palms grew sweaty. Her mother had coached her through the first episode as if at bedside in the maternity ward: *It's okay, just breathe, just breathe, sweetie, you're okay.* Now she was all right as long as she stayed off the highway and away from bridges. Funny that bridges affected her so since she had wrecked in the flattest, driest part of New Mexico, but coming over the double-decker bridge from Covington to Cincinnati before she left for the abbey had nearly made her black out.

But to lay hands on this . . . weapon. She would have no problems shooting the .45 revolver in the glove box, the gun that once belonged to Hank, but the car was something else.

"There's nothing for it," she said. "I'll just have to. I have to."

She didn't know if she believed herself.

No time for that now.

She left it crouched on its switchback as she made her way down the hill and toward the surplus store and, God willing, a phone.

Wicklow didn't answer the first time she called.

Or the second.

BY THE TIME DAYLIGHT STARTED RUNNING OUT, JUDITH'S TRAUMA AND EXHAUS-tion caught up with her. She needed to lie down. She feared sleep, not altogether certain Clayton could resist feeding on her. Would he make her a vampire if he did? Wicklow said he believed the act of transformation was both wholly intentional and rare, or else they would propagate unsustainably. Nevertheless, the idea of his teeth anywhere near her horrified her. She thought about going to the Camaro and locking herself in with the keys, but the thought of sleeping where her son had very probably died seemed worse than Clayton shoplifting blood from her. Unable to think of a better idea than locking herself in the car, she wrapped her rosary around her neck, curled up under the rock overhang not far from the vampire, and, using her new boots as a pillow, began to give in to sleep. Perhaps she would nap for a few minutes to get some strength back and, hopefully, diminish the pain in her head. She was all but certain he would not kill her, but she crossed herself and said an *Ave Maria* before her thoughts drifted into a surprisingly pleasant dream. She walked barefoot on sand beaches and spoke with beautiful colonial women like those in the beginning of *Wide Sargasso Sea*, which she had been reading when her family wrecked. The bookmark had still been in it when it was returned to her in a plastic bag, grainy with New Mexico dirt. Of course she never opened it again. Antoinette would remain on those beaches forever, never marry Rochester, leave for England, descend into madness.

She slept for twenty-two hours.

41

"YOU CAN'T HAVE IT," COLE SAID.

"Just till I get something nearly as fast."

"Well, let's get that first, then. What, a Chevelle?"

"You won't catch me in no Chevelle."

"Mustang, then?"

"More likely that."

"Fine. Let's hunt one up."

"We will."

"Bet there's somethin' in Houston."

"Bet you're right."

"Be in Texas tomorrow night."

"Just give me them cocoa keys till we find it."

"It's COPO, dummy."

"Like I said."

"Goddamn it, Luther."

"I'm the best driver, do you argue that? Better not say yes."

"I ain't sayin' yes."

"Well, there you go."

"No, there I don't go. I found the COPO, I get to keep it."

"Best driver oughta have the fastest car, that's all."

"You're always pullin' shit like this."

"Impala don't get up and go enough."

"You picked it."

"'T's all there was."

"You could have took a Camaro yourself. We were at the lot."

"We ain't gonna all drive the same thing."

"They had Chevelles."

"Fuck a Chevelle."

"So get you somethin' else."

"That Impala's like a brick on skates."

"Ain't my problem."

"Uh-huh. Give me the keys."

"No."

"Gimme 'em."

"Goddamn it, Luther Nixon."

"I'll play ya chicken for it."

"You'll lose."

"When have I ever lost?"

"You don't want to test me on this."

"I'm testin'."

"I'll burn you."

"You won't burn shit, Coley-cole. Might as well to hand me them keys and save a disgracin'."

"I'll burn you to pieces over this."

"Let's stop talkin' about it and see."

"Tired of your shit is all."

"Let's just see."

"I found that damn car. Ain't even a thousand of 'em in the whole country."

"Uh-huh. You're still talkin'."

"Any of the rest of you think this is a good idea?"

Rob said, "I'm stuck drivin' the truck. How much of a shit do you think I give?"

Calcutta said, "You can beat him, Cole. He's due to get beat up."

Neck Brace said nothing.

"Sun's comin' up. Get out here with me," Luther said.

They went out into the dirt yard of the dead man's house.

"Yeah, all right, fuck you, Luther."

"'S gonna be a hot one today."

"Now who's talkin'?"

"That little bit a' mist, wonder if that'll slow it down at all?"

"I don't reckon. I reckon it's gonna burn you right up."

"Humid as hell, too. Glad I'm cold-blooded. All them Cajuns out here paddlin' their boats around, sweatin' that cayenne pepper out."

"Shut up, it's comin'."

"I know it's comin', Cole. Them birds is chirpin'. Besides, I can feel it. Can't you?"

"I guess I can."

"You ever have that cayenne pepper, Cole? Before I fixed you?"

Cole was silent.

"Thought so. Seems I took you out for crawdads once in Breaux Bridge after a race."

"Wasn't me."

"Was too."

"We discussed how we wasn't gonna discuss this."

"That's a good burn, right there, that crawdad burn."

"You might want to pay attention, it's comin'."

"This ain't gonna be no good burn."

"Gonna sneak up on you, Luther. I don't want us both to fry just 'cause you ain't payin' attention."

"I don't need to pay attention. You're payin' attention for me. I don't run till you do."

"Bullshit, you'll run."

"Am I even lookin' east?"

"Ain't gonna work this time."

"You ever see me run inside first?"

"This time you will."

"I'm lookin' right in your eyes."

"You'll know when to turn tail. You can feel it just the same as I can."

"Sky's getting awful fiery, ain't it?"

"Look, damn it."

"Book a' Revelations up there, I'll bet."

"Damn it."

"Do you see the whore a' Babylon yet?"

"Look!"

"Uh-uh, lookin's your job."

Cole reached in his jeans pocket.

"That's right," Luther said.

The sun crowned, prickling through the bald cypress trees to the east and lighting up the moss beards as if they were ablaze. Very weak, filtered light fell on their faces and it hurt.

Cole took the keys in his hand.

"That's right," Luther said, gritting his teeth.

"Get inside, you idiots," Calcutta said.

Neck Brace loomed in the shade of the window, staring guilelessly like a child watching some unfathomable exchange between his parents. Rob, pouting about his solitary new duties as pack-truck driver, had already settled himself under the dead man's bed and wrapped up in a blanket.

"Ah!" Cole said, the thin edge of his ear starting to smoke. He swatted at it as if it were a deerfly. Then he jerked the Camaro keys out of his pocket and threw them high, toward the rope-girdled tree where the dogs used to be, and in the same motion he ran inside, small parts of him smoldering but not yet burned. Luther leapt like a wide receiver and snatched them in one smoking hand, rolling his back toward the east, landing catlike and sprinting just behind Cole, laughing.

He chucked the Impala keys at Cole and folded himself into the rusty, dry-rotted trunk he had claimed. Cole fumed until he tired of it, then, regaining some of his poise, joined Calcutta lifting up the flipped-over pirogue, the two of them nestling close but cold under the boat like two clams in one shell. Neck Brace took his oiled tarp to the chipped and stained laundry tub and, unable to fit himself in, swaddled up on the floor and turned the tub over so it sat crooked on him, covering his upper half.

"Sure am gonna love drivin' that pretty black cocoa lady," Luther said from the trunk.

"Shut up," said Cole. "Gloatin's ugly."

"You're right." Luther was quiet for a minute, then said, "Hope the old boy owned this house was as lonely as he looked."

"Wasn't no tracks on the road, and the road was dry. He didn't do nothing but fish and watch his dogs fuck."

Outside, a fighting rooster crowed in his asymmetrical cage.

Near the end of the late Barnard Gournay's dry-rotten pier, the water bubbled over him, the weight of the junked engine block pinning him down expressing the last air from his lungs. At the bottom of the brown water, the blue crabs he made his living from had found him now, and scorned the bull lip and wild turkey necks in the nearer pots on his trot line. He would not be pulled out of the bayou for three days, and though his mean-as-hell estranged brother-in-law in Grosse Tête would be questioned, his alibi would hold.

Back inside, Luther spoke from the darkness of the trunk.

"If he does get a visitor, too bad for them."

Now the others heard the sound of his pistol's cylinder spinning in the trunk, then clicking shut.

Luther laughed, but then kept on laughing.

"It wasn't that funny," Rob said.

"No, I'm thinkin' a' something else now."

"What?"

"That it's a long way to Fresno."

Luther kept laughing.

"That's not funny either."

"You know the sister's touched in the head, right?"

"You told me."

Luther snickered.

"Well, I was just wonderin' what if we turned her."

"Now *that* really ain't funny," Cole said.

"C'mon," Luther said. "Any of you ever see a retard vampire?"

Calcutta said, "Hell, I saw two of 'em standing in the sunshine a minute ago."

Luther was quiet.

Then he guffawed.

"Just shut up and go to sleep," Cole said.

The rooster crowed again.

42

JUDITH WOKE FROM A DREAM IN WHICH PATSY HAD MADE A NEW FRIEND. THE friend stood outside her window and asked to see her collection of bells—Patsy loved bells. The friend wanted inside to touch the pretty bells with their painted-on flowers and butterflies, but Judith knew her little sister mustn't open the window, mustn't invite the friend in. Unfortunately, Patsy was with Mom and Dad in Fresno and the only way Judith could warn her from so far away was to stand on the wrong side of the dresser mirror and shout. Patsy couldn't hear her very well. Every time she managed to shout hard enough for Patsy to make out the words, the special friend across the room tapped a funny beat on the windowpane and then distracted Patsy with kaleidoscope eyes straight from that psychedelic Beatles song Patsy innocently loved. The only way Judith could get her attention back was to shout even harder, but her voice was getting hoarse and Patsy went a little farther across the room with every *tap tap tappity tap.* So she broke the mirror glass even though breaking a mirror from the inside caused seven *times* seven years of bad luck, but the friend was already inside and Patsy and the pale, pale man looked at her, their arms around each other's shoulders like old buddies.

Then she was lying on a boot under a rock overhang in what looked like very deep forest. Her shirt was soaked.

"Who's Patsy?" the vampire next to her mumbled. He wore a dark shirt over his head and held his arms crossed close to his chest so that she thought of a grumpy executioner trying to sleep at the airport.

"Never mind," she said, wiping sweat from her brow. "What time is it?"

He peeped under his shirt-hood at a pocket watch he kept on a fine chain.

"I am sorry to report that it is two o'clock in the afternoon," he said, replacing the watch and pausing with the hood above his mouth until he finished saying, "I shall be better company near sundown."

He went back to sleep.

She said, "I'm taking another dime."

He murmured something that sounded unoffended, so she fished in his pocket long enough to harvest eighty-five cents in change and to make her vaguely repulsed at how lukewarm that pocket was, as though the meat of his thigh were a ham that had been cooling on the range all day; it felt very like what it was—rifling through the pocket of a corpse.

She put her boots on.

That was when she noticed the notebook and the paints.

A small jar of cloudy water sat near an open notebook containing heavy paper suitable for watercolors. On one page of the notebook she saw a portrait of herself sleeping. It looked exactly like her, so much so that his representation of her scar made her touch her nose and cheek. Clayton Birch the vampire, it seemed, was an artist of no small talent. Her realization that he was still a human being struck her in part by making her aware of its novelty—he hadn't *been* a human being to her until that moment. What had he been? An aberration, a diabolical parlor trick. Dead meat housing a damned soul, falsely alive and displeasing to God. If he was kinder than the others, and there was no denying that, it was perhaps only an echo of what the man had once been but was no more. But now. It was obvious that whoever painted that picture had seen her through a prism of genuine affection. Her own father might have painted that, so fully did it capture the peace of sleep and evoke and amplify what remained of her youth. There was something of Glendon in that picture, too.

"It's beautiful," she said, her voice shaking with emotion.

He stirred again, lifted his hood, and peeked at her.

When she saw him, she gasped.

He had taken on the appearance of a young, rudely healthy man.

Had her defenses failed her? Could she now be mesmerized?

"Thank you," he said.

"You're beautiful, too," she said, before she could stop herself, then hurried through the trees and down the switchback as fast as her insulted feet and overlarge boots could carry her.

He *was* beautiful.

She chose to see this not as some flaw in her armor, but as a gift. If she had been given Clayton as an ally, she must see him as one.

Thank you, God, she thought. *Now please let Phillip Wicklow pick up the phone.*

She got her wish.

"IT'S JUDITH."

"Don't tell me where you are."

"Okay."

"Are you safe?"

"I'm hurt, but I don't need a hospital."

"The others?"

She paused.

Looked toward the hill where Clayton waited.

"No."

"Ah," he said, and she hated how flat it sounded, like something you might say when a stranger disappoints you.

"I want to go on with the mission," she said. "I'm worried about something."

"How many are left? Of our foe, I mean."

"All five, I guess. I saw five."

She could almost hear him sorting through a drawer full of possible responses.

"Come back to the ranch."

"They got Hank alive," she said.

His silence was heavy. Hank was the most important man on the mission, more important than Lettuce. Hank hadn't been leading only because his temper ran too hot. Hank knew things.

"Yes," he said at last, "I feared as much."

"Mr. Wicklow?"

"You should really come to the ranch, Judith."

"What did Hank know? About me?"

"We can talk more freely at All Souls Ranch."

"Is my family safe?"

His silence hit her between the eyes.

When he finally spoke, she knew it for a lie.

"Yes."

"I'm not coming back to the ranch, Mr. Wicklow."

"I'm sorry if it sounded like a request."

"Help me find them."

"And what will you do when you find them? All five of them? What will you do alone that you couldn't do with armed men to help you?"

Now it was her turn to be silent.

"*Are* you alone?"

His ability to see through people frightened her. What would he do if he knew a monster was helping her? That she was beginning to feel something like affection for him?

"Tell me everything you remember about the attack, but nothing they don't know."

She did. Wicklow listened in silence.

"Is that all?"

"Yes."

"You're sure about the man in the Indian bonnet? That he was working with them?"

"I'm sure."

"All right. I have an urgent call to make. I'll give you directions to a meeting place from which I'll escort you back."

"I'm not coming back until I get at them, Mr. Wicklow. Help me find them."

"I will. With a team. *After you get back here.*"

"There isn't time for a team."

"Why not?"

"They're headed for my family."

"You don't know that."

"I do."

"How?"

"I just do."

Silence.

"Judith," he said, but nothing followed.

She hung up.

SHE STOOD FOR SOME TIME WITH A SECOND DIME PINCHED BETWEEN THUMB AND forefinger, looking at the pay phone's black slot. She yearned to call her father and warn him, but what could she say? Pack up the family and go to the Big Sur cabin because killers the police can't stop are on their way?

"Gonna use that?" an older fellow with a big watch and pants almost up to his breasts said, pointing a long, brown finger at the phone.

"Yes," she said, and dialed the operator.

An uncapped plastic pen sat near the phone, looking like a sun-dried artifact. She tested it on the skin of her arm, approved of the grainy, intermittent blue line it left there.

"Hello," she said. "I need the number of every towing service you can find near Joplin, Missouri."

43

CLAYTON FOUND THEM A RELATIVELY FLAT, DESERTED STRETCH OF FARM ROAD IN Arkansas and switched seats with Judith. She sat behind the wheel of the wicked black Camaro. A slouching scarecrow with a woman's hat faced a bean field to her right like a drunken conductor. Corn waved to her left. Breathing in through her nose and out through her mouth as she remembered her mother once told her seemed to help for a minute, but the panic crept up in her anyway.

She got out of the car and stood bent over with her sweaty palms on her thighs. She tried to focus her mind on other things. She looked at the toes of her one-size-too-big combat boots, noticed how badly her jeans needed washing. She spat dry spit and got control of her breathing.

"We should just drive the van," Clayton said.

"We don't have the van yet. And we need to go fast. We need to drive day and night without stopping."

"Maybe it's time for me to give you your present."

"What present?"

"You don't think I just sat in the car like a good boy while you bought ammunition for your sidearm, do you?"

She smiled despite herself.

"Put your hand out."

She did as he instructed.

He dropped a medallion into her palm.

"St. Christopher?" she said.

"He helps travelers, I hear."

"Put it on me, please."

He stepped behind her and put it on. She reached back to hold her hair out of the way for him, but this was just a reflex; the abbey had cut her hair just above the neck. She remembered now the dark snowfall of her tresses, then remembered even further back to the last time a man had put a necklace on her. Rob, her husband. A diamond their last Christmas together. He was a flawed, weak man, but he had loved her in his way.

"Where did you get this?" she said, turning to face the vampire, but stepping back so as not to stand too close. An owl hooted in the darkness.

"Don't worry about that."

"Religious stores aren't open at night. And you wouldn't have bought it for yourself."

"Correct on both counts."

"So did you steal it out of some nice old woman's car while I was shopping?"

"I love the way you make buying large-caliber bullets sound like a stroll through Macy's."

"You've dodged the question. I can't wear a stolen St. Christopher medal."

"You didn't steal it."

"Stolen nonetheless."

"I didn't admit that."

She made a sound like a small growl.

"And why doesn't it harm you? Or disturb you?" she said. "I thought holy objects were off-limits to . . . your kind."

"My parents failed to indoctrinate me to the mysteries of faith. Crosses have never bothered me. Even if they did, I don't know if this would have any effect since Christopher's not actually a saint anymore."

"Oh, he's a saint all right."

"Not as of February. According to what I read."

"You read hastily, Mr. Birch; the Holy Father simply removed his feast day."

"How rude."

"They had to. The calendar was getting crowded. Anyway, if you're so skeptical, why did you bring him to me?"

"It's not my faith that's at issue here."

"I beg your pardon."

"You're the one who needs to believe in this, so go ahead and believe in it."

She stared into his handsome greenish eyes, not sure if he was pulling her leg.

He looked more intensely.

"You're going to drive this car without fear. You're going to drive it skillfully and you're going to come back safe in it."

"That doesn't work on me. Or, at least, it didn't."

"What changed?"

You no longer look like a pork chop, she thought, and bit her lip not to laugh.

"I don't know, Mr. Birch. But I can't waste any more time."

JUDITH HAD LEARNED TO DRIVE IN HER FATHER'S 1959 CHEVY APACHE TRUCK, A three-speed floor shifter, so the Camaro's five-speed transmission was not an impossible leap for her. The power in the thing, however, was a different matter. She drove the farm roads of Missouri with increasing confidence, the Camaro's headlights sweeping barns and silos and the rusted hulks of prewar tractors, fireflies on either side of them glinting sweetly over low crops and in the elbow bends of hedges. Twice she almost put them in a ditch; once, her use of a hard-packed dirt driveway to turn around had summoned forth an older man who, silhouetting himself in the lit rectangle of a door and shaking what looked like a rolled-up magazine at them (had he been killing a fly? Beating a house dog?), yelled "Goddamn bums! Goddamn draft dodgers! Go to town and do your drag racing, we're Christian folks here."

Speeding away from him, Judith enjoyed her first real, deep laugh in a very long time.

AN HOUR LATER CLAYTON ROSE IN THE NEAR DARKNESS OF THE PASSENGER SEAT, consulting the careworn, rained-on fold-out map he kept in his coat. "I suppose I should invest in a new one," he said, charmingly embarrassed.

"Are we close to Joplin?"

"Yes."

"Good," she said. "It's on Independence Road. Howell's Body Shop and Wrecking Service."

"You need gas."

"So I do," she said, putting her blinker on and veering toward a big orange Gulf sign.

They parked by the pumps and, as she watched him fold away his map, she said, "I wonder how they navigate? Do they have those bothersome, hard-to-fold maps? Or do they just know where they're going?"

"No," he said. Then he sat up straight as he seemed to remember something painfully obvious. "They used an atlas."

They looked at one another.

"Check under the seat!" she said, even as he bent forward to do exactly that.

44

"THERE SHE IS. THAT'S HER," COLE SAID. "THAT* IS *ONE."

Cole held forth a copy of *Motor Trend* magazine opened to a dog-eared page that bore the legend *Mustang Mach 1* in lime-green letters.

"Listen," Cole said, and read aloud, *"You do not merely sit in the Mach One, you close the door and seal yourself away in a tiny capsule. Your eye falls on the dash and your hand reaches out instinctively to see if the teakwood grain panels are real . . ."*

"Ain't an automatic, is it?"

"I dearly doubt it."

Cole scanned the magazine, turned the page. "One in the picture here's a stick."

"Better not be an automatic."

"It's a four-speed, asshole, I'd bet on it. Look at it. Royal maroon."

"Yeah, I can see what color it is."

"Kinda makes you hungry, don't it? That blood color."

"Stop tryin' to sell me."

"You always were a Ford man."

"Mostly."

"Then you met that pretty red goat."

"Yeppers."

"Mustang's on top now."

"Some people think so. I'm used to thinking of 'em as small blocks. Little ponies."

"They were, maybe."

"'Member that greeny-blue one in New York?"

"Teal."

"Teal ain't no color for a man's car."

"Musta had it painted special."

"I guess."

"Small block."

"Well, Mach One ain't no small block. Look at it."

"I just wish they hadn't fucked up the GTO after '67."

"But they did."

"Made a goddamn hobgoblin out of it."

"Nah, they ain't pretty no more. But this one is. Even says *Cobra Jet* on the scoop. Four twenty-eight. Rob'll go nuts."

"I see it. You just want this one back."

"Bet it'll beat this one."

"You're just sayin' that. Earlier you said nothing could beat a 427 Camaro, not even a Vette."

"Bet it could, though."

"Maybe if an asshole were drivin' this one."

"One is."

"Fuck you, Cole."

"Right back atcha. You took my car. Well?"

"Sure is pretty."

"Somebody's comin' up."

"I see."

"Keys in his hand."

"I see 'em, shut up."

"Them girls with him, the one can't be seventeen."

"Good for him. Now shut up."

"Flip the lights on."

CHARLES MURPHY NETTLES WAS ENJOYING THE HELL OUT OF HIS SUMMER HOME from school. Classes at UT Austin were tough, but he paid top dollar for test answers and had just coasted through his sophomore year with a B average and minimal inconvenience to his robust social life. His roommate at the Phi Gam house had heard so much unzipping of jeans and boots coming from his bed that the other Fiji brothers had dubbed Nettles "Lord of the Flies." One of the secrets of his success, aside from the fact that he looked like a skinny, young version of Superman, was that he knew what people wanted to hear and how to say those things without getting himself on the hook. His dad, for example, had wanted to hear that he would have his brand-new Mustang home by midnight without a scratch on it, and that was what he told him. If he managed to get these two free-love chicks (one a high school senior, one a college freshman) out to the cornfield behind the Jack in the Box or the abandoned warehouse by the railroad tracks, he sure wasn't going to be watching his watch. And things were going okay. For all their talk about new America and tuning in and dropping out, they were awfully impressed with the woodgrain dash and bucket seats in the 'Stang. They had asked him to take them to a place not too far from his own home, the Catacombs in Rice Village.

It wasn't bad, but it wasn't Charlie's scene. For one thing, you had to be a member of "the club" to get a drink and the cutoff age was twenty-one. Like, you had to be *younger* than that to be a member. Charlie had just turned twenty-one at the end of June, and the bartender nearly denied him. So Charlie stood by the bar nursing his drink, listening to some band with a drummer who looked like Prince Valiant with a mustache. He wasn't worried about seeming hip. He had found that the best way to stoke a girl's furnace was just not to care. So he listened to the formless electronic music and watched the projected-light show (which looked like a brightly colored science project) and let his face read exactly what he was feeling. *This is fine and all, but we've got better places to be.*

He had watched the older of the two girls, he was pretty sure her name was Ronda, start to get drawn in by some vocal, skinny mixed-race guy who wore the ashes of his draft card in a little plastic pouch around his neck and used the word *paradigm* a lot, so he ambled over—Charlie had a flawless amble—and said, "Train's leavin' in five, ladies."

"Oh, really?" the maybe-Ronda said. "I'm kinda having a good time here."

"Yeah, man," Paradigm said, "why not be cool and hang out awhile?" Charlie knew the guy had already made him out as a poser but also knew the cruel math of car keys. Possibly-Ronda smiled at Charlie. The younger girl just held her purse and waited to see which way the wind would blow.

"My friend, I will be cool anywhere I go, and right now I'm fixin' to go to Rooster Eddie's. You been there?"

"Naw, man, I don't know that place."

"Maybe you should get to know it. They've got a band, too. And Shiner. Anyway, we're about to split. Meet us there if you want."

"Naw, I heard about that place. They're all hawked out in there."

"What?"

"Jocks and GI Joes, man."

"Ah, right. Well, I'll check it out and get back to you. Ladies? Ready to hat up?"

"Wait. Ronda."

Charlie silently thanked the hippie kid for confirming his soon-to-be conquest's name.

"Can I get your number?"

The balls on him! Charlie's respect for Paradigm went up considerably. Of course, he would still have to shut the kid out tonight—business was business.

Ronda darted her eyes at Charlie and back at Paradigm—she clearly thought about it but dreaded the awkwardness of fishing for pen and paper under her sort-of date's gaze, or maybe she imagined her conservative daddy answering the phone and chatting this kid up, but either way, she said, "I think we're going just now. But why don't you come meet us?"

Because he doesn't want to get his scrawny, draft-dodging, nonwhite ass kicked in Rooster Eddie's parking lot, that's why.

"Yeah, come meet us," Charlie said, smiling a shit-eating grin.

"I'll pass," Paradigm said.

"Suit yourself."

Charlie turned and headed for the door. The girls followed in his wake.

HE WALKED THROUGH THE KNOT OF POT-SMELLING KIDS CROWDING AROUND THE front door and crossed University Street diagonally to where his dad's Mustang was parked. As he opened the door and pushed the seat forward so the younger girl could get in, he heard the rumble of a muscle car cruising at an idling trot and saw a new Camaro with its headlights off turn the corner off Kirby (why did he have the impression it had been circling?), flip the lights on, and sidle up next to them. The driver, a bald man, leaned over his boyish passenger to address Charlie.

"That's a helluva nice car."

"Thanks."

"That all yours?"

"You bet," he said.

"Lucky kid."

"Don't I know it," he said, now letting Ronda into the passenger seat of the Mach 1.

"Automatic?"

"No, sir, standard."

"Good boy. Say," the bald man said. "You wouldn't want to, you know, do that thing people do with fast cars to see which of them cars is faster, would you? 'Cause I got fifty bucks says this Camaro's gonna get at least a car length on that 'Stang on a quarter-mile drag. What you think?"

"I don't know, man, I've got places to be," he said, giving a nod to his passengers and smiling a "you know what's up" smile at the older man in the Camaro.

"Aww, c'mon, kid. How often you think I see a car I think's even *maybe* worthy of running up against this here mill?"

"I don't want to race," the younger girl in the back said.

"Yeah, me neither. Let's go to this Rooster place you were talking about," Ronda said.

"What have you got under there, anyway?" Charlie said. "A 351?"

"Maybe, maybe not. That's for you to find out. Ask me where I want to do it."

Charlie said, "Where you want to do it?"

"Now you're talking!" the bald man in the Camaro said.

The smaller blond man in the passenger seat said, "Show me the money, boy."

"This is dumb, Charlie," Ronda said.

Ronda was starting to sound like a pain in the ass.

Charlie flashed some bills.

"So where?" he said.

"I don't know, kid, I'm a Carolina man. Where do the boys with the big britches go to lay a patch in Houston-town?"

"Rankin Road, mostly. On the weekends."

"Ain't gonna be here on the weekend. How about right now?"

"Okay."

"Let us out," Ronda said.

"No, honey, you're gonna stay in the car," the one with the dirty-blond James Dean hair said, and suddenly Ronda wanted very much to stay in the car.

"That's right," the bald one said. "What's a race without race fans? Come on, now, lead the way!"

The Mustang pulled away now, closely shadowed by the Camaro, both cars rumbling their way through the streets of Rice Village, on north toward the brand-new airport.

The younger girl, Becky Ann Davis of Tomball, said, "Where are we going? Are we really going to race? I'd rather not, please," but nobody listened. Not her gently drooling friend in the front seat. Not the wild-eyed boy at the wheel of the Mustang. Not even the large man with the neck brace who, when the cars pulled even, leaned forward from his backseat post in the Camaro and seemed, for just a moment, to be trying to read her lips.

45

THE CAMARO SS AND THE VAN SAT NEXT TO ONE ANOTHER NEXT TO A SUNFLOWER field just off the Will Rogers Turnpike northeast of Tulsa. Judith bent over a bucket of water she had half filled at the last service station and used a stolen hunk of soap to wash her hair and to get as much blood as she could out of the white coif and her novice's white veil.

Clayton sat looking at the book he had pulled from under the Camaro's passenger seat, a Rand McNally atlas that had been packaged as a *Chevrolet's Family Travel Guide*, featuring beach, mountain, and sunset vistas in the front along with helpful hints about bird watching, camping, and rock collecting. The back contained pages of car games for kids to play, including "bury the cow," "license plate poker," and the naïvely named "stink-pink," next to which someone had written

Luther's Favorite!

Stickers representing pigs and cows and other barnyard animals had been peeled out of a sheet of stickers in the back and affixed to a barnyard scene, and on another page the names of about half of the state capitals had been crookedly pasted next to their states. Whether this had been done by bored vampires or the children of some unfortunate family was anyone's guess. Clayton resolved not to show Judith any of this, nor the pictures of happy wheat-blond children smiling safely in their backseats. He turned instead to page sixty, where a dark green line representing I-40 and Route 66 crossed nearly straight through New Mexico, curving up left of Albuquerque like a snake waking up to strike at Gallup. All along this line were dots and stars in different colors of ink. Some penman with less-legible script had scratched *Moriarty* just right of Clines Corners. At the top margin of the page, *x—good mine* had been written, with corresponding *x*'s clustered southeast of Albuquerque, but especially near Thoreau and Bluewater. The word *uranium* had been scrawled near one such *x* so small as to be barely legible. Clayton knew how valuable abandoned mines were—his own fold-out map had not a few marked on it—though he favored pinholes that would show up when the map was pressed to a backlit window or laid over a bright color.

Judith came over now, her hair dripping down to wet the collar of her shirt, and peered over his shoulder, touching her fingers to her mouth at the sight of several dots near Clines Corners.

"That's where it happened," she said, pointing. "Do you think . . . ?"

"Those dots could mean anything," he said. "But one thing they certainly mean."

"This is the road they use to cross west."

"My thought exactly."

"We're ahead of them," she said. "I know it. But we need to stay that way."

"That'll be easy," he said. "We can dump the van and put me in the trunk for the daylight stretch."

"We'll need a van. Or a truck. But not necessarily that one."

"You have an idea," he said.

"You won't like it."

"The only idea I *would* like would be for us to leave the vengeance part to the Lord, as I believe it says in one of your texts, and go spend the rest of the summer in Patagonia, where the days are nice and short. Any chance of that?"

She gave him a look.

"Yes, that was a proper nun's look. Well done. I stand rebuked. What horrible thing am I doing?"

"You're joining the Suicide Motor Club. And so am I."

THEY ABANDONED THE VAN NEAR THE SUNFLOWERS.

Clayton drove for most of the night while she drifted in and out of consciousness in the backseat. The highway's white lines ran at him and ran at him and never exhausted themselves.

Their conversation echoed in his mind through most of Oklahoma. He would always remember her with her damp hair, leaning conspiratorially close while she told him what she intended to do. There was no question of him talking her out of it. Neither was there any question of his failure to do what she asked.

I would prefer not to kill any of them myself.

Will you if it comes down to it?

If it's that or watch one of them harm you, then yes.

I want you to destroy them even if I die, Clayton.

I won't promise that. So you'd better not die.

I think I will, though.

It sounds like you will.

Destroy them, Clayton.

And then myself?

Yes.

Isn't that a mortal sin?

For me, yes. Not for you, I think.

But isn't that what what you're doing to yourself amounts to?

No. It's up to them.

I still don't see what's in it for me.

Something must be or we wouldn't still be talking about it.

Perhaps.

Maybe you've caught the scent of your own redemption.

No.

You say no, but you're not sure. You're on new ground.

Stop it, please.

All right. But I can trust you? To do what I ask?

I don't know.

I do. I know.

Then why ask?

You're right. I take it back. I know I can trust you.

But if you die, all bets are off.

I understand.

I reserve the right to flee like a coward.

If you say so.

And then they stood with the night wind in the sunflowers and he touched her damp hair and she permitted this.

The lie you tell my eyes is a pretty one, she said.

As is the lie your eyes tell my heart.

They shared a gaze two seconds too long.

Jude looked away.

We can't be lovers.

Who wants you anyway?

She smiled.

He tangled her hair into his fingers and pulled a little hard. She did not wince. Rather she put her fingers in his hair and pulled it the same way he had pulled hers.

Maybe I'll kill you after all, he said.

Then maybe I'll die, she had said, offering a smile he did not return. A shadow passed over his face.

I could, you know. If I had any sense. Drain you and leave you in the sunflowers.

I love sunflowers.

Do you?

They're my favorite.

Why so?

There was a Greek myth. About a girl who loved the sun god so much she turned into a sunflower to watch him all day. I can't remember the names.

She was Klytia. He was Helios.

But the idea stayed with me. It's a beautiful image. I think about God like that.

I do, too.

Really?

Yes. Because Klytia loved a god that could not or would not love her back. She sat herself upon a hill and wasted away for eight days. No food. No drink. And all because Helios had abandoned her for another nymph. But I believe she died awfully. And the other gods so pitied Klytia, watching her brilliant lothario ride his chariot brilliantly across his brilliant sky, that they turned her into a turnsole. Not a sunflower, by the way. Sunflowers are native to North America. Ovid never met a sunflower. Anyway, there's the god you've stayed chaste for. Ever noticed how closely chaste *rhymes with* waste*? Will we really not be lovers?*

We will really not be lovers.

And yet you let me touch your hair.

Yes.

What else will you permit?

Nothing.

She drew back then.

You're using me, he said.

Yes.

He had considered this, looking at the pale, warm face of the woman whose fate suddenly mattered to him. When had that begun? The moment he saw her cross the road? When she defied Luther Nixon despite her helplessness and the murder in his heart? She had an idea about how to confront her much more powerful foes. She didn't know what would happen after the opening gambit, but she trusted that it would be pleasing to her God.

All right, Clayton had said. *Use me.*

46

JUDITH WOKE AN HOUR BEFORE DAWN, SWITCHED TO THE FRONT PASSENGER SEAT while he gassed them up.

On they rode. At first light, she would load him into that purgatorial trunk and wrap him in blankets next to the bag containing her cross and holy water, the bag they had taken from the impound lot in Joplin. Watching the ease with which Clayton charmed the night watchman out of the keys to the van and the bag, which normally would have cost them ten dollars to liberate, had been instructive—*this was how they lived among us so long without discovery, this ability to wipe or alter memory.* Was it possible that he was doing it to her? Did she now hold false memories that masked things he wished to hide from her? *Had* he fed?

No.

He fed on the night watchman, though.

He had asked her to go to the car while he did, but she had insisted on watching.

Why?

So I never forget what you are.

Despite the need for blood he shared with the killers, she believed Clayton would stand with her against them. But what did that make him? On one hand, she was grateful not to see him as a monster anymore. On the other hand, the image he projected was so handsome, so engaging, that she found herself craving his company. His touch, though she perceived it as cool, made her skin react as though he were warm. Though she knew it could in no way be organic, she wanted him sexually in a way that she had not wanted even her husband since the first year of their marriage. The realization shamed her at first, until she reasoned out that it must be part of the same illusion that made her see him as a living man of thirty rather than a century-old cadaver. It was not her fault that she felt these things—she had no more choice in the matter than a fever victim had in hallucinating. If she found him attractive, it was just a by-product of the grace that allowed her to see him without feeling a distracting repulsion. At least the good Lord had shown him to her as he truly was before setting this pleasant mask on him. And yet there was something to the way he spoke, something in his voice not unlike a purr. His intelligence was even more appealing than his wide-set, gentle eyes and thick hair. The things he said, even when she knew he was tempting her, tempted her.

When this is all over, he had said, *if we both survive, I invite you to come visit me. I have a home in New England, a place I own and pay taxes on in my own name—a place I pay a gardener to tend and a handyman to repair.*

Why don't you stay there?

It would kill me to stay still.

Literally?

I think so, yes. New experiences refresh what's left of my soul. I go home once a year or so for short visits, usually at All Souls Day.

Do you have a proper coffin?

Actually, yes.

Do you have a spare coffin for guests?

Actually, yes. Which brings me to another point.

Don't even say it.

I can make you what I am.

I asked you not to say it.

I don't want you to answer me now.

I just did.

I only propose that we consider one another's offers. You offer me eternal life, in the form of redemption and final death? Then I have every right to offer you the closest thing to eternal life I can fully believe in. If salvation is possible for me . . .

I don't know that it is.

But if it is, it might be possible for you as well, even if you join me in my night of lovely colors.

Is it lovely?

It's indescribable. But unlike your pearly gates, I can swear to the existence of the afterlife I propose.

Heaven isn't pearly gates.

What then?

Union with the divine.

We are already divine, if there is divinity.

No, Clayton. We're not. Maybe a small part of us is, but that's the part we sell when we try to make this short life better.

Theories.

Not theories. I know.

You say you know, I say you don't, and here we have the classic impasse. Faith versus reason. May I kiss you?

No.

Very well. But when this is over, should we get separated, come to me on All Hallows' Eve. If you come by night, I'll know you wish to be my lover.

How her body had betrayed her when he said that. Like a small, warm well opening in dry ground.

I won't.

Maybe. But you'll think about it.

If I come, it will be by day. To release you from this.

Very well. If I'm in my coffin at sunrise, drag it to the rear garden. Most of the grounds are well shaded, but there's a place near a statue of an angel where the sun hits red maple trees. Face me to the sun and open the lid.

Where's the coffin?

The basement.

Don't you lock yourself in?

I won't that night, or that day.

How will I know you're in there?

By the weight.

You mean this?

Yes. If I remain in my home, in my coffin at daybreak, November first, the year of our lord one thousand, nine hundred and sixty-nine, it means I've accepted your offer.

I'll pray for you to be there.

As I'll pray for you to come at dusk the night before. I've got a bed with soft sheets and goose feather pillows.

So where exactly is this home?

I'll tell you if we live.

She murmured her half of the conversation to herself as she drove.

A stranger would have thought she was praying.

HALF AN HOUR BEFORE I-40 CROSSED INTO AMARILLO, SHE GOT TIRED. SHE started scanning the road for motels but broke out in a cold sweat.

Her field of vision doubled for a moment and she saw herself seized and held by the monsters, all five of them. One had each limb. Luther had her head. They pulled her apart.

Clayton pulled over in a cloud of dust, putting his hazard lights on.

"Are you well?"

"I will be. Give me a minute," she said, her voice shaking.

"Do we need to stop? We could wait for them here."

"Not here. We need to get them near morning. They'll cross here in the thick of the night. We won't fight them here."

"Why not?"

"We'll lose."

SHE CHECKED INTO THE CACTUS FLOWER MOTEL IN THE VILLAGE OF SANTA Estrella, New Mexico, under the name Mary English. The day was bright, the temperature well over ninety degrees. She moved Clayton out of the broiling trunk by helping cover him with the tarp therein; he staggered through the burning light huddled in his rectangular oasis of shade and collapsed in the room, which she had already screened off with blinds and towels. He retched for a solid minute before he could stand again, though he stood only long enough to kiss her hand in thanks and then to blockade himself under the bed closest to the wall. The window air conditioner hummed and rattled to protest its herculean job staving off the July New Mexico sun. She put the *Do Not Disturb* sign on the doorknob, ate the rest of the hamburger she had picked up in Tucumcari, and drank from the spigot of the bathroom sink. She showered in cool water and stood naked before the mirror for a very long time, tracing the scars on her face, the slightly deflated breasts and belly she'd had since Glendon came, the hard shelves of her collarbones. She did not do this for vanity's sake. She did not know why she did it at first, but then it occurred to her that she was saying good-bye to her body.

"Thy will be done," she said, and dressed once again in the habit of her order.

Am I still a member of that order? Have they filed the paperwork with the Vatican to have me expelled for abandoning my abbey? Does it matter, so long as I have faith? I'm so very scared.

She sat on the nearer bed and opened the nightstand drawer, pulling out the brown Gideon Bible. Underneath it she found a tiny diamond earring with no back, which she did not pick up.

Do not be distracted

As much to keep her mind from fear as to arm herself spiritually, she spent most of the afternoon in prayer. At three o'clock, she fulfilled the divine office for the hour of Nones, reading the story of Samson from the book of Judges. She spoke in whispers, and when she sang, she sang her *Te Deum* and other hymns in a small voice. If any of this bothered Clayton in his blanket bunker under the bed, he had the good taste to keep it to himself.

At four o'clock, she went shopping for cans and jars.

At six o'clock, she went to the gas station and started filling them. She also bought a foldable map of the state and a couple of hard caramels.

The sun went down just before eight thirty and Clayton drove back east to Santa Rosa to charm someone out of a van.

THE KILLERS LEFT THE CRACKED, OVERGROWN TIRE SHOP AND AUTO GARAGE IN the mostly abandoned town of McLean, Texas, at eight thirty. Luther drove his new Mustang, and Neck Brace rode with him. Cole drove the COPO with Calcutta riding shotgun. Rob climbed wearily into the cab of the truck, though only after remarking that he "wouldn't drive this piece of shit forever."

He was right.

PART FIVE

The Dead

47

CLAYTON WAITED IN THE VAN, A 1960 CHEVY STEP VAN. ITS OWNER, CHUY, A MEX-ican American house painter, would not remember the nocturnal rapping at the trailer door that he answered with his double-barreled shotgun in hand, nor handing over this gun and car keys, nor going to the bedroom to fetch his visitor the half-full box of shells. He would not remember sitting obediently on the rickety kitchen chair with his chin up, like a man waiting for the barber to start his shave, nor would he understand why he woke up the next morning woozy and headachy, with an oil slick on the gravel drive where his van should have been. His wife, Consuelo, would not remember being ordered back to bed, nor understand why her pillowcase was soaked with spit. Only after they called the police to report the theft of the vehicle would Chuy notice the ten gold double eagle coins stacked neatly near his telephone. Judith had asked Clayton not to ruin anybody with his theft and had offered to pay him back for whatever he spent, should she survive. Clayton had agreed to this arrangement, but only because he wanted her tethered to the future by as many lines as possible. Her plan to deal with the monsters was as close to suicide as one could get without tying a noose around one's neck and stepping off a stool.

Clayton's role in the operation wasn't much less foolhardy, even with his ability to survive catastrophic injury and heal rapidly. He would almost certainly suffer catastrophic injury.

His signal to injure himself would be three flashes of a handheld flashlight half a mile away.

He watched the horizon all night.

It was nearly morning when things began to happen.

JUDITH SAT WITH A BLANKET AROUND HER, AS MUCH TO HIDE HER HABIT AS TO keep the desert's cold night air from sapping her strength. She sat Indian-style behind a bush, a pair of binoculars from Clayton's pack in her lap. He also had a telescope, an old brass one, he said. He liked being able to see people before they saw him. The Camaro sat behind the shell of a junked and rusted Blue Bird school bus skirted with creosote bushes and allthorn, invisible from the road. Fear of death only nibbled at her—she was all but certain she was fulfilling God's plan and trusted that whatever awaited her on the other side would be just and right. That she might see Glendon again was too sweet a possibility for her to hope for, but she weakened and prayed for exactly that. Even if she was wrong and Clayton right—that the sky was only atmosphere and the cosmos steered itself rudderless through an endless night—the prospect of non-existence seemed, at worst, bitter and bracing. She thought of oblivion as black coffee, and wondered if the peace of not-being was in fact the heaven she and so many others had been promised. Her greater fear shamed her, and that was the fear of death's pain. For as much as she tried to think of death as a sort of birth, the thought of death by fire made her bladder feel loose. She intended to wreck the '67 Camaro, with its full gas tank and trunk full of gasoline in tin drums and glass jars, only as a last resort, but if she went kamikaze, she didn't want whatever she ran into walking away after. She knew fire wasn't guaranteed in a wreck, however much gas was splashed around, but this car *moved* and she had every intention of mashing that gas pedal at her foe if it came to that. Also, she carried a Zippo in the pouch at her cincture; she did not know how many crash scenarios would leave her in any shape to operate a lighter, but she wanted the option to help the fire along if she found herself able to. Also, fire might be a fine incentive to make one of them tell her what happened to Glendon, should she find one trapped or hurt.

"Thy will be done, thy eternal will be done."

You're talking to nothing

Shut up Clayton Birch

She had the Italian cross and the remaining bottles of holy water on the passenger seat and the gun on the floor—she should not touch the pistol while she wore the veil and scapular. She would be as close to holy and pure as she could.

The gun was just in case.

The gun might be for her.

Suicide was a mortal sin, but surely God would not want her turned into an abomination. Would he? Were these things part of creation, or were they aberrations created by evil? The latter made more sense, but she just didn't know. She knew nothing but that these five monsters had to die, and if she could not kill them all, she must destroy the one whose human name was Luther Nixon.

Just after midnight she saw a car with no lights on go by, but it was a station wagon—not their style—and it was too early. She felt in her bones, skin, and hair that this place just out of sight of Santa Estrella was the place to stop, that this would bring the fight to them with sunrise at their backs. Still, she had felt panic rise up in her at the thought of driving, and so near where she had wrecked in '67. How much farther on was Clines Corners? Thirty miles? She shuddered and clutched the St. Christopher medal Clayton had given her and breathed deeply and slowly until the panic went away.

She dozed off shortly after three A.M.

48

"I LOVE THIS SUMBITCH," LUTHER SAID TO NECK BRACE. "I MEAN, I'VE LOVED CARS before, I'm a car-lovin' man, but there's somethin' really sublime about this one. That's the word for it, *sublime*. You know that word?"

Neck Brace just looked forward.

Blinked once.

"Course you do. Sublime's what you get when you put art into something. Anybody can make a fast car these days, but hell. Drivin' this car's a little like fuckin'. Not that I get to do that much with ole ball-buster ridin' wingman, not that I'd trade him. Not the first ball-buster I known, either. Other one was from Georgia, too. Bottle blonde named Dolores. Stop me if I told you all this already. You not contributin' to the conversation and all, it's hard to form lastin' memories of our talks. It's a little like these crazy old women talkin' to their cats; bet a cat hears the same story three, four, five times, more if the biddy's getting senile. You're a little like a cat that way, no offense meant. Tell you honest, I kinda like ridin' with you, not only 'cause you're a wreckin' ball on wheels, but also 'cause you don't interrupt."

Neck Brace looked forward.

Blinked once.

The road rushed under the wheels while the big engine purred, though it would have taken a vampire to see that road. There wasn't much of a moon and the lights were off. Likewise the lights on the '69 COPO and F100 truck following behind in their infernal caravan. The F100 was the only reason they were going this slowly.

Doing eighty wasn't a chore for the Mustang.

It could have done eighty in its sleep.

Luther talked.

Luther liked to talk.

***BACK IN '55 AFTER I BURNT UP THAT CARLISLE KID, I HAD JUST MOVED IN WITH** old Dolores. I hadn't never lived with no woman before or since, and that was the closest to married I ever want to come. You shoulda seen her the way I first seen her, standin' there at the Lakewood Speedway with her soda pop in her hand, that was '54, wearin' a red dress and everything. She later admitted she come fishin' for me, and damn if she didn't catch me. She had her hair all platinum blond, she called it ash blond, and I don't care who you are, you'd'a stumbled all over yourself for a chance to talk to her. I asked her why didn't she take a run at Penry Carlisle like every other head south of the Mason-Dixon, and know what she said? She said she already had him and he wasn't mean enough for her, and then she laughed so I never knew if she was funnin' me. She wasn't nothing but a kid, twenty years old. Too young for me then, I know, and the thing about a young woman twenty years old is she may have growed-up titties, although Dolores had kinda small titties, but the point is she don't know who she is yet and she's gonna find out on your dime. But you spend that dime every time. Even the way she talked was sexy, like thick honey pourin' out of her lips. She took her time talkin', gave you time to watch them lips. Thing is, that pretty little girl could drive, like no-shit drive. Just for fun I took her out on the clay track and let her run my '53 Corvette. Not that I was a Chevy man, never was, but somebody else was stakin' me just then. Stakin' me! Anyway, this girl just about creamed her* *jeans when she vroom-vroomed that motor. She took us around that track like the devil, slammin' us both around and me sayin', "Don't wreck this rod, I don't own it!" but I was laughin' it as much as sayin' it, so she didn't take me serious. She didn't wreck it, though. I think she stayed with me as long as she did because I let her drive, and I stayed with her because she* could *drive, and too well for me to treat her like any other old piece of ass. But I did anyway. I shouldn't'a never cheated on her, but I cheated on everybody, so shoot me. Well, she didn't shoot me. Know what she did? Fucked the girl I cheated on her with, if you can fairly call that fuckin'. Seems like all them slit-kissers can do is what you and me do as a warm-up. Well, me at least. I can't picture you between nobody's legs, I think that face a' yours'd close a pussy tighter than one of them diver-killin' giant clams on the sea bed, no offense. Well, old Dolores must a' drove a tongue pretty good, 'cause that other girl never give me the time a' day again. And Dolores? She said she'd always love me but she wouldn't be my lover no more, she done found out who she really was and would I please pack my shit. I thought about the way Mitch Lily woulda handled it up on the mountain. I thought about choking her little ass right then. But even if I thought I coulda beat the rap, which I couldn'ta, and even if I was sure I wasn't too drunk to keep her from wriggling out and shootin' me, which I wasn't sure, I couldn't do it. I genuine loved her. And part of her held me in contempt for not doin' it. Killin' her, I mean. Thing is, I did kill her. Later. 'Cause after I turned I didn't want to see nobody from my former life ever again, 'cept her. Only her. Meant to just talk to her but drank her dry. And she fought and cursed me the whole way down for it, and I had the feelin' she hated me for takin' her life from her just when she was figurin' out how to enjoy it, but also she loved me for bein' strong enough to do that. Which is fucked up, but that's why we ain't in the Garden of Eden no more. And the angel with the fiery sword ain't ever lettin' us back in.*

49

WHEN JUDITH WOKE UP, SHE COULDN'T REMEMBER HER DREAM, NOR WHERE SHE was. When she looked at her watch it said five A.M. and she shook it as if that might change the verdict of the hands. She broke out in a cold sweat despite the deep chill in the air. She and Clayton had agreed that one flash of the light would be a "check-in," to be answered by the other. Two flashes meant *come here.* Three meant go. She pointed her flashlight west and flashed her light once. He flashed back.

He must be getting anxious about the time. He had told her about an abandoned train car he had scouted out one exit east and two miles south on a little dirt path called Bethany Road. He didn't trust staying one day at a hotel, let alone two, what with nosy owners and curious maids. He said he had found a large tool locker in the van and set this up in the train car like a tiny coffin.

"You'd be surprised what we can fit into," he'd told her. Luther Nixon had set such a poor example that she scanned his comment for double entendre, pleased at first to find none, then ashamed of herself for thinking that way.

She peered east. First light bled into the sky, turning its eastern lip from star-shot pitch to the color of a dirty coin. A waning crescent moon rose yellow and murky a straight-arm hands' length up from the horizon.

"Major Nelson, this is mission control," she said, though she could not bring herself to finish.

Do you see the moon?

That was when she saw the needle of fire.

A shooting star over the desert, south of her.

Thou art with me Thou art

It was close enough she thought she heard its hiss and crackle, but this sound soon morphed into a metallic purr as she heard the sound of engines. Big ones. Moving fast. Getting closer.

She saw no headlights.

Her heart hammered in her chest.

Her palm was so moist she nearly dropped the flashlight.

A muted flash of dark metal shot by her, its big engine growling.

A darker car followed.

At a distance, a big pickup truck.

She broke cover and ran for the menacing black sports car where it crouched behind the husk of the bus. She ran so fast and with such pure intent that she almost forgot to use the flashlight.

Almost.

CLAYTON SAT BEHIND THE WHEEL OF THE VAN COGITATING.

Judith had just shone the light once, and he had been terrified two more signals would follow. He was relieved when they did not, gladly flashing her back as they had agreed.

To say that he was having second thoughts would have been insufficient. He was close to outright mutiny. He was actively imagining driving off, just leaving this sad, beautiful madwoman to her martyrdom and taking Chuy's van south to Mexico before word of its theft got to the border. If he survived the action he was supposed to take, there was a significant chance the others would kill him in the aftermath.

He did not have Judith's faith in her ability to deal with one vampire, let alone five, although he had once seen a priest's handiwork against the undead and understood there might be something to it. But then he had also known a woman who called herself a witch and did remarkable things, things he could not explain scientifically.

To him, there was little to choose between spells and prayer, between magic and divine assistance.

Perhaps it's a matter of will, he thought.

Perhaps some individuals cause things to happen, and whether they call it witchcraft or prayer matters little. If, for example, I saw a shooting star a moment after thinking of one, is it some communication with the divine? Or is it that time is less ordered than we think? Perhaps I knew about the event because I would witness it at some point in my continuum and my awareness somehow skipped, like a record on its track? All of this philosophy is well and good, but I have a very real decision to make about whether I am to carry forward with my quixotic mission.

"I'm going," he told no one. "I will not murder myself for a . . . doomed infatuation. One that I will scarce remember three feedings from now."

He turned the keys in the ignition switch, heard the tired rumble of the Chevy's engine—Chuy had put almost two hundred thousand miles on it. He put his foot on the brake and he was just about to put the big van into gear.

That was when he saw it.

"My shooting star," he said. A smile broke across his face. "Something remarkable has just happened." He shut the van off and sat amazed.

In the distance, he saw the flashlight flash once.

Even though he heard the engines, his mind had been so preoccupied with the falling star that he had not processed their significance.

He prepared to flash once in response to her, as he had done a few minutes before, but then his thumb froze on the switch.

She flashed two more times.

Now the sound of the powerful engines and the absence of headlights registered with him. He moved fast. Clayton peered down I-40 and saw them. Only a vampire or a night bird would have seen them, but he did.

Luther and the others driving dark and fast as if they might outrun the sun's true rising still nearly an hour hence. He started the van's engine again. It stalled but then caught the second time. He put the van in gear and trundled it out toward the highway from its side of the rise that mostly concealed it.

The time was 5:02 A.M.

50

LUTHER COULD SEE SOMETHING MOVING OVER THE ROCKY HUMP OF RAISED EARTH, and he jogged his wheel to the left just enough to miss the thing, and as he shot by he perceived that it was a big ugly van with a smiling sun holding a paintbrush, Spanish writing, a pale figure at its wheel. He hit the gas to clear it and rapidly shot his speedometer over 110.

Neck Brace had half turned in his seat but still couldn't see. Luther heard the sound of the first impact and peeked in the rearview to see the second. The COPO had spun out—Cole had nearly eluded the boxy missile as well but ran out of asphalt and got clipped hard on the right rear wheel, tearing off the rear bumper and bending his axle.

"Jee-ZUS," Luther said, still peering at the tiny drama receding in his mirror. Neck Brace hit the back of his seat twice, his eyes wide as an ape's, his lips drawn back to show his fangs and the small stream of biting-drool washing out. Neck Brace was always eager to fight.

"I know, I know," Luther said, slowing the Mustang down to eighty, seventy, fifty. "I just want to get a little space to see what it is we're goin' back there to kill."

He executed a J-turn and came to a stop facing back east, his tires pouring acrid, nose-wrinkling smoke into the night air. He saw a small fire in the distance, made out the destroyed truck and the shower of clothes and paper still falling. Now he saw movement far away, very hard to make out. Another car coming with its headlights off, but then they flicked on as it encountered debris from the wreck. Cole's old car. Not the '69 COPO Camaro. The '67 SS. The fucking Boston vampire's fucking whore nun.

Coming at him.

"I want this bitch to see me," he said. He flipped his headlights on bright.

The '67 Chevy kept coming, straight on at him.

He grinned.

"Guess she sees me," he said. "Let's see how bad she wants to play."

He screeched his tires, burning Goodyear redwall rubber off the line, throwing Neck Brace back against his seat.

The cars drove at each other.

Luther had never hit anybody head-on at these speeds.

He wasn't so sure his head would stay on.

Neck Brace looked at him from the side of his eye as if he knew what Luther was thinking.

The black Camaro came on.

Neck Brace grinned a savage, illuminated grin, as if something he had been waiting his whole life for were finally about to happen.

Luther kept the pedal down.

Back in North Carolina during the Depression, he had known a tobacco farmer who had tried to teach him what a rebel yell sounded like, though the old-timer hadn't had much left in the lungs department.

Back then, when young Luther gave it a go, the old reb told Luther he got it just about right.

Now Luther's lungs were dead, but they could still hold a lot of air.

He still had loud cords on him.

Luther sucked in.

Luther yelled.

HALF A MILE EAST, CLAYTON STRUGGLED TO GET HIS NEARLY FUNCTIONING EYE opened. When he pinched the lids open with the two fingers of his hand that worked, he could see in a sort of yellowish tunnel. The step van had been opened up in the middle like a lobster, he remembered that, but the truck had hit him so hard both vehicles had caught air and he had landed upside-down. Gasoline from the truck had spilled and a small puddle of it burned, but far enough away it might not catch either of the catastrophically wrecked vehicles.

"Here's hoping," he tried to say, but his mouth only bubbled and fizzed, showering an almost-clear liquid. He tried to laugh, but that sounded even worse. His hand was better now. He felt the wrist join back up more smoothly, it had felt badly impinged, and now his eye stayed open on its own, its fellow twitching and offering him glimpses of stereo vision. With effort, he was able to crunch the bones of his foot together and hug his tibia and fibula close enough to extricate his right leg from under the hot, hissing steel of the cracked engine block. He looked up and saw Chuy's shotgun sticking absurdly through the passenger door of the van, which was much closer than it should have been. He heard an engine, thought it was the car he had clipped, couldn't see it from its angle but heard the grinding of its hobbled wheel, the shrieking of wrecked metal. He heard car doors open and chunk shut.

He grabbed the gun.

It didn't want to come out.

He heard another car coming, squealing all the way, fishtailing, clipping something.

He pulled the shotgun harder.

It came out.

Cole yelled, "Holy fuck!"

Calcutta screamed as the car went squealing by.

He heard a vicious, rolling wreck in the distance, the screech of a car grinding to a stop on its roof or side, a moan of pain.

Cole said, "Let's get this one first."

JUDITH PULLED OUT FROM HER HIDING SPOT BEHIND THE BUS, THE TIRES SPITTING gravel behind her as the powerful car jerked forward, scratching up against a creosote bush, running over yellow grass and clumps of ephedra. She careened onto Interstate 40 dark, knowing they could probably see her anyway, but knowing even a split second of surprise could make a difference. Not long after she pulled out, she saw motion up ahead, heard the sound of a devastating wreck, yelped and jerked the wheel as a piece of camper shell hit her windshield, chipping it and spinning away. She flicked on her headlights just in time to avoid a huge piece of bumper flipping at her as clothes, paint cans, and other flotsam showered down. The pickup truck Rob had been driving had all but exploded on impact, and the van hadn't fared better. She swerved to avoid the two hulks even as they rocked or spun to their final positions, a small pool of fire flaring to her right. Cole's lamed '69 had gone into the scrub and was now fighting its way back onto the road. Judith was already too far past it to hit it on this pass, and anyway it wasn't the Beta driver she wanted.

Luther I'm coming Luther

She got clear and launched herself forward, scanning the road for him. A pair of lights came on several hundred yards ahead, floated to straddle the center line and accelerated. She punched the gas as well, shifting jerkily all the way up, biting her lower lip in concentration. Time slowed down. Her vision tunneled. Everything was the road and the enemy's headlamps.

Thou preparest a table

I surrender my body

I surrender

The road between the cars flashed away to almost nothing.

The headlights speeding at her were hot, lethal moons.

She imagined she could feel the sway of all that gasoline in the Camaro's hips.

The other car came on.

Close.

Closer.

She could hear its motor roaring in a suicidal duet with hers.

A Mustang

I'm going to be killed by a Mustang

Judith closed her eyes at the end.

LUTHER'S YELL BOUNCED AROUND IN THE SPEEDING MUSTANG.

Neck Brace had his mouth open in excitement or fear or both, looking for all the world like a mandrill yawning.

Luther was ready to hit but at the last second anticipated massive pain and maybe even death and suddenly hoped she'd turn.

Turn witch-bitch turn, he thought, and still she came on.

Then Luther saw her.

Her mouth open in a keening wail, her eyes wet with tears, her hands white on the wheel.

He understood in a flash.

This witch-bitch *wasn't going to turn.*

Not for him.

Not for the devil on an ICBM.

Shes ready to die goddamn if she aint turn TURN

"TURN! TURN!" Luther yelled, and rocked at the wheel.

But she didn't.

So he did.

He jogged right.

If she had been watching she could have turned into him and caught him, but her eyes were closed now and the Mach 1's bumper shot past the wedgelike nose of the '67 SS without a playing card's breadth to spare. Luther corrected left, but his car was already eating dirt, bucking in grama grass and rocks. He fishtailed, caught the road again, but bucked on a rock so hard it brought him up to bounce his head on the ceiling and when he came down, in his confusion and unfamiliarity with the new car he hit the gas instead of the brake. Luther and Neck Brace rocketed at the wrecked truck and van, sparks flying behind his trailing muffler. To his credit, he threaded that wreck brilliantly—a lesser driver would have caught the truck where it lay twisted and smoking on its side or wiped out on the torn skin of the step van, crushing Cole and Calcutta where they crouched down looking for the inverted van's driver, but he missed them all, though closely enough for Cole to yell "Holy fuck!" as Luther screamed by him.

But as Luther dodged the back of the van, he knew he had too much swing and now he fishtailed again. His rear tire hit a length of the van's rear axle and he rolled. Hard. The last thing he saw before he flipped was a yellowish piece of the moon where it rose in the east, and then everything spun and he was bounced and broken and cut in more places than he knew.

The Mustang came to rest on its roof, a cloud of dust pluming around it.

"LET'S GET THIS ONE FIRST," COLE HAD JUST SAID, TAKING HIS REVOLVER IN HAND and crouching as he cleared the inverted van's blind spot. He peeked under its nose just in time to see Clayton Birch aiming Chuy's gun at him. He pulled back fast, but not fast enough. The shot tore the top of his head clean off, but only the top. He fell backward, dropped his gun, blinked rapidly, and made a gagging noise as his brain tried to re-form itself.

Calcutta stumbled backward, shocked. So shocked she didn't register the sound of the '67's engine picking up steam as Judith negotiated it through the debris field. The black Camaro accelerated hard when it had Calcutta in its sights. It smacked into her at about forty miles an hour, shunting her up the hood and through the windshield.

CLAYTON, NOW STRONG ENOUGH TO STAND, SLID OUT OF THE POOL OF BLOOD AND motor oil he had been wallowing in and limped through gunsmoke toward the prone form of Cole. Judith's car had just swept Calcutta away. He leveled the shotgun at Cole's neck, meaning to give him the second barrel, but Rob shambled into sight, trying to yank the truck's shifter out of the tangle of his ribs with one hand, aiming his own gun at Clayton with the other. He fired, clipping Clay's chin, the bullet making a funny zipping noise as it spun away. Clayton wheeled and shot now, taking off half of Rob's face, spinning him so he landed in a heap around the truck's shifter impaling him.

CALCUTTA CAME THROUGH JUDITH'S WINDSHIELD IN A HEAP, STUNNING HER WITH one flailing arm, but equally stunned herself. Judith managed to stomp the brake and stop the car on the highway's shoulder, braking so hard that the cross and two of the bottles joined the gun on the passenger-side floor. A headlight was coming from the east, but she had no time to concern herself with that—the car was full of broken glass and the cold, stinking muscular thing she had just collided with. She reached under the momentarily bewildered monster half in her lap and grabbed one of the vials of Lourdes holy water from beneath her haunch. But now Calcutta turned. She lunged at Judith, meaning to bite her face, but Judith got her left arm up. A fang punctured her forearm, made it blaze with pain. She struggled to get that arm across her body, awkwardly protecting her face from Calcutta's teeth by hunching her shoulder and writhing her face away. At last she got her left hand to where her right one held the bottle, pulled the cap off. At that moment Calcutta pulled Jude's veil and coif half off and yanked her head back by her hair. She managed to get her face past Jude's shoulder and bit her savagely on the jaw. Jude made a gagging yell but, despite her bad angle, managed to splash a drop of the water on Calcutta's back. The effect was astonishing.

Calcutta bowed her back and reared her head up, shuddering. A drop of Jude's blood fell from one fang onto Jude's white scapular. Something hissed and smoked; the roof of the car was briefly illuminated as if by a sparkler. Jude tried to empty the rest of the bottle on her, but now the thing knew what was happening. She turned cat-quick and grabbed the wrist that held the bottle, forced it up the seat and away, cranked Jude's wrist back toward her so the contents of the bottle spilled into Jude's eyes and all over her white veil and wimple. She flung Jude's wrist so the bottle flew out the window and broke on the street. Now she punched Jude's face, knocking her back. The angle had been too awkward for her to break Jude's jaw or stave in her skull, as she had intended, so she instinctively reached for Jude's chest to push herself up and get good striking distance. When the palm of her hand touched the wet veil, however, she screamed. Upon contact with the holy water, Calcutta's hand burned blue-white as though it were some flammable metal ignited by a welder's torch. She scrambled away from Jude and out the passenger door, shaking her now-smoking hand to try to put it out, but Jude was up and grabbing the gun and a fresh bottle of holy water. She followed Calcutta out the open door. She wanted to shoot her, but that was animal fury and she needed something else for this. She tossed the gun down on the shoulder of the highway. She crossed herself, opened the bottle, and splashed it on Calcutta. The vampire burned as before, though now on her face and breast, and on a patch of her scalp, screaming, "Stop! It hurts! It hurts so much!" Judith splashed her again in three cruciform gouts, shouting, *"In nomine Patris et Fili et Spiritu Sancti!"* even as the vampire flared and shrieked and shook, at last crumpling into a heap at Judith's feet and smoldering like a pile of burning leaves.

Moved by something that felt outside herself, she knelt and made the sign of the cross on Calcutta's dry, smoking forehead, saying, *"Sublata est maledictio. Memoret Deus misericordiam tuam."*

A motorcycle rushed past her, its driver turning his head at the sight of her in her habit, the smoldering corpse nearby, but she could do nothing for him.

She didn't even look when she heard him crash behind her.

She grabbed the cross and another bottle and walked east toward the wreck of Luther's car.

CLAYTON SAW THE SMOKE AND BLAZE OF CALCUTTA'S ENDING. HE SAW JUDE MAKING her way toward the wrecked Mustang and knew she needed him. He saw the blinding single light of a motorcycle approaching, heard its insectile buzz. At that instant he felt Cole's hand on him. He turned his head, saw Cole, his head mostly healed, preparing to bite him. Instead of engaging, Clayton sprang right, past a bright oncoming headlamp and toward the wreckage of the van.

The motorcycle jogged to its right to avoid Clayton, making a wet thump and skid as it plowed into Cole and dragged him on the road, its driver vaulting headfirst into what was left of the truck and breaking his neck.

Clayton lunged forward, grabbed a bent door from the truck, and moved toward Cole.

Cole, dragged half out of his clothes, stared up at Clayton, too injured to do more than try to cover his exposed breast. He had taken great pains this evening, as every evening, to wind his breasts beneath a sheet, flatten them against his body so the others wouldn't see. Except Calcutta. Calcutta knew. And Luther knew.

The vampire once known as Dolores Cole, the pretty ash-blond Georgia girl who had been Blitz Nixon's lover when he raced cars as a man, the one for whom Luther returned as a vampire, didn't try to move his broken limbs.

Clayton just looked, holding the door up over his head.

Cole met his gaze and sneered, angered by how slowly his limbs were healing, angered by the contempt he imagined in the other vampire's hesitation.

"You'd just better," Cole said.

Clayton did.

He used the door like a blunt cleaver and mashed Cole's head off at the neck.

Cole's dying body arched its back and gathered its ragged knees to its chest, and then it moved no more.

The truck caught fire now.

Clayton saw that Jude had almost made it to the wrecked Mustang.

He ran to her.

It was 5:06 A.M.

51

LUTHER AND NECK BRACE HAD CRACKED THEIR HEADS AGAINST ONE ANOTHER IN the Mustang's dying tumble, but that wasn't the worst of it. Neck Brace, stretched flat over the broken bucket seat, half gutted by a piece of the roof, gathered himself together as best he could, feeling the parts of himself that had come out now running backward through his slick fingers to retake their proper places. Luther's head had been twisted all the way around but had held. He made a very wet repetitive sound with his mouth that was certainly some vulgarity, but his brain had been so knocked about even he didn't know what he was saying. Then he did and he stopped. His mouth hurt too much. Luther righted his head, crawled bloodily from the upside-down wreck, bewildered as much by the impact he had just absorbed as by the sight of the nun walking toward them with fire behind her. She held a cross before her as though she believed with all her being in its power to protect her.

"Sheeee-it," Luther drawled.

He reached into his pocket for his gun but the pocket had been torn away, along with much of the denim in his jeans, to reveal a large, white trapezoid of thigh. Neither was the gun in his blood-filled boot. At the sound of a pathetic whistle, he looked back at the wreck, saw

Neck Brace too large, hurt, and badly caught to free himself just yet, holding the gun up with his one good hand. Luther stumbled back and took it, opened the cylinder, squinted through blood to check that it was loaded, then snapped it shut.

When he pointed it, however, his target had changed. He now saw a banged-up truck door walking at him with two pairs of legs.

"Aw, fuck you, door," he said, shooting. Five pops came from the gun, to no apparent effect. On the sixth shot, the door fell.

He saw the Yankee vampire down, a neat hole just under his hairline. He saw the nun sitting on her butt, holding her stomach.

"Why!" he shouted at her. "Why the FUCK do all this!"

"You killed a boy," she said.

"I killed a lot a' boys."

"Mine. You killed *my* boy," she said, crawling for the cross, which lay broken on the asphalt.

"Yeah?" he said. "Well, *fuck* him, and fuck you, too."

He pointed behind him at the steaming wreck with the large vampire making a mess out of himself trying to get free. "I *loved* that car."

He threw the empty gun at her, but it flew over her shoulder and slid on the road. He started stalking forward. Then he saw something that stopped him. When the nun grabbed the bottom half of the cross, the broken top part skittered across the road and rejoined itself to its base.

The pain in her stomach subsided.

She stood.

Held the cross up.

Started walking toward Luther.

"Anyway, I didn't kill him."

Now Judith froze.

"Liar."

"I ain't," he said.

He walked softly closer, staring at her, trying once again to hook her eyes.

"You took him."

"That's right," he said.

"But you didn't kill him."

"Nuh-uh."

He edged closer.

From the wreck of the car, Neck Brace panted with exhaustion. Every time he tried to flatten his head and squeeze out of the aperture, his brace caught on metal and hung him up.

Clayton sat up and held his head.

"What did you do?"

"You know," he said, "that wreck musta shook me up. I don't remember."

"What did you *do*?" she hissed.

She felt in her heart that whatever power waited in the Italian cross weakened with her anger.

Pain racked her belly.

Her legs shook.

"Somethin', I'm sure," he said, stepping closer.

Clayton got shakily to his feet.

Now Rob walked up the road toward them, coming up from behind Judith, his face pinched with rage. He held the shifter that had been through him like a schoolmaster would hold a whipping rod.

"They done Calcutta," he said.

Luther's eyes cut to Rob.

Judith dared not look away.

"Clayton," she said.

"I see him," Clayton said.

"Cole?" Luther asked.

Rob didn't say anything.

"This young lady I'm lookin' at hopes you don't tell me Cole is dead," Luther said.

"Cole too."

"Gone?"

"Yeah. He . . . he's gone."

Luther nodded.

Closed his eyes longer than a blink.

He drooled, then wiped his mouth.

"You know what?" Luther said, looking hard at Judith. "I just remembered. What I did to that kid."

Take my anger away, God. Take it away I humbly pray thee.

"After we put your husband's dick in the dirt. See, I'd forgot, but I read the file on you. That husband of yours was a cheater, right?"

I am thy humble vessel.

Behind Luther, the sound of grinding metal rose up. Neck Brace had removed the brace from his neck and was simultaneously pushing the wrecked car open and getting small to free himself. It was working.

"Guess he wasn't getting enough at home, huh? Was you already practicing to be a nun, makin' sure he didn't get none?"

The vampire called Rob rushed at Judith's back.

Clayton shot forward, grabbed his waist, rolled to the ground with him. They writhed in a knot, Clayton working his way to Rob's neck, trying to bite.

Neck Brace worked most of his chest free from the wreck of the Mustang.

Sirens wailed in the distance.

The sky was lighter now.

Judith spoke.

"Peace to this house and all who dwell therein."

She moved forward with the crucifix.

Luther stopped.

"So, anyway, Glendon, that's his name, right?"

"Cleanse me of sin with hyssop, Lord, that I may be purified; wash me, and I shall be whiter than snow."

They spoke over each other now.

"So that kid. You know, scared blood tastes best, and that kid literally shit himself when we got him in that car."

"Have mercy on me, O God, according to thy great mercy. Glory be to the Father, and to the Son, and to the Holy Ghost."

She moved closer.

Neck Brace was out all the way to the navel.

Clayton was holding Rob's head down with his elbow, gouging his neck with his fangs.

"We drank him out while he yelled, 'Mommy, Mommy.' How does that make you feel? You still his mommy with all that ridiculous shit on?"

"Our help is in the name of the Lord who made heaven and earth. Oh Lord hear my prayer and let my cry come to thee."

"All that penguin-lookin' shit you wear. Ain't gonna help you. I'm gonna flipside you. You know what that is?"

"Hear us, and be pleased to send thy holy angel from heaven to guard, cherish, and defend all that dwell in this house."

The pain in her belly was all but gone.

"Maybe you don't 'cause I made it up."

Rob groaned as Clayton sucked hard from him.

Neck Brace started working his hip bone through. Judith saw him emerging naked and pale and hairy from the car, but she kept on.

"In the Name of the Father, and of the Son, and of the Holy Spirit,"

"But flipsidin' means I'm gonna fuck you livin' and dead. Once each. Don't that sound fun?"

"let there be extinguished in you all power of the devil by the imposition of our hands,"

She came closer. She was no more than five yards away.

Rob started to shudder, said, "He's killing me."

"and by the invocation of the glorious and holy Mother of God, the Virgin Mary,"

The bullet came out of her stomach, fell squat and mushroomed on the asphalt.

"Anyway, Glenny-glen."

Neck Brace was out now.

"and of her illustrious Spouse, St. Joseph,"

"After we drank him all up, he died, a' course."

"and of all the holy Angels,"

"Wasn't much in him, little as he was."

"Archangels, Patriarchs,"

"But I brought him back."

"Prophets, Apostles, Martyrs,"

Clayton vomited black blood on the street to clear his stomach so he could finish draining Rob.

Neck Brace picked up his brace, put it back on.

"I turned that cute little motherfucker just for fun."

"Confessors, Virgins, and of all the saints together."

Neck Brace stomped toward Rob and Clayton.

"Left him in a desert town to burn up."

"Lord God, who said by thy apostle James,"

"Like I'm gonna turn your retard sister, too. For fun."

"Is any man sick among you?"

"Killin' your mom and dad'll just be on principle."

She came within three yards of him.

"But that ain't all."

The lights of a police car loomed a mile away, coming closer.

"Thy mercy restore him."

"There's something you need to know."

Two yards.

"Is any man sick?"

"Somethin' I been savin' back to tell you."

One yard.

"Is any man?"

"'Cause it's funny."

"Infirmátur quis ín vobis?"

"Do you want to know?"

She stopped.

"It's somethin' you really oughta know. Somethin' that happened. With your boy you couldn't save."

"What?" she said, a tear rolling down her eye. The arm holding the cross weakened, dipped lower.

Neck Brace grabbed Clayton, lifted him up in the air, and threw him down on his head.

"What?" she said again, her voice even smaller.

Neck Brace put his foot on Clayton's head, pulled his arms up behind him. Clayton yelled. Then he whimpered. His head started to come off.

"This," Luther said.

He flashed his arm out fast, meaning to bat the cross away and then knock the nun out. Put her in the trunk of some car, maybe this police car coming. Flipside her. Leave her body out for the buzzards. Then go to Fresno and finish the job with her family.

But that wasn't what happened.

52

THE CROSS JUDITH HELD HAD BEEN MADE IN 1873 FOR THE CHURCH OF SANTA Maria Maddalena Sopra Fontana just outside Cisterna di Latina in central Italy. The craftsman who made it, Gian Carlo Orpeggio, was a devout man who had been considered the best carpenter in the village by his twenty-second birthday. He was also a gifted painter. He made the cross of rosewood painted with gold leaf, and to very specific dimensions, as it was to fit snugly into the hand of a plaster angel. This angel had formerly been holding a gas lamp but had so struck an opera singer born in Cisterna that he purchased it from a dealer in Paris and gifted it to his boyhood church. The cross was blessed by Pope Pius XI on July 22, 1874, for the Feast of Maria Maddalena, when Father Luca Morandi brought it to Rome for exactly that purpose. While cross and priest were gone, the angel's hand offered a bouquet of sunflowers and red poppies picked by young girls of the parish.

When war came to Cisterna in the next century, occupying Germans were impressed with the beauty of the angel, whom they called Magda. One rabidly Catholic young soldier, a Breisgau paratrooper and explosives expert named Karl Gerber, had become so smitten with her that he told other members of the *Fallschirmjäger* that he would become a priest after the war if they would let him take Magda to whatever church he was assigned to. Their laughter bristled him, but not so much as the news that the American army was coming in force to avenge the several hundred rangers they had caught in an open field and massacred, and that a northern retreat was likely imminent. The idea of Americans, with their farmers' hands and watered-down colonial Catholicism, flooding into this church and worshipping beneath Magda's gaze when he could not, filled him with such hatred that he decided to take measures.

His idea was to wire the rosewood cross to an eighty-eight-millimeter shell.

His reasoning was that anyone who would steal a cross must be a communist or an atheist, and that such vermin deserved what they got. He had already written a letter to the priest explaining how to deactivate the booby trap, and he would mail this later, once the main American army had left. The obvious moral and logistic flaws with this plan escaped Karl and his commanding officer because the first was half mad and the second suffered crippling insomnia since the fight with the rangers. The shell went in the platform supporting the angel and aimed into the pews, where flying wood splinters would shred personnel but, God willing, leave Magda mostly unharmed.

It was into this church that PFC Luther Nixon and three other American soldiers of the third infantry division ventured in May 1944.

That this same cross made its way into a Vatican storehouse and across the Atlantic at the request of one Phillip Wicklow is a phenomenon some would see as massive coincidence.

Others would see it differently.

If Judith somewhat resembled the dark-haired angel of the Maddalena, with her sad, pretty eyes and her fair skin, only Luther could have said. Only he saw them both. Once living, once dead. And the same thing happened both times.

When Luther touched the Cisterna cross for the second time, it was as though something even more furious than an eighty-eight-millimeter German artillery round exploded near him, and near the others. Luther took the worst of it, followed by Clayton and Rob. To catalog their injuries would be exhaustive; let us just say that they were swept aside and broken so badly that they were as formless as scarecrows. Judith, much like her plaster counterpart in Cisterna di Latina, largely escaped injury, although the concussion temporarily deafened her and she lost consciousness for several moments. The blast threw great hunks of asphalt that shredded the tires and broke the windshield of the approaching deputy's vehicle such that he skidded into the remains of Rob's truck and bounced his head on the driver's-side window hard enough to star it and black out for half an hour. A ripple in the asphalt jolted all the vehicles into the air, breaking the glass jars of gasoline in the trunk of the '67 Camaro and dropping it close enough to a worm-shaped pool of fire for the fumes to catch. It exploded with a huge, hollow *THRUMP!* that bucked the husk of the vehicle a second time, causing it to collide with and burn the '69 COPO. A mushroom-shaped cloud of fire and black smoke ascended into the still-dark sky, illuminating the debris field scattered along I-40, and all the injured and undead whose fates were soon to be determined.

53

NECK BRACE WAS THE FIRST TO REGAIN HIS FEET.

He saw the nun lying prone and moved toward her, but Clayton crawled in front of her and bared his teeth. Neck Brace, too weak to fight, looked to Luther to see what he should do. His mouth hung open in an idiot's gape when he saw what remained of Luther. He shambled to him and gathered him up like firewood, picking up one limb he might have to hold next to Luther's trunk if he was too weak to regenerate. He loped into the dying night, off the road but following the interstate west.

Exhausted from the effort of dragging himself, Clayton lost consciousness at just the moment Judith woke. She looked around for Luther. She saw a limping figure silhouetted against the eastern sky but noted it was too tall to be Luther. Damaged and mutable as it was, it looked almost like an El Greco character stamped out of pitch and held up against the cobalt and lavender of first light. It stopped and picked something up from the pavement, folded it into its pocket, then loped away.

Rob

How'd you know my name

That his name too

This was the one who grabbed Glendon's arm as he innocently planed it on the warm desert air that evening so recently, and so very long ago.

This was the one who pulled her screaming child out of her grip and into the death car—the one against whom she had lost the most important contest she would ever face.

As a novice in the service of God, she should go after Luther Nixon, the most dangerous one, the most canny and cruel. The leader.

But deep in her heart and her womb she wanted to watch the tall one die.

If it could only be one of them, she would take this one.

Rob, then.

You still his mommy with all that ridiculous shit on?

I don't know.

I don't.

She stripped off the veil, coif, and scapular so that she stood in her jeans, T-shirt, and combat boots. She ran as best she could back to where she remembered throwing the gun.

THE DRIVER OF A BLUE '68 FALCON HAD STOPPED AT THE SITE OF THE WRECK TO offer assistance. His name was Bennett Evans, and he was a thirty-four-year-old air traffic controller on his way back to Albuquerque from the home of a recently divorced Amarillo nurse. Bennett himself had lost his wife two years ago and loved the nurse with colors his marriage had been blind to. He had resisted the temptation to keep driving past the disaster, which had engulfed several cars in flames and cratered the south shoulder of the highway, despite his thirty-six hours without anything resembling sleep. The huge, pale man with the neck brace carrying his dead friend had roused such pathos in him there had been no question of driving on. When he pulled over and leaned to push his passenger door open, the big ruin of a man had dumped the small ruin of a man into the seat without a word.

"Get in the back, buddy, I'll take you both to a hospital. What happened?"

The big man stumble-ran around the Falcon's front. When he reappeared at the driver's-side window, Bennett smelled rot and gas and something unpleasantly insectile.

"Is there anybody else hurt?" he said.

The big man ignored this. He put his hand to his mouth and then moved it forward, as if blowing Bennett a kiss, but his red lips had not puckered.

Bennett recognized this as *Thank you* in sign language.

Two things happened simultaneously. The big man drew back his arm, as if about to slap a bug against a wall, and the driver gestured in ASL.

He signed *You're welcome* back at the big man, whose eyes sparkled with sudden joy at finding someone he could speak to, then clouded over as he remembered the unfortunate circumstances they found themselves in. He grabbed Bennett by the shirt and wrenched him slowly but irresistibly out of the car, but then pushed him down on the ground almost gently.

"The fuck're you doin?" the bald, half-flayed corpse in the passenger seat croaked. "We need that blood, we're dyin'."

The big man kissed at the tips of his fingers, then waved.

Good-bye.

Bennett watched his Falcon recede west as sirens sounded in the east.

He couldn't help thinking that his deaf sister had just saved his life.

5:40 A.M.

The stars were gone now, the moon a chip of white ice melting in the east. A very small town crouched close to the terra-cotta ground not half a mile away, but it slept. The vampire known as Rob, not healed yet but getting a little stronger with each step, steered for an isolated house set well back from the highway. A rooster crowed in its yard beneath a rusty windmill barely turning in the scant breeze. He was aware of the woman behind him. When he got into shade he would make her wish she had not followed him, or at least that was what he told himself to push down other, less optimistic thoughts. He just barely managed to believe himself thanks to a sophisticated formula in which he subtracted the habit from the nun who had decimated them and arrived at the lesser sum of the ordinarily dressed woman stalking him. He had seen the pistol at one point when she had gotten close, but he didn't fear it. Truth was, he was mostly just *tired* of getting shot. He still hurt from the shotgun blast he'd absorbed at the wreck. The tattooed man at the Missouri hotel had given him quite a headache with a pistol, but that had passed. He wondered what happened to that pistol, correctly guessed that it was the very one the nun was holding. Anyway, he had put distance between them since. He had hoped to get some speed back while it was still dark enough to hide him, but that prick Boston vampire had drained him, made him weaker. It was taking longer. He wasn't fully himself.

When she did catch up with him, he had a surprise to show her. Near the wreck of the truck, not far from the busted sign warning *Explosives in use, Risk of death!* he had seen a spill of papers from the file cabinet the old geezer had in Florida. Documents, handwritten notes, photographs, some of them burning. One of the photographs, lying faceup near a monkey's tail of fire, had caught his attention. When he saw what it was, he barked out a laugh despite the danger he found himself in. He folded it and put it away just in case.

Rob glanced behind him to see where the woman was. Still hundreds of yards behind him, stalking toward him. He could outrun her easily now that he felt stronger, but he needed shelter. The sun was close.

Now a big dog on a rope barked at him.

He had maybe ten minutes until the sun came up.

The house had few windows, so he approached at a blind angle.

He yipped a few times, gaining speed.

He ran to the dog, still yipping, the chickens scattering before him. When he got close, the dog gave up barking and ran up against the house to whimper and growl, jerking at the limit of his tether. Rob followed it there. The fight was brief but loud. The big dog hurt him more than it might have, but even at half strength Rob was just too strong and cold-blooded.

"Jupiter?" a voice said. "Jupiter, you get another coyote?"

The radio was on inside, playing country.

Now he took the limp dog up, a big, mostly black shepherd mix. His hand hurt where the dog had almost severed two fingers; they were already knitting on again, but slower than normal.

"Shit! Ow, damn it! Go on, git out of here!" Rob said, yipping again, kicking up dirt, and then he said, "Oh no."

"What? Who is it?" the voice from before said. An elderly voice.

"Mister, your dog's hurt."

Now he stepped into sight of a window, expecting to see a face there. No face appeared.

"Jupiter?"

"Coyotes got him, a whole pack of 'em."

"No."

"I think he's dead."

"No."

"Let me bring him in," Rob said.

Still no face at the window.

A sad, granular voice said, "Put him on the table."

Rob grinned and, invited, went into the cool darkness of the house.

A man stood at the far end of the open house, his face contorted with pain and wariness. He knew something was wrong.

Rob put the dog on a short, uneven table that looked like it belonged in a school and crossed to the man. He looked into his eyes, saw filmy white cataracts.

"Who . . ." the old man started to say. "That didn't sound like no coyotes."

"Just relax and don't talk," Rob said. "Hold still." The charm was harder without eye contact. Harder still with the sun so close, and him so weak, but at last it took. He bit punctures in the old man's tough neck and drank. The old man made little retching hitches in his stomach and grabbed weak fistfuls of Rob's shirt but didn't say anything. Rob felt better with the warm blood in his stomach, and a good thing, too.

She was coming.

He felt the sun crown outside, felt himself get wobbly.

The rooster crowed again.

"Just sit down and don't get up again," he told the blind, moist-lipped old man.

"Jupiter," the man said. "You kilt Jupiter."

"Yep. Kill you, too, in a bit. Got a gun in here?"

"Nuh."

"Oh, right. Blind. Got a big knife?"

"Drawer," the old man slurred.

Dock Boggs sang on the radio. Rob turned it up. Then he got a big knife.

He wanted to check on the woman, but the light outside would be misery and he had no sunglasses; he'd lost them in the wreck. He plucked up a deflated-looking straw cowboy hat from a shelf by the door. He put this over his face to make a sort of screen for his eyes.

He peeked out the window. In the blaze of early, orangey sun, filtered to an agonizing pointillism by the hat, he saw her silhouette. She walked around the house to where he couldn't see, holding the gun. Rob sank back into the shadows and waited.

"Jupiter," the old man said.

Rob expected her to come in the door or window at any moment, but she didn't. Finally, he saw her peek in quickly, then move away.

"Come on in," he yelled at her. "We're just listening to the radio."

She didn't say anything.

Nothing happened for several very long minutes.

"The fuck's she doing?" Rob asked nobody.

Nobody answered.

Several more minutes passed, the light outside getting stronger and hotter.

"I'm gonna die," he said.

"Yuh," said the old blind man in the chair.

The charmed couldn't help what they said and Rob knew that, but the truth of that one syllable made Rob angry. His hand flashed like the head of a striking snake.

JUDITH SAT IN THE YELLOW GRASS IN THE HOUSE'S BLIND SPOT, WATCHING HER shadow grow shorter and the ground around it grow brighter. The vampire inside had called out to her, but her ears were ringing so badly from the explosion she couldn't make out what he had said.

It didn't matter what he said.

She had stolen a glimpse inside, seen an old man with blood on his shirt sitting in a chair, looking stoned. She saw emergency vehicles and tow trucks heading east on the interstate; the wrecks were only a mile or so away. Two plumes of smoke rose up from that direction, though she had to crane her head behind her to see.

The vampire said something else.

She wanted this done before police came looking for witnesses to the explosion and fire.

How long until then? Half an hour.

Every minute she sat here, she got a little stronger.

Ten more minutes, give or take, and she would act.

She looked at her belly, where she had been shot, but all she saw was a shallow purple pit, like a scar. As if she had been shot and healed from it years ago.

A miracle.

She tried to pray but she was out of words, so she sat silently, hoping that was a kind of prayer, too.

She looked at the gun.

She had the impression that she was on her own this time, that she was no longer God's instrument.

Which might mean God was hunting on his own, too.

It was 6:10 A.M.

54

A WOODEN INDIAN STOOD OUTSIDE THE WAGON HORSE GROCERY AND FILLING STA-tion, but it wasn't the usual cigar store statuary, a mock-noble chief with a dour frown and a feather bonnet, one hand up to cover his eyes as he scanned the horizon for buffalo or long-knife cavalry. This was a brave, not a chief, and he stood not in calm observation but in the middle of battle. One hand clenched in a fist before him, while the other held a tomahawk high over his head, prepared to bring it down on the crown of a hapless enemy. His eyes were painted so the whites were prominent. An astute observer would guess the artist responsible for this figure was himself an Indian, and that observation would be correct. At 5:25 A.M., Daniel Otter Shirt sat in his wheelchair, his body a withered counterpoint to the athletic brave he himself had carved in 1943, shortly before going into the army. His nephews John and Sam ran the shop now. If his body was withered, his eyes were still sharp, and they locked on the Ford Falcon that raced to a diagonal stop in the parking lot, and on the two vile-looking men who got out.

LUTHER NIXON WAS WALKING, BUT HE WAS MILES FROM WELL. NECK BRACE WAS in better shape, but not by much. The two of them staggered past the old cripple and flung open the door leading into the small grocery store looking as though they had crawled off a battlefield, tracking blood and motor oil on their shoes.

"Hey, we're not open till six. You guys okay?" the young Native American man said, just pouring ground coffee into the coffeemaker.

"Yeah, Cochise, we're great," Luther said. "We're fixin' to run the decathlon. Now tell me where there's a good dark house or a cave nearby."

Luther stared into his eyes while he said this.

"Excuse me?"

"I said tell me where there's a dark place I can hole up, and pronto, Tonto."

The young man broke eye contact with Luther, looked at Neck Brace, and then saw his uncle Daniel wheeling in through the door.

"Shit," Luther said, seeing the charm wasn't taking.

Neck Brace pointed back out at the car, then tucked one hand in the other, meaning *trunk*, as in *Let's drive somewhere quiet and crawl into the trunk*.

"No time," Luther said, taking a shaky step forward, grabbing Sam Otter Shirt's chin and jaw.

His grip wasn't very strong yet. It would never be very strong again.

"Now tell me . . ." was as far as Luther got before the fit young man ducked out of his grasp and punched him in the nose. Luther dropped. Neck Brace charged at Sam, knocking over a shelf full of Pez dispensers, PayDay bars, and circus peanuts, but tripped over Luther and fell. He got back up fast, but Sam already had the baseball bat he kept under the counter but had never swung at anyone before.

"Hey!" Sam said, showing him he meant to use the bat, but Neck Brace lumbered toward him. Sam cracked him in the head. Normally the big monster would have shaken this off, but at nearly daybreak after suffering a car wreck and an explosion, he felt his knees buckle. Blood from his scalp trickled to the ground.

Sam immediately felt bad for whacking a guy with a spine condition, even if he was going apeshit in the store. But then his uncle Daniel spoke up in the slurred voice he'd used since the stroke.

"Keep hitting them."

LUTHER CAME TO TEN MINUTES LATER, SURPRISED TO FIND HIS ARMS OVER HIS head. He tried to move them and couldn't. Likewise his feet. He started laughing when he realized he was actually tied to train tracks, like the damsel in some silent Mountie movie from when he was a kid. He lifted his head up and saw his feet, bound with stout rope. He cranked his head to the side and backward till he saw Neck Brace's woolly hair. They were tied head to head on some old abandoned railway.

He felt nauseated from all the light—there was a dangerous amount of light in the sky. The sun was going to crown at any moment, and when it did it would crown right. Over. There.

Just past the two Indians, one sitting strokey-faced in a wheelchair, the other smoking a cigarette and squatting over a bloody baseball bat.

The back of the store was just to his right.

Come to think of it, the Wagon Horse Grocery did look kind of like an old railway station.

The young Indian spoke.

"My uncle says you're vampires. That true?"

"Well, I'd rather show you than tell you," Luther said, trying to squeeze together the bones of his wrists and ankles to slither them out of the ropes, but it wasn't working. He tried to break the ropes with the strength of his arms, but he had no strength in his arms.

"Samson with a fuckin' haircut, huh?" he said, but it didn't sound so funny with the big, burning sun just raring to come over that ridge and kill him. It occurred to him that he very well might be about to die for real and ever.

"Hey, dummy," he said to Neck Brace, "get up and do somethin', for fuck sake."

"My uncle says he's seen you before. Ten years ago. He says you beat my dad in the head with a soup can."

"Mighta, I don't know."

"You *don't know*? You do this kind of thing so much you don't remember?"

"Vampires," the old man said in a small, dry voice.

"We ain't vampires. Ain't no such thing."

"I don't believe in vampires," Sam said. "But I do believe in assholes. My dad was never right again after the robbery, if you want to call it a robbery. All you stole was gas. You could have just drove off. Why are you such an asshole?"

"I don't know. Why're you such an injun?"

"That's an asshole thing to say. I'm not an 'injun.' I'm Comanche."

"Comanche's just a kinda injun. That's like sayin', 'I ain't a bee, I'm a *bumble* bee.'"

"Bumblebee *is* different."

"How's that?"

"Honeybee stings you once and dies. Bumblebee's like a wasp. Can just keep stinging. You're not that bright, are you?"

"Fuck you, teepee nigger."

"Nope, not that bright at all."

"So, what, you're just gonna kill us?"

"Nope."

"You leave us here, you're killin' us."

"Not if you're just an asshole."

"Let me up."

"Not yet."

"When?"

"After we watch the sun rise. I think it's already up, but there's a low cloud. Should be over that in a minute. If you're okay then, I'll call the police and an ambulance. You could use both. Anyway, *they'll* untie you, not me."

"Look at me."

"No."

"How about you, old fucker? Why don't you look me in the eye?"

The old man mumbled something.

The young man passed him his cigarette and the old man took a drag.

"What'd he say?" Luther said.

"He says he doesn't look in the eyes of people who have no soul."

"Yeah, well. How about you let me up and I send you some money. Like, a lot of money. We got it hid all over."

The young man didn't talk.

"Anyway, Comanche? What the fuck're you doin' out here? Thought you was all in Kansas somewhere."

"Oklahoma. We left the rez. Dad married Pueblo."

"That's real sweet. Now how about you FUCKING UNTIE ME."

"Nope."

"It's comin'. It's fuckin' comin' for real now. I ain't supposed to die out here. With *him*. I don't even know this dummy sumbitch's name, he just showed up one night. Untie me, you squaw motherfucker. Or I'll gut you. Your cunt Pueblo whore mother, too."

"You were right, Uncle Dan."

"I'll kill you. I'll eat your fuckin' . . . I'll kill . . ."

"No soul at all."

Luther dropped what little charm he had left and Sam and Daniel

Otter Shirt saw him as he was, with his fangs and his veins and his bad skin.

He started retching.

5:50 A.M.

The sun crested over a saddle of clouds.

Yellow sunlight hit Luther on his left side.

Luther didn't talk anymore.

Luther screamed.

And Luther burned.

Together with the one he called Neck Brace.

Bright as magnesium.

Smoky as a grease fire.

And then they were gone.

55

JUDITH TRIED THE DOOR AND FOUND IT OPEN. A DEAD DOG LAY ON A TABLE JUST TO her right. Straight ahead, she saw the shape of an old man in a chair, barely lit by indirect sunlight bleeding in from a single window. She saw the object of her hatred now crouched behind the chair, squinting, his eyes watering even against this weak light. Metal glinted as the vampire called Rob pressed a kitchen knife up under the old man's jaw. The knife was smeared with blood.

"Put the gun down," the creature said.

"No."

"Aren't you afraid I'll cut him?"

"No."

He smiled like he liked that answer, then looked her in the eye. "Now put the gun down."

"That doesn't work on me," she said.

"No, I guess not."

"Come from behind that chair."

"What if I don't?"

"I'll wait."

A moment passed in silence.

"Luther told you about the boy."

"He's a liar."

"Sometimes. But we did turn your boy. Luther did."

"Come out from behind the chair."

"Anyway, there's a worse liar than Luther. You need to know."

"Just come out. Come at me."

"Look at this," he said, and flicked a photograph at her like a man throwing a card into a hat. It landed facedown. "You're working for a liar, too," he said.

Her heart beat fast. He spoke then. He told her what he had to tell. She shook her head, even though the words he said had a ring of awful truth.

"Look," he said, pointing at the facedown picture with his knife. "Just look."

It was when she reached down that he came at her.

SHE SHOT THE VAMPIRE WHO TOOK HER SON, SHOT HIM HIGH ON THE FOREHEAD. She grabbed him by the heels and dragged him toward the door. He started coming to, so she shot him again. Dragged him some more. And so it went all the way out the door and up to the frontier of sunlight pushing at the shadow of the poor old blind man's house. BANG! Drag. BANG! Drag. At the end, not five feet from the edge of sunlight blazing on the ground, the gun clicked dry and he started to grab for her. So she beat him with the butt of the big pistol. She beat him like Riley Eberhart's daughter, beat him like Glendon Lamb's mother, beat him so hard she knocked the eyes out of him, wrecked his skull without a bullet, and, while the pieces tried to right themselves, she grabbed his bootheels and dragged his legs into the sun and his legs burned hot. But he didn't go easy. He scurried back on his elbows, yelling, throwing dirt and rocks first at her, and then on his jeans trying to put himself out. In the end she dragged him into the sunshine by his hair, her silence a grim counterpoint to his dying scream. When he caught fire, she caught fire too, but she rolled in the dirt and put herself out while he just burned and burned until there was nothing left of him but echo.

She said the words then, even for him.

"Your curse is lifted. May God remember your former kindnesses. And may he one day relieve me of the hatred I bear you."

The house sat quiet, the door cracked open.

When Judith went inside, she confirmed her suspicion that Rob had cut the old man's throat. She put the dog in his lap, crossed herself, then went to the sink. She hissed as she ran her burned hands under the tap water, and she drank, and washed the smoke out of her eyes.

At last, as sirens wailed in the east, she picked up the photograph the monster had flicked at her and ran into the rocky labyrinth of foothills past a plain of tawny grass. She saw twin plumes of smoke in the west and understood Luther Nixon and the big one had died as well. When at last she felt far enough away from the business of police and fire trucks she heard behind her, she let herself look at the photo.

She immediately wished she hadn't.

She wanted to collapse but didn't let herself.

Not yet.

She had one more job to do.

BETHANY ROAD RAN NORTH TO SOUTH ACROSS THE INTERSTATE, BUT IT WAS TOO small to warrant its own exit or overpass; instead, one had to follow a feeder road to Clines Corners and then double back. By the time she found the abandoned rail car Clayton had described, it was nearly noon and her fair skin was badly sunburned. The car had been a caboose at one time. She stepped warily into the blackness offered by the tall, narrow rear door and walked into the heat of the interior, which stank of age and ancient tobacco. Numerous cigarette butts and one pair of old, soiled boxer shorts attested to the car's occasional use as a habitation, though exactly when the last squatters had squatted was not apparent. The once-white interior paint had long been flaking away to show the dry wood beneath, and the floorboards were gapped here and there by missing slats.

In the middle of everything sat a toolbox that looked large enough to hold a smallish man. She liked how slight Clayton was; he came from a time before overeating was so common, when men were considered normal at five-six. She smiled to think of the pleasant economy of his body, but then that smile faded. That he came from another time was the problem at hand. He was *undead*, his life unnaturally prolonged. However pleasant he was to talk to, and however helpful he had been, he was an abomination before God. Maybe he wasn't in the box at all. She gripped the end handle, hissing with pain when her raw, burned hand touched iron, then pulling up on it to test its weight.

Heavy.

She wanted to talk to Clayton, to tell him how sorry she was, but she couldn't have him waking up. How would he react? Would he harm her? God knew she had no fight left in her; she was bruised, burned, half deafened, half dying of thirst.

Had Clayton told her where he would be because he wanted her to do this? Or just because he wanted to see her again?

Did God want this of her?

What God? God isn't dead. He just . . . isn't.

Shut up Clayton Birch you shut up.

Oh God I don't want to do this must I do this.

Clayton had offered to make her a vampire, which meant he had almost certainly made others. Were they as benign as he? Were the ones who murdered her husband and took her boy unusual in their extreme violence?

Or was Clayton the anomaly? No matter how he had helped her, no matter how humanely he harvested what he needed, his life ran on stolen human blood. She had seen him feed.

I can't make decisions like this alone God please help me.

A scorpion made its way across the floorboards, claws out, stinger high.

That's the sign, she thought.

Poison.

"I'm sorry," she whispered.

She hugged the box, left it moist where her cheek had touched it.

Before she could stop herself, she dragged it across the caboose's floor, eased it into a bright rectangular patch of sunlight offered by a window.

She breathed in and out three times.

She glanced out the window where tall, rocky hills offered black shadows between heaps of stones. Something bright flashed there, but she couldn't make out what.

Am I really killing him after he helped me?

You're helping him now.

You're ending his curse.

She thought she should get on the other side of the chest so her way to the door wouldn't be blocked—her hands throbbed with the memory of the white-hot fire ignited by Rob's exposure to sun. Would an older vampire burn hotter and faster? More tears dropped on the box. She sobbed openly and hugged her face to it. She suddenly didn't care if she made it out of the caboose—she didn't have the strength for a hike to Pennsylvania, she had no money, no abbey to return to. And her son—she didn't want to think about her son. She had seen the vampire Rob's mouth moving, making words, telling her the lengths Wicklow would go to in furtherance of his cause.

She had looked at the awful picture he had shown her.

She would go into the desert and pray about Glendon.

The desert was a good place for understanding revelations.

Two years ago, Phillip Wicklow and Hank Calvert had been hot on the heels of the Suicide Motor Club when the vampires struck Judith's family. Calcutta had called her mother from Amarillo that night, so the Bereaved had gone to a suspected lair in McLean in the morning, hoping to catch them. They didn't find Luther and company. They were only just too late.

They found instead a newly made vampire child shrieking for its mother in the shadows of an old tire shop. A child Luther had turned and abandoned for his own amusement, knowing it would burn or starve. And Wicklow took it back to All Souls Ranch. It was precious to him, both as a specimen to study and as incontrovertible evidence that the thirsty dead were real. He kept the child alive, if barely, on the blood of deer, and kept him imprisoned.

Have you witnessed proof of evil on the earth?

I have.

They didn't show the boy to Judith, of course.

She would have known it for her son.

Glendon.

She remembered now the music from the basement at All Souls Ranch.

To soothe him.

I'm in the trunk, Mom.

Not a car trunk.

A case.

A cage.

Gimme little lovin'

Got a cake in the oven

And I'm servin' up a piece for you

She didn't know if this image was true, but she thought it was.

Rob had given her a picture of Glendon taken from the 1967 newspaper article about his disappearance, clipped out and laminated, like many of the pictures Wicklow had shown them.

The number 10 stood out in red on the top corner.

Known vampire.

It would be hard to keep her sanity but she would have to.

She would free her son from this.

She would kill Phillip Wicklow if he tried to stop her.

He would probably try to stop her.

No, to die here in the caboose wouldn't be so bad.

She unlatched the hasp of Clayton's tool chest, dug her fingers into the wood of the lid, prepared to lift.

"I'm sorry, I'm sorry, I'm sorry."

You're a betrayer.

She sobbed so hard she barely got the Latin words out.

"Sublata est maledictio. Memoret Deus misericordiam tuam."

She lifted the lid, let the sun in.

And laughed.

Paint cans for weight.

Five one-hundred-dollar bills fanned out.

A PO box address, scrawled on a notecard beneath these words:

REPAY ME IF YOU MUST.
WRITE ME IF YOU WILL.

Those weren't the first things she saw, of course. First she had been dazzled by the most glorious arrangement of sunflowers she had ever seen, their saffron petals blazing in the New Mexico morning light.

She held the sunflowers to her chest, stood in the window, looking out at the cave mouth where a light glinted—she knew he sat safe, watching her, ready to go deeper into the cave or mine or whatever it was if she came after him.

She had no bullets in her gun, anyway.

She had very little strength left.

He had outsmarted her.

Which, she supposed, wasn't very hard.

The brass telescope flashed again in the darkness.

Judith put her hand to her heart.

Smiled at him.

Blew a tender kiss that way.

She folded the money and the address into her pocket.

The scorpion raised its pincers at her.

She stepped over it.

Walked out into the sunlight and away.

ACKNOWLEDGMENTS

Sincere thanks to friend and editor Tom Colgan at Berkley for his unwavering support, and for his invaluable observations about *The Suicide Motor Club*, my favorite of which went something like "Are you crazy? Don't cut that!" I am again and always grateful to my agent, Michelle Brower, and to Sean Daily at Hotchkiss and Associates; both of you affected the trajectory of this narrative in all the best ways. For expert assistance with matters forensic, ballistic, and kinetic, I'd like to thank Teri DeWitt and Eric Wagner. Drawing on hard-won law enforcement experience, Officers Derek Conley and Kevin Daniels gleefully examined the chase scenes herein to make sure rubber met road in credible ways. Thanks, Steven Graham Jones, for lending your hawk-keen eye and coyote-sharp ear to this fable and leaving it better than you found it. If I had forgotten how thrilling and dangerous older V-8s feel with their chirping tires and lazy brakes, Corey Dickerson at Mershon's World of Cars was kind enough to remind me by letting me take a '65 Falcon for a spin on the lonely roads just outside Springfield, Ohio. (Damn, that was fun!) Thanks are due to several who helped midwife this story, as they helped with stories past; if I do not again conjure them individually, it is only in the interest of adding new names to this finite space, and in the confidence that they know who they are and how indispensable they are to me. Finally, I want to thank Jennifer Schlitt, who in her constancy, kindness, and grace informed Judith's character in ways I wasn't fully aware of until I sat down to write these final lines.